Lions & Love:
Queen Of Hearts

Sistar Sunra

Copyrights of the Song Titles Used

To Pimp a Butterfly is the third studio album by American rapper Kendrick Lamar. It was released on March 15, 2015, by Top Dawg Entertainment, Aftermath Entertainment and Interscope Records.

Good Kid, M.A.A.D City (stylized as **good kid, m.A.A.d city**) is the second studio album by American rapper Kendrick Lamar. It was released on October 22, 2012, through Top Dawg Entertainment, Aftermath Entertainment and Interscope Records.

Untitled Unmastered (stylized as **untitled unmastered**.) is a compilation album by American rapper Kendrick Lamar. It was released on March 4, 2016,[1] by Top Dawg Entertainment, Aftermath Entertainment and Interscope Records. The Act and Titles of the Chapters are Song Titles from these three albums.

King of Clubs also uses song titles from this artist as act and chapter titles. Along with **Damn** (stylized as **DAMN.**) is the fourth studio album by American rapper Kendrick Lamar. It was released on April 14, 2017, through Top Dawg Entertainment, Aftermath Entertainment and Interscope Records.

The soundtrack for the 2018 American superhero film Black Panther, based on the Marvel Comics character of the same name and produced by Marvel Studios, consists of an

original score composed by Ludwig Göransson and original
songs performed by Kendrick Lamar.

Table of Contents

Dedication

I would like to dedicate this vision to ALL the hurting little girls out there looking for a savior outside of themselves. YOU ARE A SUPERHERO!

To my beautiful daughter, Beverly…

Eye know that society makes it nearly impossible for us to be happy with the beauty we are given, but we must return to a place where self-love holds more power than any vision they try to reflect. No one can define you but yourself in this life. Don't believe the lies others may tell you about who you are! My wish is to restore faith in all the little girls who are hurt and make them believe that they can do anything they want to be happy.

Though others may tell you that you are not good enough, believe in your heart with all of your soul that you will prove them all wrong! Make them bow at your feet, but stay humble when you do. All women are queens, and all besides the only one worthy and prepared to love her with their soul must step aside!

Acknowledgments

All Praises to the Most-High Living Inspiration, My Family, Love, Musicians with words in their spirit reaching the minds of us all, and that spark of Divine the Healing Optimism contacting us all. The art of storytelling is born when the mind and heart recognize another soul and struggle in the human form connected to their own.

Light Workers, Numerologists, Tarot Readers, Star seeds, Ancestors…The underestimated, overlooked, and doubtful overthinkers that see everything with a unique perspective….My Mirrors…Eye see you in me.

The Universoul Family, mankind, womankind, and those told they are too immature…Yes, You too. This Classroom we call Earth is intriguing because of your contribution! I pray that each of you discovers what makes you shine and never stop illuminating your own paths.

About the Author

The author is a growing student of life, mother, daughter, aunt, and an optimistic lover of progressive thinking. An enigmatic, imaginative, and intuitive weaver of dreams born and raised in rural East Texas.

Her journey led her to write early in life when personal pain trying to discover the meaning of her own existence became too much to bear alone. She began to use many genres of music to inspire her storytelling. Though her views and opinions may contradict what society deems acceptable by usual standards. She only wishes to make it all make sense using scenarios considered taboo.

Sistar Sun RA seeks to entertain, nurture, and connect the minds and hearts of her readers. She means to find hope in hopeless situations and bring humor to the topics people take too seriously, using her imagination birthing lions and setting them free in the jungles of our thoughts.

Act One

Chapter One: Complexion (A Zulu Love?)

Mandisa Isoka King

"No, Tommy, we're not coming back to Paris! The last time you followed us, I told you that it was over! Look at what you've done to her! Mandisa is just a baby," Mami cried into her phone upstairs. She was arguing with Daddy again. He called at least once a week, trying to get her to come back. "I am sick of hospitals and bills for therapists, Tomny. No! Amani is not going to have a monster controlling her like Queen."

I took a sip of water to wash away the horrible dryness from all the different medications I take aside from my heart condition. I've taken mood elevators, anti-depressants, anti-anxiety. I'm diagnosed as bipolar now; It's gotten worse through the years. Being homeschooled and bullied by my father has me flying from one extreme to the next emotionally. My heart isn't the correct size to handle all the stress. I've never been healthy, and Daddy is making it worse. I'll be fine, as long as Amani is born with a whole heart. If Mami does go back afterward…I don't think I will make the trip with her back to Paris, where he can hold me hostage.

Daddy's favorite hobby would be to parade me around his wealthy strange older friends, judging my appearance.

Each time we packed our things and left, Daddy found us and talked her into moving back to Paris. He lured her home with his promises of getting help, wanting to make things right, and showering us with gifts. Then Daddy would snap. Something would set him off, and he would turn on me.

He became angry, grew aggressive, and would start talking about some doctor named Patesh. He was always surrounded by very wealthy men, and for some reason, Daddy took pride in showing off his lovely Black Queen and Princess. Then brag about how his family had always had the best taste in breeding stock behind Mami's back. He loved my mother, but he was a monster!

The first time we ran, when she discovered she was pregnant with Amani, Mami told me we needed to go, and she couldn't take it anymore. I saw Daddy and Mami fighting, and I had a meltdown. I woke up in the hospital. So, we packed as much as we could get in our suitcases and flew to Philadelphia to stay with Granny. I was so relieved to be away from him. I even made my first friend there. We were there a week, and Granny called my father to come to get us. I had met my grandmother once before that happened. When my father showed up, she took money from him, and my mother vowed never to speak to her again.

This last time we ran, Daddy did not suspect at all. Two weeks ago, Mami and I left while he was on call, we got

3

away from the hospital. Mami sold all her jewelry, emptied her credit cards, and we came here to Texas. An old friend of Mami's owned this house. He let us move in and promised not to say a word to Dr. Thomas King. I don't know what's wrong with my father, but he's changed the last few years.

It seems the older I become, the worse he treats us. I don't care what happens to me anymore. But I don't want my baby sister to be near him! Mami ran for the same reason, but deep down, I know she still loves him. I believe this hurts me the most with Amani unborn.

I know my father has been awful for years. Mami knows it too, but she's been running from him with me for so long nothing feels like home. Huh…It's so strange looking at myself in any mirror. I see my mother, and I get sad. I have Mami's copper curls, fair skin, and hazel eyes. Mami and I looked nearly identical in the last family photo we took. My age is the only difference. Mami is the most beautiful woman, she's so loving and kind, and I'm like her in many ways. It makes me afraid to talk to anyone. What if I meet a man like my father?

Daddy is so opinionated about people of color. I never heard him talk down on black women he knew, but he could be a racist white man. His family was from Macon, Georgia. All their family back down the line were doctors and surgeons. He always had money and could have anything he wanted to buy. Including my mother, Mami told me when I turned 14 that her mother sold her to my father when she was starting college. They had priorly started dating, and Daddy couldn't stay focused unless Mami was around. She went along with marriage to make her mother happy, help Daddy finish medical school, and get her life back on track after a bad breakup.

My mother is all that I have ever had. She's been there for me through the worst and at my best. But sometimes, I wonder what she's thinking. She's always looking out for others and giving until there's nothing left. How could she love a man like my father at all? He's always looking down on anyone that isn't wealthy. The words that he says and the way he says them hurt.

I've never had a friend longer than a week when he's around because he ran them off. No boy ever attempted to be nice to me, or he cut them to the quick. He scares me with his angry, violent tantrums because I know Daddy can hurt Mami now. She's pregnant, and he hit her, and she fought back this last time. I just want to be free of this one way or the other. For 16 years, he's treated my mother and me as he doesn't love us, and now he wants to get rid of me. But I can't leave my baby sister with him!

#

The front porch was my early getaway. The weather is cool and sunny here in the mornings. The yard is full of life with all the tall shrubs around the driveway. It's the perfect place to blend into nature and feel at peace. I love all the flowers. But the sunflowers and buttercups have to be my favorite. The yellow flowers remind me of the sun, but Mami says they remind her of my hair and skin.

"Queen, I am going to the market a few blocks down the corner," Mami smiled, pushing the screen open wide, holding her basketball-sized tummy in her yellow sundress and slippers as she waddled out to join me. I jumped to get up, but she shook her head. She had pulled her hair back in a curly sunset behind one of my yellow headbands. Her gray eyes flickered blue as she cuddled my cheek. "Did you take your pills, Disa?"

"I took them a few minutes ago. Are you feeling okay? You are moving slower these days," I worried as I played with her beige fingernails on my shoulder. I noticed Mami's ring and looked away.

"I'm fine, Mon Cheri. I'm just huge!" she snickered, clutching her tummy. "I'm going to get food just up the hill. You sit and relax, okay?"

"Let me come and help, Mami?" I pleaded, climbing up again.

I eased her down the steps from the porch. She smirked as she shoved my hand.

"I said I'm fine! I can go get the groceries alone, Queen! Sit and enjoy this beautiful day Jehovah 'Jah' has made. Besides, HE might come by again," Mami mocked. She grinned and pushed my arm.

"Mami!" I snorted, suddenly blushing. Mami was the one that spied that boy the first day we moved in. I noticed him running all over the neighborhood with his head so far in the clouds that he seemed like he was flying. "He soars by every day about this time. But he doesn't see me here."

"Perhaps you should make the first move! It's not the 50s, Queen! Women CAN approach men NOW. You like him, don't you?" Mami questioned me, raising her eyebrows grinning beautifully. Her gray eyes sparkled at me as her cheeks reddened pinker. Mami's golden and brown curls fought the breeze glancing around skeptically.

She knew I did! I sat out there and observed HIM jog past our house every day for a week now. However, I was too terrified to say hello. I scratched the back of my leg with my foot, still blushing deeply, and slipped my mother into the car. She placed her seatbelt as I rushed to open the gate. A quiet wind fanned my wet mane against my face. I started putting it up when I spotted HIM.

He was running along our edge of the lane on the pavement, dribbling his soccer ball with his gorgeous muscular legs magnificently. I flushed worse and moved back, disappearing behind the greenery along the fence. My eyes had never seen a brown boy so handsome. He had long brown and black dreadlocks that hung neatly in a ponytail down to his shoulders. He was sporting a red headband drenched with perspiration, and small rivers of sweat ran down his semi-sweet chocolate-colored coating. He wore a very tight black compression shirt. I could catch every muscle in his massive chest and trim torso flexing as he moved.

He was a bit taller than me with bulging gorgeous runners' legs. The black compression shorts he wore were concealed by red soccer shorts, and they were just the proper elasticity to see the definition in those thighs! His quadriceps flexed like thick logs and relaxed as he dribbled the ball.

He possessed a gorgeous symmetrical face, too. This beautiful black man wore glasses, sometimes, like this morning. He held the most adorable baby face with no facial hair but had expressive eyebrows. His eyes were almond-shaped with these clever thick brows, a wide pointed nose, and tiny round lips that looked like a heart when he pressed them together, concentrating.

As Mami started backing out, he noticed her car and quickly moved ahead out of her way. I kept quiet near the fence as he crossed the street. His concentration seemed off today as he lost pace and kept staring at his left arm. He was listening to music, and his Mp3 player must be acting up.

"Talk to him!" Mami giggled while backing out into the street gradually. "I bet he's heading to the park down the road. Just say hello, Queen. What's the worst that could happen?"

"He will laugh at me? He has a girlfriend? He's gay! I know! He's a serial killer!" I kidded, folding my arms, discouraged. There's no way Daddy would let me have another friend. A boy like that would be out of the question. One look at a black man and Daddy would go into a fit of rage, and one this pretty would drive him insane. "Daddy will chase him away."

"Your father's not here," Mami chanted beautifully before she drove off.

My facial expression must have made it simple for her to read my mind. I minded her heading up the road a moment. Then I spied HIM again as he paused on the footpath near the park. It was close enough to the house. My heart jumped, thumping against my chest like a jackhammer as I considered listening to my mother. But, instead, I rubbed my hands together and started wandering the drive.

"I can't do this," I said to myself as I walked around in a circle. As I got near the gate again, the beautiful boy was still there, distracted again by something else. "Okay, maybe I'll just say 'Hey' and introduce myself. If he's weird. I'll run away. I'm pretty fast."

I took a deep breath, exhaled, and popped a cherry-flavored candy in my mouth. I tied my hair up in a bun headed up the sidewalk. It was so breezy now. I caught sight of him near a tree trying to fix his music player. I shivered and found a tree to hide, observing him again.

Okay, I was deceiving myself. There was no way I could outrun this boy. His legs were constructed to destroy pavement! If he stole me and darted, there would be nothing I could do to fight him! But appreciating him from a distance as he dribbled his ball in place with a focused expression…I wanted to know him.

He shut his eyes for a moment and lost sight of his soccer ball. It started to bowl into the park downhill towards the pond. Hmm…maybe this could be a good morning after all? If he dove into the water to get it, I could see a lovely exhibition…. But, no, he might just abandon it. I glared. He still had his eyes closed. I decided to go after the ball.

I raced it down the hill into the park then caught it before it could spin into the water. I stooped over, seizing it, and took it between my fingers. My nails were so long they needed to be trimmed down, curling around the ball. I could feel this warm glow all around it, felt so exhilarating, as I rose up, turning around. He was gazing right at me!

He didn't speak a word. He just stared at me with those big brown eyes over his glasses. I managed to smile nervously. The wind was causing the droplets of sweat to trail down his powerful shoulders. He seemed like a melting candy bar in the flickering sunlight between the overhead shadows. My heart crashed, started again, and it sprinted away as I shuddered.

"Hey," I breathed while I clutched the ball to my heart, terrified.

"Hey," He uttered, jerking out his earbuds. His eyes exploded as his lips curled into an adorable smile, and his eyebrows lifted over his glasses. Then, he stood up straight, and his entire body seemed transformed. It was as if he was suddenly ten feet tall, grinning down at me.

"Lose sight of something?" I asked, grasping his ball. His long locks swayed, detecting his error, and he nodded gently. I love long hair on men. It didn't matter the texture, color, or style. Mami said I was a lioness with my natural blond curls, so I love manes. The longer, the more I need to touch it. His hair hung to his lean shoulders in a thick ponytail and seemed so soft. "I spotted it near the pond and saved it."

The breeze gathered up again when I hurled the soccer ball to him. I heard the solid sound of the impact. It hit him in the center of his chest, and I hoped I didn't throw it too hard. His hand caught it like a reflex then he suddenly stirred. Glancing up at me through his golden frames, which looked dazzling in the morning sunlight, his eyes grew so soft and sweet.

"Yeah, it got away from me. The breeze is a little strong," He declared. His voice was deep and kind as he leered more. He held it close to his body, and his smile swelled greater. I felt satisfied that I had actually talked to him as I glanced back toward my house. "I've never seen you around before. You have an accent. I love it."

"Oui, my Mami and I, we moved here about a week ago," I replied as I glanced back at him. He took a step near me, and suddenly I couldn't move.

"Is that right? Things are beginning to unexpectedly appear hopeful around here," he stated. His arms grew tense as he began to twirl the ball, eyeing me. However, his shoulders were relaxed, and his smile dazzled me.

He advanced nearer, holding out his hand. I was so glad he was offering to shake my hand. American boys were so very different than everywhere else I had lived. I never liked to be touched unexpectedly by strangers. I would have moved if he had come any closer or tried to touch me any other way. Instead, I drew his hand over and shook it, beaming.

There was so much warmth coming from his skin. He gawked at my hand, admiring my fingernails, and demanded, "What's your name, Sunshine?"

"Mandisa, Mandisa Isoka King, what is your name?" I requested. All I could do was smile, being close to this boy. These strange ripples were running over me as he kept my hand; his eyes plunged. They began to examine me seriously, and I felt incredibly underdressed. I had only put on my Prince tee shirt and a pair of purple leggings. He seemed to think otherwise, grinning at my slippers.

"I'm Hakim Jahlil Dunn, Mandisa. Your name is distinct and very lovely," Hakim declared to me, grinning yet nestling my hand. He looked intensely into my eyes. I felt suddenly awkward as his fingers began to fondle my hand. His russet eyes looking me over made me feel peculiar. I yanked it away, cackling anxiously.

"Very nice to know you, Hakim," I replied.

"The blessing is truly mine, Mandisa," Hakim affirmed, glaring at me again. He twirled the ball between his fingers and leered at me. "I run through this park every day. I have never stopped until today. Eight years I've traced this street, then like magic, here you are, Mandisa. That's ironic, I suppose. It's never been as lovely as it is right this minute. Huh, feels like fate."

I stretched my fingernails along my neck, giggling, "Very smooth, Hakim. I bet the girls really eat that up."

"I've never said that to a woman before, Mandisa. Not many women can hold my attention for long. I get bored easily," Hakim disclosed. He tilted his head slightly while nibbling his bottom lip, flirting with me. It was like Hakim was aiming to say something with his eyes. I wanted to head home, and he was making me worried by glaring at me. My eyes kept drifting to Hakim's lovely defined arms and legs, thinking how much stronger Hakim was than me. I thought he was sweet, and now that we spoke, we would talk again, perhaps. But I did not need to press my luck. "You're a beautiful woman, Mandisa King."

"I am only seventeen, Hakim, so I wouldn't say a woman just yet," I informed him. I gradually began to stroll up the path toward my house. "By the way, Hakim, you have a gorgeous smile."

I did it, I spoke to him, and Hakim was delightful!. That conversation was polite and well-mannered, and it was much different from any boy I had ever met in the U.S. He wasn't demanding of me or too touchy. I stepped to the park gate and peered down the street toward the house. Mami wasn't home yet. I beamed as I left for the walkway.

"Hey, Mandisa!" I heard Hakim shout as I walked. The grass near the gate had a sprinkler, and I felt the cool spray mist my face. I snorted as Hakim caught my hand abruptly. I was suspended in place as he stomped on his brakes in front of me. "Hey!"

"Oui?" I gulped. He had only gone a few feet from where I left him, but he appeared out of breath, clutching my hand. Hakim's eyes were wide as he stared down at me with a confident sneer. He touched my fingers and shook his head, beaming. He was so different from the way he grinned at me. It made me blush, and my chest began to heave. Oh, my god! How did he get so considerably intense with a full grin? His first smile was adorable, but when he flashed me those beautiful white teeth…perfection! "Oui, Chocolate Sucre…. Hakim…sorry!"

Hakim's eyebrows nearly jumped off his face, and his nostrils flared somewhat. I was ready to run. As he kept my hand happy, softly, I started to feel the urge to touch him. His skin was so warm that it was like instant happiness for a moment. It was addictive, and I believe Hakim sensed it too! He didn't intend to let my hand free.

"Do you live around here, Mandisa?" He inquired, his lips curling beautifully as he caressed my arm. Hakim had the most adorable face up close. His big brown eyes were so expressive like the Precious Moments babies Mami collected. They sparkled in the sunshine, and even when Hakim was smiling, his eyes appeared gloomy. His eyebrows emoted more than his eyes. But that smile was worth a thousand dollars. "May I, please, walk you home?"

"I live just down the road. But why do you want to walk with me, Hakim?" I requested.

"If I walk you home, then my chances of seeing you again improves. Maybe you can bless me tomorrow with sunshine as well?" Hakim responded, his light brown cheeks glowing as he looked into my eyes. Hakim seemed so serious, retaking my hand and stroking my fingers.

"You are sweet, Hakim. You can walk with me," I sighed, surrendering to his charm.

I gently pulled my arm away before following the sidewalk. Hakim walked next to me. He kept touching his shoulder into mine, getting me to smile. I kept walking, trying not to seem afraid of him. But I was terrified of that fine man! He was no boy. I knew that the moment I saw him up close. Hakim's body is absolutely Godly! Hakim is not joking when it comes to his training. He is running like he is Forrest Gump! That's what caught my attention the first day. He ran nearly 30 laps around the park. But that was after we saw Hakim up by the store. So Hakim runs for distance and speed!

He glanced up at the sky and then peered across the street.

"So, where are you from, Mandisa?" he requested. As he spoke to me, he flared his nostrils and raised his eyebrows in a silly manner. Hakim waved his head and sneered. I was trying not to laugh.

"I was born in Monrovia, Liberia. Mami and I moved here from Paris, France," I replied.

"Wow, so you've seen the world?" he queried. An impressed look on his face hinted that he maybe wanted to travel from here. Hakim liked running, so obviously, travel was something he admired. He seemed eager to keep me talking while holding all his attention on me. "I want to know everything about you."

"You could say I have seen a lot of places, Hakim. Daddy is a heart surgeon. He is very well known in South Africa and Germany, so we have moved around a lot over the years. Well, my mother and I have done the majority of the moving. Daddy is rarely around us much," I responded.

I found myself sulking. I don't know why I was talking about my father at all. He was the last person that I needed to bring up. If he knew about this conversation, he would lose his mind! I could almost hear him screaming at me about how I should never trust these 'black boys' or any man he doesn't delegate. So what that my mother was black! None of 'THEM' were good enough for me.

Hakim stopped his stride in front of me unexpectedly.

"Well, I'm glad you're here in our little town, Mandisa. It's nice to see more color in the suburbs. There aren't many black people around here," Hakim informed me. His eyes started dancing. I pushed my previous thoughts away, quickly staring at Hakim. There was something about him that made me feel peaceful.

"It's so beautiful here. It's nothing like where we've lived before. There were hardly any trees," I told Hakim, moving a branch overhead. I strolled past him. He stopped to observe me.

"Yeah, it is- perfect, really…." Hakim mumbled under his breath from behind.

"I am sorry. What did you say, Hakim?" I asked, stopping across the street from my house.

"I was just saying how beautiful it is around here. I think you'll love- it here," Hakim replied, flinging the soccer ball from one hand to the other, catching up.

"I think so too. I have never met such polite people like here in Texas. Where do you live, Hakim?" I wondered, glancing around at the rainbow-colored flowers in bloom all across the fences down Cooper Rd.

"Um, I live on the next street over, Mandisa. My house really isn't that far from here. But we- my family- we're not from Texas. We used to live in Atlanta, Georgia," Hakim added. I crossed the street and walked into the vine-covered gateway. "Is this your house? I pass here all the time."

"I know," I chuckled. I held the gate open for Hakim. He stole it, allowing me to walk through, followed slowly up the stone path to the porch. I climbed the steps and sat back in my spot on the swing. Hakim leaned forward on the porch, pushing the chain, making me sway.

"Atlanta is a long way from here, Hakim. Is it different than Texas? Atlanta is full of bright lights and noise I've heard," I started but paused. I was distracted, staring at the solid muscles in his thigh on the top step. Hakim's knees, calves, and shins were rock solid. Hakim leaned his head closer toward my face, breaking my gaze. I looked away. He started laughing and pushed the swing again.

"Yeah, it is totally different. But I've gotten used to Texas. I didn't like it at first. In fact, I really hated it here. But it's alright now. I had a few friends I left behind, but it's all good, Mandisa," He mentioned. Hakim smiled downward, watching the swing.

"Why did you move here to Longview, Texas, from Atlanta?" I raised. I reached for my book to stop it from sliding around the swing. Hakim snatched it and stared at the cover. As he glanced back at me, I motioned him to sit. He held my book for a moment then climbed the step to sit next to me.

"My parents… died a few years ago. My grandparents are the only family my brother and I have left. They took the insurance money and got us out of Georgia. My mother was born and raised here in Longview. Grandma thought Texas would be a better place to start over," Hakim answered as he glanced at my hardcover.

"I am sorry to hear about your parents, Hakim," I stated, frowning. I watched his hands stroke the cover of the book. His eyes seemed distant for a moment, lost in thought, and he peered up at me.

"It was a long time ago. But I really appreciate it, Mandisa. So, you like to read?" Hakim questioned, quickly changing the subject.

"Oui, I read when I am not busy with everything else that fills my time. I have so many hobbies," I responded, blushing. Hakim raised his eyebrows suspiciously, eyeing me. I stole my book back, suddenly feeling like a nerd. "Music, art, dance, and studying anything I can get my hands on are the only things I've been pursuing."

"Psychology is a great subject. I'm a Martial Arts/Philosophy buff myself," Hakim handsomely chuckled, reading the title.

"Really? You read too?" I demanded, giving him the same leery look. He leaned back, driving the swing.

"I read too much, Mandisa. All I do is play sports, study, eat, and chill. I'm a go-with-the-flow type of guy," Hakim answered, shaking his head getting a few of his locks stuck to the wall behind.

My hand pulled his dreadlocks away from the bricks. Hakim grew quiet, watching me as I twirled one in my fingers, admiring the spongy softness. I couldn't help wanting to feel the texture of the curls. The sun had bleached the black near his roots, and it was lighter than the ends. Hakim had red, green, and black wooden beads on one. His eyes tracked my fingertips, frolicking across the RBG flag sticker on his mp3 player.

"Wow, Mandisa, you really are a breath of fresh air. You're beautiful, you've got brains, and you've got a soft feminine form, too. I must be the luckiest man on Earth right now," Hakim chuckled, leaning closer so I could touch his hair. "You love it? It's all me."

"It is gorgeous, Hakim… It is so long… and thick," I complimented him. As I ran my fingers through his twisted-up tresses, he leaned back in his seat and stared me in the eye, smiling. "How long have you been growing your hair like this?"

"I started growing an afro when I was really young. It got so long I couldn't keep up with it. My best friend, Cyrus, he was growing dreads when we were kids. I decided to start getting mine twisted up, too," He stated prominently as I played with his rope-like twists, "That was five years ago. Now it's insanely long. I'll keep getting it twisted and lined up until I get sick of it. Then I don't know what I'll do. But I love my crown."

"It is a very magnificent mane," I thought, hypnotized. I nearly lept from my seat as Hakim reached for my bun. He was getting comfortable touching me, and it made me nervous. I couldn't help but tremble when he was so close.

"So, Mandisa, what are you hiding in there? It's pretty big," Hakim laughed, ignoring my tremors.

Hakim had a strange guise of suspicion after touching my damp hair. I was sensitive about my appearance, and I knew that sometimes people didn't think I was black. Hakim made the connection immediately. It was refreshing. But he was obsessed with my features staring at everything.

"I put it up in a hurry! It's still wet," I told him, blushing. He leaned into my shoulder, making the swing move.

"Let me see it? Or is it a weave?" He snickered, teasing my embarrassment.

"It is not a weave!" I growled, rolling my eyes at him. I took down the bun and untwisted it. I pulled away the ponytail holder putting it on my wrist. He sneered, watching me as I ran my fingers through it, letting it hit my shoulders then fall down my back.

"That's crazy," Hakim exclaimed. He glanced away anxiously, suddenly watching the road, then peering everywhere. "You're a gorgeous woman, Mandisa. So, where is your man? I get the feeling you have a stalker somewhere? Is he in the bushes? Just blink three times if you're in danger! Is that why you're so nervous?"

"No, I don't have a boyfriend! I told you I just moved here," I giggled, playfully ramming his arm. He snatched my hand and slowly pulled me closer until I could feel his next breath graze my left cheek while eyeing me. He raised his eyebrows and gazed into my eyes, making me blush. My heart began to pound in my ears so loudly I knew he heard it being so close! Hakim smiled and pulled away a bit.

"So, may I have your phone number, Mandisa? Maybe I can show you around? Could we catch a movie, or go to a concert? Why don't you let me change your relationship status?" Hakim pleaded.

"I do not know, Hakim. You are wonderful, but my father would never allow me to date. The thought of me dating strikes fear into his heart. Besides, I think a boyfriend would distract me from my music, art, and dance studies. I'd want to spend too much time with him," I grumbled.

I leaned forward, putting my head in my hands. There was no way that it would work. I wanted a friend, but a BOY would send my father over the top. Though he and Mami were separated, he would show up and chase Hakim away. By the time Daddy's done, Hakim would never want to speak to me again. It would be so agonizing to get my hopes up.

"You said you lived here with your mother. Don't you think it's alright to have an associate that's a man, Mandisa?" Hakim questioned. "You can have a friend, can't you?"

"Mami wants me to make friends! I don't have many," I admitted staring at his concerned sad eyes.

"Me either. I have two real friends and a crazy little brother. But if you want, I can be your friend, Mandisa? You're new here. You need someone you can trust to show you around town, don't you?" He posed, watching me with irritated eyes.

I glanced over at the driveway as Mami's car pulled in. She blew the horn. I got up and headed over to help her get out.

"Merci beaucoup, Queen. Ooh, my back is on fire," she declared, holding her belly, getting out of the car. I opened the back and grabbed a few bags. Hakim seized them from me. Mami didn't waste a second when she saw Hakim. "Bonjour! I'm sorry. I don't believe we've met?"

"Hello, my name is Hakim," He said to Mami, smiling as he took the groceries away from me. Hakim's face exploded talking to my mother. He was so happy it made me jealous. "You must be Mandisa's mother? I can see that beauty runs in the family. You look ready to bless the world with another beautiful child. May I help you inside?"

"Oui, oui, Hakim. It's so nice to meet such a sweet young man," Mami expressed him. She chuckled as she brushed her belly. While waddling sluggishly to the steps, Mami raised her eyebrows quickly. I assisted her upstairs, and she undid the door for Hakim. "He's so gorgeous and sweet!"

"I know," I quietly said. I held the door open. Hakim got Mami's attention first. She had pointed him out everywhere we went. Mami was trying to get me to say hello for a reason. I was happy I listened. He was charming.

"Hakim, keep going straight ahead," Mami said, deliberately later with me squeezing her arm.

Hakim was looking around at all the pictures and paintings adorning the walls. Mami loved to display and decorate with all the art she could find. Hakim seemed distracted by all the portraits, sculptures, and collectibles everywhere. I tapped his shoulder when I passed him in the den as we headed into the kitchen. He snapped back to reality and followed us.

"Hakim, do you attend school?" Mami summoned him and sat at the table.

"Yes, Mam. I'll be a senior at Washington Carver Private Academy this year," Hakim replied, entering the kitchen with the groceries.

"Queen, you're attending Carver as well," Mami inserted. "What a coincidence! Do you play soccer? I know I have seen you running every day, Hakim. You're in wonderful shape!"

"Yes, Mam, I've been playing for about six years now. I run track and field, and I head the National Honor Society. I've been studying and training my body with martial arts since I was six. I have a few other hobbies," He gushed at Mami with a shy grin. Hakim sat the grocery bags on the counter.

"That is very impressive, Hakim," Mami notified him, cheery with bright eyes feeling Amani. She became distracted as my sister began moving. I left, putting the food away, still listening to the conversation. "You're very well-rounded. So you're going to college, I take it?"

"Oh yes, I've already taken enough A.P. classes to qualify me as a second-year once I graduate high school, Mrs. King," Hakim answered proudly. I couldn't believe how absolutely perfect Hakim seemed. He was intelligent, sweet, athletic, and so very handsome in every way. He glanced over at me, winking as he handed me the eggs. "I know I'm a nerd…I'm just sort of cute…right? I get that a lot."

"Are you serious? Hakim, you are a sexy chocolate drop." Mami giggled, blushing up from her seat, observing Hakim's reaction to her interview. "What's your major?"

"Pre-law, economics, business, and African-American studies," Hakim answered. "I hope to open my own legal practice someday, Mrs. King. I've always been a debater, so I decided to become a defense attorney. My grandparents always say I should get paid for arguing and yelling at someone else besides my little brother, Lionel."

"Do you have a girlfriend, Hakim?" Mami continued drilling him.

"No, but I would love to have one if she was as sweet as your daughter, Mrs. King," Hakim confessed to Mami, embarrassing me. I blushed as he made eye contact with me. He smiled and looked at Mami again as she spoke.

"Boyfriend?" She analyzed. Her face was dead serious.

"No!" Hakim snickered. "I have a few homeboys but not that type of party. I love women! I've just never had a girlfriend."

"So, you're a virgin like Queen?" Mami persisted, her eyes squinting, but her smile faded from sight.

"You're funny, Mrs. King!" Hakim laughed, wiping a tear from his eye removing his glasses.

"No, Hakim, I'm serious! Answer the question," Mami grilled him.

"Um…no, I'm not a virgin, Mrs. King. I'm no longer sexually active, though. I used to be very wild when I was younger, running the streets. But it got ancient after years of playing the field.

"I've never met a girl like your daughter, Mrs. King. No woman has ever held my attention very long," Hakim confessed. He put his hand on the table, watching Mami. "Mandisa's the most beautiful girl I've ever seen in my entire life. The moment I laid my eyes on her, I thought I must be dreaming. I don't believe in Heaven. But a real-life angel was standing right in front of me. It scared me until she spoke to me. I thought I got hit by a car and was dead."

"I like you, Hakim. You're sweet, you like to talk, you're honest and respectable," Mami tittered suddenly, making me jump. She stood up and touched his arm as she passed him. Hakim smiled at her appearing to relax a bit. Mami grabbed a skillet and gazed back at him, "Finding good people to be friends with Mandisa is no easy task. Her father is very selective of whom she may socialize".

"He doesn't need to know all the details. I just want my daughter to have some fun and make some nice friends. She needs to be around people her own age, Hakim. Longview is very unfamiliar to us, but I hope you can show her around? School is going to be new for Queen. She's been home tutored for her entire life."

I suddenly felt like I was a burden to my mother. I only had one real friend, and she was so special to me, but when daddy met her, he told me to stop hanging around her. He said she was trying to change me into an American girl. I didn't like that at all. My father didn't want me doing much of anything involving other people. So it was only Mami and me, along with all my private instructors. I was kept away from public schools and raised with the best of everything money could buy. But I was never happy alone, and Mami had to give up her career to raise me.

I was premature, weak, and my heart never developed correctly as I grew up. I need a transplant, and we all know it, but we can't be near Daddy. It's best to hide than endure more of his torture. I know that my father is overprotective of me because nothing could fix the birth defect. But he treats everyone like he hates them for looking at me. He drinks when he's home and fights with Mami about how Amani will be raised as well. Daddy hasn't decided if I'm going to be attending college after this year. My prognosis isn't good, so I don't complain or start more problems. But it seems that no matter what I do or where we go, I always make him angry.

I'm pessimistic about things getting better with Mami close to delivering my sister and separating from Daddy. Who knows how long before he finds us and takes us back? It seems there's nowhere Mami can go to get away from him. Daddy always finds us, lies, begs, and showers her with gifts and affection. Mami always goes back, and things get worse. I've stopped expecting something to happen. I accept whatever is presented. I only want to live long enough to see Amani healthy and happy. Then I don't care what happens to me. I can't be near my father anymore.

I handed the eggs to my mother, struggling not to look at Hakim. I'm sure her little snooping session must have discouraged him somewhat by now. I was glad that he didn't use those beautiful legs to run out of the house.

"I'm thrilled that you think I'm worthy of Mandisa's friendship, Mrs. King. It means a lot to me. Can I help with anything?" Hakim offered to help at the stove.

"No, Cheri, I can handle this part. Queen, show Hakim where he can wash up. You will stay for breakfast, won't you?" Mami invited him, smiling sweetly.

"I'd love to stay, Mrs. King! I knew the moment that I saw you that you were going to offer. I'd be a fool not to try something," Hakim accepted, gawking at her. Then he quickly glared, "Wait? Queen? What's that about?"

Mami giggled, "Alex Haley, who is my favorite author, has a movie called *Queen*. I watched it when I was pregnant with Mandisa. So when she was born, I took one look at her, and she became my little Queen. It just stuck. She also has that fresh skin like Halle Berry. That's why I nicknamed her Queen."

"I've seen the movie before. I can see a small resemblance. But Mandisa has a distinctive beauty. That's even lovelier. It's rare for women these days to not rely on chemicals and artificial enhancements. I've never adored anything fake, but I can't hate anyone that does. That's what they have to live with and wake up to in the morning," Hakim chuckled, shrugging his shoulders. He was admiring my Mami's hair and nails the same as he did mine outside.

"So, you're a naturalist?" Mami requested, grinning over at Hakim.

"I would say I am a realist. I work out, don't eat red meat, lie unless it spares the right feelings, respect people until the line gets crossed, and never trust what the media or politicians say. I like to watch people. I'm really ashamed of the way black people behave in the public eye, but you can't stop people from being themselves, right?" Hakim replied with a ring of enlightenment that made me nod.

"Oui," I agreed, smiling at Hakim. "People have to make up their own mind about whom or what they become on the inside and out."

"We're not from around here, so we get looks sometimes. We do not eat red meat either, mostly seafood, poultry, and soy. Nor do we attend church services. I allow my daughter to make her own religious choices. I used to be a Jehovah's Witness because I preferred home services with family and friends," Mami explained with a tone of relief.

"That's a very admirable thing, Mrs. King. I'm not really sure I know what I believe. My family members are all Christians, but they haven't attended services since we moved to Texas from Georgia. No one has set foot inside of a church since my parents died. I used to believe.

"My mother was a devout Christian, but losing her shook us up. My grandparents are always talking about the Lord," Hakim groaned, scratching his forehead leaning backward.

"That's so terrible, losing both parents, Hakim. Are you alright?" Mami sighed as she touched his shoulder.

"I'm fine, Mrs. King. It happened when I was nine. We all took it pretty hard. My little brother, Lionel, he was seven at the time. I think he took it the hardest. He started being bad, fighting all the time, and getting in trouble at school. He's 15, doing a little better, but he's still terrible," Hakim stated, shaking his head. "I love my brother, don't get me wrong, that's family. But he's wild, he's violent, his mouth is as foul and loud as the day is long. He's brilliant, has an amazing voice, can dance, and is a really gifted artist. Lionel can sketch some of the craziest stuff I've ever seen."

Hakim's eyes drifted to the living area, adding, "But those paintings you have in the den, that's intense art! Who did those? I've never seen anything like that anywhere."

"Queen painted all those pictures on the walls everywhere in the house. All of those are her works except the family pictures," Mami answered, checking the heat.

He wrinkled his lovely eyebrows, got up, and walked into the den. Hakim pointed to the painting of a river of faces over the sofa. "Word? You painted this?!" Hakim asked, staring at the picture. I followed him into the den and stood close by. He glanced down at me as I nodded.

"I painted it after we moved from Philadelphia. We only stayed there for a few weeks during the summer. I saw so many black people there. It was the first time I lived in America. I had never seen so many people in different colors, shapes, heights, and from various backgrounds. It was so inspiring to me. I couldn't help myself," I explained, admiring the shades and tints of brown on black.

"This one?" Hakim asked while pointing to the beautiful black ballerina next to the first painting. She was surrounded by beautiful multi-colored roses. But there was darkness everywhere and eyes watching her. She had a look of sad confusion on her face crying as she looked in the mirror—a different woman in the reflection staring back at her with a frown and glowing green eyes.

"I really can't explain it. That's how I feel sometimes. I was a dancer for years. It made me feel so special to be on stage in the spotlight, but I was not allowed to perform once I grew older. If I don't paint, dance, or play music, I wouldn't know who I am as a person. A lot of times, I'm not sure who I see when I look in the mirror," I confessed, examining her miserably beautiful face in the painting. I didn't know if this girl was me. However, it felt like it could be me one day.

His eyebrows wrinkled together as his eyes grew wider by the second analyzing the last portrait.

The image of a beautiful girl wearing a black and white dress standing over a gorgeous landscape scene in the painting might disturb him like it terrified me. The beautiful hills and trees below, the night sky above, and she held out her arms with her eyes closed.

I remembered how I felt when I started it. I was so upset. My father and I had an argument about a boy that I didn't even know. The boy said hello, then without warning, my father screamed at him and frightened him away. Afterward, he badgered me in the middle of the mall parking lot. I took it as a lesson to stay away from men. I was so depressed after he yelled at me, I couldn't speak without coming to tears.

"Why is she going to jump?" Hakim probed with the most pitiful frown. He put his glasses on, carefully moving closer to the painting.

"No one's ever asked that. Most see the gorgeous surroundings, the trees below, and they kind of overlook the subject. Those that notice the woman think she's rejoicing or enjoying the breeze. But she's about to leap to her death.

"Speaking as the artist, the subject is not happy being tormented by her skin and living in her prison. She's alone, her heart is aching, and she wants to fly away. Maybe the girl is afraid of the dark and being alone? It looks like she thinks death might be peaceful," I sighed and touched her fearful face.

"The idea of there being beauty in death below is more acceptable than the harsh reality of her own sad existence," Hakim thought, stroking her clothing. "She's so beautiful but so sad."

Hakim glanced over at me from the painting. I avoided eye contact touching some of Mami's angels. I didn't like to discuss sad things, so I evaded talking too much. Especially anything that involved my father. That was a subject that I detested.

"What are you working on now?" Hakim questioned, poking me in the wing then playfully fondling one of my curls on my shoulder.

"I'll show you," I replied, smiling. I led Hakim down a hall and upstairs behind the kitchen. He trailed silently, seeing more of my sketches and pictures along the decorated walls. As I opened my bedroom window and went inside, I realized I had forgotten to air out the paint fumes earlier. It wasn't really that bad, but the oil paints I used did have a traceable odor. Hakim didn't seem to mind. He surveyed my bedroom in silence, pleased.

My art things were all in the far corner near the back window. Next to it was my stool; on the art table were some closed supplies, glasses with brushes soaking, and a sketch pad. On the easel was a painting of a gorgeous sunrise over a beach scene, a handsome brown boy was running along the sand, his long dreadlocks were flowing in the breeze, and a girl was sitting in the foreground watching him as he ran into the distance. Hakim came closer to the painting and went crazy!

"That's me?!" He asked suddenly as he leaned closer. "Wow, look at the detail of the hair!"

"It is the lion's share of what I see when you run by, Hakim," I giggled as I put a brush into the cleaning solution.

"I've seen you fly by every day for a week. You've never noticed me until Mami talked me into following you today."

Hakim stared at the girl's face. She wore a lovely shy smile gazing at him.

"He was just so busy looking ahead. If he had only stopped, he would feel like I feel right now, Mandisa," Hakim alerted me.

He stared into my eyes and explored around more. Next, he picked up one of my photographs on my nightstand near my bed. It was a picture of me when I was four years old in a ballet tutu with Mami. Finally, he touched one of my stuffed animals, a lion cub that sat on my bed.

"I have a weakness for wildcats," I informed him. Then, I showed him my lion cubs and panthers.

"My mother was a Black Panther. I can dig it!" Hakim laughed, touching my bed linens. "Red and gold, huh? Red's my favorite color besides black. But gold looks good with it, too."

I nodded, agreeing as I opened my candy dish and put a piece of cherry candy in my mouth. Hakim came close to me. His eyes looked into mine as he stood in front of me. My heart started racing, and I blushed deeply.

"May I have a piece of your candy, Mandisa?" He asked, putting his hand over mine still on the lid.

"Of course, Hakim," I replied, looking at his hand as it touched mine. He opened the lid, grabbed a piece, and tucked it into his pocket for later. Then he put the top back in place while still keeping my hand.

He saw my cell phone on the dresser near the candy dish and grabbed it. He dialed in a number, and I heard his ringtone, making me giggle, "A Tribe Called Quest, Bonita Applebum."

"What?!" Hakim asked, smiling as he sat down my phone and saved my number in his.

"I gotta put you on?" I teased him as he looked at me, impressed.

"Oh, you know about my boys, A Tribe Called Quest?" Hakim laughed.

"I'm a music lover. I like good music. Everything that gets played on the radio is not good music. Mami says I have an old soul because I like her kind of music. I love Prince, Stevie Wonder, Michael Jackson, Marvin Gaye, and The Roots," I tried to explain as I rolled the candy around in my mouth.

"What about hip-hop?" Hakim quizzed me, raising his eyebrow suspiciously.

"I like Kendrick Lamar, J. Cole, Ludacris, 2 Pac, B.I.G., Jay-Z, Common, Mos Def, Dead Prez, Talib Kwali, and lots more," I recalled as many as I could. "But I listen to all kinds of music: Rock, Disco, Country, World Music, and lots of Classical…."

"Keep going. I haven't heard anything I don't like yet," Hakim sighed. He raised my hand to his lips and kissed it. His lips were so soft and gentle that I wanted to scream. Suddenly I realized I had him alone in my room!

I gulped, still struggling to hold the remaining bite of candy in my cheek but nearly choked when his lips caressed my skin. He patted me on the back and chuckled apprehensively.

"Are you okay? I wasn't trying to make you do that," Hakim stated with a flashy grin.

"I'm fine!" I snickered, wiping a tear from my eye. "I totally disregarded it was there."

Hakim stared at me for a moment, nonetheless uneasy. I was so embarrassed. My face must have been redder than my lips from eating the candy. Finally, Hakim sneered at me and retook my hand, "You sure you're okay, Queen?"

I lingered when I heard him call me that. He stared at me and looked genuinely worried for me. I just nodded and smiled.

"You said that you love Prince? Friday night, they're showing a double feature at the old movie theater: *Purple Rain* and *Under The Cherry Moon*," Hakim chuckled finally as he nudged me in the arm, teasingly. Glancing at my tee-shirt and yoga pants, you knew I loved Prince! "You want to go with me, Mandisa?"

My beam must have been enormous as the notion made my face light up. Hakim nodded, egging me on with his attractive grin, but my spirits began tumbling again. This was not going to happen! Daddy would ruin anything if he showed up.

I did not want to hurt his feelings. Hakim was so kind to me. But I knew that nothing would come of me saying yes.

"Mami should be finished cooking. Let me show you the restroom so you can wash up? After that, you have to eat with us. Mami won't take no for an answer. She loves entertaining guests," I reacted, avoiding the subject, and left for the door.

Hakim tugged my hand; I had neglected he was still grasping it. He leisurely hauled me backward, groaning, "Mandisa, I'm not leaving your house until you tell me yes. I won't take no for an answer, either. I'm not going to hurt you or betray your sweet nature.

"I just want to spend my extra time with you. Can I put in my application for the position of a full-time fanatic, please? Let me change your mind about the whole boyfriend idea?

"Everything that I told your mother I meant. I've never wanted to get to know a woman as desperately as I wish for you. Being here with you is the sweetest dream I've ever had. So, please, don't make me wake up, not yet…?"

"Hakim," I sighed, gently embarrassed. He suddenly glanced down into my eyes with an incredible expression. His beautiful eyes sparkled down at me, and Hakim blushed.

"Repeat my name, Queen. Say it just like that," Hakim uttered, placing my hand over his heart. "Say, Hakim, like before…"

My heart was already thumping in my throat. I held my breath as I felt the tightness of Hakim's chest through his compression shirt. He shut his eyes and beamed as I said his name sweetly again, "Hakim..."

"Did you feel that, Mandisa?" He demanded. I felt his heart speeding up as he grew excited. He kept his eyes closed and put his hand over mine. "The heart doesn't lie, Queen. My heart wants you."

"My father would never approve of me dating anyone, Hakim," I groaned, rattling my head. Hakim opened his sweet brown eyes and slowly exhaled. His fingers trembled, tracing mine as he tilted his head back, thinking.

"What if your mother said yes, and we don't worry about Daddy until the time comes?" Hakim suggested with elevated eyebrows.

"I can't lie to my dad, Hakim!" I told him nervously, afraid.

"I didn't say lie. I said we don't worry about telling your father until the time comes," Hakim said, grinning back viciously. "What Daddy doesn't know what hurt him... Mami likes me, Queen."

"That's wrong, Hakim! You don't know my father. He's a crazy white man with one hell of a temper," I cautioned him honestly. Hakim had no idea how terrifying Daddy could be once he was furious. He was like a fire-breathing dragon hurling out slurs. It upset me to think that Daddy would hurt Hakim or anyone for just speaking to me. "He is a monster."

"So, you're going to just sit there and watch that sexy brown boy run off into the sunset?" Hakim asked, frowning. I nodded in defeat. I didn't want to imagine the things he would say or do to any of us. Daddy had his ways; I couldn't go against him. It could mean him hurting Mami or Amani to get his way in the end. As long as my sister and mother were safe, I'd be fine no matter what he did to me. But I couldn't involve Hakim. Mami wanted me to have a friend to cheer me up, like in Phili. But Daddy ruined that too. "Mandisa, seriously, you're that terrified of your own father."

"He's running into the sunrise because he's been with her on the beach all night," I informed him, smiling at the painting. I was done talking and thinking about that man. He made me so upset sometimes I would cry and could not stop. But, I was enjoying the day with Hakim. "Memories can be great. Even if they are just in fantasy land, I paint them."

"Is that right?" Hakim asked, coming closer to me. He took both of my hands in his. "I'm standing right here, Mandisa. That boy is right here with you now. He wants you. I want you!"

Hakim kissed my lips! It surprised me how fast it happened; he held me close to his warm solid body as his lips tasted mine. A huff of breath touched my face as his tongue glided across my bottom lip. I'd never been kissed before, though I had dreamed about it a million times. His hands caressed my back before I felt his fingers move my hips, squeezing. I exhaled and wrenched away. Hakim had a desperate expression on his face, staring down licking his lips. Finally, he held up his hands in surrender.

"Mandisa, I want you to fall in love with me so I can shower you with all the affection I've been holding inside. I know I can make you love me if you just give me a try, Queen, please?" He begged me, his eyes never leaving mine.

I was so weak from the kiss, I was entranced by his words as I concurred involuntarily. Hakim leered as he stroked my cheek. It was the magnificent grin that dazzled me at the park.

"Only if my mother agrees. If she says no, then I can't, Hakim," I warned him. My heart even now prancing as I felt my lips. Hakim nodded at me smiling. He got another look at the painting but glanced out of my bedroom window.

"Oh shit!" He snickered abruptly. He realized he had sworn and hid his mouth, chuckling to himself. I gaped at him, puzzled. "I'm sorry, Mandisa."

"What is it?" I worried, seeking to hold in my cackle at his embarrassment.

"I can see my house from here! There's my backyard right there!" Hakim hooted, pointing to the house directly behind us. I had noticed it before, but the flowers and vines over the fence made it hard to see from the street. Sometimes I could see a sweet old couple working in the garden in the evenings out my window. Our gates were linking, making me smile at the irony.

"I think I've seen your grandparents out there, Hakim. Sometimes there's a woman in the garden and a man grilling," I giggled, nudging his shoulder.

"Yeah, those are my grandparents. Granddad thinks he's Martha Stewart. He was supposed to be the gardener, but Grandma Sophie ends up doing all the work. He loves to barbeque! He even fires that grill up in the middle of winter," Hakim laughed.

"They look happy together," I reported to Hakim, grinning.

"Oh yeah, they're crazy about each other. My G.D. is an asshole most of the time. But Grandma Sophie is the sweetest woman on Earth. I'll have to invite you over one day. They'll love you. I've never brought a girl home. It might give G.D. a heart attack," Hakim snorted. He gnawed his bottom lip as he gazed at me over the top of his frames with adorable puppy eyes.

"We'd better get out of here before Mami thinks something is going on between us. I'm not trying to upset her. It's too soon for her to go into labor. She's a high-risk pregnancy because of her age," I warned him. I departed for the door. He chased me lightly and closed my bedroom door.

Chapter Two: For Free? (The Struggle)

Hakim Jahlil Dunn

The universe is so good! I was feeling some kind of way! I grabbed my soccer ball off the porch after I said goodbye to Mandisa and Mrs. King. I headed down the street, running on a completely full battery. Mrs. King cooked an absolutely delicious meal, and I felt like I had just got hit by a bolt of lightning. I was so energized.

I spent the entire morning with them, and I managed to talk Mrs. King into letting me take Mandisa somewhere for the afternoon. So I was amped! I hit a block running down Roosevelt Lane when my phone rang. Damn, who would be calling? Right…Osiris…Cyrus.

"Peace, Dunn-Sun! What's new in The View?" Cyrus bellowed as I answered, the phone still sprinting.

"Nothing much, Bro, just heading home. I've been out running. So what are you up to, Brother?!" I chuckled, clutching my phone and the ball carefully.

"I'm on my way to The View! I'm on the 20 right now in Atlanta, but I'll be there in a few hours or early in the morning. You ready to ball hard wit ya boy?" Cyrus requested. I could picture his smile through the phone.

"Hell yes, I am ready, Sir!" I snickered. "It's the summer, I ain't got no real job, I got a grip of paper, and my brother coming home?! What?!

'Bro, I just met a girl, too. I am on cloud nine, Cyrus!"

"What?! You? Hakim Dunn? You're... excited... about a girl?

"I got the wrong damn number! Let me check... I must have got the wrong, brother?

"No, it says Hakim! Who is this girl?" Cyrus snickered, nearly suffocating.

He was smoking weed and consistently elevated. That was my brother from another mother, Darius Cyrus Jefferson Jr. He knew me better than anyone else. I knew the moment I said that shit, he was going to call me on it. That's why I went ahead and got it out of the way.

"Man, she's like golden sunshine. I can't front! She's beyond words! Her body is like whoa, eyes like hey, her hair is like, what?! She is perfect!

"P-E-R-F-E-C-T...T-T-T! My brother, no lie, she is a goddess! She's so shy and sweet... I can't stop thinking about her! From the moment I laid eyes on her, it was like... Ahhhhhhh!

"That's the choir singing," I snickered as I clutched my house key from around my neck and unlocked the door.

"She got a fantastic friend?" Cyrus inquired seriously.

"She just moved here, Bro! No friends or brothers have got to her yet, Cyrus, Bro… I think I love her," I moaned as I leaned against the door frame and turned the knob. Then, I heard Cyrus spit incredibly deafening and began choking.

"What about what?!" Cyrus screamed into the phone after he caught his gulp of air completely. "Alright, I'm going to calmly and politely hang up the phone right fucking now.

"My brother, Hakim Dunn, doesn't fall in love! He never says that word! It's like sneezing on his food! Love is the most unacceptable word you won't answer to anyone but Grandma Sophie. So what the fuck are you talking about?

"I'm in my got damn car, but where's the fucking camera? Ah! Chance, you got me, man! I'm getting Punk'd, right?"

"I'm serious, Bro. I have never felt like this around a woman in my life. Of course, I've been with so many, you know that, but this girl got me elevated up. I can't stop grinning, Nigga! I'm so for real!" I informed him as I strolled into the living room, glancing around.

I ran upstairs to Lionel and my bedroom, tossing my ball in the closet and stripping my shirt.

"Bro, what's the pussy like?" Cyrus demanded. "It's got to be the best in the world if you all twisted up. When did you meet her? We just spoke the other day! You move too fast for me!"

"I just met her this morning, Bro. I ain't even aiming to fuck her, Cyrus. She's virtuous, Man," I breathed as I got down my hair. My beads smacked my shoulder, and the thought of her playing with my hair made my skin tremor. "Ooh! Damn! She's not reminiscent of anyone I've ever met."

"Yeah, that's how it always goes. All the girls are innocent until you get your hands all over them. Then you give them the package, and they go fucking crazy! So now you've got stalkers and Bush Bitches... remember the bush bitch? What was her name? Oh, yeah, Teresa!

"We went to take a piss at the club, and crazy-ass jumped out of the bushes on you? 'Hakim! Hakim, I love you! Why won't you talk to me anymore?! I miss you!'

"Does that sound familiar to you? She scared me to death, and you pissed on her! What the fuck are you thinking, Hakim... really?" Cyrus chuckled, forcing me to roll my eyes.

"No, Bro, you misconstrued me. Pay Attention to the sound of my voice...

"I said that I am not trying to fuck her, and I feel this good, not that I have fucked her.

"I met her mother and chilled with them all morning. Her mom actually adores me. I'm so in, and get this-her mom says she's a virgin!

"No one has ever touched her, Bro! I'm freaking out, Cyrus! I might just fall out and praise the fake White-Jesus right now! I think I got the Holy Ghost… nope…The moment passed!" I screamed, chuckling as I shook my head.

"I thought maybe she snuck and did something when I got her alone. Maybe her Mama just doesn't know, but no, Cyrus… she's pure, like a hundred percent Columbian!

"I could tell when I got that first kiss. It's so cute how scared the girl is of me. No one was in there but me and her. I knew she liked me, but she was too nervous to touch me. She was afraid to look me in the eye! I'm telling you, Cyrus, she's the one meant just for me! I must have been so good lately to deserve this!

"Jah! Heavenly, most divine, and supreme father above all, thank you for your perfect sunshine!" I screamed, amused, but I was genuine. I was so thrilled, I commenced bouncing on Lionel's bed.

"You lucky… ass! Alright, I… got to meet her now. Curiosity is killing me, Hakim. Oh, I'm terrified that the world might explode or World War III may jump off directly.

"My brother, Hakim Jalil Dunn, aka the Black Forrest Gump, is in love? I thought I was the only brother in this family besides Kaliah that fell in love," Cyrus thought, hacking in my ear. "Don't say her name is Jenny, or I'ma die!"

"I made a date this evening, and I need to show her a good time, so she'll know I'm really a good guy. She's not one of these thirsty chicks around East Texas. Her dad is a surgeon, so she has her own paper, but judging by how they talk about his white ass, he doesn't want anybody near her. So, I have to be careful, or her mother may cut off my visitation rights. So, I'm going to play this ice-cold, so there are no issues," I informed Cyrus.

"Where are you taking her, Bro? It's Thursday," Cyrus reminded me, causing me to frown. Fuck! There ain't shit to do in The View on a weeknight... even in the middle of June...

"I could take her to a movie, I guess... no... not until the weekend when the good stuff is playing. Maybe we can go to the mall... no... The View's mall is deadening as hell! I know, we can go to Hot Wheels!" I thought, pleased. It would be perfect for a first date. A skating rink full of kids on a weeknight was nothing for anyone to worry about with me. "I'm excited now! Let me go, Bro!"

"See you soon, Hakim! Ase!" Cyrus chuckled as I hung up the phone and flung it on the bed.

I stripped and hit the shower. The entire time I was with Mandisa, I was sweaty and hot. I knew I didn't smell, but I was tense as hell. I sweat more when I get nervous around strangers.

I sneered as I stared in the foggy mirror. Oh yes, I look good! I pouted and scowled.

Damn! I still haven't grown any facial hair… really? At least I still have a babyface. My eyebrows, sideburns, and edge-up look nice and clean, thanks to yesterday's trip to the barbershop. I'm a handsome brother, I think, and not having a beard or mustache hadn't stopped me from pulling women more than twice my age.

I dried myself off, brushed my teeth, and reached for my contact lenses but hesitated. My eyes weren't too dry, but better safe than sorry, I thought. After I tied my hair out of the way, I put on my underwear and collected up my clothes off the floor. A cherry Jolly Rancher fell out of a pocket, and I smirked as I seized it in my hand. I reminisced about the sweet and sour flavor of Mandisa's lips when I kissed her. Oh my God! I began growing enthusiastic and rested on my bed. No! Down, boy. This is not the time to be trying to get hard. I detected my phone on the bed and snatched it. Oh, a text from Mandisa?!

#

"Hakim, what should I wear? Where are we going?" Mandisa asked in her text.

"I'm taking you to a skating rink. ☺ You can skate, right?" I typed back.

"Yes, Mami taught me how to skate. So I should dress casually?" She responded, requesting.

"Just be comfy and your astounding, wonderful self," I responded.

"Alright, Hakim!" Mandisa texted me back.

"I'll be there in about an hour, Queen?" I probed, making sure.

"Okay, I'll be ready ☺" She forwarded me.

Why was I getting ecstatic over a smiley? I really hoped she liked me as much as I was feeling her. I wanted to break down those walls so she would let me in…her heart, not between her legs!

Don't be like Cyrus! He always has a dirty mind. Yes, I know you're reading my thoughts. Don't judge me…lol.

I felt like if I won Mandisa's affections, then that was all I needed. Everything else would just simply cascade beautifully in order. I'd never wanted to cling to a girl until I held her hand. Really, after I touched the ball…I needed to know her once I felt her plead on it. That's never happened before! I actually felt her sexy aura calling me closer.

I felt like I was on top of the world, and I was the luckiest man alive. Discovering Mandisa today wasn't even in my plans, but I don't even want to think about how I felt before I laid eyes on her. You have no idea how long I've been waiting to feel like this! I've honestly been happy no more than four times in my life.

Mandisa was so exquisite. She had that lovely-light creamy skin, her hair was light brown or nearly blonde with caramel coffee coils, long, curly, and natural, and her eyes were grey like moonlight. She had a gorgeous round face and soft round lips. Mandisa had the angelic face that would shut down the internet with those intergalactic eyes. Her skin was like butter, but Mandisa was a natural beauty, and she obviously was black, but she looked flawless to my four-eyes!

It was Mandisa's mesmerizing body that caught my eye at first glance! Beautiful supple curves, even though she was wearing yoga pants and a tank top, oh Jah! You could see she had a tiny waist, lovely breasts, beautifully rounded hips, and a gorgeous semicircular onion behind that made me want to cry.

She was taller than most women I have met our age, but I had her beat in height. The cherry on top, so to say, was her sweet sexy French accent! Once you add in her talents: music, dance, art, and all that intelligence, oh, Hakim was hooked!

I jumped up from my bed and started getting dressed. I put on black jeans, a red tee-shirt, black and red Jordan's, a Chicago Bulls jacket, and a Black Panther chain. It was a wrap. I sprayed on some cologne, put on my watch, and tucked my car keys, wallet, and phone. Now I was fresh to death. I looked out of the bedroom window, hoping I could catch a glimpse of her. But no, I didn't see any movement in her window. Her backyard was small compared to ours, besides a clothesline space to maybe park a car. I sneered because I was enthused about seeing that sunshine again as I glided down the stairs.

I was practically home free when my brother, Lionel, entered the front door. He took one glance at me and shut the door, blocking my exit. I exhaled and shook my head as a malicious grin curled on his lips. His pointy nose drew up with his eyebrows nodding down at me with his enormous forehead.

"Damn, Nigga! Where you going lookin' Krispy-Kreamy and dipped in hot-glaze? Is it already time to make the goddamn donuts?" Lionel examined me, his voice piercing and annoying as hell. He was only fifteen, and he was lankier than me, had a full goatee, and when I reared my eyebrows, he scowled at me. "Wait! Wait! Wait! I smell…I smell… You on a mission, Hakim? A pussy prowl? Chasing some ass? You look like you bout to pound through some panties!"

"Nope! I'm going out, and I don't know what time I'll be home, so don't stay up, Bro," I stated honestly as I reached past him for the doorknob. Lionel quickly slid the basketball he was holding in my way.

"Uh Uh, Nigga! I'm going wit you! You can't leave me home alone. Grandma Sophie said that if you leave, I go with you, Hakim." Lionel snorted, slapping my hand away from the door, switching his basketball to the left hand.

"You ain't a baby! You are bigger than me! I have a date, and you aren't invited, so no!" I chuckled as I drove his bony-ass over.

"Where are you going?" Lionel demanded, being nosy, pulling up his basketball shorts. He sat the ball on the sofa, starting toward the kitchen. Lionel was always wondering where I was going, but he started shit with anyone he didn't like if he tagged along. I couldn't afford him there, ruining my time alone with Mandisa. "You can't lie to me, Hakim. You don't date bitches. You fuck hoes."

"I'm just going ova there, you know," I thought, watching him frown at me. He must have just taken his braids down because his hair was too curly and nappy as it hung down his back. All that hair couldn't hide that big ole head underneath. He took off his shirt showing off his skinny torso and chest. My brother had let his friends talk him into getting all these dumb tattoos. I couldn't tell him what to do. He didn't listen to me about much unless it involved money. That he knew I had and was all he wanted from me.

"Ova where, Nigga?" He insisted, raising his eyebrow, scowling, with his top lip curled. He looked like Dad with really long hair and no muscle. I looked like Mama, but I had Dad's build. Lionel was always ready to talk shit or start a fight. It had been his way since Mom and Dad died. We fought before, but it got worse and isn't recovering as we age.

"Ova deez nuts, Bro! See ya!" I snickered as I ducked out the door, quickly deserting him standing, watching me.

"Fuck you, Hakim! You a bitch!" Lionel shouted as I slammed the screen door in his face.

I headed over to the garage to let my baby out. I smiled as the door rolled up. I loved my "Shun-Shun." She was a 2017 custom-made Dodge Charger, black with red racing stripes and a personalized grill. She was gorgeous sitting on her 23-inch chrome chopping shoes. Shun was the loveliest lady around the hood before Mandisa came into the picture. I leaned close to her and smiled as the sun touched her beautiful paint job.

"Now, Baby, don't be jealous. Daddy has a date, so I don't want any shit! So be good tonight, duck the police, and stop getting dirty looks with your sexy ass!" I chuckled, hitting the alarm, diving into her lovely red and black leather interior.

Shun was my prized possession. I got her last year for my birthday as a gift to myself. I had owned other cars, but Shun was my baby! I called her the "Rev-O-Lu-Shun" but "Shun" for short. Nobody in The View had a car like her.

I turned off the GPS because I knew exactly where I was going. Mandisa was going to love Hot Wheels. Everyone came to Hot Wheels to glide, show off their cars, or just chill. If you lived in The View, you needed a car. The bus was excellent if you were a kid, but that was a long-ass wait for a long-ass ride. Everything was too spread out, and the buses rarely went to neighborhoods where there weren't businesses. So you still had to walk. As soon as I could see over the steering wheel, I was trying to drive.

I pulled in Mandisa's front driveway behind her mother's car. I got out, came up the path, and was about to hit the steps when the front door opened. Mrs. King came outside. I smiled as she looked me over. She looked just like an older and more pregnant twin of her fantastic daughter.

"Hakim, a word, please?" She demanded, her cheeks blushing as she drew near me.

"Everything alright, Mrs. King?" I worried, scanning for Mandisa.

"Oui oui, everything is fine, Hakim. However, I have rules for you leaving with my daughter," She replied, gazing at me as she placed her arm on my shoulder, forcefully backing me away from the porch.

"Okay, no problem, Mam…." I claimed as she halted, staring at me carefully.

"Rule number one: Be safe, no wild stuff. I'm entrusting her with you. You bring her home in the same condition she leaves here.

"Rule two: Show her a good time. Her father doesn't let her get out much. I can't have her going around like this without friends anymore, Hakim.

"Rule three: Keep IT in your pants! Refer to rule one for more information. Have fun, okay?" Mrs. King demanded as she pointed her index finger at my nose. "If anything happens to her, it's your ass, not mine. I'll cut you!"

"Of course, I would never disrespect Mandisa. I care for her. You can trust me, Mrs. King," I assured her as she softened her eyes and smiled beautifully.

"Okay, Hakim, I trust you. Please don't let me down," Mrs. King replied, her eyes twinkling like stars as she went inside to get her daughter. I waited by the door, nervous as hell. There was no way I was going to betray that trust. Mrs.

King was so gentle and caring. She reminded me of my mom. I had never met a woman that was so open-minded and nurturing since Mama died. Most people I'd encountered were too busy in their own shit to worry about some kid running around the hood.

I was not trying to have sex with Mandisa. But if Mandisa came on to me, gave me the slightest sign that she wanted it, or even touched me the wrong way, I was going to have to bash my own damn brains in to keep my hands to myself! I'd abstain with all my might. But if I failed…I'd just have to just take that slicing and go with a big-ass smile on my face. No, fuck that! I'd marry Mandisa and lock her down…oh, Jah…I could only hope…One step at a time.

I glanced over at Shun and looked back as the front door opened. I saw golden toes, yellow heels, white leggings, and a sexy yellow flared dress. Her hair was up in a neat, lovely ponytail curled beautifully with tiny loose coils dancing at the sides of her face. I could see her eyes so clearly now because they were shadowed with smoky make-up. Her lips were shiny, temptingly delicious, painted with shimmering pink lip gloss, and tantalizing me.

Her beauty stunned me for a moment as she gleamed up at me and gazed into my eyes coyly.

"Hey," She uttered as her eyes glistened at me. Holy shit! I felt asinine staring at her now. Mandisa became a model with just a switch of clothes and a little make-up!

"H-Hey," I spluttered. I suddenly detected her sweet perfume, vanilla, and sunflowers, as she walked past. My eyes chased her as she went down the steps and stopped seeing Shun.

"Is that your car, Hakim?" She asked, admiring my ride.

"Yeah," I replied as I trailed, now staying close.

Good goddess, how could a girl so sweet and innocent have a body with her curves? She could be a stripper with her figure and rake it up! I've seen some heavenly bodies, but Mandisa was natural and untouched by anyone? Those thick tight legs in her white tights made me wish the wind would come. Her skirt coming up would give a brother a glimpse of something sweeter than that candy she was sucking between those yummy lips.

"It's gorgeous," She giggled, her cheeks glowing. "You did say your favorite colors were red and black. Wow!"

"It's not as beautiful as you, Queen," I informed her as I cuddled her arm and got her to face me. "You look divine."

"You are very handsome, Hakim," She replied, scanning up at me.

"Thank you very much," I chuckled, putting my hands in my pockets and gazing at the ground, feeling uneasy again.

The urge to touch Mandisa was driving me crazy, and we hadn't left the yard. "You look like a ray of pure sunlight, Mandisa, really."

"Hakim, you don't have to keep telling me things like that. I believe you," She moaned as she looked back at my car. Her mood dipped right before my eyes. Mandisa's eyes were like a mood ring giving away her feelings changing. When she said hello, they were bright, like the moon. But when I told her how I thought she looked, they seemed darker. There was so much that was unaccounted for, and it had to do with her self-esteem. Her father must have done a number on her.

"Hey, I told you because I need you to know that I think you truly are beautiful, Mandisa," I included as I skimmed my hand over her bare silky shoulder. "Don't you know how exquisite you are, Mandisa?"

She looked back up at me and abruptly glanced at the ground. She really had no idea what I saw when I stared at her. I glanced up at the setting sun and grabbed my phone out of my jacket pocket. I took her picture, held her close to me, snapped a few of us together, and then presented them to her. She giggled, looking at them.

"Can you see that girl with me?" I demanded, holding her close as I showed her the pictures.

"Oui," She replied, her cheeks turning redder by the second.

"Her radiance is brighter than the sun overhead," I confessed honestly as I held her near. "Your beauty is far beyond compare."

"Hakim," Mandisa sighed, looking at me.

"There you go again. You can't say my name like that," I laughed as I led her to the passenger side of my car. I opened the door for her, waiting for her to sit, and carefully shut it for her. I'm not going to lie to you; I was hoping that I could see that ass. But her sundress was blocking my view! So I just smiled and shook my head as I went around the back of the car. I sent one of the pictures I took of Mandisa alone to Cyrus and texted him. "My Sunshine!"

A few seconds later, he hit me up.

"Holy shit, Hakim!!! That's her?!" Cyrus texted me back.

"Yes, Sir! " I replied, smiling to myself.

"Damn, bro, she's not fine. She's magnificent! Not joking. I see why you're so happy! Lucky motherfucker… :P" Cyrus answered me. "Happy 4 U."

#

I dove in the car, started her, put my phone away, and buckled my seatbelt. Hot Wheels was a skating rink on the outskirts of town. All the teens and kids hung out there on the weekends during the school year. But it was summertime, so I knew it was going to be packed. The kids owned it during the day. They came to skate, dance, and play all the games. But once it got close to nighttime, the teens took over, which became a mostly all-black hang spot and semi-night club.

We all still skated, but you could dance, show off your ride, bass your beats, parking lot pimp, or whatever. Most people acted a fool at Hot Wheels because you had to fuck up for the police to come out there. That meant for every group of civilized black people consisting of ten friends, there was at least one crazy nigga full of stupidity starting shit.

But there's no such place as a black man's paradise, not here in Longview! Ain't shit in Longview, Texas! I'll say that again for the people way in the back row… AIN'T SHIT IN LONGVIEW, TEXAS!

So either you bowl, skate, shop at the wack-ass mall, or take your ass out of town to bigger and better surroundings. Maybe you could catch a movie at one of our many two movie theaters, good luck on the weekend. But you better get there early, or you will be fresh out of luck because everything sells out fast.

That's why nobody wanted to stay in The View! Once you did your time here, if you were smart, you'd go to college so you could get the hell away from here and see some shit. Most people I've met feel trapped here. My mother, Vivianne, was born and raised here. As soon as she got old enough to drive, she ran away and never came back. I understand why. After she died, my grandparents moved us back into the old house.

You know how you have that dream where you're trapped in a room or a house, and every time you get out, you find yourself right back where you started? That's The View! You can enter at your own risk, but good luck getting away for good. People always end up right back here for either family, misfortune, or just can't muster the courage to leave at all.

Me, I hate The View, and as soon as school is over next year and I walk across that stage...I'm going to hit the ground running and never look back. I don't care how much money I have. It's not worth staying rooted here.

This town is a retired person's dream but a teenage nightmare. But that's one man's opinion. Of course, I'm only seventeen, so you don't have to believe the shit I say.

I looked at the clock. It was almost five. Damn, the day must have gotten away from me when I started daydreaming at home. I parked Shun and glanced at Mandisa. She was checking around at all the cars, people and starting to get excited. She reached in her purse again and put a lollipop in her mouth as she exhaled nervously.

"You must really love candy, huh?" I teased her as she blushed, amused. "Careful, we don't need a repeat of earlier."

She giggled at me and waggled, "You're mean, Hakim…No, I love candies. I love all kinds, but it was hard to find the stuff I really like…know? So now, I go overboard, but it's not that bad, is it? Just Jolly Ranchers, Starbursts, and a sucker here and there…the cherry ones are my favorite. I have to watch my figure, so these are all I can have, but I really love…chocolates!"

"I'm watching your figure, too, and it looks superb to me," I discovered myself declaring without thinking, and I stopped. Mandisa started laughing, and I exhaled with relief. *Nothing to worry about…that only happens when I'm mad.* The last thing I needed was for her to think I was weird.

"I have to lose a few pounds before school begins, or I may have to quit ballet. Madame Olga says that I'm too heavy, but my skill is fantastic," She sighed, gazing at her long natural golden fingernails. "It is so frustrating for my technique to depend on my size."

"Madame Olga is crazy! I think you're perfect," I admitted as she glanced at me. "In fact, you can eat all the candy you want as long as you don't lose that butt! Brothers like me agree with Sir Mix-A-Lot, Queen. We love a woman with beauty and booty. Yours is like a pillow! I want to sleep on it!"

Mandisa started cackling aloud, and she covered her face, embarrassed. She took her lollipop out of her mouth so she wouldn't choke and struggled to breathe as tears ran down her cheeks. When she caught her wind, she put it back and smiled at me, "It's not that serious to me, Hakim. I only crave candy when I am nervous."

She licked her lovely pink lips and placed them on the sucker. I exhaled and wobbled my head. I wish I could be that lucky piece of candy.

"So, you said you can roller skate, right?" I questioned her again, making sure.

"Yes, my mother used to take my friend and me while in Philadelphia a while back. But that was before Mami knew she was pregnant. So now she can't get around like she used to. Amani is low. She makes Mami very uncomfortable, and she is in her 50s, so she has to be very careful," Mandisa explained.

"Amani?" I disputed, observing curiously.

"Oui, my baby sister. Her name is Amani. I picked it out. It means wishes or aspirations. I wished and prayed for a brother or sister for so long. Now I got my wish," Mandisa replied, smiling up at me.

"I think it's crazy that she would have a baby now that you're about to graduate, grow up, and go to college? Right?" I queried her, prying.

"I am not certain about college, Hakim. Mami wants me to enjoy school for the first time," She said, looking disappointed suddenly. I decided to save the conversation for later.

"I could sit out here and talk to you all day, but that wouldn't be fun for you," I stated, leaning over and nudging her shoulder.

"No, I'm having a wonderful time just talking with you, Hakim," She declared, pushing me back smiling. "It's so nice to just talk to someone else besides my mother."

"Come on, let's have some fun, and we can talk again later. I promised Mami that you'd have a good time. She won't like it if you tell her we sat in the car the entire evening, Queen. Uh uh, she ain't cutting me!" I teased Mandisa as I got out of the car, ran to the passenger side, and opened the door for her.

On the inside, the light show was flashing, the music was banging, people were everywhere just having fun, and Mandisa's eyes lit up when she witnessed it all.

"I may have to buy you some cute skates once you let me be your boyfriend. What size do you wear?" I requested as I stopped near the rental desk. She stared at me and giggled, peering toward a group of girls as they skated by. She shook her head and blushed. I was going to have to break that shy shell. It was cute, but I wanted her to feel confident with me.

"Ah shit, Hakim Dunn! What up my most militant, male, militia managing, micro-organizing, martial artist?" Stevie laughed, starting that tongue-twisting shit. "Where the hell is Cyrus-Osiris?"

"He'll be here later on. He said he was passing through Georgia not too long ago," I told Stevie as he scanned over at Mandisa.

"Who is dat?" Stevie questioned me as I rolled my eyes, playing dumb. I looked over at Mandisa, and she was all into the music. She was swaying her hips to the beat and studying people skate as DJ Khalid started playing.

"I'm on one, too!" DJ hollered, and people got crunk. I started rocking myself, and Mandisa set out flaunting her body like a pro! Mandisa dipped her back and wiggled her hips around to the beat while watching.

Whoa! Wait a minute, she had some sex behind her moves.

"Who Is THAT, Hakim?! Baby girl in the yellow dress that came in with you, look at her grooving like she moving," Stevie wondered, getting too damn excited.

"Oh, HER?! That's Mandisa, my future wife, Man," I warned Stevie, smirking.

"She's bad as fuck! Dear God, all that ass and with that skin, fresh! Makes me wish I wasn't twenty-nine," Stevie sniggered, giving me dap. "She's gorgeous…blessed nigga."

"Whatever! What you got in a ladies' ten and a half? She's tall, and I can tell she's not going to tell me her size. But I can guess. She's so fine and doesn't even know it," I disclosed to Stevie as he nearly crashed into the counter, watching her then staring in the back.

"Dunn, I got pink, white, and brown," Stevie laughed as he looked past me back at her. "When a woman is fine like that, and she doesn't know, Brother, you got to snatch her up before another nigga that won't respect her get to it."

"Stevie, ain't nobody about to snatch her away from me! I'm so serious…" I replied as Stevie accepted, smiling. "Give me the white for her, and I'll take black in size twelve."

I glanced back at Mandisa. My eyes were glued to her body. I bet she's one of those sexy shy girls that likes to watch herself dancing naked in the mirror. She could really move! I was going to have to get one dance before the night was over. Stevie handed me the skates, I dropped him a few bills, and he grinned. I went around Mandisa and bumped into her playfully.

"Here you go, Queen, these should do you right," I informed her as I led her to the lockers to change. "You can put your things in my locker."

I handed her a pair of socks. Whenever I came to Hot Wheels, I always carried extra socks because I rented my skates. Of course, I could buy my own, but I always wanted to have a reason to give Stevie and Big Mike the money to keep business going. I knelt down and helped her unbuckle her shoes as she sat down. Mandisa smiled, looking down nervously.

"Hakim, I can do this," She laughed as I helped her put on her socks and lace her skates.

"Girl, please, I know I don't have to…I want to," I taunted her, eyeballing childishly. I took off my shoes and put my skates on. She sat patiently waiting for me. She smiled, and her eyes shined brightly as she watched me lace my skates up tightly. Then I heard a mouth that I dreaded more than gunfire at a cookout!

"Nigga, where is Hakim? His car is outside!" I felt a chill run down my spine as I spotted my brother by the doorway. I hurled my head down and sulked.

This loud-mouthed, lanky-ass, watermelon-headed boy was going to ruin everything! Maybe I could ditch him before he saw me?

"There he goes! Hakim, you a ho-ass nigga! How you gonna leave me at home and come skate?" Lionel shrieked across the lobby over the music. I glanced up at Mandisa from my hiding spot tensely. She squinted over in his direction.

"Hakim, who is that?" She snorted. I stole her hand and tugged her out on the floor. I knew Lionel wouldn't follow me out there. He hated skating. I led Mandisa around the rink, trying to focus only on her and ignore my baby brother's loudmouth. She snickered at me as I skated backward in front of her. I suddenly ducked down behind her as we passed Lionel.

"Nigga, I can see you," Lionel chuckled from the carpet. Mandisa took off, abandoning me. I stood up and sneered, chasing after her as she moved and grooved that body to the beat. I smiled as I caught her again. The DJ changed the song, and Mandisa was gone again. She was all over every melody that came on. I was enjoying watching her move those hips. Oh, my word! She could move it. I obviously had judged her wrong. She skated between a group of people, and I followed her everywhere like a lost puppy.

We must have skated around that rink for at least two hours, and I was slowing down. But Mandisa was a beast out there! She was on the skate floor, the dance floor, and the skate floor became a dance floor for her. Finally, I got off the rink and stood just watching for a while, exhausted.

"Nigga, you know you heard me calling your ass," Lionel snorted as he rammed my arm.

"Oh yeah?" I demanded.

I was entranced watching Mandisa glide around the rink. She gorgeously smiled, waving at me as I handed her a sexy-eyed gaze and flapped back. Lionel peered at Mandisa, and his eyes fired up. He unexpectedly smirked and punched me but didn't glance away. I wouldn't take my eyes off of that angel on wheels for one second.

"Who that girl, Hakim?" He questioned me earnestly, still viewing her figure as she roller-skated to the beat.

"That is Mandisa, and that is all you need to know for now," I answered dangerously, still observing that sunshine complete another revolution around my world.

"You tapping that, Hakim?" Lionel asked, leering at that girl as she came by us again. "She's fine as fuck, Bro!"

"Fine as fuck? I'm not going to dignify that shit. I just met her, and she's off-limits to you, Bro. Stay away from her, or I'll break my foot off in your ass," I warned Lionel as I waved to her relaxed. She braked, approached me, and tilted over the divider.

"Ha…kiiii…iim," Mandisa chanted my name lyrically, producing a more enormous grin. "I am getting thirsty. We can get something to drink, oui?"

"Oh, I got something you can drink, Girl," Lionel went in, struggling to bend closer to her. I beat him in the arm. "Hakim, keep your hands off me! I'ma tell G.D., and he'll beat your ass!"

"Watch that nasty mouth, Lionel. Keep on, and I'll adjust that long neck of yours," I warned him again, frowning. I tilted my head, grinning toward Mandisa. "Come on, Queen, I'll get you anything you want."

"Yo, Hakim, you not gonna even introduce me or nothing?" Lionel expected as we started to skate away. I shook my head as he threw me the finger. "Well, deuces minus one, Nigga!"

I bought Mandisa an ICEE, and I got a large coke, and we shared some popcorn at the snack bar.

"So, are you enjoying yourself so far?" I wondered, offering the bag of hot popcorn. Her long fingernails took a handful, and she beamed, completing me.

"I'm having a great time, Hakim," She replied before she took a sip out of her drink. Her cute tongue wrapped around the straw, and I found myself leaning forward, gawking. "I love the energy here."

"Oh yeah?" I flirted, viewing her thoroughly. She smirked at me, and I squeezed my bottom lip and heaved a sigh to myself.

"What's the matter, Hakim?" She worried, sulking as I gaped over at her timidly.

"I'm just a little hot. What is that cherry?" I teased her, knowing the answer. I took off my jacket, sat it on the back of my chair, and shifted closer to her. My eyes stared at her resting upon those pretty plump red lips sucking on that straw so eagerly.

"Oui, it is cherry. It's delicious. But you know what is even better and I love?" She invited me, grinning sweetly.

"What, Queen?... What do you love?" I mumbled, leaning much closer now. *Come on, Queen, just go for it! I know you want me, Baby.* She giggled as she took my cup and poured some of my coke into her ICEE. "Cherry coke? I bet that flavor is so sweet..."

"Mhm," She giggled, taking another sip. Mandisa teased me with her eyes, telling me she knew what I wanted. "When you mix them together, it...is so...good, Hakim. I love Cherry Coke...The sweetness and sour make my tongue tingle."

"I see it's good," I beamed, cutting my eyes semi-closed and stretching my tongue over my bottom lip. I grinned at

Mandisa and poked out my lips mischievously, eyeing her straw. I pretended to pout and gazed away.

"Would you like a taste?" She bid while holding her cup toward me. I moved my eyes and bumped into her shoulder.

"You're teasing me," I groaned, eyeing her straw, laughing. She shook her head and sneered attractively.

"No, really, you can have a taste. Go ahead…I don't have the viruses," Mandisa giggled, tilting closer, grasping her cup over a bit more.

"Alright," I whimpered like I really didn't want any. I grabbed Mandisa's arm and kissed those soft, cold, and sweet cherry-flavored lips. I put my tongue in her mouth and tried to suck away all that delicious sugar. She pulled away, snickering suddenly. "What?!"

"You're really smooth, Hakim, too smooth," She snorted, tasting her lips with the crimson point of her tongue.

"Oh my god! I love that sight! Do that again, please?" I begged, anticipating as she ran her tongue across her lips. "Oh my goodness, that is the sexiest thing I have ever seen… So have you changed your mind yet?"

"About what?" She questioned me, puzzled.

"About choosing a boyfriend, Mandisa. I want to get that, yes. Please?! I need a sweet, sexy, and innocent thing like you to make me behave," I testified, honestly chewing my lips, wanting another taste of her cherry coke.

"Keep talking, Hakim. I'm listening," She responded. *Fine, I'm talking then, Angel...lol.*

"I'm serious, Mandisa! Give name your price, what I need to do, just give me that, yes...I'll do it. You got me open, and I'm not gonna lie.

"Look, Queen, a man such as myself, won't procrastinate or drop REAL paper without a vibe like...THIS! I WANT YOU...So, what's it gonna take?

"I'm right here, and I'll do anything, spend that amount, or run that mile. It's your world, Beautiful," I confessed. *Oh, I know you heard ME...Now that I'm talking.*

She watched me for a few moments. Her cheeks were red, her eyes beamed as she gawked at me. Then, as she uneasily held her cup, it fell over, and she spattered it on her legs. Red and brown drink spilled all over her white leggings, and she gasped from the chills as she stood up.

"Damn it!" Mandisa screamed subtly while I handed her as many napkins as I could get, holding in my laugh. She held up her dress to keep the soda from ruining all her top. "I will be back."

"No problem, Queen, take your time," I informed her as she skated to the back towards the ladies' room. I was wiping up the mess on the bench when Lionel slid over, shoving me. *NOT NOW, NIGGA...WE were so close...*

"Nigga, where your gal go?" He snorted, teasing me.

"Ladies' room, why?" I requested, turning my eyes. THIS is why I don't take my brother ANYWHERE! He is a pain in my ass, and he only starts shit. "Why are you following me anyway? How did you get here?"

"Nigga, you the one sitting over here alone looking all hurt and bitchless! I thought you dropped the ball with a girl that fine. But ain't nobody following your mean ass either, Hakim. I came here to scope the hoes, and Cyrus brought me, now what?" Lionel told me as he rolled his eyes, peering down at me insistently.

"How the hell did you ride with Cyrus? He's in Georgia, and he said he won't be here until tomorrow," I chuckled at him. The nigga loves to start shit, so we will brawl. I didn't need HIM here with all his wild energy near Mandisa! Lionel would scare her away, and I'd bash his melon head to the white meat! "You need to quit lying before your nose gets as long as your neck."

"That right?" Lionel asked, trying to steal my line. Oh, Bro, I want to fuck you up…but I can't risk Mandisa seeing me hit you. Instead, I stared up at Lionel, trying to curb my growing anger. I was enjoying myself until a moment ago. He spun my head toward a group of people near the door. "Who's that then, Nigga?"

I blinked, squinting to see…Oh Shit! Lionel wasn't lying this time! Cyrus was standing near the door talking to a large group of girls. How the hell did he get here so damn fast? Atlanta was over twelve hours away from The View. There's no possible way he got here in less than five hours unless that Nigga lied! Damn, I thought I had a little more time before Cyrus got here…shit…oh well.

"My bad! That must be some other dread-headed, joke-cracking, black wearing, bitch pulling, singing, dancing, drinking, and blunt blowing, dark-ass nigga named Darius Cyrus Jefferson Jr.," Lionel pestered me, amused as I got up and skated over to the door. Cyrus saw me approaching and hollered.

"Dunn, my sun!" Cyrus cackled, laying a blunt behind his ear, smirking at me. He gave me a hand slap, and we did our special big bro shake. "Hakim, man, it is good to see you again, Bro! Feels like forever since I've been back home. Let me guess Lionel told you I was here?"

"Right-right, you know he can't keep that mouth shut to save his own damn life," I reminded Cyrus as he checked the length of my locks.

Cyrus had been getting his hair twisted much longer than I had. His crown was too fly for words. He had grown his skinny locks so long that they almost touched his belt. He kept his shit tight and lined up like a playa supposed to do it. That is my motherfuckin, friend!

I loved his crazy black ass. He's my best friend in the universe, and when Cyrus was around, everything was better. He was so much fun, and he loved spending his money. Cyrus was like a force of nature, the walking law of attraction, he pulled everyone in, and nobody stood a chance once they got a taste of his personality.

"I thought you said you were in GA, Bro?" I chuckled, pushing his tall ass over.

"Did I say Atlanta? My bad, Bro, I was high as fuck! I must have been in Monroe, Louisiana, or somewhere? I stopped and got that power nap in. Boom! Cyrus ish herrre!" He cracked up, smiling brightly. He took a sip out of his cup. "Let me get my skates, drop Stevie some bread, I'ma tear that floor up, and then and then and then…I'ma get some head!"

Cyrus strolled toward the rental desk snickering and swaying his head. He spotted a lovely-looking sista standing alone near the snack bar, and I commenced entertaining myself. I knew he was about to score one for the home team. My boy was full of game and tricks. He was about to pull the STUNT OF THE DAY. His face said it all! So I skated my nosy-ass toward the rental desk close by and leaned backward, eavesdropping. Cyrus was about to start a seminar in Trickanomitry 101.

Cyrus ogled her up and down as he strode past.

She was light-skinned, in excellent shape, and her curly braided hair was up actually cute. I think we knew her from the cheer squad because she wore a Carver High spirit shirt and tight jeans showing off that big ole ass! Cyrus drew a step back. She was on her phone. Probably talking to her man because she looked pissed off! I leaned closer, listening in.

#

"Uh uh, no! You said that last week, Dre! I want to go out sometimes, too! I can't stay at home all the time while you run the streets with your boys. You never take me anywhere! I'm not your mama, Nigga, and I am not your wife, that's for damn sure.

"So I don't have to take this from you. If I'm not good enough for you to take out sometimes, don't call me anymore when you get horny.

"I should have listened to my mama. You ain't shit, Dre...and your boys are all broke like you! Deuces!" She shouted, hanging up her phone, looking angry as hell.

Cyrus grinned as he rammed out his tongue, considering her again. His eyebrow rose up over his forehead, and he looked like the Pink Panther as he slid around her backside and stepped up in her face unexpectedly.

"Excuse me, most lovely one," Cyrus interrupted her thinking, tapping her shoulder. She turned around and lingered, glaring up at him. My boy was smooth. I hid my mouth, amused. "I couldn't evade overhearing your terrible conversation. But once I saw your sad eyes, I had to interfere and brighten your late afternoon. I just meant to give you a smile, introduce myself, and let you know that there're some real men are out here. I would never dream about making you cry unless it was from eating your pussy until you required crutches to walk."

"What?" She demanded, mesmerized by the game. She flushed, gazing at him as he put those big brown lips on her hand.

"Ase, Most Divine, I am Osiris-Cyrus the great, and like the man that gave me my name's inspiration, I'll resurrect your heart and claim that pussy. I'll spoil your fine-ass rotten, make you my mummy, and poor Dre will have to hate from the sidelines. I will shower you with more love and affection than you ever thought you could acquire from a single man," Cyrus warned her, displaying a smile as he ran his lips across her other hand. "Will you bless me with your name?"

"Clarissa," She mumbled nervously. I rubbed my eyes, almost choking quietly, watching. "Nice to meet you, Cyrus."

"Clarissa, which is such a beautiful name for such splendor. Tell me, Clarissa, are you afraid?" Cyrus asked her, letting go of her hand, staring into her brown eyes.

"Afraid of what, Cyrus?" Clarissa sighed, totally confused.

"Well, your man seems to enjoy being around his friends rather than with you. I was just curious if you're afraid of falling in love with a real man?" Cyrus wondered, moving closer to her, and she backed up a step. He looked deeper into her eyes and smiled again, "I'm single, and I'm as real as it gets, Princess. Do you want to wear the crown and become a real Queen?"

"I-I don't know," She responded timidly. She looked nervous and down. I shook my head again. Typical lost girl. Clarissa has no idea what she wants, so she has no idea what she needs. Cyrus simply tilted his head and nodded.

"Hey, I realize you possibly have a hell of past with your man. I wouldn't ask you to jeopardize a serious relationship. But when you get tired of his shit," Cyrus started as he pulled out a gang of bills…all hundreds and took a pen from his jacket pocket. He wrote his number on one and handed it to her. Then he slowly put the rest back in his pocket. She was watching that money carefully. "Call me, Clarissa? Maybe we can go have fun? I'll take you to dinner; I can take you shopping and find something sexy by Jimmy Choo for those pretty toes. Have a nice evening. Ase, Most lovely one."

Cyrus arrived at the rental desk and bumped into me.

"What are you doing over here, spying on ya boy?" Cyrus demanded as he glanced back toward Clarissa and waved.

"She's not going to call you, know?" I teased him. "Your game was weak…weeeaaaak, Nigga."

Word? Am I getting rusty?" Cyrus chuckled as his phone went off. He stared at it. "New text…hmm…who could this be? 'Cyrus…give…me…a call…in an…hour…Clarissa.'

"Oh, that was fast! I think I got her attention, Bro! Was…that…a record?

"Wait, they're going to the tape… YES! It's a New…World…Record! I'm telling you, I'm going to get my degree in Pussyology and teach Mackanomics worldwide!"

"Bro, you're foolish as fuck! You're just flocking pigeons hoping they'll like you enough to be faithful. You know she just wants that paper," I snickered as Cyrus got his skates.

"Yeah, maybe, but I buy her a few pairs of shoes, or whatever to make her smile, see where her head really is, and she might really like me. I have a feeling she's all caught up in her feelings for her man.

"So, I'll just get some pussy, wreck it up for ole Dre with this jungle snake, and be on my merry way.

"Either way, it goes; I win. A few bills are a small price to pay when you're on a mission to find that one remarkable woman.

"Once I find her, what I buy these little girls will look like hand-me-downs from the 1940s. I'll settle for some Southern Ho-spit-ability rather than Miss Right. She'll call me again once I go deep, and her nigga can't come close to where I dig. Maybe I'll still be single when she realizes her man really ain't gonna change," Cyrus chuckled arrogantly.

"So you're paying for pussy? Trying to buy love, Bro? Tricking? That's what rich niggas do?" I taunted Cyrus, pressing him. *If that ain't the most pathetic shit I've ever heard...smh* "That's what's hot in the NYC streets?"

"I see it as spreading the seeds of love. Every time I buy a girl a gift, she has a constant reminder of the excellent nigga, with terrific hair and unbelievable dick that she overlooked for a short-stroking brother with no money, no time, and no real love to offer her.

"I didn't make all this money to sit on it! Looking for real love ain't easy, Man.

"Most of these girls don't know a good thing when it's right in their faces. They want that sorry nigga, so I let them go back to him after knocking some sense into those walls with Jody. Then I'm on to the next lovely one until I find the supreme one that really wants to love me," He respired, shaking his head, smirking at me.

"Nigga, you're silly, truly," I chuckled as I left him, skating to the restroom.

That's my fuckin friend, and we are nothing alike when it comes to handling women. *I know I'm crazy-crazy!* But Cyrus worries me with his buying-them-all-shit-for-love philosophy! You don't love all the hos, call them queens, and pretend to be happy when they don't like you in the end. He may have shit backward, but Cyrus is Cyrus. Getting him to change is as hard as getting *us* to change. It hasn't happened in years for anyone close to me. Mandisa has been the first interesting new thing in my life for over a year now. About as long as I've been abstaining and running, it's all good. With Cyrus around, things will stay positive, and I'll maintain. This is all a good thing. Cyrus can help with Lionel, too. He can keep Lionel out of my hair to have more ALONE time with Mandisa…oooh…it has been a while. She is PERFECT. Lol.

Chapter Three: The Blacker The Berry/Mortal Man

Darius Osiris Jefferson

I stood near the rental desk for a moment, sipping my fine liquor and peeping all the fine light-skinned ladies. I like the ladies lovely and light because I'm a dark-ass brother. My mother was the same color as Hakim, and my dad's darker than me. You can't blame me for loving light skin. It's a matter of contrast. For me, there's just something genuinely magnificent about creamy light-skinned women.

But I love all black women. I love gorgeous shades of brown and black. I'm a proud black man, but I just have a fetish for some very unusual things. I love it all. I'm a big boy, six feet six inches tall, two hundred and eighteen pounds, long brown and black hair that hangs down to my waist, and I pack that big ole fishing pole. Hundred percent pure dark sweet chocolate!

That's right, brothers! I'm on the prowl, I want a woman, and I will pull your girl if you come up short. I don't care. She can be tall, short, thick, or chubby. If she's a good girl, I want her.

I prefer the thickness. Skinny girls can't handle what I'm packing, so don't try me if you're not ready for a workout.

Trust, I'll kidnap the pussy and hold it for ransom. I'm sure you can't afford to get her back either.

Hakim knows it too. He was just like me. He has it terrible for redbone girls, but I've seen him with all shades of black and brown. One thing about us that we have in common, we cannot get down with the snow. Sorry Jenny, Rebecca, and Melanie, I can't do it! It had never turned out well when I tried. I can deal with being called the 'N word' by my people most of the time, but when it comes from another race, oh no. Every time a black person says it to another, it can be harmful or good. But any time another color says it…it's always awful. Come on, let's be honest; there are too many ways to hurt a black man. I'll be ya nigga, friend, brother, homeboy, or that unknown black man.

I can't be an ignorant Negro or your field nigger (niggar).

Cyrus can't pick your cotton, Massa. Slavery is dead, and people are too worried about the wrong shit these days. You need to get like me before you die on your knees living by the erroneous rules. There's freedom and slavery, and money is the whip-toting master…how man manipulates master determines the amount of liberty he acquires. You can't learn how to make any master respect you, shit he'll kick your ass your entire life…along with your kids…for generations.

Get your money, live your life, and stop waiting for someone to give you anything. That's the ignorant mentality that is holding *us* all back. We want something…NO ONE is gonna just give it to you because you want or deserve it. But you don't have to TAKE anything from the master if you can pimp him to your objectives. Take notes, ladies and gentlemen, you roll with Cyrus…I'll learn ya sumthin…not preaching or teaching…just meeting and seeking myself. I've got many teachers.

#

I put on my skates and peered out on the floor and got baffled when I saw Lionel out there chasing some girls around. Li-Li doesn't skate! He says it's for girls and kids. Hmph…funny. Not me! Not Hakim! Women loved to watch us glide around and act a fool. It was too much fun, and in The View, you had to make the fucking best out of the situation.

It was nothing like my hometown, Brooklyn, New York. Too much shit for me to get into there. Besides, I wasn't trying to wear out my welcome! Every time I got around my old colleagues back home, I'd end up practically going to jail.

So, The View was my actual home. I had been in NYC for a school year because I got accepted into a famous dance school, and I didn't want to waste the opportunity. So I got what I needed out of it, and now I was back to graduate with my brother.

I skated to the barrier and looked around for any sexy ladies skating alone. I was about to head out to make a few rounds when I saw her! She came out of the ladies' room, a high-yellow, long-haired, delicious vision of loveliness in a short golden sundress. She tossed something in the garbage, looked around lost, and smiled beautifully as people skated by. Her legs were long, juicy, and muscular. When she waved at the skaters, I saw long beautiful gold fingernails, and I was stuck. I had never in my natural life seen a woman so beautiful!

Her eyes danced like stars in the sky when she skated by me. My eyes followed her, and she smiled. I thought I would die. Literally, my heart tried to blast out of my chest. I stopped inhaling for a second. I clutched my shit and wobbled my leg.

Wait! I had seen her someplace before, but I couldn't remember.

I took a deep breath and slipped over towards her as she got on the floor. She moved across the rink, wiggling that physique like alchemy! I chased those hips and succulent thighs. As I caught up with her, I skated over and grinned, making eye contact. She giggled at me as I moonwalked in front of her, following her dance.

She waved her head, dipped down low, and rocked her hips right on time. I sank down and did the same changes she did, but I kept facing her. I winked, getting her to eye my footwork about the floor. Her eyes twinkled as she glided in a circle, beaming at me like my future wife! I spun about as they started playing The View Skate Clap.

"Come on, Baby," I shouted to her, demonstrating how to glide and when to clap. She got into the song after she learned the moves. Then we were all over the floor, going hard. "Move them hips, Baby girl, now! Snap! Clap! Clap! Snap! Glide!"

She laughed and grooved with me as I danced all around her, laughing. I caught her soft hands and swirled her around and whipped her across the rink, chasing her down. Her eyes flashed like rainbow VVS diamonds when she leered, and as I retook her hand, she gazed up at me and blushed so exquisitely.

I was disoriented… It felt like a beautiful hallucination being near that vibe. The music seemed to feel amazing on my skin. The light was following the both of us and lifting my mood by the second. Each smile, giggle, or glance in my direction drew me nearer until I had to touch that queen physically!

Dear, Jah, I need this woman! I've never felt so happy just being with a girl doing basically nothing.

She started off the floor as the song came to an end, and I pursued her. I just needed a name, age, or a number. I couldn't let her get away, not yet.

"Hey," I beckoned to her as she glanced back at me and snickered nervously again.

"Oui?" She requested as I paused near her. I felt jumpy as hell when I heard her speak. Her accent sent chills down my spine, and I smirked immediately. Her gorgeous creamy cheeks reddened as her eyes danced up and about my face.

"You were outstanding out there. You learn well. I'm Darius," I reported to her as I presented her with my hand. She gaped at it for a moment, and I was worried. Maybe she didn't speak English.

She grabbed my hand, and her lovely curved nails softly scratched my palm and made me shudder. Her skin was so soft I found myself staring closer at her. "I know great dancers when I see them."

"Merci beaucoup, Darius," She giggled sweetly, peering everywhere.

She was flawless! As I admired her body, I couldn't find anything not to love. Her sweet baby face was round, and she had the curves of a goddess beneath that short yellow sundress. Her legs were thick and tight, which told me that shorty had some skills. Not to mention I was smitten by the sound of an alluring French accent that made my dick as hard as a brick. Terrible, I needed to find anything to get my thoughts off my lower head. That was when I noticed she looked disappointed.

"Is everything alright, Baby girl? You look worried," I invited, waving to break her gaze and get her attention. Her doll-like face smiled, glancing back at me hesitantly.

"Man-DEE-sa, my name is Mandisa, and I cannot find my friend," She sighed sadly, and her lovely eyes grew dim.

"What does she look like? Let me help you find her?" I requested, aiming to lift her spirits again. However, she was even more lovely when she sulked. It was similar to the sweetest kitten viewing her eyes and stunning golden curls searching timidly!

"Him…*his* name is…Hakim," Mandisa informed musically. I practically lost my damn balance! I felt paralyzed suddenly! My heart stopped as my jaw fell wide open. "He brought me here, and I have not seen him in a while, Darius."

"Did you say, Hakim?" I questioned, genuinely tense.

"Oui, Hakim," She blew out, disappointed, checking around tensely. "I hope nothing awful has happened to him."

"Hakim… Dunn?" I continued interrogating her as my heart started battling my stomach, then twisted up in knots as the realization began.

I blinked when I grasped where I knew her from. The fucking picture Hakim sent!

Oh my, Jah! Mandisa was the girl Hakim was talking about!?

Maybe there was still hope for me. Just say no!

"Oui, Hakim Dunn, you know of him?" She begged me, inspecting my expression now.

"Yeah-yeah, I know Hakim Dunn. He's in the restroom. He'll be right back. He might have fallen in. You want me to go find him, Mandisa?" I mumbled like Future on Percocets, feeling suddenly nauseous but attempting not to let it display.

She screened her mouth as she snorted at that corny joke… Her face was so lovely and pink. Oh Jah, help me!

What the fuck! No!

How could this happen to me? Shit!

"No, if he is in the restroom, leave him alone. You will stay with me, Darius? I don't know anyone else here. I hate being alone," Mandisa pleaded, sulking. Her eyes appeared to switch gemstones in the light to emerald! They were so bright, green, and sad in the flicking light. I nodded in submission to her sweet cry. Suddenly I wanted to lift her spirits and keep her talking just to hear her accent.

"Sure, I'll wait with you. So, where did you learn to move like that? You can groove like water. Not many people can ride the beat like that," I flattered her dancing skills. She stared at me, appearing confused.

"Ride the beat?" Mandisa repeated with puzzled soft green eyes.

"Yeah, you know, ride the beat? Move, sing, or flow like you wrote it yourself. No one else can do it like you…it's like you have the beat moving through you. It's a part of you." I explained to her. She nodded, understanding, and glanced to the left. I could smell cherries. It was so sweetly mixed with vanilla. I bit my lip and smiled at her. When Mandisa was listening to me explain things, her eyes seemed to stare directly into places unknown. She didn't have a problem making heavy contact with those beautiful things, and the longer I looked, the harder it was to look away.

"I think I understand. I suppose I learned to ride the beat in dance lessons. I used to watch videos and mimic the steps. Sometimes I watch my body move in the mirror. I've been a dancer for years: ballet, jazz, hip-hop, and street. It's fun and unpredictable. Hip hop is my favorite, it really pulls you in, and there is so much that you can do with your body. You move like every song is made for you, Darius," She giggled, caressing my elbow.

"Yeah, I've been dancing since I was in diapers," I laughed, looking at her hand on my skin. It seemed so right to me. "My mother saw I had a gift and put me in every dance class she could afford. I dance for fun, but I've studied professional dance and choreography. It's a hell of a lot of fun, Mandisa, especially when you have a really great partner. It can be magic."

DJ got hype again and played a perfect song, and Mandisa grabbed my hand. "I love this song!" She screamed, her eyes shimmered, and she took off moving. She was on that beat, and before I knew it, I was tearing up the floor with her again.

"Ooh, baby, you want me? Well, you can get this lap dance here for free," Mandisa giggled and sang as she rolled around the rink.

She had no idea how bad I wanted it. She kept giggling, dancing, and skating. I clutched her close and skated with her. As I moved and grooved, she followed me. The more I vibed with her, the more I loved it. We skated a while longer, and I spotted Hakim. He was leaning against the barrier, watching us, grinning. When the song ended, I glided over to him, and Mandisa chased me.

"Bro!" Hakim snickered. "I see you out there!"

I managed a smile and gave my brother a clasp. Mandisa skated beside me and humorously yanked my locks.

"Queen, I see you met my Bro," Hakim informed her, and she colored pleasingly, appearing lovable. Hakim glanced down at her legs, and a huge grin formed across his face. I gazed away, pretending not to observe. "What happened to your tights, Mandisa?"

"The drink ruined them. I had to throw the pants away. That stuff really stains. It's alright, they were old. It's been time to go shopping for new clothes. I'm glad Mami is going to let me pick my own things. This is her dress," Mandisa sighed, blushing as her lovely golden nails touched the ruffles above her creamy knee.

"Maybe you'll let me take you shopping? Mrs. King looks like she wouldn't last around a good mall…Not The View's mall! It's lame, but we can hit the twenty and head to Dallas. You'll die. All the bad stuff girls are wearing they have there," Hakim contended, signaling me as he caressed her golden ringlet ponytail. Hakim had a smile on his face the moment Mandisa appeared. My brother was not lying to me. He was in love!

Hakim Jahlil Dunn does not fall in love. However, it was written all over his pitiful face. That fascinating girl that had me star-struck was the first woman to make Hakim act like me!

Wasn't this the same brother that just told me that my game was weak offering to take a woman I just met shopping…? Now, I'm intrigued! I know why he was signaling me. My brother knows who to talk to when it comes to the drip…and he will want my professional opinion. Oh, of course, I'm going to take the bait just to see what could possibly happen? Obviously, Mandisa had no idea about Hakim's shady past, and he really seems to like her, but once he's bored, he's another person. Perfect timing, Cyrus. Let's see how my brother behaves with feelings he claims to never experience. I'm in. She's sweet and seems pretty innocent. What harm would it do for me to hang around and see what develops from the negatives Hakim tends to capture?

"I'll ask her and see what she says. I'm sure she won't mind if I'm with you, Hakim," She answered, touching his dreadlocks sweetly between her fingertips.

"You know I love to shop, so I'll make that drive with you two if you don't mind the extra company," I posed, glancing at Hakim.

Oh, Hakim! I have to be there to see it in action. Indeed, my brother can prove me wrong. I know Hakim better than anyone. He doesn't have to be faithful because he never commits! They don't require a commitment when you do it big like my little brother. And he said she's a virgin! Oh, I don't think Hakim has ever been with a virgin. Is he playing around with her to see if he can get it, or is he serious? The only way I'll know for sure is if I keep a close set of brown eyes on him with her. I'm no hater. I hope that he's serious.

"Hell no, I don't mind, Cyrus. The added company would be cool, Mandisa?" Hakim tempted her, and I stared at her. Hakim obviously had told Mandisa about our friendship. The moment that I made the connection, Mandisa missed it because of one simple fact.

"Darius… Cyrus?" Mandisa cross-examined me, grinning.

"Osiris-Cyrus, or Cyrus, but I let the sweetest ladies call me by my first name, Darius…Queen," I joked her, laughing. The way Hakim stared at me gave me a strange familiar vibe…I thought it was gone…but…it was totally different? I was playing off what I thought I was reading in his eyes and expressions. No one here would even know if they didn't know what I knew about my best friend.

Everyone knew Hakim wasn't a nice guy to be fucked with. They knew that he was super intelligent, but they didn't understand that Hakim had a sickening sexual addiction and was mentally ill. I only wanted to make sure my brother didn't fuck this one up! "Darius Cyrus Jefferson Jr., Brooklyn, New York, Flatbush!"

I moved about and found a spot to sit and remember. Hakim and Mandisa came and sat next to me. I tried not to look at them because the more I looked at Mandisa, the more I wanted to talk to her. Hakim was acting differently with her. He wasn't talking shit. He wasn't ignoring Mandisa or trying to disappear like he usually did when he knew a girl liked him. Hakim never had a problem pulling fine women. The problem was he didn't have to.

They came on to him! He'd been with more women than I could count. He never wanted to be in love, and he let them all know upfront. They didn't even care! The women still chased his ass.

Me, on the other hand, I loved being in love. I got so much joy from being a lover and provider that it made me sick in the head. If a woman treated me the way I wanted to be treated, I'd give her anything to make her happy. What I saw now was really out of character for my best friend. But I wanted him to really find that one special girl, fall in love, and maybe one day get married. Now that I had met Mandisa, all these feelings started developing inside of me. I just didn't want my brother to fuck up and hurt her like all the others.

I sighed and looked at my phone. Five missed calls from…Ms. Clarissa? I gazed around to see if she was gone. Then I detected a very familiar face talking to a group of niggas. She was all cuddled up with one guy. It must be Dre.

Oh well, I'm not out of hardly anything. But why do girls do that? If you're not going to leave your sorry nigga, then stop trying to get a real man's attention. The Friend Zone is not my favorite parking space, especially if you ain't being a real friend to me. I observed her thinking to myself as she went to the ladies' room, and a few ticks later, she called me once again. I disregarded it and cut my eyes.

"You want to go outside and smoke that, Cyrus?" Hakim raised, interpreting my attitude.

"Hell yes, I need to get my head back right. I lost all my peace of mind in just a few moments," I snorted, thankful, ready to get my shoes. "Where's Lionel?"

"That's what took so long. Lionel got in a scrap with a buster in the men's room a while ago, so I carried his crazy ass back home," Hakim groaned, glowering as he opened his locker and took Mandisa's shoes.

"Are you serious? We've only been here for a little over two hours, and that nigga already got in a fight?" I questioned Hakim, glaring.

"Yep, he's at home. He's grounded, and if I get back and he's gone, I'm going to snatch all the hair off of his melon head, I swear!" Hakim informed me as he sat down, shaking his head. Mandisa raised an eyebrow at Hakim and seemed disappointed. Mandisa sat nearby and took off her skates, and Hakim hurried and put his sneakers on.

I stared at her as he took both of their skates back to the rental desk. I know this seems impossible, but it's like that girl gets lovelier every second! All I needed was one flaw, and I could move on! Ugly feet was my stop sign, so I knew if I saw a bunion, corns, or jacked up toenails, I was home-free! I was begging Jah for Mandisa to have ugly feet, and I have never asked for that in my entire life. It was always the other way around!

As she took off her socks, all I saw was soft yellow skin and pretty golden toes that matched her fingernails. Her feet looked so smooth; I just wanted to touch them, smell them. I pretended to drop my phone, and it landed right by her foot. I got down on my knees nearby and quickly snatched my phone and sniffed her feet. They were just a little sweaty, not sweaty enough for me, though. She slid on one heel and had trouble buckling it.

"You missed the hole. Need some help?" I requested, glancing up from my knees.

"Would you mind, Darius?" She invited me as she held out her foot, struggling to see.

"No, I don't mind at all," I breathed, glaring at her beautiful foot. I grabbed it in my hands, rested it in my lap, and stroked her toes with my fingertips. I pretended to ease her shoe on tighter, but that was just a ploy to rub her foot on my leg. Damn it! I wanted to suck her toes badly. Instead, I put the strap back through the buckle and tightened it slowly as I held her calf, staring at her muscle. I suddenly had to hold my breath because I could see her pretty black lace panties as I glanced up! Now I knew I was being punished for something. I pretended to have to scratch my neck and placed her foot on the floor. "I think you're good to go, Queen."

Mandisa peeked down at me, brightly with those green stones whispering, "Merci beaucoup, Darius...Cyrus?"

"Just Darius, please, Queen?" I requested as she grinned at me so innocently beautiful. I chuckled back at her as I saw her feeling my locks. I watched her twirl one around her sparkling fingernail, and I blinked, needing to look away. Mandisa was taking my emotions on a trip!

"So, you are Hakim's best friend, the one he calls his brother?" She questioned, watching me as I started taking off my skates. I groaned, laughing at her attempting to ignore her accent. It was ringing in my ears like music...I concurred, nodding.

"Hakim and I have been friends since I was eleven. We've done everything together. Hakim used to be mad all the time and very discreet. It didn't take me that long to break that wall. He's really cool when I'm around. But Hakim's ecstatic now since meeting you, Mandisa.

"He talks about you like you're the most wonderful girl in the world. I see why," I finished plunking on my boots. I raised and exhaled, eyeing down at her. "You're really amazing and good for him. Hakim needs you."

"Darius?" She muttered, gazing up at me, sulking. "Do not talk like that, please? You sound so sad. We were having so much fun. What is the matter?"

"Nothing is the matter, okay? I'm happy for Hakim. What I said is true, Mandisa. You're beautiful, fun, and so sweet. Any man would be blessed to have a woman like you. Just being around you is uplifting," I admitted as she stood up, observing me, puzzled. Her eyes seemed concerned and sad. "I'm going to go outside and smoke this good weed and get my shit together. You're going to spend time with Hakim so he can really get to know you. You need to get to know him too."

"Darius, you're sweet and fun, too...I like...being around you. I want you and me to be friends, like Hakim. I'm here to make real friends, and I've never had any male friends. Dancing with you has been magical and so much fun, so bless me with a smile?" She implored, elbowing my arm.

"Anything for you, Mandisa, anything," I mumbled, feeling great but suddenly dissatisfied. I don't know why this happened. I'm not even sure how. But I found that I unexpectedly had fallen in love with this girl. She was with my best friend, and I would never betray him. One side of me wanted her so badly that it couldn't stand to be around her. The other half needed her so much it hurt to be away from her. I felt like I was literally being plucked apart by two different people.

"Darius?" Mandisa inquired, glancing up at me.

"Yes, Queen?" I replied, spotting her serious face.

"Stay around, please?" She requested elegantly as she unexpectedly scratched my crown mischievously. I snickered, but it really felt good, and I didn't want her to quit.

"Oh, fa sho! I'm finishing school here at Carver with Hakim. I'm in Madame Olga's dance class, and I'm always around my brothers," I assured, aiming to keep her off my trail. I surveyed all over the place, grinning.

"Madame Olga is also my dance instructor, so we will see more of each other after school starts. What I meant was…I hope that you are around…for the summer," Mandisa responded, moving in front of me, coercing me to look at her face.

"Oh yeah! I'll be around. I said Hakim's my bro, so we do everything together. The Dunn family is my family. So yeah, no worries, I'll be around…but…

"I don't know if that's a good thing or a bad thing!" I thought, abruptly boosting my voice. I was getting upset as I threw my jacket over my arm and headed towards the exit. Hakim was by the snack bar as I went out the door.

This girl was mystifying the fuck out of me! It was like she was flirting and being too friendly. I didn't know what to believe. I didn't mean to yell, but I don't think she would have left me alone if I didn't ruffle her feathers. There was no way in hell I was going to step on Hakim's toes.

Yes, I had feelings for her unexpectedly. But I know how bad it feels to really love a girl, and she was just using me. Hakim has never been in love. If I had acted on my emotions, I'd never have forgiven myself. Mandisa was sweet and innocent. I don't think she would hurt him. But the longer I was around that girl, the more I wanted to stay, which equals pain for someone.

I parked near my truck and lit the blunt; I hit that shit like it had the cure for cancer. I was trying to get so high that nothing could bother me. It wasn't going to take too much either. I only smoke what we grow, and we produce the best. Yes, that's how we make our money, and don't call us drug dealers because it's all legal!

Let me tell you about myself, my friends, and our business ventures.

#

When we were kids, we were all poor as hell. My dad worked two jobs, sometimes sixteen hours a day after my mom died. He moved us here to The View to take a job at the local chemical plant. I hardly saw him except to eat and sleep, and then it was right back to work.

Hakim and Lionel's grandparents moved back here and raised them with very little money. But they did the best they could. Mr. Dunn was disabled from a bad injury from working years ago. Part of his leg was lost from faulty equipment when a press malfunctioned and crushed him underneath. He was lucky to still be alive when the machine flipped over on him. Grandma Sophie is a nurse. She's been working at health clinics for over forty years.

When Hakim and I became friends, his grandparents accepted me as their own. They started keeping me while my dad worked. We really did grow up together. We would take these trips to different places during the summer when the Dunns' grandparents were young enough to take us. Man, those were the best times. Those long car rides made us see that the bus was just a distraction.

To really see something, you had to have a car, money, and a destination. So, when we got home to The View, we all hit the streets running. Hakim, Lionel, and I wanted to see it all! We got maps of places we wanted to go, wrote lists of things we wanted to do, and found pictures of all the shit we wanted to own. Lionel used to make these scrapbooks from magazines, and they were dope.

Me? I wanted it all, everything that I couldn't afford. I enjoyed the money, cars, clothes, and especially all the fine women. If love wasn't an option, I was going to pull the finest women I could find. I had so many lists of shit I wanted; it was scary. I added more as my tastes evolved.

But not Hakim... No, Hakim wanted to change the world. At first, he had crazy ideas about growing the city and making his home more comfortable. All Hakim dreamed about was the ultimate comfort. He wanted the perfect house, to drive the most luxurious cars, and he wanted the perfect woman... My brother didn't like girls...he wanted women! Hakim had the most exquisite taste.

He wanted to pay for his own education and everyone else's. He chose to take his money and make more money. Hakim and our friend Kaliah are certified geniuses. They read books about everything, especially business and marketing. Hakim watched the news all the time, and his favorite shows that weren't sportscasts were about finance and world news. He could quote numbers and guess changes almost perfectly. Hakim would call Kaliah, who was in college at UCLA. They bounced numbers off of each other every morning for months.

It freaked everyone out how he could sit in front of the TV and quote the numbers as they showed up on the screen. Mr. Dunn saw that shit, and when Hakim turned thirteen, he gave him some savings bonds that belonged to his deceased father. It was worth more than ten thousand dollars! That, along with some insurance money, got the ball rolling. Hakim and Kaliah turned that money into over two hundred thousand dollars in three months!

When I told my dad what Hakim had done, he gave Hakim every penny of our savings, and they flipped it. Kaliah was unbelievable! He's a human calculator, and he could memorize anything once he read it or saw it. He started going to medical school at the age of sixteen and took a pharmacy job. Kaliah started telling us about medicinal marijuana co-ops, pharmacies, and dispensaries.

Kaliah had started growing for a farm and cross-breeding strains as well as developing seeds. All the while, he and Hakim were still flipping paper on the market! They had almost two million dollars in a year.

Soon the brokers started getting nosy because Granddaddy Dunn was too old. They wanted to know where he was getting his information. Hakim and Kaliah decided to pull all the money out of the market and move into the marijuana business.

Kaliah used his botany, chemistry, medicine, and business degrees to develop some crazy shit, and we wanted to use our money to back him. He was selling his plants to co-ops, and then inspiration hit. Kaliah and Hakim took their money, bought a farm, and grew in Kaliah's hometown in Jamaica. I took my money and paid for development, distribution, and in the next year, we split five million dollars three ways! We kept buying more and more farms in different countries, and in states that allowed cultivation, we stayed on top of all the laws and bills being passed, so we knew our limits. Kaliah invented more ingenious, specifically potent strains. Now we split about nine million a year…that's net income. For an 18-year-old…that's gross.

Hakim and Kaliah handle all the legal aspects of the business. Hakim had his grandmother take ownership of all his legal contracts until this year, when he turned eighteen. So nine times out of ten, if you get your weed from a pharmacy and it is mind-blowing, it came from us. Kaliah has even obtained medical endorsements for some strains by testing cancer patients and people with other terminal illnesses.

We have all bases covered! All of us are multi-millionaires, and only Kaliah is over the age of twenty-one. We each have an accountant who covers our taxes, and any issues we have involving the law, we have a legal team standing by for that shit, too. Hakim was determined to make sure that his family's best interests were utterly taken care of for now and the future.

"This really isn't a job that you try to make a life-long career," Hakim always says.

But I feel, "Nigga, get your paper... Why are you bullshitting?!"

We're good at what we do, so why not try to get the most out of everything? I say do it big! But this was all Hakim and Kaliah's operation. I financially back them, I respect them, and so I listen to them...I just can't live like them.

Once we saw all those zeros, we lost it...well, I did. But I promised that I would not go spend crazy. We did not want police in our business. So we play it cool. I've only bought one vehicle in the last two years, Mercedez, my truck. I own a nice set of condos on the west side of town, and I have more clothes and shoes than a person can wear. What would you buy?

But I ain't spend crazy! No one could guess how much money I am actually sitting on by looking at me or my possessions.

I never carry more than fifteen hundred dollars cash. I don't drive crazy anymore, I still tote weed most of the time, but the police will need a welding torch to find it. I'm the only person that knows where and how to get around my truck. Good luck, pigs!

I didn't live with my dad anymore. We fell out after the money started coming in, so I gave him a huge chunk and skated back here. No biggie, I hate drama.

I had spots all over, so I could move around when shit got hot in The View. But this was home to me. Hakim, Lionel, Grandma Sophie, and Mr. Dunn were my family. As soon as I start the car to leave…I'd miss them and want to turn back around.

We had our disagreeing moments. We fought like brothers, but after we chilled, everything was fine. That's how you know someone really cares about you. They can squash anything because no matter why you fight, it ain't worth saying goodbye, not for good… We started out as neighbors, became best friends, and grew into a family. I love them all.

Hakim, my brother, he's been through so much shit in his life he deserves some happiness. Since I've known him, he's always been the responsible, cool, and protective one. I bring him laughter, I can make him smile, but he has never been ecstatic. Never! Money can't make you grateful. It can't replace what you've already lost, and he's hurt. Shit, we all are, but you can't stop. You got to keep moving forward, right? I live my life like Puff in the 90s because it was *lit* to have paper and be *that* nigga with the bag.

Hakim's nothing like me when it comes to money. When we got paid, Hakim didn't buy a lot of shit. He remodeled his grandparents' house, bought both Grandma and Granddad's new cars, paid all the bills, and still does. Hakim gets all of Lionel's clothes, too, but he never goes big on anything. Lionel's head is not ready for anything expensive. He's crazy! Hakim is terrified about his baby brother. I know why…you'll see, too. We'd only been here for one hour, and Lionel was already fighting. I don't know. I love baby bro, but he doesn't listen to anyone, especially Hakim. Maybe he'll talk to you later.

#

I stood up, leaning against the truck, watching some guys trying to bop, and I chuckled. I took a few steps toward them and stayed back, watching and listening to the beat. Next thing you know, I was in the center of them, demonstrating how you were supposed to do it right. They were trying to copy my footwork.

You can't move like Cyrus on your best day, baby. I got this! I've danced everywhere, and I'm all over the internet in videos tearing it up. I'm arrogant about my skills because it's the truth. I got a swimming pool full of Hateraid for you ignorant niggas…want a taste? Don't start sipping. It's addictive, and I got a line of y'all already drinking from the diving board…LMAO!

I looked at my watch. It was close to ten. Hakim came and chilled with me while Mandisa was talking to some well-dressed sistas about their clothes. He took off his jacket and sat it on the hood smiling at me like a lovesick puppy.

"So, where did you find her, Bro?" I sweated him for more information. I took a drink and shook my head, watching her as she glanced in our direction, blushing.

"I told you, Cyrus, she lives right behind me in that white and yellow house on Cooper Rd, the one with all the flowers everywhere," Hakim stated, leaning closer to me as he took my cup and stole a sip. We both loved Crown Royal, and I realized he only wanted a taste because he was on a date. That's how tight we are. We share everything. "She just moved in last week. I ran past her house every day, but I never saw her. When I bumped into her at the park down the road, I felt like I had won the lottery. She paints these amazing pictures, and she's just so incredible. I have to keep Lionel away from her, he's too rowdy, and he'll scare her off, no respect."

"Yeah, baby bro can be a handful. He's a good kid, I'll talk to him, but he's just always hyped up. Once he calms down, he's cool," I chuckled, getting my cup back. I glanced back over at Mandisa as she knelt down, taking a rock out of her heel, and I saw those calves flexing. I breathed cumbersomely, staring back left field.

"So you like her, Cyrus?" Hakim grilled me seriously.

"Oh yeah, she's cool, Bro," I fantasized, striving to seem nonchalant, glancing at Mandisa again. "So, you really are trying to cuff her?"

"I want to so badly, but she's scared of her father," Hakim groaned intensely, stroking his stomach, observing her closely. "She got this spell on me, Bro. I can't stop thinking about her. When I close my eyes, I can just see myself with her. I know if she'd only give me a chance…I would make her mine. I'm not even talking about sexually! I just want to hold her, you know?"

"You're really in love, Hakim… Wow! I never thought I'd see the day. As many fine women I've seen you fuck, this is a totally different side of you. I'm terrified! Hold me!" I chucked, lighting another blunt and giving him a squeeze. I blew out the smoke and handed it to him, and he grabbed a puff. "Does she trip over you smoking?"

"No, her mom is totally cool, and Mandisa is open-minded like us, but she doesn't smoke. So weed doesn't bother her at all," Hakim told me, grinning. Most women hated brothers that smoked weed like I do. That's my major vice. I've been smoking weed hard since I was thirteen, and I loved it. I smoke weed daily. Don't judge me!

"That's fucking crazy, Bro!" I exclaimed, shaking my hair as he passed it back to me. "She's remarkable, really."

My phone was going crazy, suddenly, so I gazed at the screen. It was 10:30 pm, and now I had ten missed calls! All of them from Clarissa. She even texted me, which I hated doing, about six times. So I read a few, and she was just telling me to call her, and she had seen me still at Hot Wheels.

The funny thing her calls and texts were spaced the same amount of time apart. Which usually meant she'd call, then text…go chill with Dre…Then call, then text again…but she could have been chilling with me the whole night if she was serious. But I could see the game she was playing, so I snubbed her thirsty ass.

Hot Wheels closed early since it was a weeknight, which meant it was time to shake the spot anyway.

"It's getting late; I better take Mandisa home so her mom will trust me to take her out again. What you going to do, bro?" Hakim started prying as he saw me eyeing my phone.

"I'm going to chill until Stevie closes, then head to the crib," I replied as I scratched my forehead and handed him the weed one last time. He took a few puffs and passed it back.

"Alright, Bro, give me a call when you make it in? I'll come through and chill for a minute," He told me as he strolled over and got Mandisa's attention. I observed for a second and peeped around, feeling really lovely now. I beamed and waved to a few sistas about to leave.

"Darius," I heard Mandisa cry from nearby. She snuck up on me as I was floating. I flinched, and she snickered at me. "Mami told me that I could go with you to the mall. So I'll see you tomorrow, oui?"

"Oh yeah, Mandisa, bright and early. Dallas is a two-hour drive, so the sooner we leave, the sooner we can hit the racks! I'm telling you I'm a shopaholic, so you better bring your A-game, Girl," I mocked her, beaming.

"Oui, you're so cool!" She giggled as she tossed her arms around my waist and squeezed me. I held up my hands apprehensively as she tugged away, smiling. She was actually just a sweet innocent thing. I couldn't believe she just did that to me in front of all those people. I didn't want to touch her so they would get the wrong idea about us.

"I'll be ready. Just give Hakim a…here. Let me give you my number," I thought as I found a piece of paper. I wrote my number, handed it to her, and she grabbed her phone and saved it immediately. Next, she took a picture of me, then Hakim, and finally all of us together. Hakim took off to get the car, and she looked up at me.

"We're going to be terrific friends, Darius. So you have to teach me how to move like you!" She giggled as she put a piece of candy she got out of her purse in her mouth.

"May I have one?" I asked her just to see if she would give it to me. She colored and happily handed me a piece of cherry candy. She beamed at me as I put it in my mouth, and I noticed she was playing with one of my dreadlocks again. She swirled it between those lovely golden fingertips, and I analyzed her staring in my eyes. "You take care of yourself, Queen. Have a good night. You'll see me tomorrow, okay?"

"Oui, Darius, you remain…sweet, good night," She responded as she gazed into my eyes. Her candy-coated lips parted to say something. But Hakim pulled up, and Mandisa instead waved as she walked to the car. I couldn't take my eyes off of her. As they tore away, I remained there, just stalking them with my eyes silently. I'm not the sharpest knife in the drawer, but I'm pretty sure she was flirting with me. Interesting.

I took another sip out of my cup and glanced over, spotting Hakim's jacket on the hood of my truck! I felt the pockets. His phone and wallet were inside. I threw it in my window and started the car, and tried to catch up with them. I couldn't believe they didn't notice me behind them all the way from the East Side! Hot Wheels was almost near the city limits! Hakim must be high or in his own world to not even see me. They got it all the way to Mandisa's house on Cooper, so I just parked on the side of the road and waited to give him his jacket since they were enjoying a moment.

I leaned back and closed my eyes, trying not to be nosy, but it didn't take long for curiosity to make me watch anyway. Mercedez was hidden by the vines on the gate, so they couldn't see my truck. Shun was parked near the mailbox just ahead of me. I leaned forward in my seat so I could tell what was going on.

Mandisa was standing on the porch close by Hakim on the steps. She played with his hair as they talked, just like she did with mine a moment ago. I unpredictably found my fingers twisting the same one she had handled. I wished I was standing in Hakim's shoes right then.

"Take the fucking hint, Bro! She wants you!" I thought to myself, wishing it could reach his ears. Hakim took her hands, holding them smiling, and he pulled her into a hug. My heart was on speed, and I wanted that hug. I couldn't look away as he started to let go. Finally, when he changed his mind, she kissed him.

I smiled and peered away, sitting back in my seat. Finally, at least one of us was getting what we wanted. I would give anything to feel that good again. Being in love with a beautiful girl that loves you back is the best feeling in the world. You can't experience anything but bliss when she looks at you. Man, if I could go back, I'd do it all over again, just with a girl I knew actually wanted me.

#

The only girl I ever really loved, I wanted her so badly. I'd known her for years, and I thought because we were friends first, it could work. I was wrong. She wanted Hakim so much she used me. She kept telling me she loved me, but she did really evil shit behind my back. She started saying really underhanded shit to get Hakim's attention, and I went with it until I realized what was really going on. Hakim was a real brother to me. He hipped me to the games Samantha Reed was playing.

"Yeah?" Hakim answered his phone, putting it on speakerphone so both Lionel and I could hear. Then, he put his finger over his lips, telling us to shut up.

"Hakim, what are you doing?" Sami demanded.

"Nothing, just chilling at the crib. I'm getting ready for my game. What's good, where is Cyrus? I haven't heard from him in a few days?" Hakim answered her, making small talk. It was true I had been with her constantly for a week because her birthday was last Thursday. It was close to Christmas, and she was lonely because her father had been working a lot more since her mother left him.

"I don't know, and I don't care… I'm talking to you right now, and that's all I worry about, Hakim," Sami sniggered

120

condescendingly. Hakim glanced over at me as I sat on the bed, snooping fatally now. Hakim glowered and wobbled his head. "Whoa, Sami, that's my boy, and y'all supposed to be seriously together. Everybody knows that shit, girl! So how you gonna front like you don't care about him?"

"Cyrus is sweet, he helps me out a lot, but he's too immature. (Okay…I thought she liked how I cheered her up?) I need someone more grown-up and intellectual. We've all been friends for years, Hakim, so why are you acting like you not feeling me? Before Cyrus moved here, we hung out all the time… There used to be this strong vibe between you and me,…then you just cut me off," Sami groaned woefully. (I didn't know that Hakim and Sami had anything before me. He ignored her.)

"Because you started fucking around with Cyrus! You smile in *my* brother's face and talk shit behind his back to everyone! I'm not messy like that. You ain't my friend, and I'll tell Cyrus the shit you always spitting," Hakim bellowed, scowling gravely.

"He won't believe you, Hakim. Darius loves me. He'll consign anything I tell him. (Whoa! Wait? What?) You're still running from us, but that's cool. There are lots of niggas that want me. Cyrus is just trying to be you. (That's a fuckin lie!) He's a cheap substitute, but at least he pays what he weighs. (She's laughing hysterically suddenly! Wow!) He lost all that extra weight running with you. He couldn't afford me if he was still fat like he used to be when we were kids. Maybe he can try to look like you, but he's still slow. (SLOW?! Of all the…okay…fine…whatever…)

"That's why he's always cracking jokes and shit. But that's okay…I'll just keep spending his money, and maybe I can learn to love him. (Learn to love yourself, bitch…I'm outie…) He might have some good sex, but it's lame once he starts talking. You want me, Hakim, I know you do," Sami chuckled, and I rose up and glared. I was pissed off entirely. I loved that girl with all my heart and soul. Hearing all that broke me down. I was ready to hurt her.

"Yeah, whatever, Sami!" Hakim exclaimed, hanging up on her. "I told you, Man! Three years calling, coming by, following me, and she's just a gutter-mouthed ho! Every conversation the same, and she won't stop. Chick calls Lionel, Sophie, G.D., and she leaves long-ass messages all over my voicemail. She's fucking crazy! I have never touched her!"

I just stood there. I couldn't believe that was the same girl. My girl?!

When we were together, she was so different and sweet, but now I saw the real her. I hated that bitch! I packed my shit and went back to New York. I had gotten accepted into

Julliard, but now I had to get away from her…and away from there.

I called Hakim a lot. Lionel and I had our bro time, too, but I didn't talk to that girl. She still calls from time to time, and I ignore her number. I wasn't going to uproot my family and friends by changing my number because of her! Hakim is my best friend, and he could have had that girl, but he never even considered it because he knew how much she meant to me. It petrified me how women gravitated to him. Even when we were kids, he had this strange aura that attracted women.

Hakim and I had been through everything together. He had his moments, but I knew that Hakim was just crazy. My friend was a sad and lonely kid. He was always mad. He never had fun, and all he did was read and plan. For what? I have no idea. But when I first met him, he had me concerned. I couldn't help but talk to him.

I was sitting on the porch in front of my house and saw him running down the street. He was sprinting like he was being chased by someone, but I didn't see anyone. He slowed down in the street up the road from my house, and his brother, Lionel (who I didn't know at the time), rode his bike past. Lionel brushed Hakim's arm as he dodged being hit.

Hakim dropped the book he was carrying in the drainage ditch and dove down to go get it. Hakim looked like he was going to fuck his brother up, but he went home instead. I was ready to go speak, but I decided to let him chill. I sat down and played my Game Boy some more.

But a few minutes later, Hakim came back out of the house. I stood back up and decided to go see if he was okay. He walked down to the end of the block and sat at the bus stop. I caught up with him across the way.

"You live over there?" I questioned, seeing him sitting and waiting for the bus.

"Yeah," Hakim replied, staring up the road, sulking.

"What you so mad about?" I demanded as I came across the street.

"What are you so damn glad about, nigga?" He tested me, still staring away.

"I just came out of your grandparents' room. Your grandma was giving your granddad head, and I stole her teeth out the jar. So here you give them back to her," I laughed, putting the toy on his lap. He looked down at it and started chuckling when he saw those jumping teeth.

"Nigga, you're silly," Hakim snorted.

"I know, but at least I ain't mad like you," I stated as I sat next to him. "Why you so angry anyway?"

"Because life here sucks, why else? I'm sick of niggas being happy about dumb shit they should be angry about. White men don't give a fuck about us. I hate this town! I want to go home!" Hakim groaned and frowned. "I miss…Georgia."

"Don't they have white people in Georgia?" I asked, chuckling. "They in New York where I'm from, and it's more niggas and Puerto Ricans there than anywhere."

"Yeah, but at least back home, I can be close to…never mind," He said, looking down. "Why you got them snakes in your head?"

"My mama, she used to have long dreadlocks, and she died from breast cancer. So she lost all her hair, and I'm growing it back for her," I replied, pulling his hair. "What's your excuse, Don Cornelius?"

Hakim stared at the ground for a moment and didn't say a word.

"You miss her?" He finally managed to ask me.

"I miss her every minute of every hour and every day…I wish I could just see her again," I groaned, touching my hair.

"I miss her just like that too, Man!" Hakim told me, his face sorrowful and weepy now.

"How you know my mama? Your name Big Willie? My daddy says you owe him some child support if it is," I snickered, struggling to cheer him up.

"Nigga!" Hakim chuckled, elbowing me.

"What's your name, Bro? I see you around all the time reading and shit! You need to have some fun or at least one friend?" I thought, kicking the curb.

"Hakim, and I got a crazy-ass brother, so a friend probably wouldn't matter. I like my privacy, so I can think about shit," Hakim replied honestly.

"Cyrus is my name. You can think when you sleep, read when you're bored, but can't you have some fun? It's good to be smart and read, but if you just get mad and do nothing, why get so worked up in the first place? I see your brother. He plays ball, rides bikes, and he talks more shit than me, but at least he's living. What are you doing? Waiting for an answer to a question that doesn't have one? You're missing it all," I warned him.

"What? What am I missing?" Hakim demanded, rolling his eyes.

"Fun!? What fun memories you got?" I requested, pushing him.

"I don't know!" Hakim thought, becoming annoyed. "None, I guess!"

"Then we need to make some now, don't you think? Look over there! You see those kids playing in the street? They ain't worried about what's wrong with anything.

Because to them, everything is fine. Yeah, you're smart, and you know better, but we are kids…what can we do now?

"Nothing, so just hold off on shit and stop being so mad. I used to be angry all the time too, but being upset doesn't fix shit. So, get up and do something or scratch your black ass and get glad like me," I chuckled, getting up. I was about to go back home and get my Game Boy.

"Cyrus?!" Hakim called me as he got up.

"Yo?!" I replied back.

"Come get your ass kicked in *Street Fighter*?" Hakim challenged me, smirking. I nodded and went back and followed him to his house.

"Oh hell no, Hakim! This ain't a daycare center!" Granddaddy Dunn yelled when we came inside. "Who the hell is this burned nigga? Sophie is at work, and I ain't watching y'all badasses!"

"He's Cyrus, just a new friend from down the street. We just want to play the game, G.D., alright?" Hakim explained calmly, and his grandfather looked at me.

"Alright, come here, let me check you for guns and drugs. I don't play that shit, Hakim! Lionel's little friends get the pat-down, too!" Mr. Dunn said seriously, getting up and going through my pockets. I was terrified! "Wallet, key, gum…condom?! What do you need that for, little boy? You too young to be doing the nasty!"

"Better safe than sorry, sir, you never know. The girls on this street are hot, like that light-skinned angel across the street from me," I reported to Mr. Dunn.

"That's Samantha Reed," Hakim uncovered, glowering. "She's cool, but she's too clingy like static from the dryer."

"She can cling to deez- she is certainly nice-looking," I stated, correcting myself, gazing at Mr. Dunn. "My dad told me pretty girls like that are like sunshine. If you don't catch them shining now while they are innocent, you have to go through a storm later when they all messed up."

"I like you, Cyrus. You're alright. At least you've got respect and listen to your elders," Mr. Dunn declared, nodding to me as he staggered back to his chair, sitting. "Hakim, where the hell is Lionel's badass? He was supposed to go to the store for me. Find your brother, then come back and play."

"Yes, Sir," Hakim responded, going back outside the door. I chased him.

"Man, your grandfather is loud. His voice is high as hell, too! Why he yell so much?" I chuckled, forcing Hakim. "He talk like that all the time?"

"No, just around boys and other men. Women come around, and he's a pussy. Grandma got him so whipped he doesn't even curse when she's around. He doesn't like kids," Hakim informed me. "If you gonna hang around us, you need to know my grandparents are not married. They have been together for over twenty years, though.

"G.D is my dad's father, and Grandma Sophie is my mama's mother. It's a long story, but they love us. They loved their kids, and they love each other. No incest…I've heard it all."

"Nigga, what?" I requested, perplexed as fuck as we walked down the street around the corner heading to the park.

"They can tell you better than I can explain. But we don't ask. All I know for sure is that my dad and mom grew up around each other and fell in love first. They were classmates, and shit just happened. I think G.D. started trying to see Sophie when mom and dad were kids, but it didn't work out," Hakim exhaled, confusing me.

"Why do you call him G.D.? Is that short for granddad?" I questioned, trying to change the subject.

"His real name is Gary Dunn, but we don't call him by his first name," Hakim stated. "Grandma Sophie's last name is Clark. She's not a Dunn, not yet. I think they're gonna finally get married one day. They both moved in together when my mom and dad got killed in a car wreck last year. But they were together before all that happened."

"I think I get it...losing both their kids brought them closer together for y'all? That's kind of deep," I thought as Hakim glared, still going.

He stopped by the entrance to the park and waved his head, seeing his brother throwing hands in the middle of a massive crowd of black and white kids. It seemed like Lionel was fighting four white boys and an older brother with long braids helping him. He looked like he was 16 or maybe older. The older guy was really tall and was shredded! He had an enormous grin on his face as he pulled two dudes off of Lionel.

"I'm not gonna let y'all fight my little homie! Shit, fight fair if you ain't scared! Four of y'all against just his ass... that's foul! You want to fuck him up.... All of you gonna have to go through me. I promise none of y'all want any of this," He hooted, scanning all of them.

Lionel's lip was busted, and he was covered in dirt. There was a cute little girl nearby the older boy. She was cocoa brown, short, and had Indian braids. She was trying to help Lionel up and make him leave. But Lionel wanted to stay and fight.

"Fuck that little nigger! He ain't nothing but a loud-mouthed piece of shit!" A white boy with blond hair and green eyes cried. I glanced over, and Hakim was gone!

"What you say about my brother, Bitch!" was all I heard Hakim say. That boy was fast as lightning! He punched that boy in the mouth, and he went down like curtains. Another one tried to grab Hakim, and he pulled a short blade out of his pants as he flipped him over on his back. "Come after us again, and I'll chop you up like a white onion! It's over! Take your wicked asses home, or I'll start a lynching like it's the 50s in Mississippi for white boys!"

"What the fuck? Bruce Lee?" That was what I thought when I saw Hakim move and those white boys scattered like roaches.

"You better watch your back, Dunn! Your brother can't always save you!" The green-eyed blond boy yelled.

"Watch your back, Cracker-Jack!" Hakim shouted after them as he tucked away his blade.

"Man, didn't nobody ask for your help, Hakim! You ain't no damn ninja! I can handle my own shit," Lionel exclaimed, appearing pissed.

"Yeah, I can tell," Hakim replied, glancing at his brother.

"Hakim! You were everywhere, Nigga!" The dude with the braids snorted, whacking him five. "I had Lionel's back, though. They love to jump kids if they can catch you alone, especially that racist asshole Kayle Bennett, Amber's big brother.

'They daddy got him brain-washed. Amber is cool, but Kayle's an asshole. May-May and I saw that shit from the front porch. They followed Lionel down here. I wasn't going to let that shit go down."

"Yeah, they follow us around at school, too," May-May blabbed, shoving Lionel's head. Her voice was high and cute. She smiled sweetly as she dusted Lionel's shirt off and stared at us. "I tell him to ignore them, but his lips start flapping. You know Lionel."

"Yeah, thanks for looking out, J-Rock," Hakim expressed, nodding.

"Fasho, little bro, but we got to go! Aunt Key-Key is undoubtedly pissed! We are not supposed to be outside. We've got stuff to do around the house," J-Rock cackled, putting a blunt behind his ear and striding by me. "Sup, Homie, be easy, Bro!"

"Yeah, you too," I answered him as he gave me a pound.

I glanced at Hakim, and he glowered. I had never seen a black man fight like that in real life, only in movies! May-May ran behind her brother after she waved bye to Lionel, and he just nodded to her. I was like, 'Bro, she's feeling you,' but he was too damn hard to say shit to her. She was so cute, too. But she was way too young for me, but she was the perfect age for Lionel.

Her brother, J-Rock, was a big Nigga, though! I have no idea how old he was, but he looked like a grown man. He was cut like he had been in prison or was a defensive lineman for a pro football team. But if he was so old, why was he helping Lionel? I had no idea at the time, but later on, J-Rock and I got really cool.

"For real, Ha-kim, don't do that shit no more. You're making me look bad!" Lionel expressed, pushing his bike behind us.

"You want to look good and get fucked up, fine… I'm out of it," Hakim answered, walking on ahead. I followed him closely. "G. D. is looking for you. You better get home, or he'll crack you with that cane."

"Man, you the only one scared of that cane, Nigga. If you ran from him like you run from everything else, he wouldn't hit yo ass. But you stay and take that shit!" Lionel laughed as he looked at me. "I know you! You live down the road in the blue house. I see you dancing in the yard all the time. You got skills."

"Yeah, Cyrus," I uttered, smiling back at Lionel. "Come by, and I'll show you something. Girls love brothers that can dance like niggas on TV. Ayo, Usher, Soulja-Boy, and ya boy got the moves!"

"Right-right! But I ain't got time for no hoes. I'm all about making money and handling my business," Lionel snorted. "Oh, and chilling with my niggas on the block."

"What money? What business? What niggas? You're broke, you're always at the house or on that bike, and besides me, J-Rock, or Maya…you ain't got no real friends!" Hakim revealed, busting Lionel's bubble. "Just because Jamire lets you kick it doesn't mean he's a real friend. Yeah, HE, has paper but he ain't eating with you…some friend."

"You're just a mean-ass bitch, Hakim, that's why don't nobody wants to kick it strong with you. You so damn busy being mad you ain't never gone make no money or pull no bitches. You a pussy-ass hater," Lionel ridiculed his brother, chuckling again.

"That didn't look like no pussy-ass nigga I watched save your ass a minute ago," I interrupted Lionel. "Hakim was like Jackie Chan on those white boys!"

"Yeah! Yeah! Yeah! Hakim can fight, thanks to dad, but all he does is talk shit down. He ain't got one positive bone in his body. He scared of pussy, and I think he's gay!" Lionel started rolling, holding his stomach.

"I'm not gay! I just don't need a girl under me all the damn time, like Sami or May-May. Sami's too immature, and she gets on my last nerve. Hakim-this! Hakim-that! Do you like my hair? Aren't my new shoes cute? Can I have a hug?

'Girls always want attention, and I can't give that. I'd rather read a book, watch a movie, or take a nap. At least then, I get something out of the time I spend. If girls don't want to break me off something, why waste my time? Why are you in my face if you are not going to give me some? Girls don't know what they want," Hakim moaned, rocking his curly afro.

"That's true, though; they act like they like you, then get shy. One minute a girl is chasing you…then you have to chase them? When you try to touch them…they run! That's why if I can't at least see something, I got to go," I chuckled, stirring my locks.

"I don't have time to give to girls," Hakim groaned as he stopped near the bus stopover. "Now, that right there is what I am talking about!"

I saw her, and Lionel spotted her too! She was tall, light-skinned, had thick thighs, and twisted with her book bag on her shoulder. Her tight red dress clung to her body, and you could see it all. She had a switch in her stride, her hips shook as she strode, and her skirt was shorter than summer break. She suddenly noticed us and beckoned.

"… Angela," Lionel sighed under his breath slowly.

"That is all, woman! Ain't nothing on her little like a girl," I whispered as she started across the street for us. My eyes were on the prize… Those thighs...

"Hey, Lionel, how you doing, Sweetie Pie?" She sang as she bent over, caressing the top of his crown. She ran her fingernails through his curls, and he smiled, glancing up at her breasts. "It's almost time to get it braided. You're growing it out long enough… Jimmy said you want some braids like his?"

"Hey, Angela, I'm doing good now that your fine ass said hi," Lionel said without hesitation. My jaw dropped. "You going to do me like you handle J-Rock?"

"You're something else," She giggled, moving her fingers around his afro longer than Hakim's hair. But Lionel's was fine like light-skinned boys. He was a bit darker than Hakim and looked like a girl at first glance. When I heard Lionel talking shit, I knew he was no girl. Lionel loved to sneak up on people and fuck them up if they said anything he didn't like. He was knocking some big boys out until they started jumping him with three or more. Lionel didn't act like a kid either. That little girl was the only kid I saw him kick it with. This was the first time I saw him with his brother. "Call me. I'll fix it up for you, okay?"

"Yeah…but you need to let me fix you up down below first? You let me sit between your legs anyway. You won't be sorry if you allow me to turn around!!" Lionel said sincerely.

"There goes that mouth again," Angela giggled, rolling her eyes at Lionel and shaking her head. "Hakim, you're not going to talk to me today?"

"Do I ever speak to you, Angela?" Hakim responded, staring down the road, scowling.

"You could attempt to be nice. You never know what you might get if you were kind to me, Hakim," Angela giggled, flirting with him! I watched him smiling, amused as hell. Hakim acted like he didn't care right now, but he was drooling over Angela a minute ago!

"I will get into a fight with Lester the Molester. He will get his ass kicked, and you will finally GET something in your life that would tame that ass. But I don't want to do all that, so I won't say hi," Hakim continued rolling his eyes, examining her, then back down the street. Angela's cheeks turned red, and she beamed. That woman didn't know what to say to him. Then she glanced at me!

"Who are you? I've never seen you before," She questioned me. Her voice was shaken, and she seemed uneasy now.

"Cyrus, I just moved down the road. So you can take a seat on my face and call me your chair," I chuckled. "But if you sit on this dick, I'll have to call you an ambulance!"

"Oh shit!" Lionel snorted, whacking my arm. Angela stared at me, grinning. She was too old for us, but it was nice to pretend we had a chance with her. Angela realized it, too. She loved the extra attention.

Angela shook her head, crying, "Call me when you get about 18?"

"Shit, I got 11 right now! Can't we make a deal?" I teased her, and she snorted, running down the street. She hopped into a black Expedition with a red-headed white guy and flew off.

"See what I mean?" Hakim questioned me. "They love interest, even if it's from us. So, if I don't give it to them, they choose me more. It always ends up this way. Give them attention, get dissed, but disregard them; you get the pussy. I wasn't cruel, nor did I disrespect her, but she was gobbling up my remarks. I compelled her to want it as well as consider me more than she planned."

"Hakim," I snickered, giving him dap. "You got some game! That's the most real!"

"Y'all niggas are dumb. A bitch ain't going to fall for that shit! Keep it 100 percent! I want that ass! Now, we can do this the easy way or the hard way! I hope you want it hard, Girl," Lionel displayed, smirking viciously.

"Nigga, that's rape!" Hakim giggled, and Lionel retreated unexpectedly.

"What?" I demanded, confused.

"Shit, I got scared. Hakim doesn't laugh or smile," Lionel informed me, seriously nervous.

"Shit changes when you roll with Cyrus, Baby Bro," I chuckled, messing up his hair as Hakim shook his head. We spent the rest of the day playing video games and laughing at Dunn's house. Soon, I never wanted to be away from my brothers. I was an only child, and I always wanted a brother or sister. Unfortunately, Hakim and Lionel had one another and didn't seem to get that memo. So I hung around because they were cool when we just had fun.

#

I got out of the car and walked over to Shun to put Hakim's jacket in the seat through his open window. I saw him smiling as Mandisa let him go. I nodded and got back in my truck quietly. I backed up to the corner and headed home. I got comfortable, had a good drink, smoked some terrific weed, made myself a snack, and lay in front of the TV. Trash TV was my shit at night.

"Baby, you know I love you, right?" The ole girl lies, murmuring.

"Yeah, I love you, too, Baby," The unsuspecting brother tells her, smiling.

"I brought you here to tell you...I have been sleeping with your best friend, Marcus!" Ho reveals, and the boyfriend seems upset.

"Let's bring out Marcus," Jerry announces. The audience boos and throws shit as Mark-ass comes out with an attitude and pride about how he fucked over his friend?!

"Man, fuck y'all, you don't know me!" Marcus hollers at everyone. The audience keeps booing, the ho tries to hug Marcus, and the unsuspecting boyfriend goes berserk. Finally, they fight over the ho?

No! A real brother would fuck her shady ass off! But, yo, she came between you and your best friend, Bro! She is smiling while you all are fighting over her. I bet she doesn't want either of them, and now they're mad at each other.

"Shaunda, don't you have something to tell Marcus and Jacoby?" Jerry goes on to say.

"Yeah, …I'm sleeping with Tiffany, my hairdresser, too!" Shaunda says, and shit goes crazy!

"Oh shit!" I screamed aloud. I sat up laughing. "At least it's a girl! One for each of y'all!"

I smirked, tossing the remote across the coffee table as I sat up on the couch. That's a surprise a nigga can overlook, some shit a brother can handle if the shock is worth it.

If I was in Marcus's shoes, I'd be like, Jacoby, you take Shaunda. I'm going to take Tiffany, and we can watch them together. If Jacoby's cool, he'll be like fuck yes! End of story!

But if Jacoby all twisted up over Shaunda and she's just a whore, then you got to have your boy's back. You can't mess around with your best friend's girl and still be cool after that when your brother is all in love. Even if she is just a whore. To him, she's not.

Now what? No girl, no friendship, and no possible three-way? All that's left is a bunch of anger, hate, drama, and messed-up hearts. I'm Cyrus, not Marcus, Jacoby, shit… I feel your pain, brother.

Some bitches are shady; niggas too, but a female has way more game than any man can kick. If I were Jacoby's friend,

I'd be like, 'Yo, Jacoby, let's hire some crazy females to mess her up! That ho broke your heart...Let's get 'em both...Marcus got to go!' I'm petty, I know, but fuck it. A friend is going to be there, and a nigga is going to set you up every time!

I sat back on the sofa, smoking, and thinking. Then, I picked up my phone for some reason and saw two new texts.

"You... home... Bro?" Hakim's text read.

I frowned. Hakim knew I hated reading, but he insisted on texting rather than calling. I shook my head and slowly answered.

"Fasho!" I text back.

The other was from an odd number. I opened it, and it was a picture of Hakim, Mandisa, and me at Hot Wheels.

Mandisa! I saved her number, and I texted her back using voice chat.

"Thanks for the memory...Big fun, Queen!" I texted her.

"Oui, big fun, Darius. I cannot wait to see what you know about fashion. I need help!" She replied.

I grinned, getting excited, and sent her pictures of the hot stuff I'd seen girls in New York rocking, made by black designers and shoes. I thought her feet would look hot in.

"Omg! That's what I need! You have to help me pick out some stuff? Please!" She pleaded.

"I got you, Queen, I got you! I'm all over it. You gonna kill em' this summer! :P" I taunted her.

I heard a knock at the front. I put my phone on the charger and ran to the door. Hakim was here smiling up at me.

"What up, Bro?" I demanded, blinking playfully, knowing what he had been up to with Mandisa. "You are looking ecstatic and enthused. What have YOU been doing on a lovely summer evening?"

"Cyrus… I had to go anywhere. I can't go home right now! I'm too hyped up!" Hakim glowed as I let him in. He rested on the love seat, and I returned to my place on the sofa, grinning at him. "Bro!"

"What?" I answered, demanding.

"Cyrus?!" Hakim bellowed.

"Hakim?!" I hollered back. "Uh, Nigga, if you don't spit it out, I will choke you! You've got my energy anxious with all the hyperactivity…spit that shit…out...Nigga!"

"Bro, I have never felt this good before!" Hakim screamed, falling over on the loveseat, almost tumbling to the floor. "I need her bad, Bro! But she's still hiding behind that anxiety. It's so electrifying just attempting to get closer! I'm going to get her, and she's going to be mine! Ooh, when I do…ooh!"

"It's nice at first, but how do you think she feels about you? You think you can trust her with your heart?" I questioned him, my eyes half-closed.

"Bro, she's not Samantha Reed. She would never hurt us like that," Hakim replied, causing me to raise my eyebrow at him. "I meant me… Mandisa wouldn't do that shit. Sami was crazy, Bro."

"Yeah, all around the world, it's the same song. This isn't about me, Pac. You might be all into the feels now. But what's going to happen when you get bored, and our 'other friend' shows up? He's going to get around like the underground, Shock-G! You will hurt Mandisa. Are you going to tell her?" I catechized, receiving a dangerous face in response.

"Bro, don't do that shit right now. I haven't had an episode in over a year since Courtney. It's over! So, let's drop it, alright?" Hakim requested, sulking.

His eyes dipped down as he looked me over. I know my brother…He seemed sincere this time, so I exhaled and glared. I'd drop it for now, but I knew Hakim was lying. I heard Hakim's phone and rolled my eyes.

"It's her texting me!" Hakim chuckled, reading.

"What did she say?" I requested, getting excited but pretending to not really care. I was dying to know what she was asking him.

"She says she wishes she could be here with us. But, she knows we're having fun," Hakim recounted, grinning.

"Wait, what?! She knows you're here with me?" I questioned, staring confused.

"Yeah, we talked on the phone all the way over here," Hakim chuckled. "By the way, that shit you sent pictures of is what I want to see her rocking. She looks good in everything, but that shit is dope! Her hips in tight jeans, and those beautiful breasts in something strapless or those thin little straps! Oh my goodness! I'm drooling worse than you when you're sleeping!

'Okay…okay…breathe…Hakim, breathe! Ugh!"

"So you knew she was texting me, and it didn't bother you?" I demanded, glaring folding my arms.

"Why would it bother me, Bro? I trust you," Hakim told me, smiling. "You don't have a foul bone in your body, Cyrus! But, come on, man, I thought you knew me better than that. I would never think you were trying to do me dirty."

"I know! I mean…yeah…fuck! Sorry, Bro…You know how I am. I have that jealous streak, and I just assume everyone feels like I do about certain things. I'd never do you dirty, Bro," I groaned as I heard my phone. I went to go get it.

"Any more ideas?" Mandisa asked. "Can I ask you something? Do you think Hakim would hurt me? I'm afraid…I feel something when we are together, but sometimes he seems…different. It troubles me."

"Hakim is crazy… about you, Queen! You should relax and see…stop worrying so much," I told her.

"You really are a great friend, Darius! Sorry…Hakim has a great friend in you," Mandisa responded back.

"No, I'm your friend too, okay? Just think of me as a straight-girlfriend-guy friend," I told her.

"LOL! What?!" Mandisa asked me.

"Never mind…You have a good night, Queen! See U early…;)." I told her, smiling.

"Night to you, Darius, you R an 0:)," Mandisa said, flattering me.

If I could blush, I bet I'd be as red as a rose.

#

146

I walked back into the den, and Hakim was sitting on the couch with a blank expression.

"What's up, Bro?" I demanded nervously.

"Mandisa replied she wants to be my girlfriend," Hakim exclaimed, beaming unexpectedly. "I've been sweating her to tell me yes all day, and now she just said…okay."

"I wonder what could have happened to possibly change her mind….?" I teased him, smiling childishly. Then, I tossed him my phone and let him read our texts.

"Cyrus! You talked her into it!" Hakim snorted, gazing up at me, amused. "I could kiss you, Bro."

"Uh uh, not on the lips. I go a cold sore, and it might be contagious," I snickered as Hakim screamed, hugging me. I held up my hand and made a circle over my head. "See my halo! I'm a crispy angel! Hakim!...Wait!...Hold on a minute…Bro?

'Mandisa doesn't know about the money, does she?"

"Nope, not a clue. She just thinks I'm a normal dude off the streets. But after I lace her fine body up tomorrow, she'll know I'm the real thing," Hakim chuckled, rubbing his hands together, grinning.

"Oh, now you trying to spend some paper on a woman like your lovesick homeboy?" I cried, putting him in a headlock pulling his dreadlocks.

"She's my girl, Cyrus! She's not a stranger on the streets or some thirsty female. Why don't you stop chasing these boogers and find a sweet chick?" Hakim inquired as he leaned back, conceivably feeling pleased.

"I'm trying, Bro, I'm trying," I replied, crossing my arms pondering.

Hakim might be happy now. But I was hoping that Mandisa was the real thing for him…if not, we all were going to see. Everyone knew my brother was a hazard to niggas, but he was far more perilous a horror to any woman he found attractive enough. I overthink things too much when I'm uncertain, which always puts me in unbalanced spaces. I just got back home, so I'm going to roll with the flow and take things slow…we'll see where shit goes. I have to make sure shit stays honest with the fam, but Hakim wouldn't hurt her if he really loves her…I hope?

Chapter Four: Hood Politics/Institutionalized

Lionel Eugene Dunn

"Lemonhead?" She beckoned me from the sidewalk ahead on the street. It's always dark in this dream. That weird green glow is always covering her in her blue plaid uniform. Her long pigtails were hanging beneath a pink Hello Kitty backpack. The odd colored waves on the walls tell me I'm dreaming as I walk toward her voice. "…Lionel?"

"Yeah?" I replied as I stared straight ahead, glaring. Ordinarily, in this dream, I can't see her face when I look over. Instead, there's this horrible blur of black and brown when I look at her. I hate it here.

"Look at me!" She demanded as I blushed and turned my head, looking over at Shamaya?! What? This time her pretty brown eyes gazed up at me as she glowed. She looked even sweeter than I remembered. "You miss me?"

"Yeah, I miss you, Girl. You were my best friend, and we did everything together. There are only a few people I'd give anything to be with right now.

'I miss my mama, I miss my dad, and I miss you, Maya," I admitted miserably to her.

She looked over and smiled at me, and her eyes sparkled. Her Indian braids fell down her back, her skin glowed like dark brown sugar, but her eyes shimmered like brown sunshine dipped in honey. Her voice made me grin, her smile made me weak, and whenever she touched me, I felt embarrassed.

"I miss you, too, Lemonhead," She giggled, her voice high and happy like always. She put her hands behind her back. "Will you walk home with me? I don't like to walk alone."

"Yeah, Girl, I'll walk with you," I decided, moping at what was to come.

I always had this dream. I hated it. I knew what was about to happen, and I wanted to wake up before stepping off the curb. But I knew I was going to have to see it through again.

There I was, 15 years old, now. Talking to a girl I hadn't seen since I was 12. But, in my mind, she was still that same little girl. I couldn't get over her, and I just wanted to wake up!

Here we go!

I watched her step off the curb onto the street, and she started skipping as I took that step. I paused as she sped up; I slowed down.

I tried to run after her, but she was too far ahead of me. People just started walking in the street all around me. People to the left, on the right, crossing the road, and they were going so fast I couldn't move without hitting someone!

"Maya? Where are you going?" I called for her. She was right there! Right in front of me, but as the people knocked me around, I lost direction. I couldn't tell which way to go. She went-? "Maya!?"

"I'm right here, Lionel!" I heard her laughing, but I couldn't tell where she was.

I just frowned, appearing confused. Then, just when I was about to step back on the curb, I saw the light! This wasn't the same dream I had before. It was bright and golden, just like the sun! It came close to my face, and I tried to touch it. But, it was so warm and beautifully blinding. I had to look away for a moment! Then, it launched, flying away, and I chased it.

It led me right to Maya, and as I stepped onto the street… I started sinking! The road was like black quicksand. The light tried to save me, but I couldn't hold it. Maya stood on the curb. Her back was still to me. As I sank under, everything grew darker and went totally gloomy.

But the light waited with me in all the darkness that generally swallowed me in this dream.

"Lionel…we'll find her," The beautiful light hummed to me. Her voice was so warm and soothing. It reminded me of-

#

"Mama!?" I shrieked, wakening up in the bed.

It was dark as hell in the room, and the only noise was from the air conditioner. It was early in the morning, too damn early for me. Hakim sat up from his bed, gazing at me in the darkness. I pretended I had to go to the bathroom and shut the door.

Shit! I hated that damn dream. All those people were everywhere, and no one had my back. No one offered me help! They all just watched me fall and drown in that dark pit.

Discourteously, like when I used to run with cliques and them bastards would get me excited to fight; they'd dip out on me once the brawling started.

Maya? She was the only real friend I had my age growing up. She and her brother James always had my back no matter

what. Now they were long gone and nowhere to be found. We were kids, but everything about her made me happy to be here. I never knew a girl like her. She was so sweet but so hard. She could fight like a man, but she was always so happy, and she was just a joy to be around.

Yeah, she was a tomboy, but Shamaya Lockhart was still beautiful in her own way. She had all that long hair, and she never wore it down because girls picked on her. They called it a weave, pulled it all the time, and made fun of her because her family was poor. But I didn't care, she was always full of fun, and she had this contagious laugh. Her giggle was so funny it made all of us laugh. I had a crush on her, but I never told her how I really felt. That fact alone pissed me off.

#

"You see that faggot out there with that long hair like a white bitch? I almost died when he rolled by me. He's pretty as a female. If he didn't have a beard, I would have sworn that was a tall flat bitch, yo! If it was any darker out there, a nigga might try to get the digits. I like my bitches to have long hair," the Dude stated as I sat trying to fix my zipper.

I just took off my skates, and I didn't want to fall. My temple wrinkled, and I realized that nigga was talking about me! I waited in the stall listening.

"Nigga! That's Hakim's brother!" Dude's homeboy replied. "Shit, Hakim will kick your ass faster than you can slap a bitch about your money, Ace, what...I'm out!"

"Fuck, Hakim Dunn! He's been a bitch since we were kids. He thinks that Kung-Fu shit works against REAL NIGGAs. Bruce Leroy fucks with Ace, and he's going to have to really catch that bullet.

'This ain't no movie! I'll show that dread-headed nigga who's the master and put his brother on the streets with my hos. But, of course, he'll be bringing me my money," Ace chuckled.

I leaned against the stall, inspecting through a crack for him to walk by. As soon as his ass got close enough, I kicked that damn door open right in his face and broke his nose, attacked his bitch-ass, and slapped that bloody mug right into the nasty floor.

"You ain't got to bother with my brother, Hakim! I got what you need right here, Ace! You want to fuck somebody? I got your number right here, Nigga!" I snickered, kicking him in his ribs. "You are the biggest faggot in here talking about somebody looking like a bitch! You are just a PO-ass pimp! Talk that shit now, Do or Die!?"

I was tearing that ass up when Hakim pulled me off of him. Then, he yanked me out of the bathroom and outside.

"Lionel!?" Hakim howled at me, holding my head and locking my arms so I couldn't move.

"Let me go, Hakim! That nigga asked for that beat down. He was the one talking all that shit! I'll make sure he doesn't talk about fucking me or clapping you again!" I shouted as he lifted me, so my feet were off the ground. "Put me down, Hakim!"

He carried me across the parking lot and leaned me against his car. He pinned me down on the hood for a second. When I finally cooled down, he let me go. Hakim stared at me for a minute and sneered.

I leaned backward, anxious.

"What the fuck are you doing, Lionel?" He hollered at me, resting in front of my face.

"I WAS minding my own damn business when that foul-ass nigga started talking shit!" I roared back and tried to go back inside. Instead, he chased, remaining right in my face.

"What you gonna do? Fuck up everyone that says something wrong about you? You ain't bad enough to fight the whole damn world!" My brother shouted at me.

"Niggas going to talk, Bro, you can't stop niggas from talking shit! That's what niggas are programmed to do! Are you too dumb to realize that? All the shit you talk about, everyone? You should get jumped 80 times a day. Fuck them!

"You are letting meaningless words, anger, and jealousy from complete strangers kill your vibe and mine. I'm on a date! I was too fucking embarrassed to even introduce you because of your crazy-ass ways! So get in the got damn car!"

"No, …I'm going back inside!" I screamed, scowling. I wasn't hearing anything Hakim was trying to kick in my ear. He was just a hater because he's been scared to fight since he went to jail last year. But, I ain't afraid to stand my motherfuckin' ground. That nigga, Ace, and his boys was going to catch as much fire as I could unleash at Hot Wheels once I got past my nosey-brother!

"If you don't get in this car right now, we are going to fight right here and now!" Hakim hollered at me alarmingly. "You're going home, and you're staying there all night!"

"Hakim, I-" I jerked, gasping, getting upset. Hakim locked up his right fist, relaxed his left hand, took a step back from me, and waited. If Hakim fought me like I knew he could, then we both were going to wind up fucked up. I didn't want to fight Hakim. I was pissed off at that nigga talking shit about clapping Hakim and trying to fuck me. But Hakim doesn't understand shit about loyalty. So I get down for mine. He's constantly bailing on us.

"Lionel, get your ass in the car, now!" He barked at me again. He wasn't going to let me go back. Hakim seemed ready to toss one of his wild strikes. He would distract me with his hands and then kick the shit out of me if I made a sudden movement. I gave up as I opened the car, frowning, then sat shutting the door. He started the car and headed for the house. "I can't believe you, Lionel. When are you going to calm down? You have been pulling this shit for years! G.D., Sophie, and I are tired of this shit! You need a fucking hobby or get some pussy. You need me to call a bitch for you?"

I rolled my eyes at him, "I don't need you to do shit for me, Nigga. Ain't you done enough?"

"What the fuck is that supposed to mean?" Hakim demanded wide-eyed.

"Man, you act like you're perfect! You make good grades, you got bitches, money, a few cool friends, a car, and you always come for me! Yet, all I do is defend your ass. Niggas don't just be talking about me! They are scared of you, talking about catching bullets and shit. What did we do to them?" I requested seriously.

"We were born, Lionel. Don't you know the truth? Nobody gives a damn about you or me unless you give them a reason to care. Kicking their asses only adds more hatred.

If you fuck somebody up, you'll see who your real friends really are. Most of the time, when niggas are short-fused like you, they can't be trusted. Who wants to be around somebody that gets set off over everything?" Hakim catechized me, glowering.

"What the fuck-EVER, Hakim," I stated, leaning back in my seat. "If I wanted a speech, I'd watch the goddamn Learning Channel or PBS. The damn muppets are more convincing than your act!"

"Yeah, whatever, Lionel, why do I even try to help your ass anyway?" Hakim replied, rolling his eyes at me driving.

"You wanna help a nigga, give me some fucking money!" I sneaked him seriously.

Hakim laughed out loud and almost choked.

"Fuck no!" Hakim thought critically. "I give you money. It goes to your already swollen head. So you buy a bunch of shit you don't need, get shot, stabbed, or end up dead. For what an expensive material possession that you value more than your own damn life?

"Money doesn't fix your problems, but it can make more significant issues if you can't handle the burden. Money sure as hell won't cure YOU. I don't know what will, Bro, but I'm not going to do that.

"I thought about it seriously, but it takes maturity to handle the kind of cash we have. I didn't earn it all to lose your ass for a few damn dollars or fucking chain! Fuck that shit, Lionel! Mama would never forgive me if I lost you.

"I could never tolerate myself if I lost you."

I leaned back against the headrest and exhaled. I felt awful, but I didn't say anything. Hakim just got quiet and drove until we got home. I already knew G.D. and Grandma Sophie were gone. They went to Shreveport to the casinos Thursday until Sunday morning every other weekend. Hakim sent them twice a month to get away from us. But I hated being home alone!

"Go into the room, look under my bed, and find the red box with the green leaves. Smoke a blunt, calm down, play the Xbox or whatever, but don't leave this house! Don't call Jamire or Lester! You can't have any company, Lionel. You're grounded!" Hakim commanded me.

"Nigga, you can't ground me!" I chuckled, mocking him. Hakim's face remained so stern as he gripped the steering wheel, I eased up. He behaved like he was going to knock me out. I hurried up out of my seat, "Alright, man!"

"I won't be much longer. I can't keep Queen out too late, but if I get back and you ain't here…I swear, Lionel, you'll wish you could still get your ass whooped by G.D.," Hakim avowed gravely.

"Yeah," I consented, frightened as I went inside the house and locked the door quickly. When Hakim was like this, he wanted to seriously fight me! I knew he didn't hold anything back, and the last time the cops had to break us up. It wasn't worth it so soon in the summer break. I'd wind up grounded the whole time while Hakim got to run the streets with Cyrus doing it all. He's about to turn 18…I know he's going to turn up now that our big brother is back. I can't fuck up my chance to ball with the big dawgs.

When Cyrus is around, Hakim will actually spend if I get him feeling some type of way about Cyrus's tastes. I know it's fucked up, but it's the only way I can get Hakim to spend a penny of his bag. Hakim thinks he's the shit, and it pisses me off. But Cyrus isn't always around to keep Hakim off my back…Like now…Cyrus wouldn't have taken me home. We would have just bounced somewhere else together. Hakim loves to bail on people to do his thing. It is what it is…

I flung my jacket across my bed in the room, investigated under Hakim's, and found the red box. I opened the window. I didn't want to stink up the house, but G.D. didn't mind if we smoked at home. We stayed calm and didn't fight when we were all high. Granddaddy said the weed made us rich, kept us quiet, and instigated us to have fun, so he didn't care. Once Hakim and Cyrus started making paper, G.D. and Sophie began kissing their asses, and I became Flavor Flav, the annoying frontman of Public Enemy number 1. I can't do shit right, so I don't try anymore. I don't care what anyone thinks, as long as they don't say shit around me.

I sat in my usual spot near the window, in the chair, by the computer, and got blown. Hakim was right, he was… always right, and I needed to chill out. I wasn't 16, and I had fought more niggas than I could count. At first, getting my ass kicked because of my size and my mouth got me in trouble. But once my body caught up with my chops, I became a savage.

But winning wasn't the point. I like the rush of adrenaline I get from getting hyped up. It feels terrific, and I am centered once I get going. There's this phenomenal feeling that takes over once I get angry, then I just have to fight! I can't run! I've tried to control myself, but my mind just shuts off, and I react. Sometimes, I can't keep shit from coming out of my mouth when I'm angry, scared, or sad.

Hakim had never been on a date before. So I guess I fucked it up for him and ole girl. My bad...

I looked up at the moon and frowned, "I bet if you were here with me, Maya, we'd be on a date too. I'd go skating with you. I bet you would have fucked that nigga up with me too."

I chuckled and hit the blunt again, about to reach for my wallet. But, instead, I looked out the window to blow out smoke, and I saw a pretty lady in her backyard in the full moonlight. She was hanging some blankets on her clothesline and struggling with a heavy one.

I put the blunt out and went downstairs. It was only 9:15 pm, and I never came home early during the summertime. Jamie and Les would show me a good time if I called them right now. As I opened the backdoor, I hesitated to grab my phone. But I spotted the lady again and changed my mind. It was kind of dark out there, so I turned on the party lights in our backyard so she could see.

She glanced around and smiled as she noticed me. Damn, she was beautiful! She had long-ass curly brown hair, light skin, and her eyes lit up like a Christmas tree when she saw me. She looked kind of familiar, but I couldn't remember where or if I had seen her. She was a new neighbor, so maybe I just saw someone that resembled her.

"Hey, you need some help, Mam?" I offered, walking to the gate and staring at her.

She glanced at me for a second and agreed. I jumped over the fence and took the blanket from her, tossing it over the clothesline for her. She watched me for a moment, then clipped a few clothespins on the cover.

"Merci beaucoup, Dear. Thank you very much," She told me, grinning, grasping her back, and resting a bit.

Her belly poked out from her shirt, and I leered. I didn't know anyone pregnant but Mama before she died. If my mother didn't die in the car wreck with my father, I'd have a little sister. Mama was hilarious, approachable, intelligent, and she was always singing to us. The last time I saw my Mama was a few days before Christmas when I was seven, and she was close to having the baby. No one survived the accident when that man hit the ice and went into traffic head-on. I didn't know this woman, but something about her made me think of Mama when she smiled.

Beneath the moonlight, her hair, eyes, and skin looked insane. I got a chill as the temperature seemed to drop, talking to her. She didn't look like Mama in any way. This woman had nearly blond hair, and she looked mixed or white from afar, but her eyes did this crazy thing when she grinned. They started out with one color but switched. I only one other person's eyes do that....Kaliah! It gave me a calm feeling seeing the similar appearances she had to my other big brother.

"No wonder you struggling out here! Are you having twins?" I chuckled, moving closer and offering my hand to help her to the stairs. There was no way she was going to make it back alone. Every step she took seemed like it caused her discomfort!

"No, no, dear, she's just a big low girl. She's number two for me. I haven't been pregnant in so long. It feels like the first time," She giggled, taking my hand. The woman smelled like she knew her way around the kitchen! My stomach started rumbling as I picked up the smell of something sweet from her hair. It reminded me of apples and cinnamon.

"Where's your husband?" I pondered, helping her to the steps and overlooking my stomach.

"Tomny is occupied overseas. He's a surgeon, so he's here and there," She replied gently. She stopped at the door and giggled, hearing my stomach, glancing around. "Oh, the basket! Sorry..."

"Oh yeah!" I recalled and ran back to get it for her.

"You're a sweet young man. What's your name, dear?" She comforted me with her sweet nature. She was so warm and happy taking my hand.

"Lionel Eugene Dunn," I replied, smirking. Her face suddenly became genuine as she looked me over.

"Lionel, a sensational name you have! It's powerful and proud. It means regal or royal lion, a prince," She giggled at me, blushing. "You look like a lion with all that hair! Your mane is huge!"

"Uh, thanks, I think…is that a good thing or a bad thing?" I worried as she opened the backdoor.

"Lions are proud, beautiful, and strong beasts. Their manes are symbols of their royal blood. Black men with strong emotions, deep heritage, and noble family values are lions. So your mane, name, and skin; tell me that you are a lion, Lionel. I'm sorry!

'My name is Ninon Isoka King. It's a pleasure to meet you, Lionel Eugene Dunn. But you can call me Mami, all the young ones that I meet call me that or Mama," She informed me as she held the door open for me. My stomach told me her house was where I needed to be as I followed her inside.

"You're really trusting. I mean, I could be crazy! What if I were a thief or something worse?" I questioned her, looking around at the pictures on the walls. There were these incredible paintings in all of Mami's rooms. The kitchen was lit up, and she stopped in the hallway in front of me. "I'm not, but I could be someone trying to hurt a nice woman like you."

"I know you're not a bad person. You're Hakim's brother, Lionel," Mrs. King laughed as she slowly walked like a duck to the laundry room. I followed, carrying the basket. "It would not be intelligent to harm someone that lives right behind you. There's a brain under all that beautiful hair."

"I see, you know my brother. He's never home, so when did you run into Bruce Lee Roy?" I groaned, rolling my eyes. It's always like this. Everywhere I go, someone is talking about or knows my brother. I couldn't get out of the nigga's shadow, and I'm taller than Hakim. All the women wanted him, the guys wanted to be like him, or they hated him. That left me the one to catch the backlash. "You one of HIS friends?"

"No! He is friends with my daughter, Mandisa. They went skating a while ago," She replied, laughing at my suspicious gaze.

It hit me when I gave her the once over again!

"Oh, yeah, HER?! She's your daughter? I see it now. You look just alike…accept the baby belly," I chuckled, thinking back to earlier. "I think Hakim really likes her."

"Is that so?" Mrs. King asked with my suspicious look from before.

I glanced around their pleasant house. It was well decorated, lit up brightly, and smelled so sweet. You got this warm feeling the longer you were around Mandisa's mother. It made you relax, and you couldn't be angry. The moment I walked inside that kitchen, I couldn't stop smiling and joking with her. I wished she was my mother as she served me a plate of thin pancakes full of cream and covered in fruit. They were so good I ate about seven or eight of them. She smiled up at me, enjoying a bite.

"You love crepes, too, Lionel," She said, tossing a blueberry around her plate with her fork. Her grey eyes twinkled as she frowned a bit. "I didn't like them until I got pregnant with Mandisa. Now, I love them. She's loved them since she was a baby because of me."

"They're good like sweet little blankets. Make me a big one for my bed so I can sleep and eat at the same time," I laughed as I finished the last bite.

"You and Hakim look very much alike, very handsome, but you have a beard. Does Hakim shave his off?" Mami giggled as she wiped whipped cream from my chin-chair.

"Uh-uh!" I died laughing. "Hakim can't grow a beard! He's been trying for years and nothing. It pissed him off when mine grew in at 13!"

Mami laughed at me, shaking her head. I covered my mouth as I realized I cursed in front of her. I couldn't help it. Whenever I talked about my brother, I got excited, and words just came out. Mami saw my reaction and grabbed my hand smiling. She rubbed it, and I relaxed a bit.

She caught her breath grabbing her belly, and said, "Lionel, that's terrible to tease your brother because he can't grow one yet. Boys are so different from girls. All I worry about with my girls are the boys.

'Everywhere I go, I meet so many sad little boys that can't get along. It upsets me when it comes to us, black people as a whole. You lack compassion for your brother, but you envy them. It breeds a strange relationship with your ideal of who you are deep down. Doesn't it?"

"We fight over stupid stuff all the time. That's what brothers do. It's been that way for who knows how long. Guys just have to prove themselves to everyone that tests them. Women don't want weak, soft guys, so it's kill or be a virgin till you die!" I laughed, catching her hint.

"Hakim said you were intelligent. I could tell that you play like you can't see things, but you're afraid to be yourself.

Siblings can bicker, Lionel, that's normal. But if there is no love after the fighting, then are we being loyal? Shouldn't we love before the fighting sometimes? I don't know. I am glad I am having another girl. Raising a boy in this world would be very hard with my husband. He doesn't see things the way we do, Lionel. Men that do everything for money and recognition for others are slaves to approvals never meant for them," She told me, frowning more and more. "A man that can't be his own master is a slave to what controls him. I was never a slave before marriage. But Mandisa has become one in my stead because I could not take my freedom."

"Mrs. King, are you gonna be okay? You look upset?" I worried, feeling her squeeze my fingers. The vibe in the room changed the moment she started talking about her husband. It gave me the creeps the way she said, slaves and masters. It sounds like she was tired and was overthinking. I was going to let her rest until I noticed the paintings on the wall in her living room! "That's crazy! Look at all those faces melting together! Each one looks like a different person…it's so realistic!"

"Oh, you like art? Disa has been drawing, painting, sculpting, dancing, singing, or anything I could talk Tommy into. He didn't let her do much except study art and dance.

All private tutors…her entire life, she's been kept under lock and key. I'm fatigued with Amani on the way.

'This year will be the first year Mandisa will be around kids her own age. Hakim is the only person that has seen these aside from you, Lionel," Mami sadly sighed as she pointed to the painting of a ballet dancer looking in a mirror.

The girl in that painting had the prettiest made-up face, but her face was sad. Then canvass was black, and there were these eerie eyes all in the darkness around that mirror. The prettiest object was the sparkling multicolored roses in a glass vase next to the mirror. There was a heart-shaped locket I noticed on the stem of a rose's thorn. Why did it look like the roses were trying to protect the girl from the eyes that were everywhere? It was deep and so detailed that I tried to touch the tears on her face. They looked so real!

The painting over the sofa was incredible! It was a beautiful night mountainscape. All those dark blue tints made the sky and the valleys below look like a vortex of confusion. The moon was pretty, and it seemed tame until you noticed the girl about to jump from the cliff! She's so insignificant, but you can see her in that dress that looked ghostly black and white. The tortured expression on her face said it all. The word is vast, I'm small, and I don't matter…I'll just jump.

"She's in bad shape, huh?" I asked Mami staring at Mandisa's face on that painting.

"Lionel, I love my babies. I'll do anything to save them. That's why we moved here, and I believe that is why you're here also. I know Queen better than she knows herself. Being alone all these years hidden away from the world has injured her soul and broken her spirit.

"Mandisa has had one friend her entire life. It broke her heart to leave Philadelphia. I can't do that to her again. They haven't been able to make contact since we got away from Tommy this last time, Lionel. We had to leave so much behind when Disa tried to kill herself. But I won't let him keep hurting her anymore. I thought I could rely on my family to keep us safe, but my mother was never nice, and money meant more to her than anything. So, it will be the three of us until Tommy comes and takes us away. But I hope that at least I can be a better mother for my children than mine was for me," Mami explained with a look of exhaustion in her hazel eyes.

I watched her go sit at the kitchen table, rubbing her belly. Staring at those pictures on the walls around the den made me frown. Mandisa was alone in all of them except the ones with her mother or both parents. In the pictures with her father, Mandisa looked so sad. The older she got, the look in her eyes changed, and she looked angry in the last one!

"Don't worry, Mami, she's in good hands. Hakim really likes her. He's never cared for a girl before until he met Mandisa. He wouldn't hurt her, and neither would I. She seemed really sweet, and I'll be her friend, too, okay?" I assured her before I left Mami to rest.

"I should get home. I'm not supposed to be out. Hakim grounded me, and I don't want to fight anymore tonight. But I'll come back and visit you soon. If you want?" I added as she took my hand. She stood up, showing me to the back door.

"Anytime, Lionel, next time, I will have something wonderful prepared for you to try," Mami said, waving as she watched me jump the fence.

"I'll be back tomorrow!" I laughed as I watched her shut the door, and I headed home.

Mrs. King reminded me of my mother so much it was insane! Mama loved to feed people with food and knowledge. She was an Elementary school teacher and taught fifth-grade kids. Every morning, she made Hakim and my breakfast, helped us get ready, and then took us to school. Mama used to ask us what we wanted to be when we grew up, and I never had an answer. I didn't know shit then, and I still don't know eight years later.

Hakim would look Mama in the eye and say, "I'm going to be a King, Mama."

I used to laugh at him for that shit, but he never lost that mentality through the years. He's self-educated, stacking his paper, overseeing his friends, and now my brother has a girl named Queen. If that ain't some King Shit, I don't know what is. Hakim was trying to be like our father.

I don't remember much, but he was a police officer in Atlanta. I remember Dad was always working long shifts, rotating days and nights, and chilling with everyone. When he was home, he was all over Mama. He was crazy about her. We had an incredible family life when our parents were alive. Maybe that's what Hakim means by King. He just wants the fabulous home and wife…the perfect life! I don't blame him for that shit; I'd be happy if I could come home to the only woman I wanted, and we had everything we needed.

Kaliah and Cyrus are always talking about finding a woman that gives me a vibe. I can't take advice from two brothers that clearly are not happy in their relationship statuses! Kaliah has been married to the craziest bitch on the planet for over five years. I love my mixed-up brother and miss having him around! Kaliah is so much fun, and he makes everything better for us all. But he's always fighting with Ms. Trisha, his wife! She gets fucked up and shows her ass more than some dancers in Magic City! Kaliah keeps saying he's done; they separate a while, then he's right back with her ignorant ass again! A month passes, and he calls again, saying he's done! Wash, Lather…Rinse…Repeat…Really?

I don't care how fine a bitch is or freaky. I'm not letting a woman talk crazy to me or disrespect me in public the way Trisha Myers runs over Kaliah. I don't understand why he keeps trying to love a bitch that crazy, but she's got a hold on him. It can't be the pussy I know that much! She's tried to throw it at all of us at least 3 times. I don't like bitches on her level of psycho! Cyrus runs when Kaliah comes to town because he can't stand Ms. Trisha. I avoid her crazy-ass. Hakim will fuck her off. He's never had a problem hitting a bitch that hits him first. He won't start shit, but he loves to finish it and put a tag in it. Kaliah has moved to Los Angelos and keeps calling, wanting to come to visit.

But he respects our family too much to come with his wife following his ass! She will show up uninvited and ruin everyone's fun just to piss Kaliah off. She has issues, and I'm not reading one page of full-on fuckery. Hakim tells Kaliah that he loves him, but as long as Trisha is riding shotgun…Our brother can't come to kick it with the family. We all agree on that.

Cyrus can't keep a girl either. He switches women like drawers but claims to be searching for a queen. I know that you can't find a Queen using bitch-bait! Cyrus is flashy, and I ain't mad at him for showing off what he got! I'm trying to get like Cyrus! Shit, Cyrus has his own spot wherever he goes, he's got the best of everything Cyrus wants, and he fucks the finest girls.

But Cyrus loves to trick off his paper on any bitch trying to make her a queen. Most of the time, they love his ass for a minute, but Cyrus suddenly loses interest like Hakim when it comes to women. Both of them are alike mentally in some areas, but nothing alike, and nearly opposites. I watch from the sidelines while the pros play until it's my time to shine. All I needed was for Hakim to put me on or give me a few racks. I can flip it because I got connections. But my brother is the ultimate hater of Team Lionel! All he buys me is food and clothes and talks down on everything I do.

Hakim believes he knows everything. Yeah, he's a genius, but so is Kaliah. They made money together, but Hakim seems to be the brains behind the shit, and I don't understand how that works. Kaliah is older, more educated, and he's the doctor and grower. They don't tell me enough…I have to eavesdrop on calls and guess because Hakim doesn't trust me to cut me in. Cyrus and Kaliah keep their lips shut unless Hakim tells them.

You know what, I really don't know my brother that well. I know, my brother! But we don't hang out together, not unless Kaliah or Cyrus is in town. If neither of them is around, then Hakim is gone, too. He only comes home in the morning, and he's gone after school. Once he got his first car, Hakim was never home, and since he was paying the bills, no one asked. My grandparents think Hakim walks on water and can do no wrong. I'm the fucked up failure that can't do anything right.

There's a lot of shit that I might be holding against my brother, and I know he means well. But he's walking around like he's perfect, and I'm the family's disappointment. I hate that condescending tone of his and his as a matter-of-fact attitude. At least with Cyrus around, I won't have to fuck his ass up on sight. Cyrus keeps Hakim mellow and happy with the jokes and games they play. I love kicking it with them, but I don't know what the fuck is happening with Mandisa. Hakim is acting like he is actually in love. I've never seen him with a bitch that he was fucking, twice. He doesn't date. My brother used to have bitches lined up looking for his ass. Mandisa is fine, but I'm talking about grown women. I bet he hasn't told her shit about them hoes, either. I said to Mrs. King I would be Mandisa's friend. I may have to protect her from my brother if he gets bored.

#

I had fallen asleep in my clothes on the bed, and that dream was different than before. I looked in the mirror and scratched my head, dandruff; time to rewash my hair. I went ahead and got in the shower to get it out of the way. Hakim was up, and I was avoiding him for now. I squeezed my crown as dry as I could, twisting it upside down. It's so long now if I don't get it braided back or wear it in a ponytail, it's hard to keep it from getting caught on shit. Hakim and Cyrus's hair is curlier than mine, so mine won't lock without lots of extra work. I love my hair too much to have to cut it off if I decide to change it up. I know it's just hair, but I haven't gotten a haircut since my Dad died. He was the last person to take me, and I didn't want to cut my hair.

Hakim and Cyrus are the same about their hair. Hakim's had an afro since Mama was alive. She had a huge afro, and Hakim loved it. But when he got tight with Cyrus, Hakim got his shit locked up to grow it longer. It's long for only developing a few years of growth. The longer our hair gets, the prouder we feel about the shit we do. I understand Mrs. King on the lion talk. I've always thought like a prince. My crown makes me feel like a King.

Back in our bedroom, Hakim was putting on his running shit. He looked up at me as I frowned down at him. I was still mad about last night, but I was gonna squash it if he didn't start no shit at 5:30 in the morning.

"You running at the track today?" I asked, already knowing he ran the track at school on Fridays so he could count laps.

"Yeah, Cyrus and Mandisa have to work out for dance class. I'm going to get my laps in, then we're gonna change and hit a mall in Dallas. You should come? It's good for you to stay in shape for basketball. You'll build up your wind if you run with me," He chuckled, putting on his running shoes. "You know I run for speed, though?"

"Yeah," I replied, holding the towel around my waist suspiciously. "But you've never invited me to run with you before."

"You don't like to get up early. I'm up at 5am most mornings, and you sleep until 10," Hakim laughed, pointing to a drawer near the closet. "Extra stuff is in there if you want to come. But it makes you sweat more, so you'll need a shower afterward. That's why I wait until after I run. Better put some clean clothes and shoes in my bag since we're heading to the Galleria."

"I can go with you?" I asked, reaching in the drawer and putting on Hakim's tight-ass shirt.

"Yeah, I just invited you, didn't I?" Hakim snickered, grabbing a bag out of the closet and tossing it on his bed. He grabbed shoes, clothes and neatly put them inside. I put my things in with him and finished getting ready. Hakim looked at his phone a moment then made a call. "You on your way? Yeah, Queen's on her way through the back gate. I'm gonna meet her. Lionel's down to roll. We'll all change at your place and hit the highway from there. Ase!"

Hakim hung up his phone and went back to packing shit in his bag. Then he reached up in the top of the closet and pulled out that damn safe! I could never get into it! It was locked tighter than Fort Knox. Hakim got it open and turned back, tossing a stack of cash against my leg as I sat on my bed.

"What's this?!" I asked, eyeing at all those blue-faced bills locked together in some different band. It didn't have an amount on it but was colored like a foil rainbow and had BKM. Running my fingers through the bundle told me that it had to at least be 30 thousand dollars in cash! "You're giving me some racks?"

"I'm giving you that to buy some summer gear and shoes for school. That one is 32 thousand. You can't go shopping along with Cyrus carrying less than ten. He'll embarrass the hell out of you. You should be straight with that much, but no jewelry, Lionel! I don't want you getting charged up by some nigga about some ice," My brother explained to me as I stared at those stacks he had in that safe. I know I saw about

8 more of those and lots of paper and envelopes. Hakim snapped his fingers, and I looked up at him. "You hear me?"

"Oh, yeah! Shit! I'ma tear it up!" I laughed, putting it in the bag under my clothes. Hakim took out a few credit cards and stuck them inside his wallet. Then he tucked it under his clothes for later. "Let me hold one of those since you're feeling so generous?"

"Nope, the limits are too high on these. I don't want you to lose one. Show me you can do what I say with that, then I'll see about getting you one issued for your birthday in October. You have to earn your way up to it.

"But I feel I have to be nicer to you. Thank you for looking out for Mrs. King last night. Mandisa said her mom really likes you. I don't know what you did, but you're all she talks about, Lionel. That's a good look, Bro," Hakim complimented me, making me grin.

"We just talked, and I helped her with some laundry. Mrs. King is sweet. I like her, too," I told my brother. I heard a knock on the door.

"Damn, Cyrus is too fast!" Hakim laughed as he locked up the safe, put it back on top of the closet, jumped over my bed, and vanished.

A few minutes later, Hakim came back with Mandisa following behind him, glancing all around. She looked nervous as hell as he pulled her into our bedroom. One look at me sitting on the bed, and she was as red as a cute cherry. I tried not to laugh as I waved to her, smiling.

"Hey, Mandisa," I playfully sang to her so she wouldn't make a run for it.

Mandisa's red cheeks and pretty grey eyes made her face look like a Teletubbie! Po, Mandisa was so shy around men, she didn't know what to do. I stood up and came closer and offered her a handshake so she would calm down.

"Hello, Lionel, Bonjour," She replied, holding out her pretty hand for me. I took it and rubbed it for a second while staring into her eyes. Mandisa looked exactly like her mother. When I kissed her hand, Hakim pushed me off of her!

"Nigga, she liked it!" I yelled at Hakim while smiling at Mandisa, blushing by the door.

"Stop playing, Lionel!" Hakim said with a frown going into the bathroom. "Just have a seat anywhere, Queen. I'll be right back!"

"You better brush your teeth! Your breath smells like Doritos and thunder, Hakim!" I yelled, putting my wallet inside his bag, but paused. I flipped my wallet open and slid out the picture of Maya and me. I only looked at a second and smiled, putting it away.

Mandisa looked around our room curiously as she strolled by Hakim's bed. She turned on the lamp on his nightstand and flipped open the book he was reading. It was something about James Bevel. I don't know, I don't ask, and Hakim is always reading some book and talking shit. My brother can be a big mouth when it comes to talking about white people and the law. He became obsessed with reading when Mama was alive, and he got so bad when she died, he had to wear glasses.

Mandisa held the book turning the pages, and said, "It is not watered down at all."

"What?" I asked as she wrote a note to Hakim, putting it inside and closing it.

"I will not bore you, Lionel, but that man was on to something big. Anyone close to Dr. Martin Luther King Jr. was either a good friend or great enemy to the cause. When people continue to be a problem with specific social ideas, there will always be someone watching and waiting to put them away. They will drag your name through the mud, make you appear crazy, spread rumors, fake lawsuits, or threaten you until you give up or no one respects you or your work.

'That is if they do not kill you first. Hate is contagious, Lionel. It spreads faster if surrounded by fear and misinformation. Fear of the unknown can create mass levels of hate, and it could spread like a virus when fed to the ignorant," Mandisa explained, watching my response.

Mandisa was smart like Hakim, Kaliah, and Cyrus. They talked about Black Lives Matter and Black Power like the Panthers back when we were kids. Mama was a Panther in college, and Hakim loved that shit and ran with it. Folks were always talking about being "Woke" all over the internet these days. It seemed like a fucking fad for niggas to jump on the bandwagon to make more money for the white man pulling all the strings. If they really gave a damn about us, why didn't they change all the laws everywhere?

If they fought England and wrote up the Declaration of Independence for freedom, then fought the Civil War because they were divided by Capitalism like Kaliah tells me, then slavery is suddenly abolished, but white people still see us as the cause of their problems when we did shit they don't want to do for nothing. We get Jim Crow and fake Civil Rights with integration. They get more taxpayers to test their pills, vaccines, and phony food while getting more prosperous.

I don't know shit! I'm the crazy stupid brother. I don't listen to shit...lol.

"Yeah, I know, I got haters everywhere! People I haven't met hate me! All my Facebook, Twitter, and I have strangers on Snapchat hitting me with that bullshit all the time. I cuss them out, and if that doesn't work, I block their dumb-asses," I laughed, nodding.

"Do you not realize that is the worst thing to do, Lionel. You are feeding the fire and making matters worse. The best thing you can do- Negative attention that is fed with negative action leads to," Mandisa seemed to be frustrated getting out her thought. Maybe it was the silly face I was making to get her to calm down. I hate when niggas get all militant and self-righteous without warning. Hakim is always doing that shit, and it has been getting on my nerves since I was six!

"Getting your ass kicked by Lionel Dunn is probably what you were going to say. I don't play that passive shit. If someone comes at me, then they have to kiss my fist. I'm not bowing down to anyone that thinks they're better than me," I chuckled as I started looking around for my cigarettes.

"Lionel, violence will only lead to more violence. Do you not believe in karma?" Mandisa asked me.

"Yeah, a nigga that fuck with me got an ass whipping coming! That's called karma!" I died laughing.

"No, Lionel, fighting makes things much worse unless in defense of attack. So you kick some ass now? But they will be back. What do you do when hate brings the big guns? You give them something more significant to hate about yourself...the hate turns into admiration," Mandisa elaborated with a smile holding Hakim's book. "The more people admire you, the more you inspire. People are willing to stand and fight next to a man that has a worthy cause. Jealousy is merely expressing love and hate due to an imbalance of reason. I read in a Psychology book. One man cannot face the world, but an army of followers inspiring others can transform the world into true believers. That is what I believe."

I stared up at her in silence. Mandisa sounded like my Mama. She used to preach unity and family to people at church. Mama was an activist and tried to get others involved with raising the kids in the community. I caught sight of Hakim standing in the bathroom door eavesdropping. Mandisa picked up his glasses and put them on her face.

"I look sexy, oui?" She giggled, pouting her pink lips at Hakim.

"Hell, yes!" Hakim laughed, going over and taking his glasses. He leaned in closer, looking her over. "Hey..."

"Hey..." She giggled, pushing his hair behind his shoulders looking at him. "You are very sexy in glasses, Hakim."

"What?! Glasses don't make niggas sexy!" I laughed.

"Not everyone, but some people link glasses with intelligence and find the connection sexy," Hakim blabbed at me. He looked at Mandisa winking. "I fell in love deeper listening to you talk, Woman!"

I grabbed Hakim's glasses off his face and put them on, laughing, "See! Glasses don't do shit! It's just an illusion!"

Mandisa looked over at me, smiled, blushed, and looked away. I paused and looked in the dresser mirror. Shit! I looked good in glasses! Hakim died laughing, "I told you, Nigga. If you could only back up the look with your brain, you'd kill em!"

Hakim took his glasses, putting them on the nightstand and snatching up the photo nearby of us when we were kids. Mandisa started laughing as she took it, touching Hakim's afro in that picture.

"So cute! All of you! Lionel, your smile is so adorable when you show your teeth! That is Darius!?" She giggled louder, holding the framed picture next to Hakim's face. "Why do you look so angry? You have not changed. You are taller, built, with more hair, but look at your baby face, Hakim. Darius looks so innocent here, nothing like now, too funny!"

"Oh, you like that?" Hakim sarcastically chuckled, grabbing the photo album out of the nightstand drawer. "Bam!"

Mandisa took the photo album and died laughing, "Oh, God! Lionel, is this you?"

She held up the baby picture, and I rolled my eyes. I sat down and put on my shoes. Hakim started clowning and stuck out his tongue at me.

"Look at him! Lionel's so cute in pampers," He teased me. He turned the pages for her making her eyes brighter with each picture. Then Hakim stopped her. "That's my favorite picture of us."

"Your mother was so beautiful, and look at that hair! It is so curly and thick! That is a sista!" Mandisa gushed with her eyes glowing.

I looked at the floor, not wanting to see the picture, thinking aloud, "Yeah, Mama loved her hair. I guess that's where we got the crown pride. But G.D. hates our hair."

"He's been trying to get us all to cut it off for years. G.D. says only girls and gays grow their hair out. It feels like a way of conveying my honor to the world. I don't care what people think about it. They can look away if they don't like it, right?" Hakim added, smiling. I nodded, agreeing.

"You have such gorgeous, strong hair," Mandisa giggled, playing with the damp curls on my shoulders. She ran her long fingernails across my scalp, and I had to move around. It turned me on when girls messed with my hair. Damn it! She was too fine! Now I saw what Hakim liked about Mandisa.

After meeting her mother, seeing those paintings, and talking to her, I was feeling weak. She was so sweet. It didn't help that I loved her mother and handled all the pain in those pictures. I had to watch myself. I don't like redbone girls like that, but she was growing on me. Hakim would fuck me up if he saw me get excited when she touched me. This compression shit is tight in the wrong places!

Mandisa was fine! Every time I saw her, she seemed unique and prettier, too. Her long hair was up in a bun, and she wore those tight dance leotard things, and I could see it all in black! The tiny skirt couldn't cover an inch of her perfectly round ass. While Hakim was distracted, showing her more pictures, I enjoyed the view from a safe distance.

I kept wishing Mandisa would bend over so I could see those titties pop out. Boy! Those suckers were big and sweet.

I love breast-esses! I bet her skin everywhere was as soft as her hands, and she smelled like a damn fruit salad!

When I saw her last night at Hot Wheels with Hakim, I knew it was a wrap. Hakim doesn't hang on to bitches! He doesn't date anyone. Grandma Sophie thought Hakim was a pimp. He had so many women calling and coming by at one point. Then one day over a year ago, Hakim stopped going out. He was always around the house or running everywhere. Cyrus wasn't here, so he didn't have a reason to hang around or party. Hakim was mad or sad, and Grandma Sophie made him go see a therapist. Now he's good.

I go too. Those niggas are stupid if they think I'm gonna tell them all my business. Fuck that! I sit there for an hour fucking with my counselor's head. He thinks I'm really crazy. He is always giving me pills I don't want, and I ain't gonna take. Shit, legal drugs don't cure shit! Most of the time, they make you 10x worse. Look at the commercials!

The side effects to some shit will kill you! I got asthma, and I don't need the side effects of my inhaler to be rapid heart rate, shortness of breath, or light-headedness. That equals death, and a nigga just wants to shoot hoops and breathe easy.

Thank the good Lord that I ain't had an attack in about a year. I just take the inhaler everywhere in case shit happens.

But I hid that shit from Hakim cause he'd never let do some shit if he knew I could break down. My attacks were terrible when I was twelve. Now I don't worry much, but Hakim will stop me from doing me if he finds out.

I tucked the inhaler inside my socks as he stole a kiss from Mandisa. He had her in a mad liplock, and I acted like I wasn't watching as he rubbed that fat ass! I couldn't look away, so I snatched the zipper, shut the bag, and threw it over my shoulder, making a run downstairs.

I stood by the front door thinking while I waited for Cyrus.

"Damn it, Hakim! Why is he always so damn lucky?" I thought to myself, rubbing my chin. I rolled my eyes and leaned back against the door.

If Maya were here, I wouldn't even be thinking about Mandisa. Maya loved playing in my hair. She loved it so much she learned to braid watching Angela. When Angela left to go to college, Maya braided my hair for me. She was outstanding, too. Nobody made my shit look like Maya could catch my hair. It used to get me excited when she yanked it too hard, trying to get me to be still. My thoughts got interrupted by Cyrus blowing his car horn.

"What up, Baby Bro? You still on that bullshit like last night?" Cyrus demanded, rolling down his tinted windows.

He opened the back for me with a gigantic grin, ready to roast. I put the bags inside the trunk and sat in front next to him. His crispy ass gave me a goofy look. "We just got in the spot, and you had to go and lose your shit. You do that everywhere these days. If it's not with Jamire, Lester, or some random nigga co-signing you…What are you on?"

"It ain't like that, Cyrus. I was just feeling some kind of way," I groaned, staring left. As I put on my seatbelt, Mandisa came outside. She came over to the truck waiting for Hakim to lock up the house. Mandisa leaned in my window, waving to Cyrus with a great big smile. The tops of her big ole breast-esses were pressing into the glass. I bit my lip, gazing at the ground.

"Morning, Darius," She giggled with red cheeks and that cute smirk. Cyrus glanced over and saw what I was trying not to see and grinned as big as fuck! He was talking to her chest rather than her face when he greeted her.

"Hey, Mandisa, how are you this morning, Queen?" He asked, talking slowly. The grin growing on Cyrus's big brown lips was infinite. Mandisa was so tall that if she leaned a little stronger, those bad boys could just explode out of that tight gift wrap and make my day. Cyrus let the window all the way down, and Mandisa leaned inside as Cyrus took her hand, smoothing it. Breasts are my weakness, and I don't give a damn what anyone has to say about this situation.

Hakim is my brother, and I understand he has it bad for Mandisa.

But those babies were perfectly in my face leaning over me! I sat forward and put my face right in between them, grabbing both!

"Oh, my God!" I yelled, sniffing that sweet-smelling coconut oil and caressing her softness with my face. It felt like Christmas came early that year! They were perky, and it felt like I was squeezing the warmest set of water balloons. "Thank you, God! Won't HE DO IT!"

Cyrus smacked the shit out of my head plus yanked my ponytail back to the seat. I saw stars a second when my tail bounced off the headrest. Cyrus looked pissed, his eye narrowing down at me, but he resisted hitting me again after seeing Mandisa's terrified face in retreat.

"Nigga, are you fuckin stupid?" Cyrus hissed as Mandisa tore back, covering her chest, flushing, totally embarrassed. "Hakim is already near strangling your ass out, Lionel!"

"I'll take that blackout! Them shits are so soft, and they were right in my face! I ain't gay! Mmm...mmm....mmm, they feel just like a warm set of memory foam pillows," I groaned, smiling as I licked my lips in her direction. Cyrus walloped me in the back of the brain again. "Ow! Nigga!

You would have done that shit, too! Lie and say you weren't looking at em'!"

He jerked my head across and laid his arm over my throat, and flexed his arm, suffocating me.

"Apologize to her before Hakim gets to this truck!" Cyrus grunted in my ear, choking me.

"I'm so sorry, Man-Disa…sowoory," I cried as Cyrus tightened. He sluggishly let me go and lay back in his seat.

"I should have known better. I was not thinking," Mandisa breathed from a safe distance protecting her chest.

Hakim appeared, opening her door for her. She climbed in behind me, along with Hakim behind Cyrus.

Cyrus kept glancing over at me the whole time he drove. He seemed more pissed off. I raised my brows at him. He didn't want me to open my mouth or catch my hands if I felt like throwing bows. Cyrus was a big brother, but he couldn't fight! Hakim and I have saved his ass more times than I can count. He didn't want me to retaliate, so he looked at the damn road.

Yeah, recognize Cyrus!

I know he's Hakim's boy, but why the fuck was he so mad at me? Cyrus was thinking the same thing I was when I did that shit. It was written all over his dark-ass face. His smile was growing the longer he looked. He wasn't fooling me with his fake-ass chivalry. He's a man-whore like Hakim and trying to use me as bitch bait. He thought putting hands on me was gonna win him Brownie Points with Mandisa, but she didn't like violence! She felt terrible for me when Cyrus clucked my noggin. He was gonna keep his hands to himself if he wanted me to keep my mouth shut about his little crush.

Hakim was all over Mandisa as I gazed back. She was smiling while chatting with him. But Cyrus kept glancing at her from time to time, plus making eye contact with Mandisa. She would blush, smile, or giggle at anything he did. What the fuck?!

I ain't as dumb as I act, sometimes. I'm smart enough to notice there's chemistry between two people. Cyrus was feeling Mandisa, and she knew it. But did Hakim know was the real question? I rolled my eyes and stared back out the window, pretending to listen to the radio. I don't know shit, and nobody listens to me anyway. I can see this shit won't end well. But Hakim's a big boy that can take care of himself. Cyrus was probably not thinking of doing anything foul. I hope…

Chapter Five: These Walls

Mandisa

Hakim and Lionel ran the track outside while Darius and I used the studio to work out with the other dance students. Madame Olga opened the studio for all her pupils to practice during the summer. She was a very dedicated instructor and supportive of all the serious dancers. We ran through several different types of dance choreography, and I was finished. Two hours of exercising and constant repetition had worn me out. But Darius was a great ball of pure energy! He was here, there, and everywhere showing off his skill and technique mastery. Madame Olga loved Darius!

"Cyrus, you are too much! Please calm down! No one in the room can keep up with you and your skill. Give the other students a chance to learn the routine. I know you're a memory master from the previous times you were in my classes. That's why I was overjoyed when I learned you were coming back your senior year. But-" She giggled, seeing him making expressions. He started dancing in slow motion taking her words literally and making her laugh hysterically. "Cyrus! No! What am I going to do with you?"

"Let me teach the class?" He requested kidding.

She gawked at him for a moment and was seriously considering his suggestion. She leered to herself and replied,

"You know...I was thinking of letting you and another student choreograph the Spring Dance Explosion. Would you be interested?

'Your hip-hop, jazz, and modern techniques will blow everyone away once you get your music choices and dance numbers together with the rest of the class," Madame Olga questioned him very seriously.

"I'd love to, M.O. It's gonna be dope to show people my crazy ideas on stage," Darius laughed as he stood up straight and quietened down, smiling.

He rose over her and joked with her hair bun. She giggled and glanced up at him smiling. Darius was much taller than most of the men I had ever seen. I shook my head and continued my cool-down stretching.

"You will need to learn more ballet positioning and movement. Perhaps you can persuade Miss King to offer some of her expertise?" Madame Olga suggested as I peered, overhearing her. Darius stared a second, then sneered.

"She's a sweet friend. I'm sure she'll be cooperative, M.O.," Darius answered her honestly. "But seriously, I'm a musical movement master of memory, and Mandisa can move. But you think I'm that bad in ballet I need a tutor?"

"Your ballet technique is subpar. Everything else you dominate! You're even a masterful tap dancer! But Miss King is a superb ballerina, and once she gets her figure perfect, she'll be a pristine dancer," Madame tried to whisper, but I overheard her.

I paused and frowned. Darius glanced over at me, and I turned, pretending to not be listening. I didn't want them to see how upset I was getting. I had been painting more and dancing less. I gain weight because of my medication and hospital steroids. I took this class because Mami thought I missed dancing. I did, but I felt like people were judging my appearance one way or another. Hakim was the first boy that did not mind my height or figure. But this was not the first time my weight has come up with Madame Olga. Why would she tell Darius anything about my size?

"Maybe I can be convinced if I had a demonstration of her ballet expertise, M.O. If she's going to teach me, I need proof of her abilities," I heard Darius tell her.

"Mandisa, will you come and provide a brief exhibition of your ballet dancing technique for the group?" Madame Olga called me as I exhaled away the frustration and smiled, looking back.

"Oui, Madame, what should I do?" I asked, trying to maintain my expression.

"How about the piece from Giselle that you performed for your audition? I was very impressed with your graceful movements. Just a small portion is all we need to see. I only want the class to see the beauty of your ballet technique," She instructed me with a smile. She went to the stereo and found the music I used and nodded.

"Oui, Madame," I agreed, smiling as I moved to the center of the floor and posed in a bow, sighing to myself.

My father never wanted me to dance. My mother was once very gifted, but she gave it up for medical school. My father told my mother that I wasn't built to dance ballet. All the other students were so thin. I wasn't fat, but my weight and height always seemed to be an issue around people of the white race. Black people thought I was too thin. So, I was perplexed. What was I supposed to be? But all that clutter made me more determined to prove them all wrong!

I felt the routine run through me as I gracefully escalated to the melody. My arms glided delicately at my sides as I sauntered like a posing doll beaming. I shifted my legs playfully, posing with each step as I traced a circle and spun, stopping. I held out my arm and slid my leg to the next position. I began to leap around as I danced mischievously.

Giselle was a very whimsical character, and I loved how happy she always seemed. I danced around smiling as I twirled once, posed, twice, posed, thrice, and leaned low, posing again. I grew spinning on my toes in a perfect twirl then stopped suddenly skipping across the floor. While on my toes, keeping my back straight, I made tiny kicks, landing playfully.

I leaned low and bowing once again to the left, booted, lept to the right, kicked, arose up tall on my toes, and turned in a circle once more. Upon completing the final twirl, I strike high, holding my leg in pose behind me, and bowed.

"Beautiful, Mandisa! That was simply beautiful!" Madame Olga applauded along with the rest of the class. I bowed again.

"Merci," I thanked everyone for feeling much better now.

"I want everyone to get a genuine feel for the ballet in this year's lessons. Mandisa has been dancing for years. She's an excellent addition to this program. I want you all to get to know her. I hope to see you a few times a week to work out and work together outside the class. Have a wonderful weekend. Mandisa…thank you so very much for that. You made me feel like a little girl again. Watching you was like the first time I saw Giselle when I was six."

"Oui, Madame, I was four when I saw Giselle, and I knew I wanted to dance just like her," I stated as I walked toward the back to take off my toe shoes and put back on my sneakers.

"Queen!" I heard Darius call for me. I sat on a bench and started unlacing my shoes from my calves. I glanced up, and he smirked down at me. His eyes appeared sad.

"Oui, Darius?" I asked, taking a deep breath, trying to push what Madame Olga had said out of my thoughts.

"You're a fantastic ballerina. I didn't know you could move like that! I've never seen a black woman move like that, Queen. Giselle is super technical, so I know you were holding back because of the lack of space here. I bet if we got you into some authentic choreography, you would blow everyone away! M.O. is a little white woman, so she thinks anyone larger than her frame is overweight. But you're perfect just the way you are!

'If you were too big, there's no way you could move like that, Mandisa! The way you move is beyond explanation. Ignore her ignorance, okay?

'I like M.O, but she doesn't understand us," Darius showered me with compliments. I smiled and nodded. He knelt down, looking me eye to eye. "Queen, you are gorgeous just the way that you are! Don't listen to that negative shit, okay?"

"Darius, she's not the only one that has told me the same thing. I've heard it since I turned 13," I informed him with a sigh. I stared at my legs and hips, frowning. "I was great until I got all this! But now, if it is not one thing…it's another wrong with my shape. It is very discouraging sometimes. That is why I always diet."

"What do you think about how you look, Queen?" Darius asked me as he sat on the floor nearby. He had a very concerned guise on his face. Then his eyes scanned up at me as if he was agitated. Darius reached over and began helping me take off my toe shoes. He gazed down at my feet and started rubbing my left sole, suddenly smiling again. His personality changed in that instant. "Answer the question, Mandisa. I can rub your feet, can't I? You have really exquisite toes."

"Okay…um…thank you?" I replied, a bit confused as I examined him. "I think that I do not know what to think. I am very comfortable with my size, but I could lose a few more pounds. It would not kill me to be a bit leaner."

Darius glanced up at me, nodding. He grumbled to himself while he rocked his head, rubbing my foot, "If you're happy with what you are, then fuck what anyone else thinks. It's your body! Nobody can make you or break you unless you let them. Shit, Hakim ain't complaining, and I love you…I mean, I love your size!"

Darius got very quiet suddenly. He continued massaging my feet for a moment, and I blushed. His fingers gently caressed the sole softly and rolled his thumbs over the ball, relieving a lot of pressure. He was sighing and staring at my foot, lost in thought as he shifted his fingers hypnotized. He rubbed my toes mischievously and started breathing heavily. I began to think weird when he suddenly pulled it close to his cheek and smelled it! He tried to kiss my foot, and then I pulled it away quickly!

"What are you doing?!" I laughed as I tucked my leg under the bench away from him. He looked at the other foot and tried to grab the right. I quickly sat on it.

"Damn it! I forgot you're flexible," He laughed, pretending to be angry, closing his arms. "I'm sorry, Queen. I lost my cool for a second there. Put your foot back down here? I just want to rub it again, okay?"

"Why?" I asked him, struggling not to chuckle. He rested back and leaned his head over, peering around as a few other students walked by, noticing us. He groaned and shook his head.

"You have the prettiest toes. I can hear them calling for my attention. I'm not sick, okay?! I just really like YOUR feet. Let me finish, please? I know you'll like it," He begged me under his breath, desperately.

"Oh, God! You're one of those foot freaks that love to do nasty things to peoples' feet!" I chuckled as he appeared embarrassed and frowned. He pouted his lips and wobbled his head.

"No, not like that at all! I don't do this to everyone!" He wailed and stared away for a moment, then looked back. "I like rubbing...YOUR feet, okay? There's nothing wrong with that, is there? I can like feet and not do anything sexual to someone, right?"

I rolled my eyes at him and crossed my arms, laughing aloud at how ridiculous this conversation was. He was totally embarrassed, and yet he didn't mind anyone seeing him. I was so confused.

"Mandisa!?" Darius begged as I stood up. "Come on, please? You'll love it. I promise! Free massage...How you gonna pass that up?"

"I know, just like Lionel's free face rub?" I reminded him as I shook my head, blushing. Darius's mouth dropped wide open, and he covered his lips. "You are all so bad. Why?"

"I'm not bad, Queen. I just want to rub your feet! There's nothing bad about that?" He tried to convince me, but I was not buying it. I leaned against the locker and put my socks and sneakers on very quickly.

"You were getting excited by my feet, Darius," I grumbled under my breath as I saw Hakim and Lionel nearby. My heart started racing very fast as they came over. Hakim smiled at me and took my hand.

"We saw you dancing a moment ago, Queen. You looked beautiful twirling and spinning around like a star," Hakim flattered me, and I flushed, staring at his sincere grin.

"How long were you watching?" I asked, suddenly worried if they had seen Darius's groveling session.

"Long enough to see you dance and watch Cyrus try to eat your feet!" Lionel laughed with a very evil grin holding his stomach. Hakim started laughing and looked innocently at the floor. Darius fell out on the ground laughing. I shook my head, feeling silly, and tied my sneakers heading outside. Darius chased after me, still laughing.

"I'm sorry! I didn't mean to do you like that, Queen. I saw Hakim watching, and I couldn't resist teasing you. He knows about my little foot thing. He thinks it's funny as hell!

'I wasn't trying to rape your foot. I just got a little carried away. I used to always play with my mama's feet. So when I see women with sexy feet, I want to spoil them.

'I won't lie to you, though; it can get intense if there is sexual tension. But it's just a thing I like to do," Darius confessed, laughing as he got in front of me for a second, blocking my escape. He smiled at me very sweetly and winked. I was so humiliated. I was with Hakim now, but Darius kept giving me these wild, silly, and happy feelings. I stared at him, and he made a moping face pretending to be sad. "Please forgive me, Mandisa? I was just having fun."

I laughed, folding my arms, "It was innocent, and it actually felt nice until you started acting weird."

"So, are you going to let me rub them again?" He asked, becoming excited again. I rolled my eyes and moved away. He kept teasing me as I quit. "Come on, Baby-cakes! Let Daddy rub those tootsies?"

I giggled and jogged away as he hounded me outside. I was burned out because of the workout and stood waiting for Hakim and Lionel. They were both having a colossal laugh at my expense as they caught up with us.

"Mandisa, if you would have let Cyrus put your foot in his mouth, I'd have died! I would have literally fallen over and croaked like a frog!" Lionel teased me, making me blush deeper. "Cyrus, I've said it before, and I'll repeat it. You are a freaky-ass nigga!"

Darius stood off to the side of the entrance to the football field, shaking his head. He was listening but ignoring Lionel's taunting. Hakim suddenly grabbed his little brother locking his arm around his neck from behind. Hakim was shorter than Lionel, but he was obviously stronger! Lionel's knees bowed, and he dropped down as Hakim put pressure on his neck.

Hakim yelled in Lionel's ear, laughing, "What about you, Titty Rubber! You thought I didn't see that shit you did at the crib?"

I shook my head, walked out into the sunshine on the green grass, and smiled, looking around at the vast stadium. The bleachers were so high it was like they went up to touch the sky. I couldn't believe so many people could fit in one school. The football field was so enormous, I had seen games on television in college stadiums, but this was different.

Darius came close by and leaned close, whispering playfully, "Hakim said that you've never attended school before. Are you sure you're ready for this? It's really crazy! You're lucky that Carver High is private. You wouldn't last at L.H.S. They would have you ran back into the jungle with the tamer monkeys, Jane."

"I only want to feel normal. I've never been to a school before," I told Darius frowning.

"Normal is over-rated, Queen," He replied with a worried look on his face. "Being crazy is so much better. That way, the normal people look crazy."

Darius walked ahead. As he headed toward the gate, a group of girls stopped him. Hakim scampered up and paused close by, eavesdropping.

"I told you Cyrus is a trip. But this might be the most serious I've ever seen him. Usually, he's so full of laughs it's almost sickening. I think he's been away for too long. But he'll find his groove soon. When he does, be prepared," Hakim warned me as he bounced into my shoulder.

"He seems just fine to me," I said to Hakim smiling. My eyes drifted over to the girls talking to Darius. Each of those girls was close to my complexion, and they had cute colorful tracksuits. Lionel was eyeing them from behind us, grinning. Those girls were beautiful with their adorable matching braided updos. But Darius didn't seem very happy speaking to them. I didn't know how to feel when one girl tried to get close to him. "Who is that?"

Hakim looked ahead at the girls talking to Darius, and a huge smile grew on his lips. The girl with light hair like mine was dangerously close to Darius, appeared vaguely familiar. Hakim grabbed me and sped up, whispering to me, "Shh… that's the girl from Hot Wheels last night. Let's be messy, Queen! Cyrus runs game like a King!"

I did not understand what Hakim was saying. Darius was playing a game with the girls? No one looked like they were enjoying the conversation as Hakim pulled me near the wall. He jerked Lionel down and covered his little brother's mouth. Hakim raised his eyebrow and winked at me.

"What happened to you last night, Cyrus? I called you, but you never answered. You had your game down tight, but then you got scared. I saw you with another girl skating. So that's what you like to do?" The pretty girl asked Darius with a distraught look on her face. He glanced at the other two girls with her and smiled charismatically. "One second, you treated me like you're a real King, but as soon as you found someone lighter, you ghosted me."

"Many apologies, Clarissa, but I got discouraged when I saw you hugged up on your man. I hope you didn't get the wrong idea about my approach, Queen?

'I asked you if you wanted to wear the crown. I'm not in the business of hiring hoes anymore.

'Yeah, I can take you around. I can show you a wonderful time, then buy you some expensive shit.

'But if you are looking for a sucker to play retarded while you're cuddled up on Dre, you got the wrong brother. Cyrus plays the lead, not the background.

'I believed you could tell how sincere I was by how I put the mack down?

'If you can't show me you're interested in getting to know ME, then we don't have anything to discuss," Darius explained eloquently, polite to her. She examined him. She was upset or baffled. "Tell Dre I said what's up? Clarissa, Ashe, Queen."

Darius walked away as they stared after him. One girl with Clarissa stated, "I think you just fucked up, Clarie. You know Andre ain't shit. Mama told you to find a good guy and leave his sorry ass alone. I think you just missed the boat playing around."

Hakim stood up straight and appeared stumped. He frowned and watched Darius walking away. Hakim folded his arms, raised his eyebrows, and mumbled aloud, "Damn, Cyrus was cool until last night! Now he ain't down anymore? What changed?"

I didn't even notice Lionel standing behind us, listening as we watched Clarissa and her sisters stomp away in another direction. Lionel got close to Hakim, gazing around, and laughed, "Clarissa and her sisters are all gold-diggers, Hakim. I've known them since last year. She only got with Andre because she thought he would get a basketball scholarship and go to college at A&M.

'Every school was looking at his ass to go to the NBA. But he got hurt, and now he ain't doing shit! He dropped out of school and can't even get a G.E.D because he can't read. He was 19 then, so being 20 in high school ain't a good look."

"That's deep, Bro," Hakim said out of character for himself. "Cyrus must have peeped the vibe and shook the spot on her. But I thought he's at least seal the damn deal. Hmm…"

He swiftly took off sprinting after Darius. Lionel and I trailed behind. He bumped into my shoulder and frowned, saying, "You know you got him all twisted up with all that giggling and blushing? Cyrus is always catching feelings not thrown at his ass. If you want to be his friend, then you need to chill with that cute shit! Nigga's gonna keep fallin for you, Mandisa. Then Hakim's gonna start fucking people up over you. I know my brother, Mandisa."

"Lionel, I am nice to Darius because he is kind to me. I only want to be friends with you all. Hakim and I are taking things slow, so nothing bad happens. There is no need to worry about Darius nor me," I replied, watching Hakim dive on Darius's back across the football field.

"Alright, don't listen to me…I don't know shit like Hakim says. But I can see what the hell is going on, and you're going to wind up looking suspect, Sissy," Lionel chuckled, rolling his eyes and running after his brother.

Lionel was confusing me with his accusations. I was not... It could be possible I was too nice trying to get everyone's approval. I did not think that Hakim would become jealous if I befriended his friends. I thought Darius was so sweet, silly, and fun. When we skated together, it was the most fun I can remember. I didn't want to stop, but I promised Mami that I would only stick with Hakim. I was lucky someone so nice was Hakim's best friend. He didn't seem interested in trying to break up the two of us. I thought Lionel might be teasing me again. I might have rug burn from his chin between my breasts. He can be a loud pain. I can see why Hakim worries about him.

#

Darius lived very close to the school. It was only a few turns away. He stayed alone in a lovely condo with apartment complexes across the street. His home had two floors plus a patio. He liked privacy because he had no neighbors, and all the houses on the block were for sale. I thought that was a bit odd.

"Location, Location, and Location!" Darius laughed as I peered across the driveway. "When I sell all of them, I'll be even richer. The area here is in high demand because of the school and shopping centers nearby."

"You own all of this?" I questioned him, considering each newly built home.

"The whole street is mine. Jefferson Drive sound familiar to you?" He laughed as he took my bag from Lionel and tossed Hakim his keys. "I've been living on my own since I was 15 years old. Before that, I stayed with the Dunns. My dad was always working, so I just decided to emancipate myself after he moved back to NYC."

Darius's place was very nice! He had a lot of furniture, a few pictures on the walls, some black art, and more electronics than I had ever seen. It looked like a bachelor's pad like in the TV shows and movies. You could tell he lived alone—most of the interior of his condo was black, gold, silver, or glass.

"You can change upstairs, Queen. There's a guestroom and a private bath. I'll help you with your things. The rooms are kind of tricky. But make yourself at home, Mandisa. Mi casa es su casa, si?" He laughed as he hauled me, opening the door to his guestroom for me. "If you need anything, just ask, alright?"

"Si, Darius, muchas gracias," I told him as he sat my bag on the bed. He opened the bathroom door for me, made sure it was clean, and stood in the entrance staring at me, smiling. "Darius?"

"Yeah, Mandisa?" He answered, eyeing me about to go out the door. He raised his eyebrows and smiled beautifully. Standing next to the white door, Darius's brown skin stood out. But it was lovely. He had beautiful dark chocolate skin. His face was so expressive because he was always smiling, and his eyebrows led when he talked. Darius had big round lips beneath a handsome thin goatee. His eyes were shaped like almonds the same color. When he smiled at me, he got these adorable lines in his cheeks, and his nostrils drew up. His eyes would twinkle like his expensive diamond earrings.

He kept his ridiculously long dreadlocks braided down his back, but he rolled them up under a scarf when he was in dance class. He was so tall and slim when he talked to me, he had to look down and put a slump in his shoulder, or he would change his stance playfully, making me look him in the eye. I had never seen a man so sweet and dark. The more I tried to pretend I didn't like Darius, the more I did. Each smile or joke… made me want to talk to him more alone.

"What you said in the dance studio. It was captivating. You made me feel much better," I heard myself stalling. Why did I stop Darius? I just felt I needed to say something.

"It's the truth. You're the most beautiful girl. I don't believe you need to change anything but the way you look at yourself, Queen," He started looking down at the floor. "Hakim is fortunate to have found you…first."

"Darius, that is not nice!" I scolded him, frowning. He leaned back, shutting the door. I sulked, and suddenly I wanted to apologize for raising my voice. I grabbed the doorknob, running into Darius, who was standing just behind the door. "Darius, I am very sorry for being upset with you. The way that you speak to me when we are alone is very affectionate. But then it is like you become mean just to upset me purposely. Why? Do you not want me to be your friend?"

"I'm sorry, Queen. I don't know how to handle this. I could keep back peddling to myself because I'm used to doing it. But I can't lie to you.

'I've been the other man to so many women that I thought no one cared about me. I'm just a sucker for love and fall in so fast.

'But I can't hurt my best friend. Hakim is my brother, and you're his girl. I want you so bad that it hurts. But I want him to be happy.

'You're everything I want in a woman except one thing…

'You're not single. Now that you belong to HIM, I have no right to betray Hakim like that.

'No matter how much I may love- want you…

'I can't lose my brother. I need him, and he needs me. I am sorry…I've already said too much. I'll see you after you change, Queen," Darius professed to me and quickly exited before I could even respond.

He was gone quickly, leaving me alone to keep running his words through my head over and over. As he headed downstairs, I watched that beautiful man with dark hair and skin run away from me like a sad kitten. I went into the bedroom and shut the door. My heart was racing as I leaned back against it holding my chest blushing deeply. He did it again! He told me twice today that he loved me… I needed to hurry and take my medication!

Act Two

Chapter Six: For Sale?-(Literally)

Hakim

After my shower, I felt golden. But I was starving, so I went to the kitchen and Mandisa had cooked! There were pancakes, eggs, and potatoes. She had made more than enough for all of us! Cyrus was in awe when he came behind me in the kitchen from the extra shower. Lionel was already eating.

"This is so good! Everything was delicious," I complimented her cooking as I enjoyed another plate. "I haven't had a meal this good since your mother made breakfast yesterday! Before then, I can't remember. Grandma Sophie only cooks for the holidays, and she is always trying to get me to eat meat. I can't do it!"

"I am glad you enjoyed it. I love to cook," Mandisa giggled very adorably as she watched Cyrus and Lionel go in again for more food. She seemed astonished watching them scarf down everything so quickly. I remembered that Mandisa had never been around any boys at all. That excited the shit out of me!

"Will you marry me?" I asked, teasing her, but I was gauging to see her honest reaction. She turned a darker shade of red and nervously chewed a bite of food, laughing. "I'm about to go get a ring."

"Better hurry," Cyrus mumbled into his fork, looking down at his plate tickled. I raised my eyebrows curiously. Lionel made eye contact with me, slammed a whole pancake in his mouth, and then looked over at Cyrus. Mandisa just shook her head and drank some orange juice.

"What?" I asked Cyrus to repeat himself, smiling.

"Nothing, Hakim, I'm extra like always," He lied, staring at his plate. Cyrus never makes eye contact with me when he's lying. Cyrus had been acting weird all day long. It was 11:30 am. He wasn't cracking jokes, which meant he was uneasy about something.

I stopped listening to the voice in the back of my head that told me that Cyrus was falling again. I suddenly believed what it was saying. What worried me the most was the fact that Mandisa knew what was happening too. She kept giving me these hints that she was on to him. Then I noticed how she looked at him.

There was something there also, but she wouldn't act on it. She wouldn't even give Cyrus a hug unless I was there, and it was okay with me. It was like she could feel my dominant side saying no. It was the same with Cyrus. It was like they both were just torturing themselves to make me pleased. I cared about them both. Observing their off behavior made me want to say something, but I wasn't giving Mandisa up! Fuck that! I found her first!

Then there was Lionel, but he was just an asshole. Plain and simply put, he was still a mannish little boy trying to act like a man. I wasn't worried about his mouth, but I didn't trust his actions. Earlier, he didn't know I had seen his little game. I was very close to fucking him up.

Everyone was fortunate I wasn't still that angry kid I used to be. I would fuck them all off and still get my girl. She still wanted me. Anyone could see that, but something was off.

I knew she wasn't a ho. But being alone for so long made these empty holes in her heart, and she needed to fill them with more people. Her mother said she needed friends, and now that I had my way in, I wasn't going anywhere! Fuck it!

If I could have Mandisa, I'd play along as long as everything stayed cool. You don't know how long I've waited nor the shit I've been through to find this one particular girl.

The thing about me no one ever gets is I've never been selfish or jealous because I have something no one around me has…that's confidence in myself.

Yeah, I was horny, but I knew how to control that urge now. I was in love for the first time. But I could see she wanted me to tell her what to do to make her happy. I liked that shit a lot! I actually fed off of it. So, I'm going to wait and see what happens.

Is she going to be straight up with me? I feel there isn't a cheating, back peddling, sneaky bone in Mandisa's body. I want that heart along with her body as the bonus!

I've never said this before, but I want her as a wife! Fuck this girlfriend, boyfriend, and child's plaything. I could tell the moment that we met that she's the only one for Hakim Jahlil Dunn! If I let her get away...no! I'll never want another woman as bad again. I know what I feel.

A woman like Mandisa could bless me with family, happiness, and everyone would love her! People everywhere we went noticed her. When you have a beautiful woman, all the men want her, but she doesn't even know how beautiful she actually is, then she's worth even more.

Once she realizes her real value, oh God, she'll be the most formidable force on the planet! All eyes were always watching us as we walked by. I know once she gets over her shy girl phase, she'll be fighting niggas off. But she'd still be begging for my attention because I treated her like royalty when she had no clue of her worth. I'll end up with a wife that every man wants, but they couldn't pull on their best day!

I don't think you fully understand me yet, but you will and soon! When you have been with as many women as I have or turned down as much sex as I've done out of boredom, then you will understand how happy I am to actually have a woman that has me begging for her affection! I'm not giving this up!

#

After everyone finished eating Mandisa's excellent breakfast, we piled back in Mercedez and were off to Dallas. It's a two-hour drive west on the interstate highway, but we had lots of music and too much to talk about.

Lionel was sitting up front with Cyrus. I sat in the back with Mandisa. She was silent and distant for a while. She seemed to be appreciating the scenery, but there wasn't much but highway, cars, and forests as far as I could see.

Lionel was quiet, too. That was really out of character for my baby brother. He was into the music one second, then he would look back at us, but after I gave him a 'what you looking at' glance, he would make a face like he wanted to say something. He suddenly turned back in his seat and touched Mandisa asking, "Yo, Mandisa?"

"Oui, Lionel?" She replied as the wind blew through her hair. She let the window up, nearly closing it.

"Why did you try to kill yourself?" Lionel asked her, and she peered back out the window, remaining quiet.

"Nigga! Where did you hear some fucked up shit like that?!" I yelled at him about to cock back my fist and slug him in the shoulder. Mandisa looked at me suddenly and frowned. I put my hand down.

"Mami told me! She said that Mandisa has hurt herself before," Lionel explained, frowning at me scrutinizing closely.

"It is very complicated, Lionel. You would not understand," She finally answered with a sigh, still looking out the window.

"Try me!" I growled, watching my brother's face. Cyrus looked at me in the rearview mirror and peered back at the road. Mandisa exhaled and nervously looked at her long fingernails.

"My daddy…" She began but paused. Her face became red, and she covered her mouth. She shook her head and took a deep breath. "He tried to marry me to this older man when I was just 14 for money. He told me that I am only allowed to live the life that he chooses for me. I am supposed to earn his honor and respect with his colleagues by marrying a doctor.

'It is a very sick tradition that has been going on for generations in his family. He is a member of a group of doctors and surgeons from all over the world. It is like a sick fraternity. Their father's all bought or arranged their marriages for them, and the women were all young girls. They were women bred to be artists, musicians, or intellectuals with a certain level of beauty. The only rule they really told me of is that I have to be married before I am 19 years old. But my father has had many offers, and now he is just taking bids for who will be my husband."

"They still arrange marriages? I thought only Indians with the dots on their foreheads and Africans- Oh, you're from Liberia!" Cyrus suddenly yelled.

I felt my heart drop down into my stomach. As I leaned back in my seat, I glowered and crumpled my arms, thinking aloud, "Wait…If your parents have plans to just marry you off for money, then what is this then? What about you and me?"

"This is my mother's way of letting me live just a little before I am sold. So far, there has been no exchange of money, but it looks as if I have until I graduate, and then it's a done deal," Mandisa sighed, shaking her head sadly. "My grandfather purchased my mother for my father when she was just 18. She knows how I feel. She let me dance and wanted me to have friends because…her mother wouldn't let her have her own life.

'It's not mandatory for us to fall in love. Love is optional for girls like us. That is why I just sat and watched you run by without speaking. I am doomed. But now I can say that I felt something beautiful for once in my life before I died. Once school is over and I graduate, I am off to Europe, and you will never see me again."

"What?!" I screamed as I pulled my locks. I felt so sick I wanted to lose my breakfast. Cyrus suddenly pulled the jeep over. He got out of the truck and started pacing the side of the road. Lionel shook his head and turned around in his seat. He frowned and hit the dash throwing his head back. Mandisa had tears streaming down her cheeks as she leaned her head against the window, losing control.

Cyrus halted, getting back in the truck. He had a pitiful look on his face as he glanced around. Shaking his head, hitting the steering wheel, he finally moaned, "This ain't right! How can your father just give you away for money? He sounds like he doesn't give a fuck about you, Queen!"

She shook her head as she gasped, "I am so sorry. I wanted to tell you! But I was just having so much fun with you. If I let things go too far, my father will send me away immediately. That is why I haven't had friends! I lose my value if I have been touched.

'My great-great-grandfather was a surgeon and down the line with all the sons. My father is the only surviving son of my grandfather. He has no son.

'So I must marry a doctor, or he will lose his place in the organization. Mami was purchased high; therefore, I must sell for the same amount. I do not understand the conditions or why my father wishes to be involved in this arrangement, but I must. If I say or do anything my father dislikes, he will send me away to live alone again."

"Shhh," I said, hushing and tugging her into my arms. I held her close to my chest. My heart was beating so fast I could feel it in my ears and fingertips. I was in panic mode! I didn't know what to do right then, but I was going to stop this! "You're not going anywhere! I'm not going to give you up! I don't give a damn what your father says. We just met, and I've never felt this way in my entire life. Just stay calm, and when the time comes, I'm going to prove to you that I'm honest.

'Just trust in me, Queen?

'Cyrus, drive the car! Nothing has changed!

'As far as I'm concerned, your father doesn't run shit! I respect your mother for loving you enough to give you some freedom. She gave me a chance, and I'm not wasting it! I'm going to make you believe me! I love you so much! I can't go back to living my life like before! If you care anything for me, please, believe in me, Mandisa."

"Hakim?!" She sighed, touching my face. She stared into my eyes, crying helplessly. "What are you saying? I love you!"

I closed my eyes, nodding, and stopped her from saying anything else. I was so relieved that she said those words. I was afraid that she was really willing to just go along with her father's wishes. I didn't have a plan. All this was happening so fast I couldn't think straight. But I am going to think of a way to save her.

Lionel was pissed off! He looked back at me and gave me a glance, and I nodded, telling him that I knew what he was thinking. But running away wouldn't work. Not for this moment! She'd miss her mother, her baby sister, and we would probably end up bringing her back in worse condition than she was.

If she was suicidal, that means that if we can't save her, it won't be long after she's taken away before hurting herself. She's tried before, but once she feels completely hopeless, she's going to try again until she succeeds or gives up. I couldn't believe that her father was so evil. He was crazy! I thought slavery was dead?! Sex trafficking is illegal here, but I don't know about other countries.

Cyrus looked at me and cried sadly, "Hakim, if anything happens to her… What are we going to do? We can't…."

"Nothing is going to happen to her!" I screamed as I felt my temper about to slip. I paused as I realized that she had cried herself to sleep. I held her close and calmed. "Her mother must know a way to get through to her father. Maybe if we talk to her, she can help us. She opened up to Lionel, so she wants to save Mandisa."

"Mami is really scared, Hakim. I don't know if she can do anything. I think that she is worried about the baby, too. Dr. King must want to sell them both! But Mami knows that if someone doesn't help Mandisa, she's going to try to hurt herself again," Lionel added as he stared at me, wiping his face.

"Listen, we don't treat her any differently. That's why she doesn't have any friends. She's afraid that once they hear that she won't be around long, they stop coming around. Her father kept her away from the world for so long that she's terrified to reach out! No wonder she was so afraid to just go out with me when I kept asking her. She knows there's no future," I cried, unexpectedly breaking down. Cyrus was already there once reality sat in. The thought of never seeing her again scared the hell out of us. Maybe I had my doubts about Cyrus's feelings for her before, but not anymore. He's in love with my girl, but he's too afraid of losing my camaraderie to say anything.

"Why would her father mistreat her?" Lionel cried. "She looks like she hates him in some of those family pictures, Hakim. I saw how messed up Mandisa is.

"He's a fucking slave master that fell in love with a black woman. It's as simple as that! Mandisa may be his daughter, but she's just a brick to building up his name. Her mother must feel so helpless because she can't stop him," I reported gazing down at Mandisa. I loved her. I'd never loved a woman before. I meant every word that I said. No one was going to take her away from me. I looked around at my brothers and frowned. "We'll make a pact right now! If you really are my brothers and you love me like I love both of you, then you'll do anything to help me save her! Cyrus?!"

He looked up at me and nodded sadly, "Hakim, I'll do whatever it takes, Bro. I don't want to see her sold off. She'll kill herself! Mandisa's so sweet, Hakim. She doesn't deserve this!"

"Lionel?!" I asked my brother, scowling harder.

"Hakim, I'm in, too. Mandisa is the nicest person that doesn't hit me. Her mama is so scared. If you would have seen her face last night...No games...I'll do whatever you say, Bro," Lionel said through his tears. He was dead serious. I could tell he meant every word by his tears. Lionel doesn't cry unless he's terrified.

I exhaled and ran my fingers across her cheek as she slept, "All the years I've tried to save strippers and girls, I didn't even care about being arrogant. I don't deserve her. But I am going to do whatever it takes to make her happy.

'Cyrus, you're my brother! I trust you more than anyone. If I didn't, you'd be gone!" I announced to him, then stared at Lionel and shuddered. "Lionel, don't fuck me on this, Bro! I need you!"

"I'll do anything you need, Hakim! I promise I'm not going to drop the ball," Lionel replied, eyeing me. He nodded. After that, his ponytail got stuck in the seatbelt.

"Cut your hair!" I taunted him, seeing him try to get it free.

"Hell no! You cut your locks off!" Lionel yelled back. Cyrus finally started the car laughing. Lionel was still worried. His face never relaxed. "For real, though, Hakim, what are we going to do?"

"For now, nothing changes. Mandisa's never had friends, fun, or any freedom. We act like normal, and I'll think of something. She's safe, and her father doesn't know shit. I will talk to Mami soon, so not a word to anyone unless I say so! We roll on my wheels!" I informed them, both scowling. "Let's take her shopping. She can have the whole damn mall if it will make her happy."

"Fuck yeah!" Cyrus agreed, frowning at the steering wheel. "She's my friend, and I care about her. I'm with you no matter what you want to do, Hakim. This is fucked up! I owe you too much to not help."

I knew my best friend was in love with her and my brother was a jerk, but if I could trust any two people, it was Cyrus and Lionel. Mami was going to be my only lead if I could get her to tell me everything. Mandisa was not talking, and she was afraid to say more. When her father came up yesterday, I should have known when she got depressed. Dr. King was married to the kindest, most beautiful black woman and using her as a baby factory? If her father got his way, Amani would meet the same fate, I'm sure. Over my dead body! She's all I've ever wanted, and I wasn't going to give up this feeling.

#

230

The Galleria Mall was packed that summer Friday afternoon. People were everywhere. Families, groups of people of all ages were running wild. The shopping centers in Dallas were like Mecca to us from The View. We could get lost and fantasize about life when we were broke. But not now, not us, not ever again. We had money, so the malls became our personal playground. I personally enjoyed the idea that if I want anything I can buy it.

Mandisa was blown away by the multiple floors of window-shops and the friendly people walking by to say hello. This isn't New York! We might seem country, but down south, many of us have manners. We're family-oriented, love showing Southern Hospitality, and we make the most of so little. Don't get me wrong, there are some decent people on the East Coast, like Cyrus! But many are consumed by the paper chase to the point nothing mattered more than the hustle. You can respect a noble brother with that kind of mentality, but those raised in these kinds of environments are the brothers labeled "Thugs" by the media when the shots get fired.

It wouldn't matter if he was a good guy that made a wrong move. To those that hate our existence, we're all unworthy of humane treatment. It pisses me off that some people treat their pets better than others and train them to hate. Ignorance is a global pandemic that needs a cure. A vaccine would take too long for people to reach my level of not giving a fuck.

It doesn't matter where we came from if we're not going anywhere. If black people don't have anywhere to go or a plan of escape, what's the point of debating in a broken system? I've been planning and saving to make my goddamn flight my entire life. As mentioned earlier, I want to practice law as a defense attorney to save brothers from that fate.

When you're preparing your mind to utilize the law to modify the flawed system, you must have a detailed execution strategy. The farms, dispensaries, and labs were Kaliah's doing once we made money flipping stocks, and my brother was growing and blowing since 14! He used his extraordinary mind and educational experiences along with connections to start everything up. Once Kaliah began producing seriously, he had buyers lined up. But he wanted to own everything!

He sold most of what he grew to buy a more extensive farm, and he began writing his research papers. My brother's scientific studies, testing methods, and designer stains are winning more awards and recognition than natural herbs. Kaliah's synthetic strains have more or less THC depending on his growing processes.

The country has been bumping heads for generations about the purposes of marijuana, and Kaliah is breaking myths and stigmas about the medicinal effects of the many types of oils, pills, and topical ointments he's developed for patients for pain management, sleeping, eating, and nervous disorders. Kaliah grows the best weed that intensifies relaxation of some regions of the brain while raising serotonin levels. The side effects are always the same. With Kaliah seeking endorsement from the FDA, we have been raking in money like Gang Busters. The work he's doing has blessed our entire family exponentially. My brother is on a quest to apply his enhanced intelligence to take on Western Medicine and mankind's disrespect for alternative medicine.

Cyrus is the only one of us that doesn't have a plan for the future. He seems to be stuck with the mindset that you do whatever you want once you make money. Cyrus dances, and he's always been gifted with the moves and silver tongue. But he doesn't plan to do anything with his skill besides show off or goof around. He hates school, studying, and won't read to save his life. I barely get a response if I text him. Cyrus will call before he texts unless he is in his feelings. He hides and runs off when he can't hold his shit together. It makes us worried if we can depend on Cyrus in the long run.

My brother, Cyrus, lives for right now but has no dream for the future besides spending all the money as fast as we can make it. Kaliah talked him into buying the condos to have a place to stay when he flies off on a whim. I love my brothers, but they are slaves to their emotions, and it seems like they look to me to make serious decisions because they don't trust themselves outside of their hobbies.

Kaliah and Cyrus have a love/hate relationship because Cyrus can't stand his wife. None of us like Ms. Trisha, and we have our reasons that Kaliah pretends not to see. He's been with that crazy woman for a few years, and I realize she is beautiful.

At first glance, I thought she was Lisa Raye McCoy with her pretty hair, skin, and eyes, but when Trisha Myers opens her mouth….That bitch will make you hate her! We keep telling Kaliah that a woman with multiple sources of attention was a bad look. She was a dancer for attention alone and never needed money. She was married to a white man, and she turned into a savage when she got divorced! Kaliah thought he could tame her, but he regrets that shit now!

Kaliah's not going to want to keep growing weed forever. He's got a dream to change the way the world views the human body's healing factors. Marijuana growing was just his thing during college! He graduated a year ago and hasn't stopped working. I know my brother never wanted to be a surgeon or Western doctor growing up. He smoked too much weed and always talked about Psychology, Sociology, Metaphysics, Astrology, Ancient Civilizations, and Physics…Kaliah was not the typical guy, but he was so approachable that he made friends with everyone with no effort. Kaliah and I talk about how we want to change the world's problems, make plans, and follow through. I hope I can get Lionel and Cyrus on the same level as us, at least when it comes to the nation-building shit. I don't care how they spend their free time, but I can't watch them spend up all the money waiting to be taken care of by us.

Cyrus and Lionel have similar tendencies to not give a fuck when they get in their feelings, and I can't lose my brothers over this paper, either. It'll all be for nothing without any of them. But they need to grow up while they have a chance to get shit right. I'm putting away money for Lionel, but I get tired of telling Cyrus to ease up on his flexing. He's got Lionel ready to spend everything I have, and I have to hide shit from my own brother because I can't trust his mouth! Lionel's no thief, but he talks too much, trying to get niggas to like him. I hate that shit! Niggas are gonna hate you when you have something worthy of their attention.

I'm not afraid of anyone out here but the police! Anyone else I encounter is fair game to receive the karma I deliver.

I'm not going to lose my freedom, but I don't play the passive enlightened brother, like Kaliah either. Any man that fucks with mine around The View knows Hakim Dunn will come to find you if you touch his shit or step up. They love to test Lionel because Lionel loves to talk shit and listens to everyone who talks! Lionel gets into fights everywhere we go together, so I leave him home alone to think. Then he runs off with his homies and comes home fucked up. He's out of control, and I think I know why, but he'll never confess.

I can't force my brothers to tell me what's really bothering them. We're men, and our bonds get tested all the time. We always seem to find reasons to stay tight, so it has to mean we need to be close after all we've been through getting this far, right? Now that I've met a girl I feel is worthy of my time, energy, and devotion, I can't let their immature mindsets dictate the future. I'm serious about Mandisa. I've never been more serious about anything I've charted out for the future.

Okay, I have to confess that I planned the perfect existence that I wanted to manifest on this planet in this life as a kid. Yes, that also included the woman I wanted to marry, and though I was just a kid messing around with shit in a scrapbook tearing up magazines...I think I made Mandisa! Her hair, skin, eyes, body, and accent...were all the features that I used to fantasize about as a horny little kid! I think I became obsessed with the perfect woman that I never thought existed until I saw her in the park yesterday. I can't kick the idea that Mandisa is going to be it for me! I don't need sex. I've had enough for now. I need her to be mine! I'll do anything…she's too special to let vanish without a trace.

#

"Finally, the herbs come around. The high grade when me a look for me get it by the pound yeah. Sweet Sensi a come around," My cellphone rang while I walked with Mandisa glancing at the shops hand in hand. Only one Jamaican made my phone ring like that. I smiled as I pulled to the side to answer Kaliah. "Ha-KIM! Bro, what's gud on da south side, eh? How come yuh nah call me?"

"Kaliah, Bro, everything is everything in the great Lone Star State. What it look like over yonder?" I teased him.

"Oh, eh, aye?" Kaliah asked, making me laugh. His voice was high-pitched over the phone, and I caught it. He must be stressing again. He couldn't control his rage when he was emotional. "Dat right? Cyrus called me, say him gonna be back in Longview? Wat happen in NYC? Michael Blackson get arrested for stealing cars with him old homies again, or fight wit dad comes running back in a year?"

237

"No, none of that, at least I don't think it was serious. Cyrus said that he just missed being around and wanted to finish school here. I think he's getting bored dancing, and Julliard wasn't what he thought it would be," I replied, looking over at Mandisa as she glanced at a kiosk with sunglasses and novelty stuff trying on things in the mirror. She was so cute, waiting patiently for her man to get off the phone. I'm telling you, Mandisa is so damn sweet and submissive…Oh my god! "Cyrus is gonna do Cyrus, Kaliah. You know how he gets when he's in his feelings. Why do you sound like you swallowed a squeak box?"

"Tired…no sleep in days. Mi working all di time. I'm stressed out beyond comprehension, Bro. Sick of this bitch! Trisha was gone for the entire weekend, and we had peace, Nigga. She walked through the door Monday morning, raising more hell than Pinhead!

'The bitch was so fucked up…I can't explain the shit I've been through this week. Been at the lab, don't go home, and har crazy-ass came ere talking shit, Hakim! 'Kaliah! Kaliah?! Nigga, bring yo ass back home! I want to fuck and you playing with weed! That's why you ain't shit! You're always high! Your Mama ain't shit! Your daddy sure ain't shit! If I could find the nigga I'd fuck him and compare the different types of shit that you ain't!'

"Bro, she's getting worse! Trisha stabbed me a month ago when I walked upon her in a parking lot to get her drunk ass home. She's got one more arrest for possession or public indecency, and they're gonna throw the book at her. Mi done.

'Stanley is out. Nikki is the only one that still cares. I don't know why I thought I could make shit work or fix her....But nah...Dat woman really insane, Hakim. Mi fuckin nuts! But har on anotha level of crazy I never wanna reach. Anyway...gonna go home, spend time wit Mom. Har call tells me har sick, Hakim. Liver terrible, all the drinking...been helping wit tha Cancer and pain, but Mom so stubborn. Still drinking when har upset."

"Do whatever you need to do, Kaliah. I thought Mama Louisa was doing better?" I groaned, worried.

"She hit a wall with her treatment, Hakim. You can't force someone to listen to their doctor's advice to stop drinking....even if your son is your doctor. Don't know how much time she's got now. Can't deal with losing Mom and psycho Bitch Barbie all at once. Pick and choose yuh battles, Hakim, aye?" Kaliah growled. "Oh, where's Lionel? He mentioned me coming to visit soon. Thinking bout things once mi checks in wit Mom. Too stressed... I need a damn vacation. Shit, Bro, been working for nearly 4 years nonstop."

"I think a vacation is a good idea. We all need to get away from shit. I'll get back to you on making something happen. There's shit going on here," I started glancing over at Mandisa. "We'll talk later, Kaliah. I've got to go. Take care of your mom and leave that crazy bitch alone! Love you, man!"

"Oh, eh, aye? Care to share, Brother? Sounds more urgent than the shit I have to handle. I need to get new gloves for all the shit I carry. At least I know you and Cyrus don't have the issues I fuck with, and that gives me some peace. Do I need to book a flight to Texas before Jamaica, Hakim?" Kaliah wondered curiously.

"No, not yet, Kaliah. I'm gonna fill you in on the details once I get home later. For now, we're flying under the radar. I'll let you know when we need to make some wind," I replied, hanging up. I wasn't going to keep Mandisa waiting around, and I didn't need Kaliah worried about what was happening here.

The last thing we needed was for him to come flying here trying to save the day and being stalked by his wife! I'd have to kill that bitch! She really is insane. When I say crazy, I mean talking to herself, fighting men and women, and staying high with meth or speed so she can't sleep, or knocking herself unconscious with pills and liquor so she can sleep without the nightmares.

We do not go around that woman since Kaliah married her. She's always talking shit to everyone because she knows she looks good, and people want her. The bitch thinks she can fuck anyone she wants when she feels like it. I've fucked up Kaliah's wife about trying to get Lionel. That's why Kaliah will not bring that bitch here anymore. He married her, trying to save her wild ass. Hoes like that can't be saved. I cannot stand evil bitches like Ms. Trisha. Mandisa is the complete opposite of that, and if Kaliah sees her, I'll have to kill him!

Kaliah may be the only brother I will admit is better than me in some areas. But no…we don't want Kaliah here with his wife still hot on his tail.

Mandisa glanced through a rack of women's tops. Her face seemed puzzled about what she needed. I'd never shopped for a girl before, so I was lost too. Cyrus ran off with Lionel shortly after we arrived, saying he'd catch up with us. My call with Kaliah didn't take that long, but they vanished on us just before finding this trendy little shop.

The store clerk was busy hanging up a display when he noticed me signaling for help. He was another tall, dark brother, but bald, older in age, maybe he was 30, he wore a nice dark designer suit, and had swag as he walked over spotting Mandisa and freezing.

I was the one that signaled the man, but he was stuck looking over Mandisa like I wasn't there. I wanted to fuck him up because he was staring at her like he was taking in every part of her for memory.

"Need help finding something, Sweetie-cakes?" He asked Mandisa, getting her attention. I actually took a step back, trying not to laugh. The man looked like a brother, but I knew he liked the brothers when I heard him speak. His brown eyes grew wider as Mandisa looked over, seeing him. "Good Lord…what's the matter? You look so miserable! You're in a clothing store with your figure, and you are upset? Uh-uh, talk to Antoine and tell me what's wrong?"

"Everything looks nice, but I have no idea what I'm doing. I have never bought my own clothes before. Women in America are so different than those in Paris. I don't want to look terrible," Mandisa sighed with an angelic pout to Antoine.

Antoine's face exploded, listening to Mandisa with wide eyes. He covered his big brown lips with a graceful wave and offered her his other hand to her, noticing me watching. Antoine looked me over a second and smiled, saying, "First thing you've got to do is smile, Precious! You are too gorgeous to be inside my store and not have a smile on your face. I'm going to help you find anything that makes you feel as pretty as you look. Tell your friend to go play for a while...."

"I'm not leaving Mandisa with anyone, Bro. Her mother trusted me to keep her safe. She's never been allowed much freedom at all. I love her, and I only want to make her happy. I'll buy anything that makes her forget the shit she has going on in her life for now. I'll sit out front if you want to play dress up."

"I thought you might be a little uncomfortable being the only man here. You're welcome to stay with your sweet little flower. I was just thinking....Man-di-sa, was it?" Antoine chuckled, looking at me.

"I'm Hakim Dunn. Mandisa is my Queen," I replied, realizing that Antoine wasn't trying to sell us clothes at all. "This is your shop?"

"Yes, Hakim Dunn, this is my shop, Zola. I designed the majority of the original fashion showcased here. I have many partners that have their independent lines I market in my stores. I can't get over this fresh, natural, innocent, shy, but clearly womanly vibe I feel looking at you...Man- No! You're Paula! Gorgeous, radiant, and just what the doctor ordered with your height and figure!" Antoine honestly replied, looking us over. "I have to dress you up and see what develops. One look at you, and I see Zola's new Lola!

Queen...Paula...the fresh young face rocking my designs for each season with those hips...Lord...I'll be rich! Robin, may I borrow Paula for a moment and work my magic? If you don't like what you see, then I'll let you have anything from the store as a gift from me."

"You want me to...wear your...." Mandisa sighed, understanding but lost.

"He wants you to model professionally for his shop, Queen!" I yelled, shocked entirely. I thought the brother was up to something because he was staring at her, but I didn't know he had that kind of clout! "You're serious, Antoine? Mandisa doesn't need anymore blows to her self-esteem."

"I never joke about money. Paula is going to be my money magnet...I can see it! Oh, we will have to sign a contract...I'll get Lena, my manager, to get all the paperwork for you. I'm willing to put my money on these features," Antoine chuckled as he touched Mandisa's curls. "It's all you...oh! We are going to make a lot of money, Paula! Come with me...I want to get your exact measurements! I can see inspiration hitting!"

I smiled to myself as Antoine led my Queen to the dressing rooms. Antoine was exactly what Mandisa needed to break that shy shell and help her realize how beautiful she actually was. We only walked in to buy a few things, and it felt like the universe was working with us. I have to be on the right path if things keep going my way. If Mandisa was allowed to be a model by her mother, then I'd support her 100 percent. Once I talked to Mrs. King about everything, she would let her daughter do this. How is it possible that the model wife I built as a kid was coming to life right before my eyes? I was starting to get excited. What could possibly happen next?

#

"Presenting my latest creation, PAULA!" Antoine yelled while dragging Mandisa from the back.

I had been sitting on my phone for over an hour and stood to stretch. But one look at Mandisa coming from behind Antoine and I was so weak I fell to my knees! She had on beautiful gold and pink heels. Her jeans fit perfectly on her hips, a sheer pink and golden halter top held her soft breasts, belly chains, bracelets, earrings, and Antoine pressed her curls straight and gave Mandisa the badest updo. Her face was softly colored, with dark blue eyeshadow like her jeans, but her lips were pink and golden. Mandisa looked like she was about to walk onto a TV screen as she nervously waited to hear me say anything.

"I think my heart just stopped," I groaned, trying to breathe as my dick got so hard I couldn't see straight.

Mandisa smiled and blushed. I couldn't get up off the ground as Antoine spun her around, and that ass looked like a ripe Georgia peach! Oh my god! Everything was nicely put away but on display with living color. "All of it! I want whatever you have in her size! Pick it all out, Antoine!"

I grabbed my wallet from my back pocket and tossed it on the floor at Mandisa's feet. I kept rubbing my hands on my knees to pull myself together. When I smiled, I found myself so nervous I couldn't look at her.

"Oh, I think he likes what Antoine sees, Paula...." Antoine giggled, hitting Mandisa on the shoulder and making her belly chains jingle. "You better get that wallet! He meant that shit, Paula! I will give you this outfit, hoping that you'll talk to Mami about seriously modeling exclusively for Zola. I don't want you to break Robin's pockets trying to look as cute as I can make you for free!"

"Hakim, get up! What are you doing?" Mandisa giggled, grabbing my wallet from the floor as I noticed a group of people in front watching us.

"I am worshipping my Goddess! I don't think I can feel my legs," I told Mandisa, unable to stand yet. She bent down, trying to help me up. I saw her breasts up close, and her belly chains rolled against my arm, and I moaned. It's been over a year since I've touched a woman I swore I would not go back down that path that nearly fucked me off. How did Mandisa become so beautiful that now I was afraid to touch her? I felt like she was too good for me! I wanted her before the makeover. Now…I needed that girl.

"Somebody is a bigger drama queen than I am," Antoine chuckled as Mandisa handed him my credit card. He looked at it and fell over the counter. "Nigga! You have a Black American Express Card? You don't look like you have that kind of money….well….I could be off on my money meter. When I saw you come in with the other tall brother dressed up in Gucci…I had a feeling you had some paper. I overlooked Paula…I was trying to see the one with the long hair to his ass with the pretty teeth."

"That's my brother, Lionel, and he's just 15. I wouldn't tell him you were looking…he fights anyone that says shit he doesn't like," I told Antoine seriously.

"No, not the skinny one that looks like you, Hakim…Mr. Gucciman? He's got the long braided locks down to his fine hips, and he's pure dark chocolate wrapped in the sunshine with that golden glow all over him," Antoine chuckled, rolling his eyes.

"Darius! Antoine…I never would have thought he was your type!" Mandisa giggled, turning red as Antoine covered his mouth, laughing as I frowned.

"Cyrus is not going to want to know that shit either. Keep it in the closet, Queen," I laughed.

Antoine died laughing, "You can keep it in the closet all you like, Michael, but a brother that tall, dark, and handsome with a smile like Lance Gross has got to be packing severe heat. The sweet ones are the ones you want to notice you. He looks like he's got money and loves spending it."

"Yeah, all of that and that last part," I chuckled under my breath as Mandisa and her new friend had their back and forth and picked out more hot shit to dress up my wife. I was in love all over again, and I didn't care anymore what anyone thought.

Chapter Seven: We Gonna Be (Alright)?

Cyrus

I was in the Armani Exchange with Lionel looking for anything to distract my thoughts from drifting back to Mandisa. Today was taking a toll on me. I was fighting all my feelings for Mandisa and originally wanted the best for Hakim. But after seeing her dance for Madame Olga, I realized Mandisa's a better dancer than me, and there was a newfound admiration. I didn't know Mandisa was so gifted.

Then I fucked around playing and touched her feet. Why did I do that? I had to lie about everything once I spotted Lionel and Hakim watching me. I know better than to think I could be attracted to a woman and be her friend. Meeting Mandisa made me want something more profound than just a physical thing. I wasn't trying to fuck her. However, I wanted to worship every part of that girl. After hearing that messed-up stuff about Mandisa's father and seeing Hakim's reaction, I need to stay away from her. It seems like the deeper Hakim falls, the more I feel for Mandisa. I hate it here! I may have to rethink my plan to finish school here if Hakim suddenly flips the script on me. He's a rookie in love. If his feelings get hurt, who knows how he'll react.

Lionel came out of the dressing room looking fresh to death in blue and black. His skin was made for dark colors. However, I look crazy in too much black, but I love the color.

"I know…just say it," Lionel laughed, holding up his arms flexing. He was so skinny I didn't see enough bicep for a baseball game. I nodded. "I'm black-boy fly! We gonna hurt em' all this summer, Bro!"

"Right-right, Fasho!" I laughed, looking around. Some kids were playing near the store entrance, but they all stopped suddenly. Lionel smiled, staring in the same direction. It reminded me of us when we were kids, all hanging out at the mall with no money. We were just happy to get away from the house. It felt good to be here spending money rather than daydreaming. One little boy that kind of looked like me was staring at something. "Mall cops probably on their asses?"

"Yeah," Lionel said as I spotted a pair of jeans that would fly at the club. I was about to grab the hanger when Lionel snatched my hair and made me look back. "You see that shit, Cyrus?! What the hell happened?"

Hakim came toward the store entrance, and all the kids were surrounding Mandisa. Hakim tried to drag Mandisa away from all the kids trying to give her hugs. People were gathering around watching as my jaw fell open seeing that woman. Mandisa bent over, giving one little boy a hug, and got damn! She was a pink and golden vision of sheer perfection, and Hakim couldn't stop smiling.

Mandisa was superb beforehand, but a few changes, and she looked like a supermodel! When she spotted us, she waved at me. I felt like I didn't know her! My hands got sweaty, my knees felt weak, and then I lost all my swag when I attempted to wave back. Seriously, I was as nervous as my eleven-year-old self around her! Mandisa terrified me. All the bags and boxes I was holding for Lionel had hit the floor, and I didn't notice until a shoe fell out. I quickly knelt down, picking up everything, but I couldn't take my eyes off of her.

Hakim dashed over toward us with her in tow. He spun her around, screaming, "Do you see this?"

Mandisa was blushing with her softly made-up face, but those eyes were dangerous now. They were pulling me in like a starfield as she smiled with those luscious plump pink lips. Her face was stunning! She nervously asked, "Darius, do you like it, seriously?"

"You look amazing, spectacular, delectable, shit I almost didn't recognize you if not for Hakim," I told her, glancing at Hakim. "What happened? We left you a few minutes ago."

"Antoine happened, Bro!" Hakim gushed like a kid swinging her hand. Hakim glanced away and handed me a business card.

"Zola? What's that? Sounds like a soda for vampires…drink…Zola!" I chuckled.

Mandisa giggled at my nervous outburst, and my heart stopped as she playfully patted my arm.

"It's this hot spot that just opened here. They sell the fliest gear for ladies with a body, Cyrus. The kind of body that Mandisa has, and Antoine wants her. He's the owner and designer and offered her a legit contract, Bro," Hakim squealed, trying to contain his excitement. I could tell by how his squirming and smirking at Mandisa that he felt just as bitch slapped as me! His fingers played with her bracelets, getting them to twist on her smooth wrist. "My wife is gonna be a model."

"Are you serious?" I asked as it set in. "You're gonna do it, Queen?"

"If Mami says yes, I would love to model Antoine's beautiful designs. He has a wonderful vision to use all women of color in his ads, but he wants me to be his Paula. I like him. He is funny as you, Darius. I think Antoine likes you a lot," Mandisa replied with a gorgeous smile.

"Yeah, Antoine loves men with long hair. I had to fight him away once he got comfortable around me. I'm not homophobic, but I don't like them touching me!" Hakim chuckled, turning his eyes. "He's a big dude, and he made me uncomfortable trying to feel my legs. Eww..."

"Shit, you should have busted him in the lips!" Lionel laughed, rolling his eyes then frowning. "The big ones will try to make you gay if you're too nice!"

"See! That's the shit I'm talking about, Lionel! I hit him for coming on to me, and it'll ruin Mandisa's shot at modeling and being happy for once in her damn life! You don't think at all, do you?" Hakim groaned.

"Shaniqua, you need to stop playing and tell Mandisa the truth about us!" I teased Hakim putting my hands on my hips and waiting.

"Cyrus....do...don't...not now...." Hakim laughed and shook his head. I was not going to have them fighting around Mandisa.

"Oh, so I should go talk to Antoine? Fine, I see how you treat all your bitches," I growled, pretending to be hurt.

Mandisa turned so red I was worried if she could breathe! Hakim and Lionel knew that was one of the go-to moves when they started in on homosexuals. I have nothing negative to say. I don't like to hear anything negative either, so I use it to make them shut up. It's worked for years on Lionel and Hakim. Kaliah hates that shit. So I do it even more around him to piss him off. Sometimes when Hakim is high, he joins in, and it is hilarious. I do my best to flip negative scenarios positively.

"Mami will say yes once she sees you, Queen," Hakim sighed, falling under her spell. "It's like watching a butterfly come out of its cocoon. Fly, Baby, fly!"

As Mandisa laughed at Hakim's excitement, I couldn't look away from her either. She was the most delicate red-boned sister I had ever seen, with skin like honey flowing down to her lovely toe tips. She was sweet before, but now it was like the first time I opened a magazine and saw a REAL model. I don't mean Sports Illustrated or Maxim....I'm talking about the women in Thick Magazine.

Most don't know some men love sisters with the body. I love my ladies with the thickness. It's an obsession, and I am not ashamed to like it all. I just want a woman that will smother me with her softness and take as much of these 14 inches as she can take. So far, no one can handle it, and I have to keep trying to find my ankh. I'm not saying I will not love a thin sister, but she better be ready if she wants to play with Cyrus. I play for keeps, and I've never had a complaint in that department.

I could see Mandisa on a beach backdrop wearing a pink bikini and heels crawling around in the sand on all fours. Ooh shit!

"I can't believe how much you changed with just some clothes and make-up. You look so much older now!" Lionel exclaimed, shaking my arm.

"I did not believe it either, Lionel. When Antoine turned me around in the chair, I felt like someone else," Mandisa confessed.

"You were beautiful before, though," Lionel told her. "Now it feels like someone's gonna hit me for looking at you!"

"Yeah," I agreed to go to pay for the things I was holding.

It felt weird being near Mandisa. My little crush on Hakim's girl was replaced by complete infatuation with everything about her. When I looked back at her as I strolled away, I nearly lost my balance and tripped! Mandisa hadn't changed at all on the inside; she was still quiet, shy, and sweet like before. But her appearance was more vibrant than ever, and it made every male within striking distance notice.

At the register, I tried to pull myself together. I caught sight of Mandisa walking by, looking at a pair of sunglasses with Hakim trailing on her lovely rump in those fitted designer jeans. As he grabbed her waist, her adorable golden belly chains made me shiver. I reached to get my wallet, dropping it in my haste. I knelt down to grab it and saw her splendid heels caressing her feet. Fuck me! Her toes looked so cute in those straps and chains. The only thing missing was a toe ring for me to kiss. I'd probably destroy this damn store if she wore toe rings and anklets.

"653.75," I heard the clerk say. I snapped back to reality. I turned around and ran into the counter head first. As I fell backward on my ass, Lionel laughed so loud that everyone in the store noticed.

"Damn, Nigga! You missed all that counter?" Lionel taunted me as I tried to shake off the stars before my eyes.

I completely forgot I was kneeling and slammed right into the rim of the checkout! I couldn't play that off, so I fell back on the floor a moment until I could see straight.

"Bro, you alright?" Hakim laughed at me as I struggled to get up on my knees.

"That was not funny!" Mandisa said, helping me get up. She frowned, poking out her lips looking at my forehead. "Are you okay, Darius?"

"Yeah…I'm good. I wasn't watching what I was doing," I told Mandisa as she touched my forehead with her fingernail wrinkling her nose. "I'll be fine."

"You were paying attention to the floor and those feet when you should have been watching out for your head!" Lionel snorted, pushing Hakim. Hakim wrinkled up his nose and shook his head at me. Both of them died of laughter.

Mandisa grabbed my chin, forcing me to look at her.

"You are going to have a knot there. A lump is popping up, and it looks bad," Mandisa sighed as she opened her bag, put a bandage over my bump, and pressed her soft pink lips to it. "Do you feel better?"

"Much better now," I replied, staring at her lips.

My heart was dancing the Mambo, and now I wanted her to be my partner. I don't know why the thought of Hakim kissing Mandisa last night popped into my mind, and I craved it so bad. I glanced away a second.

"Sir, should I get a manager for a statement?" The clerk asked, watching closely.

"No, no! I am good! Just clumsy for some reason today that's never happened to me before. I'm usually light on my feet and unstoppable," I laughed off the moment. I quickly paid for everything and put my wallet away. Mandisa tried to grab my bags, and I stopped her. "Uh-no! I can carry my own shit, Queen. Where are your clothes? You didn't buy but the one outfit? Has Hakim fucked up and dropped the ball?"

"No! Antoine is personally going to deliver Mandisa's things to her house tomorrow so he can meet her mother. He's serious about getting her to model for Zola, Cyrus! For your information, I bought my girl enough clothes to make it Her Hot Girl Summer! She's going to be the sexiest woman in THE VIEW!" Hakim moaned, rubbing his hands together. "A fucking model, Cyrus! You know what this means, right?"

I stared at Hakim's enthusiasm and couldn't help but feel him. There was no way I could be a hater. He's always been my friend when I found one I thought was IT for me. Hakim was the one that knew exactly what he wanted, and I understood. Maybe this was his year to get it all. He was making all the right moves while I kind of drifted. My brother was going to be a successful lawyer soon. Hakim was determined to make this world a better place. It was Hakim and Kaliah that did the majority of the work to make money. My job was always finding ways to transport before we got legal. I did a lot of shit to establish our connections from coast to coast, but Hakim and Kaliah had words about how things were split. Kaliah thought I should get less.

Hakim went to bat for me, and Kaliah caved. I couldn't fuck over my best friend like that.

#

We walked around checking out more stores. Lionel was buying everything he could fit. I'd grab a few things here or there.

But Hakim was buying Mandisa all kinds of expensive gifts. Hakim bought makeup, perfumes, lotions, soap, expensive hair styling tools, and anything that Mandisa looked at. Mandisa didn't ask for it, but my brother blessed that girl with anything he could to make her cheerful and beautiful. She was so grateful for his generosity that she couldn't keep herself off him, and Hakim was relishing every touch. Mandisa told him no on much of it, and he'd still get for her. She'd ask him to stop, but smile giving him kisses, and he kept spending. It was like this all day. Hakim turned into an atm, and Mandisa paid him back in affection. Why? That was all that I wanted!

Now you trying to pull a Cyrus, Hakim? No one does Darius Osirus 'Cyrus' Jefferson Junior, like the master! Allow me to elaborate on my point? A King does not just buy his Queen everything money can afford. No, he must cater to her needs and desires. What good is it for her to have her closets full and her passions left unsatisfied? I can demonstrate this without stepping on any man's toes. This is Chess, not Checkers when it comes to love. You do not make a move that leaves you unprotected or the Queen open for capture. No King wants to adjust his strategy once the Queen is taken due to his carelessness.

Shit, now I wanted to lace her with something just watching her reactions. Women I took shopping would say thank you, but they seemed to feel I owed it to them. There were times I'd take them shopping, then others out to a movie, and the attitude is totally different. I know from last night at Hot Wheels, Mandisa is not that kind of girl. She's not using Hakim or anyone, and I hate to say it....She is perfect in every way, and if Hakim marries her, he will be the happiest brother alive. How could any man resist a girl so humble, beautiful, intelligent, talented, and sad?

I glanced at things thinking of what to gift her. It was too soon to shower her with anything expensive. That would give the wrong impression. I noticed these cute golden anklets, toe rings, and matching bracelets. Then I found lovely waist beads the ladies wear and found myself unable to say no. I didn't think they were too expensive compared to what Hakim was dropping. I grabbed a few sets she could wear with all her new clothes and tucked them away after I paid. I'd find the moment to give them to her. She had us carrying enough of them.

We had to return to Mercedez to unload some of Hakim's gifts and Lionel's things. I barely bought anything. That seemed to shock my overspending brother. I am full of surprises when I want to be. I saw a nail salon and paid for Mandisa to have her nails and toes done while Hakim was distracted looking at cell phone cases. She was so happy that I got a hug and kiss on the cheek. It was just my way of seeing to her needs. She mentioned they were getting too long, and I wanted to see her toes with a lovely design, so I spared no expense. They were happy to take care of Mandisa while we checked out the neighboring stores.

#

"Hakim, why you spending so much money on Mandisa?" Lionel sweated his brother the moment we were alone. He took off his shirt and grabbed another off a hanger.

"I'm buying Mandisa what she deserves. She's not any female to me, Bro. Mandisa's my queen now. When you love someone, you give them anything to see them happy," Hakim told his brother, sighing.

He rubbed his eyes under his glasses and sat for a moment. He frowned and looked in the mirror, thinking. Holding his glasses while folding them, Hakim put them in his pocket. He took out his contact lenses, hesitated, and smiled at me. His grin was off a bit. It must have been the way he was leaning as he sat.

"Hakim's right, Lionel, " I added, seeing Lionel roll his eyes. All women love to be spoiled, and the ones that don't ask for much deserve it all."

"I understand that, but I've seen you spend all kinds of bread on bitches that didn't deserve shit!" Lionel chuckled, and I frowned.

"That's not true. All women deserve to be treated right, Lionel. Some take your kindness for granted. But I bet every woman I've ever blessed is still holding on to anything I gave her. She may never get something that nice ever again," I defended myself.

"No, no no, no….NO! Some women are bitches and only want your paper, and if I can't get no head, she's better off dead," Lionel laughed, putting on a pair of Ralph Lauryn pants.

"Some of that is accurate, Cyrus," Hakim stated out of the blue.

"What?! I know you didn't take Lionel's side on that ignorant statement, Hakim Dunn?" I chuckled against my will. I threw my shirt on the hanger trying on another.

"I'm not saying they're all bitches, Cyrus. But some bitches are bitches, Bro. A good girl can turn into a savage if she gets dogged out. I'm not one to lie to a female. I'm honest about my intentions from the jump. I've never promised a bitch anything because I didn't need a bitch. You don't promise shit you don't intend to deliver," Hakim chuckled, standing up and grabbing a shirt from a rack. "However, I'm feeling very generous as of late. I wouldn't worry about how I spend my money."

"Since you're feeling so fucking friendly, can the fam hold a card or what, Nigga?" Lionel charged up Hakim unexpectedly. Hakim glanced up at Lionel and raised his eyebrows with a severe gaze. Lionel's face dropped, and I suddenly felt worried. I hoped Hakim was not going to fight Lionel if he mouthed off here. Fuck! I like this store…They have all the Versace shit! My other trick wasn't going to work.

"I tell you what…If you're only buying clothes, shoes, and whatnots, then I'll pay. But if I see any ice, then bet's off," Hakim told Lionel with a smile.

"Yeah, Nigga!" Lionel yelled, slapping my arm. "I'm gonna be like Hammer! You can't touch this!"

"Hammer blew all his money, Bro! Pick a better role model…what the fuck?" Hakim groaned, shaking his head.

Hakim tried on the black and gold Versace shirt, shocking me. Oh, are you going to jump up to my level of drip as well, Hakim? I playfully grabbed the sleeve looking at the detail, asking, "What is that? Vercases, Vasauces? It looks like that shit I got at the swap meet, Shaniqua. You sure it ain't a knockoff, Bitch?"

Lionel hit the floor, cackling in his high voice. He was always doing that shit to make us all snicker. It never failed if Lionel fell out; Hakim was going to laugh. Hakim died giggling and wobbled his head, "Versace, Nigga, stop playing!"

Lionel got up and grabbed the tag on Hakim's shirt, saying, "That's an 800 dollar shirt, Hakim!"

"I know," Hakim replied, looking at himself in the mirror. "I never get to spend money on myself. But if my girl is gonna look like a million dollars, I need to step my wardrobe up a little. I can't look broke next to her in Antoine's custom stuff. His store is high-end, Bro. It has the best designers to kiss the curves on a queen."

"That shit is fly as hell. You need to wear that to Gucci's! Everyone will drown in haterade!" Lionel said, sticking out his tongue.

"It's not about generating hate, Lionel. I just want to look like I belong with her. When you find a real one that makes you happy, you will always have someone watching and waiting for a chance to shoot their shot, Bro. So you have to elevate with your Goddess or be left to pick from the peasants. I'm not going to go back to that shit now that I've found her. Good luck finding yours...." Hakim chuckled with an arrogant tone I didn't like.

"Ooh, all I'd need are some stones like your shit, Cyrus. I'd blast these niggas in the chest like Voltron!" Lionel said, nodding at me.

"No!" Hakim shouted angrily. "Next, you'll be asking for me to buy you some heat to protect that shit. Forget it, Lionel, you fight too damn much! A few diamonds ain't worth getting shot over!"

"You got a gun, Hakim, and you do too, Cyrus," Lionel fronted us out with a frown.

"I've never had to use that shit, Lionel. It's to keep niggas off me and mine if it gets too hot to handle," Hakim stated with a grave glare. "I don't start shit like you. I haven't needed it because niggas don't test me anymore, Bro."

"You use your heat, Cyrus?" Lionel pried, killing my vibe.

"Yeah...and..." I said, moving my hair over, taking Hakim's Versace shirt to try on. "I fired it at some niggas that tried to steal out of my truck in the Bronx. It was self-defense because they shot first when I chased them down. I have papers to carry and conceal in every state I have a house. Kaliah told me that shit when he got me out of trouble the last time. I operate legally no matter where I go now."

"Mhm, so you're saying you'll never buy any jewelry, Hakim" Lionel asked, folding his arms.

"I didn't say that," Hakim replied, getting upset again. "I said you can't buy any! You're unstable! Show me some responsibility and maturity for once, and I'll get you something that will blow your wildest dreams away.

'But as of right now, the only thing I see you need is clothes. If you get jumped over a pair of shoes or a jacket, so the fuck what? We get another. But a nigga will blast you over a watch or chain. We live in the country, and people do stupid shit when they aren't thinking.

'Think about how many enemies you've made over the years? I figure you've got all of them because of your mouthpiece, so you have all the pieces you need until you find some inner peace, Baby Bro."

"True that," I agreed with Hakim. "How many fights you see me get into, Lionel?"

Both Lionel and Hakim cracked up laughing at me!

"Nigga, you can't fight!" Lionel cried, grabbing Hakim's arm, trying not to hit the floor.

"What?" I asked, staring at them, offended.

"Cyrus, it's okay, Bro. We know you can't fight. But you're pretty, so it never mattered to us," Hakim taunted me, wiping the tears from his eyes, trying to save his contacts.

"Fuck you with two dicks, Hakim! I can fight. I don't like to throw blows because I get emotional and need to chill afterward," I explained. Lionel was rolling on the floor like a bony-ass log in a Polo shirt. Hakim was crying, holding his stomach so loud people were watching. "Both of you can choke on this dick!"

Hakim's face was red, wiping the tears laughing, "Cyrus….remember when Toby Reese stole your brand new bike the day after Christmas? Who fought him to get it back?"

"You did," I admitted folding my arms. That was one time when we were kids. Toby Reese stole everything that wasn't locked up. I had words with him about stealing shit out of the yard, and we fought a few times, but when he took my bike…My Dad told me to stop because I was acting like Lionel. He was right. Both of the Dunn boys influenced me, but I learned. "Toby and I fought a lot. That was one time when I didn't want to fight him."

"Wait, Wait, Cyrus!" Lionel cried, leaping up. "What about the time when them niggas at the club jumped Stevie, and you tried to help?"

"That was five niggas! You can't count me getting jumped, Bro, really?!" I groaned, getting pissed off. Lionel smiled viciously and shook his head. Hakim bit his bottom lip and raised his eyebrows, looking away. "You really think I can't hold my own?"

"Yeah...naw...who saved your ass that night, Cyrus," Hakim chuckled, rubbing his forehead signaling his brother. I hated this shit! Lionel's grin exploded as he manipulated himself in his pants and nodded. Hakim indicated Lionel and died laughing.

"Lionel," I mumbled, rolling my eyes. "Are you done?"

"No, wait, Cyrus! What about the time Catrina Bradley cracked you in the park and gave you a black eye?" Hakim chuckled, sitting holding his gut. Lionel fell over on Hakim's shoulder as they both had their giggle fit. *Cool...I see where this is going. I'll play along.*

"I don't hit girls, Hakim, you know that shit!" I yelled, pretending to be offended but wanting to see why he brought it up after agreeing with his brother before.

"That was no girl! That was a dike!" Lionel cried, hitting the floor. "Hakim knocked her lights out. She went down like Ronnie from the Player's Club! I was so proud of Hakim that day."

"She talked more shit than Lionel and kept getting in everyones' faces starting drama. 'Fuck you, Hakim! I ain't scared of you, Jim Kelly! You ain't Bruce Lee!' (*He struck her so hard she hit the sidewalk, breaking her nose!*) I felt bad that I lost my temper, but watching Catrina's loud-mouthed ass hit the ground made me smile," Hakim snorted, thinking back.

"I still can't believe you hit that girl like that, Hakim," I sighed, shaking my head putting another shirt on.

"Catrina kept putting herself in a man's place. She picked on everyone because she was older, and she knew the boys wouldn't fight her back. I let her make it for months until I saw that black eye. The bitch did that shit being evil. Then she dared to talk shit to me for asking her why. Fuck that." Hakim grumbled with a nonchalant expression. "Grandma Sophie saw me come home one day. Catrina had scratched my face up, trying to get her off Lionel. Sophie was the one that said if a woman hits you too many times, then she's just a bitch and to fight back. She could kill you. G.D. told me to get that bitch, or he was gonna beat my ass. He didn't have to threaten me; I wanted to fuck her up. So the last time she fucked with one of us, I confronted her about your eye."

"Ooh, I didn't know G.D. told you to hit her, Hakim. Grandma told you to fight her too? I wish they would've said that shit to me," Lionel laughed, cupping his mouth.

"It's not cool to hit women. I know you were looking out, but I think it messes them up when you beat them. Black men are here to protect women. If we turn on them, who can they trust?" Hakim said, frowning. *(Says the brother that broke a 13-year-old girl's face because he didn't know his own strength at 11.)* "That was something that was going to either end with her taking shit too far or my kicking her ass like a man so she would let us be men. Catrina wanted to be the first to test that part of me so desperately, so I introduced her to Hakim's boot camp for bad bitches.

'A woman doesn't have to worry about me for long once she pushes me too far. The minute she raises her voice at me for nothing, I give one warning, then I'm gone. 'Where you going, Nigga? I'm not done with you yet!' Yeah, we're done here. I gotta GO!"

"Shit, I love a woman with some attitude. If she starts popping her neck and rollin' her eyes at me…oooh, I am so ready for you, Girl! I know what you want, and it's right here, Baby.

'The girls that love to argue just want you to fuck the shit out of them. Once they start all that shit-talking, I grab that ass, get those clothes off, and go to work. Next thing you know, they're crying, apologizing for the toilet being dirty, and making me a sandwich," I disagreed with Hakim with an evil thought.

"What?" Lionel asked me, laughing. "That shit doesn't work…does it?"

"Hell yeah, try it and see, Baby Bro! I don't care what she's mad about. The only thing I know it fails every time with is cheating. Nothing fixes that shit for good. If you get busted for cheating, just buy all the roses and diamonds you can and hope for the best. A woman will never forget how you treated her like she wasn't enough, no matter why you did it," I told Lionel, nodding. "I've never gotten busted like that, but a few errors got confronted by their men with me. I act crazy or gay, and he believed I was just there."

Hakim plunged his head between his knees, chuckling so hard his locks were shaking like a seizure.

"I poke and move on these hos, and I ain't gonna tumble in no tricks. I always use rubbers and bring my own shit too. You can't trust a bitch you don't know. That's how Jamire got caught up by his old lady. He assumed he could leave his condoms at her spot.

'You know how you be in a hurry and don't check for shit? Well, his kept popping, and one day we found an open box. That bitch had poked tiny holes in all his condoms! Now she's pregnant and laughing all the way to the bank. He's 16, and she's 22 with two kids from another nigga she doesn't take care of. I know she did that because everyone knows Jamire and Les's family have money.

'That bitch set my nigga up! I don't trust none of these hos. You can't fall in love and get soft, or they'll make a fool out of you."

"What about Shamaya Lockhart?" Hakim catechized Lionel with large eyes staring up thoughtfully.

"What?" Lionel replied, faking he didn't hear.

"You heard him," I co-signed Hakim with a chuckle, bobbing. "Little May-May, your pretty brown shadow?"

"Oh, Maya, naw, it wasn't like that. We were just friends. I was 12, and she was 11, so it doesn't count if you're kids," Lionel responded with an annoyed glance at Hakim. Lionel took off the pants he was trying on and put back on his shorts, glaring. Obviously, Lionel was lying. It's funny when a brother is too hard to admit he has a heart. It's always written all over the ugly face he makes when the girl he loves is mentioned. "Besides, you all know Maya was a tomboy.

She fought niggas that tried to touch her, and James didn't let anyone near her."

"J-Rock was like your brother, Lionel. I know better than that shit. Did you kiss her?" I demanded seriously.

"Yeah, but I didn't know what I was doing the few times she kissed me, so I never kissed her back," Lionel exhaled as he put on his shirt. "We were kids."

"Maya was constantly with you, Lionel, from the instant we moved here. She was there cheerful, playing with your hair, and riding bikes everywhere with you," Hakim reminded us, teasing Lionel in his discomfort. "Sounds like love to me."

"Yep, it sounds like a first love to me. I remember May-May. She and James were there when we met. Maya had those long pigtails, that cute giggle, and a pretty smile. She was so cute. What happened to them?" I agreed as I pushed Lionel's shoulder.

"She moved," Lionel mumbled with a deep raspy groan, looking away.

"There are ways to find people, Bro. You can use the internet, phone books are still around, have you talked to her relatives or tried social media?" I suggested trying to help.

Lionel flared his tiny nostrils and ground his teeth, shaking his head.

"I've tried to find her for years, Cyrus. It's like Maya dropped off the planet. She didn't have family here once her mama died. Her Aunt Key-Key moved out and left them, and that bitch hated me. She was mean to Maya and fucked with James all the time. Their mama was too strung out to stop her from getting fucked up and hitting her, and James kept trying to protect her from shit. He tried to work at a factory, and they fired him because some dude hated him, saying James was stealing supplies.

'James wasn't no thief, but he'd fuck a nigga up for starting shit or fucking with his baby sister. He sold weed and was always working with Lester, then he went to the pen. He got an assault charge from that nigga Miles that sold that shit to his mama. James found out that nigga tried to get Maya's mama to sell her for some dope. He lost it and went after that nigga, and turned himself in when they took Maya away," Lionel explained and looked away. "She came to school that last day, and then she was gone. I found out everything from Angela after J-Rock got locked up and Maya was gone. I have been trying to find James, but you know he can't read, Cyrus?

'You both used to smoke together, so I thought you might have something about your boy. But you don't talk about

274

him. It's like the minute they were gone, you all forgot they existed. I never forgot them. They were like family to us, and you bailed on them too, both of you. You wonder why I question your loyalty all the time…shit like that.

'I loved her, so? Find her for me if you want to help a nigga. You don't see me over here throwing nobody's feelings bout love in their faces. I'm just fucking with the woke brothers…Right, Kung-Fu Kenny…? Huh, Andre 3000? I think yall niggas playing woke with all that damn money and no sense of real family. Why you ain't been calling Kaliah, Cyrus? You don't care about the cash cow suffering from that bitch as long as he stays far away and keeps making money! But he's both your brothers, and you won't cut me in the business. But I appreciate your concern, Hakim. You pretending like you give a damn, so I guess Mandisa making a man out of your bitch ass…About time!

"You always trying to front me out, well it backfired on both your asses this time. I'ma go pay for this before you kick my ass for speaking MY truth for once."

Lionel stared at Hakim and wrinkled his forehead walking away. Hakim didn't say a word to his brother.

I wasn't going to argue with the truth. For once, Baby Brother was absolutely on the money. Hakim would be a fool to start that shit and lie his way out of it. Lionel was pissed off and sad simultaneously, so he might swing, cry, or both. Hakim would fuck him up, reminding him that he's faster and more brutal. I'd have to pay security not to call the police or grab everyone and make a run.

Please, no! We'd have to disturb Mandisa's pretty new pedicure. Lionel walked toward the front of the store when Hakim did nothing. Once Lionel was out of range, Hakim stood up and looked like his entire body turned into a statue.

"That's fucked up, Bro…." I sighed, realizing what was pissing him off for so long. "All that happened while I was in Brooklyn?"

"When you left, he got worse. He started skipping school, stopped playing ball for a while, and wouldn't draw anything. He was flying off the handle when anyone said anything to him. We had to get help, you know…Lionel and I lost it, Cyrus," Hakim confessed, looking up at the ceiling.

"You know that I love Lionel like he's my blood, Hakim," I groaned, scratching my head worried. "You're all my brothers. Fuck! He's right about Kaliah! I can't stand Ms. Trisha, Hakim. I run when that bitch shows-I mean. Kaliah's wife is crazy, and I don't want to be near her…ever…EVER!"

"I hate admitting that Lionel is right about anything he says, but I can't kick his ass for putting me in my place. He's

276

been watching me closer than I thought. I haven't been watching him at all and thought I was helping by staying on him," Hakim groaned, clenching his fists across his knees. "It's got to get better, Cyrus or I'm gonna lose Lionel."

"I'll do whatever I can," I vented, wanting to go check on Lionel.

I'd never seen Lionel that messed up before, and he's never talked to us like that…Intelligently…I mean.

He always talks shit. I think it astonished us both that he called us both counterfeit, and he was appropriate. We were hypocrites and attempted to inform him how to be good. No wonder he had the where do you get the fuck off telling me anything attitude toward Hakim. It also explained why he liked having fun with me, but Lionel thought anything I said seriously to him was a joke like my usual fuckery. We needed to make changes, and Lionel pointed out the critical factor we missed glorifying our minor victories. The money made me think I was better than everyone else, and it was a slap to reality for me to hear Lionel correcting me for once. Fuck Kaliah's wife, though! I mean that from the darkest part of the crack of my ass.

The few that had the terror of meeting that bitch know the definition of a ho! I love a wild woman with a mouthpiece on her fine body. Kaliah's wife has the body of heaven, and everything else about her is hell on Earth, literally. He won't leave her, and the bitch scares the shit out of me. I'm just gonna be honest. You get around that woman when she's fucked up, and you'll hear voices coming out of her. I didn't think that shit was funny. She tries to fuck anyone that gets close enough. Once she's made up her mind, she is going to fuck you; she doesn't care what it takes to get hold of you. The bitch came after me in the bathroom at Kaliah's birthday party when we met her, and Hakim had to knock that bitch out!

I needed to seriously get out of my own head about a lot of shit and try to fix what we fucked up being so selfish all these years. I knew Hakim felt the same way. His tears as I left him alone in the dressing room told me. At least we knew that Lionel wasn't as stupid as he pretended to be for so long.

Chapter Eight: Wesley's Theory As Told By

Lionel

Being in school was boring when I was in middle school, and I hated going. We went to a private school, so there were more white kids than us. But Grandma Sophie said it was good for us to be in a private school because we got a more genuine education from more involved teachers. A Few were good, but others were assholes like in public schools. Several privileged bastards looked down on anyone that didn't come from families with paper.

White kids were trying to act black around us, and that pissed Hakim off. Most of the black kids that went to St. Luke's were getting picked on, like James and Maya. They went to our school because Hakim begged Sophie to let them come with us. We didn't know anyone else there. Cyrus and his dad had moved back to New York.

James was a football star. He was accepted there for his athletic abilities but wouldn't go if Maya couldn't. Hakim cut a deal and paid for Maya, and James went. That was when they started making money. Hakim was helping everyone back then.

Though we were at a good school, we had problems because we were different from everyone. We didn't belong there, and everybody knew it. Girls used to pick on Maya, calling her names, torment her hair, and those were the black girls. Maya got fed up and started fucking up anyone that touched her. Hakim fought a lot, too, but he was battling for attention. When niggas started shit or tried to jump someone, he'd make an example out of them in front of everyone.

Hakim had the faculty afraid to break up his fights. Hakim is a beast when he lets loose, and I love to fight with him. Maya, James, Hakim, and I piled up niggas in the park that started shit or chased us home from school. I miss those days the most.

Shamaya followed me around and laughed at my jokes. She was always there. When we moved to Longview, she stood on the corner and saw me bringing out my bike. She came by on her bike and asked to race. We rode everywhere. She'd chase the ducks at the park or sit in the yard with us talking.

James was around the way, and he was there from day one, keeping the neighborhood clowns off us. He had long braids, and I quit cutting my hair once we left Georgia. When I saw how long James's braids were on his shoulders, I wanted my hair braided up too. He turned me on to Angela, and the rest is history. James used to sing all these songs, and girls loved him. But he only cared about getting money to take care of his sister.

James was a few years older than Hakim, but he couldn't read well, so he got held back in school. He was swollen like a bodybuilder at 14, but he looked 20 years old. He never got carded for anything, so when he bought cigarettes, Maya and I would sneak them to smoke in the backyard. James was a fighter and a powerhouse and knocked grown niggas out cold for fucking with Maya. James started selling weed to buy shit for the house and get things for Maya. He was always smoking it too, and when Cyrus came around, those two were always talking. They're almost alike in a way as far as personality. But if I were to think which brother reminded me the most of my locked up homie that's out here…it's Kaliah.

Kaliah's the only play-brother I have that I wish was my real brother. Yeah, he's got a psycho bitch for a wife. Let the po-po lock that bitch up and walk! But Hakim and Cyrus used the hell out of Kaliah, and all he wants is to be close to the only people he considers family. Kaliah went to school to be a doctor to heal everyone with his intelligence. It makes a hell of a lot of money, but Hakim acts like he hates Kaliah sometimes. Cyrus will tell Kaliah he can't stand him or his wife, but he makes friendly because Hakim and I are close to Kaliah. Cyrus is cool with Kaliah, but they got that Team Light Skin vs. Team Dark Skin shit going on. Since Kaliah committed to Trisha, they feel he'll stop them from having fun. Shit, Kaliah is more fun than both of them when his old lady is blacked out somewhere else.

Kaliah used to stay with us when our parents were alive in Georgia. Mama knew he was gifted and had him tested, and he wound up going to High School before he was ten. But Kaliah was messed up because he saw a car hit and kill his twin brother. Kaliah had terrible mental health problems and was trying to find ways to heal without dangerous drugs. He started the weed cross-breeding shit because his mother got diagnosed with Breast Cancer while he was in college.

She needed money, and he used what he knew to make as much as he needed to take care of her, but she used his shit because it helped with the pain. Kaliah is blessed with brains, and he's always trying to help the people he cares about in any way he can. Hakim and Cyrus treat him like shit because they are scared of his wife, and they're both so jealous of him that they are afraid he will steal their shine. Yeah, I said that shit. Tell them, I don't give a fuck, right now after the shit Hakim tried to pull bringing up Maya.

Everywhere I go, I hear shit about my brother and all the bitches he's fucked, or nigga's he's terrified. I'm not afraid of Hakim. I respect my brother; there's a difference. I don't like him or the way he believes he's smarter than people. Mandisa is the first person I've heard him compliment besides Cyrus or Kaliah, and she's making him soft.

I'm glad that he's finally starting to feel something, but he's not gonna keep treating me like a little kid. I told you I'm not stupid. But him finding a girl doesn't give him the right to come for me about my feelings when he never gave a fuck before. He did that shit trying to entertain Cyrus, all the while too dumb to see Cyrus about to risk it all for his girl. I'm the only loyal nigga in this family besides Kaliah, and I'll dare them to prove that shit if they deny it. I get pissed off thinking about Maya.

#

We were waiting for the last bell of the day to ring starting summer break. I was in the seventh grade and happy the year was over. I planned to ask Maya to go to the movies. I managed to save a little cash mowing the lawn and raking the leaves. Hakim only let G.D. and Sophie spend the money back then. They put it away until he had a way to make more. I wasn't allowed to get shit unless I worked for it.

Maya was sitting in front but moved to an empty desk behind me when Ms. Scott wasn't looking. I was so bored I pretended to be sleeping. Maya giggled as I quietly snored under my breath. Her laugh was like a high squeak or a stuttering chipmunk. It made me smile every time I heard it. She leaned forward and pulled my braids, and my head whizzed around. She was smiling up at me with her sweet face. I rolled my eyes, giving her a warning not to do that shit again, but I liked it.

I leaned down, pretending to be listening to Ms. Scott as she glanced up from reading, noticing me. Maya started playing with my hair again. I moved my leg and scratched my chin because she was making me excited.

"Shamaya, stop that shit!" I mumbled through my teeth, blushing as Ms. Scott looked back at her papers.

"Liiiiionel," Maya sang to my ear. "I need to talk to you."

I slouched down in my seat while Ms. Scott glanced back at me. I frowned at her nosey ass. She set her papers down just in time to catch the bell. I grabbed my backpack and slid out of my seat. When I turned around, Shamaya was there.

"What up, Maya?" I asked, trying to remain icy.

"Can I walk with you as far as the bus stop? I want to talk to you about something important," She asked beautifully.

"Yeah," I replied, nervously thinking she might try something different than hitting me in the nuts if I touched her. I was happy as hell when she took my hand and walked with me. "So, you going to be busy tomorrow? I know your mama don't like to let you out the house much since J-Rock ain't around."

Maya pulled herself ahead of me, moving out to the street. She walked in front of me, and I wasn't mad watching her strut. Her ponytails had cute little curls today and danced on her shoulders as Maya marched. She stopped nearby the bus stop and waited for me.

Usually, we rode the bus together, but I saw her looking toward a black car parked back by the steps. I heard the horn, and she waved to them. Maya grabbed me, and my hands got sweaty as she stared up at me, happy.

"Lionel, have you ever wanted a girlfriend?" She asked, moving next to me clutching my hand. I wasn't that tall back then.

"No, but I ain't a virgin if that's what you want to ask next," I lied about to talk shit.

Maya shut her eyes, listening to me, then threw her arms over my neck, paralyzing me! She never got that close to me without hitting me in the stomach for talking too much. I remember her hair smelled sweet, resembling something tropical, and it was the first time Shamaya held me like a girl and not just a friend. I dropped my bag as she ran her tiny fingers over my braids, and she kissed me.

I wanted to hold her too, but I knew she would run by how fast she was going. I shut my eyes for only a second enjoying her soft lips on mine. When I opened my eyes,

Maya's smile told me that I could have been her man all along, and I felt so stupid.

"We've been friends a long time, Lemonhead, but you seem mad like Hakim. I think if you had a girlfriend, you'd stop worrying about him and be happy. I wish you liked me the way I like you," Maya breathed, stroking my hair again with the saddest expression I had ever seen. It fucked me up. Maya was always happy no matter what she was doing. She even smiled when she fought niggas. That was the first time I saw her cry, and I lost all my shit.

"Maya, you make me laugh, and I think you're sweet. I don't know how- Girls don't like fu-," I started as she covered my lips with her hand. Maya gave me an envelope and grabbed her bag from the sidewalk.

"It's okay, Lionel," She assured me as her pretty smile returned. But I didn't feel better, though I was trying to tell her how I felt. I needed Shamaya to feel normal. Maya had no idea that she was the only person I trusted, and I would do anything for her. But I was scared because I knew James would fuck me up if I ever hurt Maya, and I couldn't bring myself to ever piss her off. Maya was the only girl that kicked my ass, and I didn't fight her back. She had her reasons for putting her hands on me. I knew I took shit too far if Maya swung on me. I guess I always knew how she felt about me, but I didn't want to look soft, saying she was mine in front of everyone. We were too young, and I wasn't going to fuck off the best thing that happened to me since we moved here. I always believed Maya would always be there, and we'd grow up together. "I wanted you to know that I think that you're a sweet, shy, and cute guy deep down. I like the mad boy that likes to fight and the nice one that lets me braid his pretty hair. I wish I could stay with you all and see how you change. I'm being put with my granny in Virginia until things get better with Mama. With James in jail and Aunt Key-Key long gone, I don't have a choice, or I'll be taken by the state. My brother knew this was gonna happen, and it's my fault he's gone."

"Maya…what happened? Why didn't you say something about how fucked up it was if it was that bad? Hakim has money. You know he wouldn't let this shit happen if you said something!" I groaned, about to cry, seeing her wipe her pretty sad eyes. "It ain't your fault, no matter what you believe. You always do the right shit. You're smart. I could have-"

Shamaya ran her fingertips across my lips, making me smile, and quickly took my picture with her camera. I was going to tell her how I felt, but she ran away. Maya was always taking pictures back when we were kids. Now I knew why. She was keeping all the memories of us together. Maya ran back to that black car and dove in, and she didn't look back. I wanted to chase her, but it felt like my legs were glued to the ground.

The second Shamaya Renee Lockhart was in that car, it was as if the lights got turned off, and it didn't matter what I did. I blinked when I realized the car was gone, and I was still standing at the bus stop alone. The bus was long gone, and I didn't know how long I had been standing there. My chest was burning, and it started to hurt as I took a breath. The more I struggled to breathe, the more the tears fell, and I was so mad I tried to walk home, knowing I couldn't make it. But I didn't care anymore. I wanted to go home and talk to my Grandma. Granny Sophie would make me feel better.

Jamire's brother, Lester Woods, saw me walking and offered me a ride home.

"Lionel, why you looking so fucked up, Nigga? Get in!" He yelled at me so loud his ass turned red. Lester was Jamire's older brother, but he was white and had a different mother than Jamie. Jamire and I were always playing together, so Lester was my boy too. But Lester was running hos for paper and in the trap houses all over the place making money. He didn't let people get close, but he liked all of us for some reason. "Lionel, Bro, it's gonna be alright. Here, man, give me a call if you want to come chill or whatever. Shit, we can go get fucked up or something. You out here looking like Hakim said he gonna fuck you up when you get home. Is that why you walking slow and shit? You want me to scare the shit out of him with my gun again?"

"Thanks, Les," I replied as he stopped at the house. "I ain't mad at Hakim. I fucked up this time."

"What's up, man? Don't tell me May-May got took away from her Mama now J-Rock's on lockdown? Sylvia fucked up. Damn! Angela mentioned that May-May was gonna have to get out of there a while back when Key-Key was still around. You know that bitch was beating the shit out of Maya, and she was fucking James. He kept getting away from her, and Key-Key was holding his sister hostage so he'd come back. Bitch was evil, but she made me a lot of money, so fuck it!

'You're kids, Man! Love is a fucking practical joke that everyone knows how it ends but keeps going along with that shit, thinking the punchline will be different. Nope! Once you have a kid, all that love shit goes out the window, and you just got a girl that wants her life back while you try to guess what will make her happy. You are better off staying single and fucking these hos with no feelings. They don't know what the fuck they're doing, and none of these hos really want love. Give em some dick and keep your money until you're ready to go down with the ship. Or even better, find you a bitch with her own paper and let her fuck and pay you like James was doing. He didn't mind getting down to get some cash."

I couldn't believe all the shit Les knew about James and Shamaya's peeps. Maya never told me any of it, and I realized that I wasn't a good friend to either of them, and it fucked me up worse. I got out of Lester's truck and went inside the house. No one was home yet, and I was alone. I wanted to talk to somebody. I found Maya's note when I threw my bag on the bed. She had made the envelope herself out of her stationery and drawn candy and ice creams on the front. But on the back where it opened, she wrote both our names and drew a heart around it. My fingers wouldn't steady as I opened it to read:

"Lionel, you're the funniest, cutest, and freshest friend I've ever had. I'm so happy to know you. I'm sorry we couldn't talk about our feelings. My grandmother would never let me have a boyfriend. But with all your pictures, I feel like I'll always have you with me. One day…I'm going to see you again.

'But until that day comes, I hope this reminds you of me and the time we had together. Don't forget me! I'll never forget you, Lionel Eugene Dunn. You're my best friend, and no one will take your place, never….." Maya.

Behind Maya's letter, underneath the fold, was a picture of us together in Home Economics class. I remember Mr. Owens took the photo because Maya poured flour over me for rubbing her leg. She laughed, but she still threw the bowl over my head, and I looked like a damn ghost! The whole class thought that shit was funny, and I laughed because Maya didn't hit me.

Someone opened the front door downstairs, and I was so upset I locked myself in the bathroom and cried looking at the picture. I searched everywhere for Shamaya. Her mom was no help because she was too far gone. People talked about Maya a lot once she was gone. They said her mother tried to sell her for rocks. I heard she tried to run away once James was gone, and that's when her grandmother showed up. We never knew any of their family besides Key-Key. She was just a ho begging for money and trying to get the attention of any nigga she thought had money. If only Hakim or Kaliah had known. Kaliah would never have let that shit happen. He was crazy about Maya and James, but Hakim didn't want Kaliah around when all this happened.

If I talked to Maya again, I promised myself to tell her how much I loved her. I didn't care how long it took, two years or twenty…. I had to let her know she had my heart, and if she wanted to keep it, I didn't want it back. If Maya still loved me, I'm marrying her and making her happy because she made all the fucked up shit seem normal. All she had to do was smile, play with my hair or chill. Her presence was missed the instant she was gone. She gave me a vibe that no other girl could touch. So no other girl was worth more than a fuck to give.

So, I was mad, but I was lucky, too. I know my brother never had that kind of shit with a girl before. So I was happy because Mandisa is a sad, hurt, pretty girl like Maya. She didn't ask for her fucked up life, but she kept trying to make the best out of it. I understand how a nigga can get in his feelings over a good girl, but I can't give my time to a ho or a bitch. Hakim's lucky as hell because Mandisa was perfect from the beginning, and she keeps getting better. He's only known her for one day, and he's talking about getting married! Well, Hakim has always been over the top, spontaneous, and he's got an ego the size of Texas. He loves Mandisa, for sure, but I think the only reason he finally gives a damn is that he knows she's so fine every nigga will want her.

But Hakim tries to play conscious King, talking about elevating her and keeping up. Shit, Hakim thinks he's better than everyone, so Hakim's using her to generate the hate he likes to pretend he doesn't crave. I know my brother, Cyrus, Kaliah, and most people better than they know themselves because I'm not back-peddling about who I am. I just watch them lie to everyone else while they guess about what they think they see. I play stupid, crazy, and act like I don't give a fuck because nobody around me really gives a fuck, so I'm not gonna go out of my way to tell anyone shit until they piss me off since they really don't care. They just get their rocks off feeling intelligent and righteous trying to lead me somewhere. I ain't going with them acting like bitches. If you awake, then you don't fuck around like Hakim and Cyrus.

Kaliah's the only woke brother I got. Hakim's faking the funk for attention. Cyrus is bright but trying to be evolved and still missing the damn boat because he ain't doing shit, either. Cyrus has never picked up a book and read shit. He listens to Hakim and Kaliah talk and runs with it. At least Hakim has a plan for his life. He's saving his paper, going to college, and sticking to it. But he's so stingy and manipulating when it comes to being honest about his side ventures. I know my brother did some dirt, and I've been trying to uncover it. Cyrus and Kaliah know but won't say shit. Making all this money turned my family into a bunch of confused clowns. But at least now, Hakim is spending some of it on me.

I don't know what I want to do, and I don't even care right now. If Maya ain't in my life, then I don't give a fuck what they do as long as they stay off of me.

"$1307.56 is your total, Sir," The clerk said, smiling at me as I handed her Hakim's credit card. She ran it, handing it back, and the white girl looked me over. "You look like you lost your best friend."

"Maybe I did," I said, taking the card and snatching the bags.

I stood by the store entrance waiting for Hakim and Cyrus. I needed a cigarette so bad. But I lost my train of thought as a group of girls walked by the store and noticed me there. Two of the four girls were staring at me.

"Sup?" I said, nodding as they stopped.

"Look at all that hair!" One of the sisters laughed, eyeing my ponytail down my back. "Are you gay?"

"Hell, naw, ain't nobody gay over here!" I laughed, frowning as the same girl looked closer at my hair. Her cute chocolate friend was who I was curious about. Now, when I saw brown girls with long hair, all I could think about was Maya. If a girl had Shamaya's features, I was down to see if she was real, but most were on some bullshit. No girl was like Maya, even if she kind of reminded me of my girl. "Hey, come talk to me, Chocolate Star. I'm trying to see if you can give me the munchies like Bootsy Collins?"

Cocoa shook her head, acting shy, and I smiled, glancing at her and scratching my chin. The girl looking at my hair was smiling at me. At the same time, the two older girls were talking to themselves but watching.

"It's so soft, long, and thick," The light-skinned sister looking at my hair, laughed, telling her friends. She was hypnotized playing with it. My hair had the same effect on most people. They saw it, thought my hair was fake, or believed me a girl until they saw my beard, then they assumed I was gay. Cyrus got the same response once his locks got so long. Niggas always think a brother that grows his hair longer is checking for their asses. I think it's the other way around because most men love women with long-ass hair. So, they are just sexually confused about what they are seeing and what they want. I know I don't need no more dick in my life than I got, and I don't need a nigga trying to touch it. I want a woman, and if a man tries to touch me, I might mess him up depending on my mood.

I don't like gay men that try to take shit from me. It's happened before, and I had to fight a big nigga off of me in a club. He thought he could take me because of his size. I knocked his teeth out of his face and left him with the transgender home girl he was using to pull young boys in. A nigga named Sweets that lived in the hood turned out young niggas and tried to pay them to fuck for money. That nigga

Ace from Hot Wheels worked for Sweets before he got locked up. That's how I knew he needed a beating. He was serious about fucking me if given a chance! Hell to the no! I'm not going to fuck no dudes, and If I'm getting paid to swing my pipe, I want all my money for every pump I kick at a bitch.

"I got something else that's long and thick, but it won't stay soft for long if you keep playing in my hair with your fine ass," I flirted, tilting my head and grinning at her. "You scared?"

"Scared of who, you?" Chocolate Star asked, giggling, keeping her distance.

She was too cute with her long straight hair, brown skin, pretty light brown eyes, and she dressed like she was one of those girls from a Cheer Team. They all had matching tops and shoes, but she wore short pink hot pants, and I could see her sexy brown thighs and wanted to touch those legs.

"Yeah, why you standing way over there? You want me to come over and talk to you alone?" I asked, taking a step closer. She stood there watching me for a moment as I leaned closer, pouting my lips at her and raising my eyebrow. "I love melanated sisters with their own hair and style, Girl. I won't bite unless you like that shit. Then you can call me Jaws because I'll dive in that water and eat your ass whole."

"You've got some swag, but all that hair makes you look like a fag," Chocolate Star tried to roast me! She giggled at the two older girls watching and walked away.

"Brianna! You're so immature!" Her friend that loved my hair called, but that girl was too busy being stuck up to hear. "Sorry, Bria is a bitch sometimes…no…all the time."

I wasn't paying attention to the nice girl because I was watching Brown Bria, but I suddenly noticed her when she stood up for me. She had spunk. She was cute too. This one was tall, thick with hips, brown-skinned, with glasses, and had her hair braided up in a bun.

"I'm Emma, that's Tiyanna, and Jazzy…you've met Brianna. They're my sisters," Emma told me with a pretty smile. When she smiled, she was even cuter with that mole on her chin. She was in love with my crown, and I wasn't mad at her sweet ass. "I love hair. I want to be a hairdresser."

"Must be my lucky day. I don't come here often, but today I met three cute sisters. I need to come to the mall more," I flirted with her, smiling.

Emma was all smiles as her other sisters came closer, looking at my hair with her.

"Where are you from?" Tiyanna, the other red-bone with Emma, asked. She was cute like Mandisa with her green eyes and brown curls, but too skinny and short.

"I'm from Atlanta, Georgia, but I stay in Longview," I told her, looking down at Emma's hips.

"I'm from Longview! I go to L.H.S. Why haven't I seen you before?" Emma asked, blushing.

"I go to Carver. L.H.S. is crazy! I've heard stories," I laughed, vibing with Emma.

"Whatever, Nigga. School is school. I can't wait to graduate. So you go to Hot Wheels?" Emma laughed, trying to get the business. I was feeling generous today suddenly.

"Oh hell, yeah! I'll go gliding sometimes. Maybe we can slip and slide together sometime?" I asked Emma messing with her glasses.

"Mhm..." Brianna grunted. I ignored her stuck-up ass and turned my attention to Emma.

"Maybe; what's your name, cutie?" Emma giggled, giving me that adorable smile. I wasn't looking for a girl, but Emma gave me the feeling she was feeling a nigga. She liked my swag, and I wanted her to smile. It reminded me of Maya looking at those adorable high cheeks and pretty teeth.

"Lionel Dunn," I told her, playing with her micro braids in her bun. I love messing with girls just to get them laughing when they're cute. I love the hair too, and my mama had natural hair. It didn't matter to me what a girl did to her hair as long as she wasn't gluing that shit in. I wondered if Emma wanted to braid my hair? "You know how to braid, Emma-Pie?"

"Wait?!" Tiyanna's ass yelled at me. "Dunn, from Longview? You have a brother?"

"Yeah, Hakim, why?" I asked curiously.

"He's kind of tall, has long dreadlocks to his shoulders, sexy, kind of looks like Trey Songz but no beard, and built like a brick wall?" Brianna added, coming closer looking at my face. Tiyanna looked me over, folded her arms, and seemed upset. "Oh my fuckin' God!"

"Your brother used to come to the club where I work. He used to try to collar my sister, Nicole, but she ran from him. He fucked her, and she went crazy. Nicole went to college, quit dancing, and he's all she talked about for about six months!" Jazzy groaned, shaking her short Indian braids. "I saw him fuck her...He's a beast! I know why Nikki ran...Every girl he fucks falls in love if they take his money. He's got a nasty mouth too. I heard the shit he said to Nikki, and I liked it."

"So what, you the Hakim Dunn Fan Club or something?" I laughed, already knowing that shit.

"No, Nicole talked about Hakim so much that we've been trying to see him in person. Is he here?" Emma asked me, folding her arms and smiling at Tiyanna for some reason. The vibe changed immediately, and suddenly that shit didn't seem right. "Hakim paid Nicole's college tuition after he did some crazy shit to her."

"Oh yeah?" I laughed, covering my mouth, unable to believe that shit! I looked back, spotting Hakim and Cyrus heading over. "Oh, there go Hakim right there! Why don't you say hi, Tiyanna? You must know him if you not saying nothing."

One look at my brothers, and all those girls were giggling and huddled up, moving back. The fuck was that about? Hakim alright, but he ain't that fine. He got muscles, his hair tight, and he got a babyface, but he was short, and Hakim's ego was a turn-off.

"Ase, Ladies," Cyrus said, grinning at each of them. The girls stared up at Cyrus, stunned, and Emma looked like she was gonna die."You look lovely in your matching school spirit."

"Some friends of yours, Lionel?" Hakim asked, looking around at each girl. Suddenly, Hakim raised his right eyebrow, and Cyrus moved over next to me. Cyrus looked at Tiyanna and frowned at me.

"No, we just met," I told Hakim, grinning, seeing something about to happen. "Tiyanna, Emma, and her sisters say they know Nicole…Do you know a girl named Nicole that goes to college, Hakim?"

Hakim looked at the girls, and his eyes glanced over each of them for a second and said, "I know a lot of girls in college, Lionel. I paid for them to go—my way of supporting the future goddesses of tomorrow. I can't say I remember Nicole. But if she's from here and is in college and started out a dancer…I probably helped her aim higher than the strip club ceiling for a contract or game. There's no love involved in that shit…It's just a game I play when I'm bored with my money.

'No bullshittin,' really. Everything was consensual, and I got the contracts and collars as proof. But honestly…too much paperwork to go through to remember one girl.

'Sorry, Ladies, If you're looking for a collar, I'm out of the game. I got a real Goddess, and I'm not interested in slaves anymore. Just pretend you didn't see me so you can sleep tonight, alright?"

Hakim glanced at Cyrus with a weird grin, and Cyrus shook his head. Hakim started off to get Mandisa, I guess.

But he was not talking to those girls. He was gone and not waiting to hear shit anyone had to say. It was like he turned into a nigga that had no time for shit but what he wanted. He wasn't even ashamed about what he confessed in front of me.

That wasn't what got me tripping. That girl, Tiyanna, tried to go after Hakim. Cyrus shook his head and said, "Lionel, prepare yourself. Don't say shit to Hakim until he is smiling again. He is very pissed off."

"The fuck you want, Bitch? I know you aren't deaf! I said the fucking game is over! Step!" Hakim yelled at Tiyanna when she grabbed his arm. Hakim reached back like he was gonna swing at her and froze! His eyes were so open that they scared me. Tiyanna backed up but was smiling and waiting for Hakim to hit her! Hakim shook his head and pulled back. "You almost tricked me, Bitch...I knew you wanted it when I saw your hungry eyes. You forgot that I don't give a fuck what you want! I said, STEP!"

That didn't sound like Hakim. That nigga was really gonna hit her! What I didn't get was why the fuck did all the girls think that shit was sexy? All their faces were locked on my brother as he walked away. Tiyanna came back over to us and looked up at Cyrus. She had tears in her eyes and asked, "He's seriously done, Cyrus?"

"You heard him, Yana. He said he was done last year and hasn't gone back, so I think he's serious. He LOVES her," Cyrus told Tiyanna. "He's really in love with her."

"What? ELYEUH doesn't...." Tiyanna cried, and Cyrus backed up.

Cyrus motioned me to move around quickly. Tiyanna grabbed Cyrus's shirt sleeve, and he smiled and said, "I don't know what to tell you. You signed it, and it's over. You all knew what it was with Hakim, and he told you what he wanted. I don't take ownership of nobody. He's my friend, and I just made sure he was safe in his little games. I don't fuck around like that, but you take care. Sorry, Ladies, slavery is over for Hakim. Lionel, let's bounce, now!"

#

"Lionel, what the fuck are you thinking? There is no way that you didn't see that shit coming. He was already pissed off about the dressing room, and then that shit?" Cyrus groaned, dragging me into a hallway. "What are you doing?"

"I WAS trying to get a number, Nigga. Hakim's name came up, and those girls all turned into straight TRL groupies. I didn't know that shit was gonna happen. I had a feeling something was up. Everywhere I go, somebody talking about Hakim. What the fuck is he doing, beating on bitches for fun?" I replied, looking around. Shit, Hakim looked mad enough to murder a bitch, so I know he'd fuck me up if I said any shit to him. "How she know your name, Cyrus?"

"Didn't you see her face, Lionel? Hakim hasn't hurt her in any way that she didn't want. She's heartbroken that he doesn't need HER anymore. That's his little secret. When he wants sex Hakim plays with girls' affections for money, and they know they can't make him love them, but they try.

'Some quit, most keep trying, but Hakim is picky, and if he doesn't want to play, they get mad. He cuts them all off, and then they try to find them. He's been doing this shit since we were kids. He doesn't lie to them, but they try because they want to be the one to wear the crown and not a collar. I know what Hakim did because it was my thing to help find the girls that Hakim liked. We got to fuck many fine women, but Hakim takes things to a level I can't go. He's disrespectful, and he will hit them, but only if they ask to be hit. Hakim's sexual addiction is dangerous, Bro. He's been with so many; I don't know. I wasn't always around. I only know the ones I've met or any that came looking for me to find him.

'Hakim is lying about Nicole. He remembers her….she's the one that got away. She broke the contract after she got the money and ran for it. Hakim respects her for doing what the others won't. The game is a mind control thing for

Hakim. He controls them until he gets bored, hoping they'll realize Hakim isn't going to love them if they don't run…He runs from the game.

'When Nicole ran, showing him that she never wanted him, just the money…It fucked up his ego, and he quit. Now he's in love with Mandisa, and this shit happens everywhere. Hakim's scared she's going to run like Nicole. Hakim doesn't love Nicole, but he respects a woman that knows what she wants and will ignore him. He wants Mandisa more than anything, and he quit the game and is serious now that he has her. I believe he's done. But you just have to understand that your older brother has some serious shit going on, and he doesn't like to talk about that shit. I keep my mouth shut, but you're old enough to know how fucked up it is being me for once! I know you know how I feel about Mandisa, but I would never hurt Hakim.

'Too many blows to the ego fuck him up, and he starts drinking a lot, then the drugs. Then you don't want to be around him or hear shit that comes out of his mouth. He's not my friend when he's low like that. You want to front him out and get revenge, but you have no idea what monster you're going to get once Hakim stops responding to Hakim and calling everyone a bitch. Trust me, Lionel, you can't win a fight against him when he's furious. As long as Hakim's running, training, meditating, or not fucking…He's good. But if he feels the itch…then Hakim has to move around."

"The fuck you say? Just because he been with a lot doesn't mean he addicted." I laughed. "Hakim's just a bitch ass nigga that can't handle rejection!"

"You don't get it, Lionel! Nicole is the only one in too many to count that actually took the money and ran. Any girl that Hakim wanted, he fucked, and he let them go. All I could do was watch them all fall for the game, take the money, and wonder why.

'You finally will get it once a girl you really love falls for the game, and he fucks her crazy too, then tosses her. Every One Of them talks to you about him, comparing you to him, then laughing at you behind your back.

'You might be lucky May-May isn't around. He'd have fucked her cute ass, and you'd hate him. Think about it," Cyrus sighed and took off to find Hakim.

This sounds like some perverted slavery BDSM shit. This ain't 50 Shades of Hakim! What kind of games is my brother playing, making all these bitches crazy? If he is fucking girls' brains out, then he doesn't need to touch Mandisa. She might kill herself!

Aww, hell naw! I think I get why Cyrus is just keeping close. If Hakim is that crazy…aw shit! I need to find time to talk to Mami and Mandisa alone. This couldn't end well if Hakim gets bored. What if all those girls find out who Mandisa is and come for her? She's too sweet for this shit, man. This is what my brother was doing with his money in secret? He was playing Captain Save-A-Hoe, using Cyrus to pull them, and talking shit to everyone else? He's got Cyrus playing Charlie Murphy to his Rick James? Damn, they should have never gave this nigga money!

Chapter Nine: Loving (U) Is Complicated

Mandisa

My nails were nearly dry as I admired Mr. Lee's work. He smiled at me through his glasses and nodded, saying, "You love the colors, Queen?"

I giggled at Mr. Lee agreeing. Darius told Mr. Lee that he was to address me as Queen, and he took it literally. Mr. Lee had drawn a gorgeous dark galaxy on my nails with a golden sun. There was a shimmering pink aura beneath the sun's black shadow because of the blended colors I loved.

"They look so realistic," I replied as he checked my toenails. The golden flakes on the black foil looked beautiful. Darius demanded that my toes have gold somewhere. Mr. Lee said the man that pays had the final word. I did not care. I had not had my nails done in months. My friend in Philidelphia styled my hair, did my nails, and we tried on all the clothes we could find in Mami's old closets. I began to miss my sweet friend. Instinctively, I nearly ruined Mr. Lee's hard work reaching to get my phone. "So close…What am I doing…?"

I hadn't talked to her since her number was disconnected in Spring. When I missed her, I would dial her number, hoping that she would answer. I needed to stop that habit.

"You about dry, Queen?" Hakim asked, coming into the shop and looking around. Hakim came over and knelt down next to me, looking at my hands and feet. I smiled down at him as he looked up and smiled beautifully. "They look beautiful...You're so beautiful, Queen. You know I'm serious when I say I love you, right?"

I blushed as Mr. Lee stood up and gave us some space. He had the silliest look on his face after hearing Hakim talk to me.

"Hakim?" I sighed to him as he ran his hand over my jeans. His face was so soft as he looked up at me but began to stroke my thigh with his fingertips. He chuckled to himself and put his lips to my knee. "What are you doing?"

"Cyrus isn't the only brother that thinks you have beautiful feet. Everything about you is perfect to me, Mandisa. I want to worship every part of you and make you happy until the day I die. Do you believe me?" Hakim begged me, getting up to his feet but taking my hands carefully. "I don't want to mess up your fingers. I just need you to feel me, Queen. I'm so serious about the way I feel about you."

"I believe you love me, Hakim. I love you, too, and I am so very blessed that we met. I have never had such a wonderful time just doing things normal people do. You are a perfect boyfriend to keep me smiling, so I do not imagine the bad," I replied, stroking his cheek so he would relax. He suddenly became so tense holding my hands. "Is something bothering you?"

Hakim bit into his bottom lip, and I stirred his eyebrow. He closed his eyes and stated, "Mandisa, I can't lie to you about my past anymore. Things keep coming up that I thought would be buried, and I don't want you to believe that I'm the person I used to be."

"What are you talking about, Hakim? Everyone has a past and secrets. Look at mine? I have lived my life like an animal inside a cage poked at and put on display. I have issues, and I know this, but I do not ask any of you to do anything more than be my friend," I explained, pulling him closer for a hug.

Hakim pulled away from me and said, "No, Queen, I understand your issues because of your father and family situation. But I have no right to ask you to love me when you don't know anything about me. People talk, and I'm known for the way I treat women...I used to treat women...before I calmed down a year ago."

"I'm confused, Hakim. What do you mean? You said that you never had a girlfriend, and you messed around, but nothing serious. Do you have kids or something like that? I don't think I could-," I began.

"I have a terrible sexual addiction and a history of mental illness, Queen," Hakim confessed, looking only at my nails. "Can we find somewhere to sit down and talk? Things have started bugging me, and I don't want to flip out in a store."

"Okay," I replied as he hauled me out of the nail salon.

#

Hakim and I met up with everyone else, and we sat down in an empty restaurant. Lionel and Darius were quiet while Hakim tried to relax to talk. He was unhappy and looked woeful, not wanting to make eye contact with anyone.

"I'm gonna order some food while you make up your mind. We haven't eaten since we left Longview! I'm so hungry I'll eat some pussy!" Lionel groaned, grabbing the menu from near Hakim's hand. Hakim's eyes locked on Lionel, and Hakim scowled. Darius snatched a menu and nodded to Hakim. Hakim moved, stood up, and walked away quietly. "Damn! Hakim looks like he's gonna sprint through a wall. That bitch pissed him off like that?"

"Lionel!" Darius grumbled, looking at the menu. "Everyone order something, and you, shut the fuck up!

Queen, let him tell you the real. Your nails look beautiful, by the way."

"Merci for getting them done, Darius. You know what Hakim is talking about?" I fretted as Darius lifted his eyebrows and stroked his chin.

"Worth every penny! Don't mind Hakim. He's upset about some bullshit that comes with the territory. I can fix him, but he's gonna need some weed soon to relax. His anxiety is high with so many people around, and he hates being touched when angry. I was amazed to see him let you hold his hand when clearly Hakim is so furious he wants to run," Darius said with a charismatic smile, glancing at the menu. "Order something to eat, Queen. It's my treat. We're going to need to hit the road after this shit."

He winked at me and tapped his pocket on his black St. Laurant shirt, where he had a blunt. Lionel looked at Darius and bobbed with a smirk, saying, "The ultimate cure-all if that's Kaliah's shit!"

"Most definitely, Baby Brother, roll wit yah boy, Cyrus. I know how to get Hakim back elevated," Darius chuckled. He glanced up a moment and smiled. "Can you please fix your face, Nigga? You have Mandisa and Lionel thinking you're going to redecorate an IHOP."

I hadn't seen Hakim standing behind me as I looked back. Hakim stared at Darius for a moment and looked at me, saying, "I'm sorry, Queen. I've been good for so long. I thought shit was fine. It'll be fine once I get to the truck. Cyrus always has the medicine with him when we roll together. He's always known what was up. I'm gonna sit down and eat. Then we'll talk in the car on the way home. I just want to enjoy the rest of the trip. I've fucked up a really great day with my shit."

"That sounds like my brother," Darius said with a smile. Hakim sat next to me and looked across at Lionel hesitantly. Darius pushed to menu toward Hakim's hand, distracting him from Lionel. Hakim peered at the menu a moment. "Get some pancakes with blueberries, a cup of orange juice, and chicken wings as always."

"Right..." Hakim chuckled, ultimately relaxing and grinning. I saw that. I do not know what it was, but when Darius told Hakim what to eat, Hakim seemed lost as his eyes grew wide and sad. "What are you having, Queen?"

I didn't know what to say. I quickly looked at the menu and said, "I think I want the veggie omelet with spinach, mushroom, onions, and swiss cheese, and wheat toast."

"I think I want that. God, you are perfect for me!" Hakim chuckled, nodding to Darius. "What you going to get, Cyrus?

Don't tell me you going with the Double Bacon Burger as always?"

"Don't judge me, Prince Hakim. I enjoy sucking the grease from crispy swine, and you won't hate on my burger when it gets here, Nigga. Or I will order a side of grease and put it in your sweet tea!" Darius humorously groaned with a clearly fake insulted gaze.

"Ooh, a bacon burger with everything on it and extra bacon!" Lionel squealed, looking at Darius's choice.

I spun my eyes as Hakim teased my hand, stating quietly, "Don't tell them anything about eating right. It's like trying to sell ice to an Eskimo. I can pack away some food. Those two eat enough for 6 brothers…Watch this. (Hakim raising his voice). I might get the omelet and the chicken wings so I can have something crispy. I like having different textures in my mouth at once. My palate might be a bit more refined…We are at an IHOP."

"That's why you gotta get the onion rings, jalapeno slices, and everything, so you get the best of it all in one bite. Oooh…I can taste the cheese melting on that bacon. I'm drooling!" Lionel hollered. Darius gave Lionel a pound, and he gazed at me and began laughing. "You nasty, Cyrus!"

"Why are you having that fodder, Queen? Yes, men should watch their daily consumption of animal proteins and fats, but that doesn't mean you have to turn into a damn rabbit. Clearly, you aren't vegan, but I'm curious if there are spiritual beliefs behind your diet choices? Or are you still thinking about that bullshit M.O mentioned," Darius asked me with a severe glance? His face was so relaxed. It was so inversely handsome than his happy-boy face he always wore. I leered and wobbled my head, peering away from his lovely brown lips and twinkling eyes. "Do you believe you're fat, Mandisa?"

"I eat what is filling and does not make me feel sluggish. All that red meat is bad for you, and I have heart problems that I must take medication for, so why would I risk it?" I clarified.

"What?" Both Hakim and Darius demanded, hearing forward.

"Now you understand why Daddy was more possessive of me. My heart was defective at birth. I had many surgeries as a baby, and they said I would not live to be 13. Mami wants me to have a life and fun. Daddy wants me protected in case my heart stops. I take all these pills each day, and one I keep with me if I have Cardiac Arrest that goes under my tongue. Surprise. I'm dying…so I guess that no one else's secrets are worse than that…oui?" I told them.

"Oh, fuck me! No!" Hakim growled, putting his head on the table in frustration. "The painting!"

"She's going to jump because she doesn't want to wait all alone to die when her heart breaks on its own. Daddy's a Cardiologist, and there's been nothing he could do but wait for me to grow up to see if I survive long enough for a heart transplant. But things went so bad, I told Mami to just run with Amani! I don't care what happens to me…Amani cannot be like me! If her heart is like mine…Daddy will treat her so cruel, and it will kill Mami!" I sobbed, dropping my head.

"I don't care what's wrong with you. You're mine, and I'm not letting you go, Mandisa. Nothing is going to take you away from me! Nothing changes… Can we please talk about anything else?" Hakim cried, shaking in his seat.

"Fine! But this conversation isn't over," Darius sighed, wiping his face. "Fuck!"

Darius got up and walked to the men's room. Lionel chased him down after he touched my shoulder.

"So who is this bitch that got you all worked up?" I asked Hakim seriously.

Hakim gazed at me in shock and chuckled, "Oh yeah? Where did the attitude come from, Queen?"

"I only want you to tell me the truth and stop dodging the subject because Darius is around. He seems to know more than Lionel. I want to know why he seems afraid of you, but you are afraid of some random bitch?" I giggled, tilting my head smiling.

"Not here, Queen. I'm going to tell you everything when we're in the clear. I can't lie to you," Hakim promised.

"All of you are going to tell me everything," I giggled as I smiled at the waitress bringing our drink order.

"Whatever you want, Queen," Hakim replied with a smile, and his cheeks blushed deeply, growing round.

I sat quietly and watched those boys scarf down enough food to feed an army. I couldn't finish my omelet, and they were still ordering and eating food. Each time the waitress came back, she was running for refills or taking another order! I was so embarrassed by how much food was consumed. I never saw boys eat like that before, so I just smiled, blushed, and stared.

Darius ate the most. He ate two cheeseburgers, 3 orders of fries, onion rings, a salad, and a chocolate cake. Then he finished my fodder, checking to see if Hakim left anything. Lionel ate two burgers but got full. Hakim had two omelets, pancakes, wings, and had a milkshake. Okay, Hakim ate the most, but Darius was still trying to find something once he stopped ordering. That's why I gave him the crown.

I tried not to laugh at his sloppy table manners. He enjoyed his food too much and didn't mind making a mess. He had chocolate cake and icing on his shirt. Hakim was laughing as he tried to lick his shirt to get the last bit of chocolate. His tongue was out when he realized he was being watched.

"I might need a bowl of chili or something. I'm still hungry?" Darius groaned, glancing across again.

"What?!" I laughed, putting down my fork. "You cannot be serious, Darius?"

Darius moped down at me and said, "I'm sorry. I know I'm a pig, but the more I do, the hungrier I get. I burn carbs in my sleep. I have a very high metabolism because I don't eat red meat all the time. Only when I'm having fun around Lionel.

'Now I can pack away food like a garbage disposal. When I was young, I was a fat boy, so I had to learn how to keep eating like one and keep the weight off. That's why I asked about your diet."

"I've never seen anyone that can hang with Cyrus's table muscles. He should be a competitive eater. Hakim is close, but if he has breakfast, it's a wrap. I've seen Hakim eat enough to shut a chicken place down when he was training for track season. He runs for distance, so he packs in the food!" Lionel laughed, pushing Darius's shoulder.

"I'm six feet six inches tall, and I work out constantly, so I'm hungry!" Darius groaned. "I only have red meat on occasions, so when I get some, I want as much as I can have to satisfy me until the next taste. It's how I get through months of avoiding the sweets I crave. I'm a Chocoholic, Queen. How do you think I got this dark?"

"Big boys need more food, I guess," I giggled, avoiding looking at his smile. I loved Darius's dark skin tone. It reminded me of dark chocolate candy. He was just as sweet-tempered when he was joking with his friends."Growing boys gotta eat too, right?"

"Does pussy count as red meat?" Lionel wondered out of the blue, shocking me.

Hakim choked as his forehead slammed into the table, covering his mouth with his napkin, then excused himself. I blushed, trying not to laugh at Hakim's giggle fit.

"No, Nigga, pussy is a sweet fruit! It's a delicious gift from the highest," Darius laughed, rocking in his seat.

"What's it taste like? Some bitches fruit smells spoiled," Lionel asked Darius. "You say it's fruit...I think it's fishy."

"What?!" Darius asked Lionel, seriously looking him in the eye. "Nigga, all the girls I know you done fucked- I mean, sorry, Queen."

"It's fine," I reassured Darius as I rubbed my forehead, snickering at Hakim pacing behind the table. "What does it taste like?"

Both Lionel and Darius stared over at me thoughtfully. I took a sip from my straw and giggled nervously. Lionel's eyes got enormous as he smiled at me, declaring, "Damn, Sis, you trying to get down for the crown or somethin'?"

Hakim remained quiet, viewing Lionel teasing me. Darius waved his hand, acting like he was about to hit Lionel. Lionel, who was trapped in the booth, nearly hit the wall. Hakim covered his face laughing hysterically again. I covered my face laughing as he realized he couldn't run and shut up.

"Pussy is good, really good. But the flavor varies from queen to queen. The more you like her, the better it tastes and the sweeter. But it has to be clean. If it's foul, a nigga like me can't fuck with it.

'Like this girl I met. I thought she was so beautiful, and I took her out. But when she sat in my car, I kept smelling something. She lived in a dangerous neighborhood; therefore, I thought the air was foul because of a nearby plant. The air over the entire house was horrible.

'Come to find out that she didn't have running water. I went inside her house; dirty dishes were piled up, clothes everywhere, and no one had bathed in days. I felt so bad I gave the girl money to pay the bills. When I checked up on her, I learned she spent the money buying more clothes instead of paying the fucking water bill. Then she wanted to go out again and see if she could get more. I didn't want to fuck with her after the first date. I was just looking out for a sister that needed help. I left her alone because her priorities were fucked up if she'd rather step out in a pair of Jimmy Choo's than step into the tub."

I panicked as Lionel fell under the table and hit the floor. He was laughing so hard his head hit the tabletop while crying, "How you gonna buy Gucci when your house smells like dookie?!"

I covered my mouth as tears fell out of my eyes, watching Lionel rolling on the floor. Darius wasn't laughing at all. He took a sip out of his straw and shuddered.

"That's nothing," He exhaled, glowering. "I'm a good guy, and I'll give a sweet girl a chance. But some women have done some really nasty things I won't even say. They think that because another nigga likes it, I'm gonna do it too? Shhh, I dated a girl that always wanted to fool around on the rag, ugh!"

"Fuck, no!" Lionel shrieked, getting up. "You do that shit. It looks like a massacre took place! It's nasty!"

"Some men don't care as long as they can get some. They'll take it any way they can get it," Hakim thought, resting down in his seat and closing his hands on the table. I shivered the thought off; I'd never heard of such things before. Darius frowned, staring at the table. "How did you get on this subject?"

"Cyrus was telling his American Horror Stories! He's King Simp of this episode." Lionel laughed, hitting the table. "I just needed to know what pussy tasted like. Now, I'm frightened of pussy. I may never fuck a bitch again after that shit!"

"I've got a lot of stories. Women can be devious, but men are bad, too. I've heard niggas say some horrible shit. Some things are too nasty for virgin ears," Darius grumbled, lifting his eyebrows gazing into nowhere. "But you really want to know it all...Hakim's the Pussy Monster."

Darius stared at Hakim with the same dangerous expression from earlier, and Hakim gazed over at me and grinned half-heartedly.

"Why do you always cover what you up, Hakim? You don't lie, but you conceal the truth…it's the same shit," Lionel hooted, staring at his brother. "You acting good because Mandisa's here? She wanted to know too. I'm a mouth virgin like her, nigga, help us out! Cyrus says, you the Mouth Master?"

"Shut the fuck up, Lionel! You know you're not a virgin. You've been going hard since you were 13," Darius groaned.

"I ain't ate no pussy, so that makes my tongue a virgin! You scared to talk about sex, Hakim? You get quiet when the subject comes up. I had to learn from G.D. and Sophie you were fucking!" Lionel exclaimed, moving in Hakim's face across the table, laughing.

Hakim looked down at the floor as if he had dropped something and blushed like a little boy. He pretended that Lionel wasn't there and scratched his neck. A group of various people, maybe a church group, walked by our table, eyeing Lionel. Hakim waited until they went to sit, then grabbed his brother's shirt, pulling him down to the table.

"This really isn't the place to have THIS discussion, Lionel! You're too fucking loud, and whites are listening.

Act like you have some home training, idiot!" Hakim whispered, yelling and slapping Lionel's head.

Lionel leaned back in his seat, staring at Hakim. Hakim glanced at Darius, and Darius got up and left to the front with the ticket.

"I ain't dropping this shit, Hakim," Lionel stated, clutching his head with a huge scowl. "When we get to the truck, you gonna spill it, or I'ma tell Mandisa what I do know about your ass. Niggas talk too, and I've heard stories. So, either you tell me, or I tell her! You said that we were supposed to protect her, right?"

Hakim acted as if I heard anything about his past that I'd break up with him. How bad could it be compared to what I told him? I'd talked about sex before with people online. The internet was graphic on discussion boards about situations. I didn't care for pornography either, but I had seen movies. Most of the time, I was just curious.

Mami and I talked about sex vaguely. But I only wanted to know how it felt. It didn't mean because I had never been with someone physically, that I was ignorant. I didn't understand why people were so ashamed of their sexual behavior if it was natural. They all seemed so apologetic to talk about things. Well, Lionel, not so much embarrassed as flamboyant in his delivery.

"I know I bought a lot of gifts for you, Queen. But I wanted to get something as sweet as you to remind you how much this day meant to me. It's not anything crazy," Hakim told me as he stopped me about to get in the truck. Darius bumped into Hakim playfully, handing him something behind his back. I saw the box and giggled. "My bad, Queen. I suck at surprises."

Hakim offered me the opened box with the lovely heart-shaped cake covered in candied strawberries and cherries. Someone wrote, 'I love you, Queen.' In chocolate and whipped cream. It was so sweet and beautiful. I couldn't resist taking one of the cherries to taste it. They had a tart, crunchy shell covering the juicy cherry, and the flavor exploded like happiness inside my mouth biting down.

"Oh, Wow! That is so good it should be illegal. I'll eat it all," I giggled, wiping my lips.

"I'll pay you to eat it just to watch you make that face!" Darius moaned, pushing Hakim to get in the trunk. "I need to smoke after that shit! Claude, have mercy!"

"She swallowed that whole cherry like she got fired from the Sperm Bank for drinking on the job! Damn!" Lionel growled as he spotted Hakim gaping at him. "What would you do for a Klondike Bar, Mandisa?"

Hakim covered the cake and lept at Lionel. Lionel scampered, moving into the front seat. He shook his head and smiled, declaring, "You don't have to eat it all, Mandisa. Save it for later to share with Mami and Amani. I know she'll love the cherries as much as you. She might turn a cartwheel and make Mami go into labor....You eat the cherries...I don't think Amani's ready yet."

"That's so sweet, Hakim. Merci Beaucoup, Mon Cheri," I thanked him, watching him put it away. He reached for my hand and helped me sit in the backseat of Darius's truck. Hakim instead sat in the from since he agreed to drive back while Darius sat next to me. He sat forward and pushed the back of Hakim's shoulder. Hakim looked over at Lionel suddenly as Lionel turned around, smiling at me strangely.

"What, Lionel?" I asked, noticing him reaching down.

"You like Cyrus, don't you?" Lionel demanded, glaring at me.

"We're friends, Lionel. Stop being nasty," I replied, frowning.

"Yeah, yeah, say that shit! But I'm not stupid. You laugh at everything he says, plus you make sexy eyes at him all the time," Lionel snorted, reaching between the seat, grabbing my heel, and pulling my foot.

"Lionel, shut the hell up!" Darius yelled, taking off his jacket and setting it on the floor.

"Why you want to sit in the back with her, Cyrus?" Lionel questioned Darius, still swinging my foot by the heel of my shoe.

"To keep your filthy hands off of her while Hakim drives us home! After the shit, you pulled you think we trust you? You don't have any respect," Darius laughed, pushing his hair over his shoulder. Then slapping Lionel's hand.

"Exactly," Hakim agreed over at Lionel. "Look at you touching her without permission. Don't think I've forgotten about this morning, either. That shit wasn't cool, Bro!"

"She likes me, too, I can tell," Lionel laughed, sticking his index finger between my big toe and making lewd gestures with his face. "You like that, huh, Mandisa?"

Darius and Hakim slapped Lionel's head at the same time.

"Nigga, you're too young for her," Darius laughed, shaking his head.

"Age ain't nothing but a number, Nigga!" Lionel yelled, grasping his head smiling at me. Hakim glared at his brother for an instant, and Lionel bowed, facing forward.

"Thank you!" Hakim sighed, his face growing upset. "Don't make me drag your narrow ass out of this car and paint Dallas with your face, Lionel."

"Oh, so it's okay for Cyrus to spend on your bitch, but if I touch her, it's a fuckin' problem?" Lionel argued with Hakim angrily, and I glanced away.

I know my expression changed when Lionel called me that. No one had ever said that to me before, and I didn't know how to respond. I don't think Lionel meant it. He was angry at Hakim and Darius for picking at him so much. I figured out that Lionel lashes back furiously when they offend his pride. Hakim seemed to set Lionel off when someone said anything about him that he didn't know.

Hakim moved so suddenly I didn't see it until it happened. Lionel's head slammed against the passenger window, and his face fell forward into the dashboard. Darius stared at the both of them nervously and unbuckled his seatbelt. Hakim took off his seatbelt to get out of the truck. Darius leaped out and blocked Hakim.

"Hakim, he's stupid! He didn't mean that shit, Bro! Calm down," Darius said, grabbing Hakim's shoulder and yanking him back into the seat. Hakim's face was red, and he had a dark look in his eyes as he struggled with Darius trying to get to Lionel. The truck was rocking from the two of them, going back and forth. I covered my face as Darius slammed Hakim through the door and made him sit down. "You better apologize and make it fast, or I'm gonna let him go, Lionel. I told you to stop that shit!"

Hakim's face shot over to his brother, and Lionel spun back in tears. He held his red face and sighed, "I didn't mean that shit, Mandisa. I'm sorry, you're not a bitch, okay? I let my mouth fly before I think sometimes. My bad, forgive me?"

I nodded, understanding, "It's alright, okay. I know you didn't mean it."

There was so much tension in the silence as Darius looked over at me, and I stared at Lionel. Hakim gawked ahead, pondering.

"Is everyone okay now?" I asked, attempting to calm them down. "I'm fine. There are worse things to be called than a bitch."

"Fine, Queen," Hakim surrendered, grinding his teeth looking out the window, upset.

"Apologize, Hakim," I said, observing as he turned, glancing back at me.

"What?" Hakim demanded, frowning. His forehead rose as a look of shock appeared. "I'm not apologizing to him for that shit, Queen!"

"You hurt your brother, Hakim. Apologize to him!" I cried, raising my voice. Hakim's eyes glanced at me decisively and examined Lionel sulking. "If you don't tell him you are sorry, Hakim, I swear I will never forgive you."

I was weeping and disappointed. My voice was trembling. I hated the way they fought over such little things as words. Hakim reached back into the cooler and offered Lionel a bottle of water, saying, "I'm sorry for losing it, Bro. I wish you'd watch your mouth."

"I know, I'm a dick, but I didn't mean to say that. It was foul, and I'm really sorry," Lionel apologized, taking the water bottle and holding it to his jaw.

Darius stared at me and smiled. He nodded and patted my hands, telling me, "Don't do that, okay? They're sorry, so don't get upset, Queen. I've been trying to keep them off one other for years. It's a full-time job, Mandisa."

"You're family. There should not be so much anger between you. I could never hurt someone I love like that. I love Amani though she is not born because I've always wanted what you have and seem to hate. She's my little sister. I don't want her to be alone, sad, and afraid like me.

Even if you don't like it, you have each other at the end of the day. That is more than I had," I sighed, wiping my tears.

"It's okay," Darius comforted me with a smile. "I don't have a family, so I understand how you feel. That's why I'm always with these two. They make me feel needed. So, you never had any friends?"

"A few months ago, Mami and I ran away to stay with her mother in Philidelphia. That's where I met the only friend I ever had. She lived in the apartments across the street from Grandmother's house and was a few years younger than me. But we vibed from the first day. She was so mature for her age and had confidence around people. She went to school and worked at the same time. Mami loved her so much.

'We did everything together when she wasn't busy. She was always pushing me to try new things," I remembered growing sad again. "We lost touch when Daddy came for us. He took my phone and Mami got me another, but when I tried to call her....it's disconnected. I miss her calling me Beyonce and showing me the dances like the girls in the videos."

"I bet she's fine too!" Lionel groaned. "Fine girls always run in packs like sexy beasts!"

"She's the cutest thing I've ever seen," I replied, blushing. "Every time I'd tell her how cute she was, she would laugh at me. She thought that because she didn't have money like we did, she didn't matter. But Mami spoiled too. I told Mami I'm going to find her one day."

"Keep trying. You'll find your friend," Hakim said, starting the truck. "I know we'd love to meet her if she's as sweet as you."

"We're all here for you, Queen," Darius chuckled, unbuckling my shoe.

"Oh, no, you don't!" I snorted as he pulled the straps loose.

"Oh yes, I do!" Darius hooted, sliding off my shoe. "Look at these pretty colors. The golden flake over black looks hot! Good, Goddess!"

"Darius, no!" I screamed as he tore my foot into his lap. He tickled my feet, making me giggle as I tried to stop him.

"Cyrus, you are a freaky-ass, Nigga," Lionel cackled, watching Darius as he began to squeeze my feet. Hakim was chuckling, trying to drive and observe.

"She's smiling, isn't she?" Darius said sarcastically as he cuddled my foot smiling. "No woman can frown when you enjoy her feet. Look at this...."

Darius leaned forward and pressed his warm lips to my toes, kissing sweetly. My legs started to tremble as he flicked his tongue over the top of my foot, and I screamed so loud that Hakim's eyes shot wide open.

"Ooh, did you hear that shit?!" Hakim snorted. "I'm going for the feet next time!"

"I'm the Foot Master," Darius groaned as he ran his tongue beneath my toes and pulled them between his lips, and sucked.

I leaned back in the seat and moaned softly. Darius's mouth touching my skin and staring up into my eyes made everything go crazy inside me! I covered my eyes, blushing with embarrassment as my entire body shivered with excitement. My face flushed as I felt my heart thump loudly for a moment, and it got so hot between my thighs my knees buckled.

"Damn," Daris mumbled with a vicious grin watching me. "I think she likes it. Did you just cum?"

I gasped, not saying a word, holding my chest, and looked out the window. I felt so uncomfortable and embarrassed by losing it. My thighs were burning as I tried to pull my foot away, but Darius kept smiling and rubbing, refusing to let go.

"Oh shit!" Lionel chuckled, mocking me. "Cyrus, you made her bust a nut by sucking her toes?

Eww…Mandisa…your panties are probably wet now…huh?"

I shifted my weight, sat up, and pretended not to hear him still looking away.

"It's alright, Queen," Darius whispered, still caressing my feet. He leaned closer, lowering his voice. "You like it…I love it. I wasn't striving to do that, but I'll take the victory."

"Ugh, if I could be those blessed panties," Hakim breathed, peering at me in the rearview with glowing eyes. "I bet it's so sweet and sticky like hot buttery syrup."

"Oh my god!" I screamed as he winked at me and ran the tip of his tongue across his top lip slowly. Darius grinned, biting his bottom lip, watching my expression as I blushed. "You're so bad. Hakim, stop it."

"Damn it! I shouldn't have volunteered to drive," Hakim bellowed, trying to concentrate on the road. He leered to himself and turned over his eyes. "Don't be ashamed. You know you're sitting on a honey pot, Queen Bee. I'm just a drone trying to get a taste of that golden sunshine between those silky thighs…mmm…shit! Let me…calm down. It's been so long since I've had a taste."

"Hakim!" I screamed, laughing timidly. "STOP that!"

"Alright, I'm just talking. You know I can't reach you way up here, but if I was in Cyrus's seat…think of the trouble I could cause if I got you out of those sexy designer jeans. He's licking toes…I like licking…." Hakim groaned deeply. "Ice cream…"

"I'm not playing with you, Hakim," I giggled, staring out the window noticing the sky growing darker. "Weren't we supposed to be talking about you anyway, Hakim?"

"That's right!" Lionel cried, looking at his brother. "I ain't forgot shit, we on the subject now, and you can't run, Hakim."

"What do you want to know? If I feel like answering, I will. I'm apt now, so ask away, but if you go too far, I'm cutting the conversation short," Hakim warned Lionel but grinned strangely. Hakim's smile at Lionel was very fake. It was nothing like the smile Hakim customarily used.

"I'll know if you lie, Bro," Darius said, pulling Hakim's hair backward. Hakim's neck snapped forward, and he frowned.

"Nigga, stop that shit. I don't have to lie about anything. I just don't answer if it gets too personal," Hakim replied, eyeing at the road.

"How many girls you fucked, Hakim?" Lionel started. He went for the kill on the first shot! Lionel glanced over at Hakim and grinned, sticking out his tongue.

"Too many to count. Next question, please?" Hakim responded quickly.

"No, Naw, that's not good enough. Let's hear a number, Hakim. You're avoiding the answer," Lionel said, raising his eyebrows seriously looking upset.

I didn't care. It was before me, so why did it matter so much to anyone else? Hakim was with me! Why was he afraid to talk to me about these things? He wasn't telling Lionel, either, but Darius seemed uninterested in anything at the moment other than rubbing my feet. Darius was suddenly using much more pressure on the balls of my feet, listening to Hakim and Lionel with nervousness in his sad eyes.

"A number, Bro," Darius added, agreeing with Lionel making me pull my leg. He frowned and raised my foot back to his long leg. Darius gently traced my toe tips with his fingers quietly and motioned with his head toward Hakim.

"I don't fuckin know!" Hakim yelled suddenly. He frowned so severely that he looked like he was going to hurt someone. Hakim slammed his fist into Darius's dashboard. He gasped, suddenly looking over as Lionel flew against the window, thinking the worse. "I lost count after 70, but I used more than 1,320 condoms a year before last. I kept the fucking receipts just to be nosey. I did a lot of fucking just trying to feel something other than anger."

Lionel glanced over at Darius, and Darius nodded. Hakim's eyes met mine, and I could see the growing shame in the rearview. I attempted to smile at him and bowed. He didn't seem convinced that I was all right.

"Damn, Hakim! You were that busy?" Lionel asked, amazed.

"I have been clinically diagnosed by several Psychiatrists as having a sporadic condition that we can't pinpoint the origins, but it has the symptoms of PTSD, OCD, Schizophrenia, and Bi-Polar Disorder. Sexual addiction was derived once puberty set in, but I was at it before then. The problem is that when I have extreme emotional swings...

'All my reasoning goes out the window, and I feel like a kid again, unable to control my actions, thoughts, or words. I've taken meds to control the urges that trigger me, but when I feel upset, angry, or someone dies....I can't remember what I do.

'I'm not normal, and I know I'll never be normal. Normal is one, two, or if you're a boss, three at women once. I was sometimes tossing five or more at one time in a night that begged to be there. Sometimes, I knew them; other times, I didn't. I have a sick deep-down desire to seek pleasure from women I'm attracted to physically so that I can feel in control over the shit I can't handle losing. It happened when I was nine and got worse once I lost my virginity. After turning twelve, I went wild, and Cyrus caught me at a function that he thought was a club. But when Cyrus found out I was too far gone, I pulled him into the game. That's how he knows.

'It destroys me once I'm done, and the drama starts. They love me, but I hate them all for letting me treat them that way. I didn't care about one of the women I slept with. It's just a sick game to me. I'm constantly destroying women's minds, bodies, and expectations with sex. It wasn't until I stopped when I realized how bad I was.

'I nearly killed a girl, and it scared me to death. I couldn't do it anymore," Hakim elaborated, watching the road.

"What happened to her, Man?" Darius asked, putting his hand on Hakim's shoulder leaning forward. Darius clutched my feet to his thigh, still stroking slowly. "That's the one you called me when it happened."

"She stopped breathing on me! I panicked, and I almost killed her trying to give her CPR. She came back, but I hurt her badly. I didn't know my own strength. I got her to the hospital and just ran," Hakim groaned, rubbing his forehead. "The next day, I started fasting, meditating, and I found a therapist. I run every day, and I don't think about going back as long as I run.

'The meds don't work. They make it worse, and my blackouts are dangerous to everyone that pisses me off on them. I've been to jail a few times for fighting under the influence. I got locked up in a place a few weeks when I was 15, and they know not to fuck with me. I'm crazy, okay? I've been this way since as far back as I can remember.

'That's why I'm so hard on you, Lionel. You don't want to be fucked up like me. I don't think I'm better than anyone. I just don't need anyone close to me to lose because of the shit I attract with my fucked up karma. Cyrus is grown, and I never forced him to do anything. He probably kept me from hurting a lot more. I can't remember once a blackout is over. The memories sometimes flash before my eyes when I see faces. I don't know what I did. I can only remember the names of the girls before I started the game.

'After the games, it was not Hakim. That's ELYEUH. He's the part of me that hates love and feeling inferior to anyone for any reason. My therapist triggered HIM, and she switched my doctors after meeting him. It's scary shit listening to a recording of a voice that the doctors say is you, but it doesn't sound like anyone you've ever heard.

'Kaliah knows, and he triggers HIM, so I keep him away. His wife elicits HIM, and I can't stand her. I don't know for sure, but I think Kaliah's wife made HIM. I haven't been able to find balance since I met that bitch," Hakim went on with the saddest eyes. His voice began to shake, and he glanced at me.

'It's different this time, though. I don't think about doing it all the time anymore. I've been daydreaming about hugs, kisses, massages, and making love. I've never thought about things like that because I never wanted it. I didn't care. I couldn't feel love at all for any of them. But you….

'Mandisa…you…I. Now, when the dark, scary shit starts coming back, it changes to something sweet. I need to be near you to feel happiness. I haven't felt happy since Mama and Dad got killed."

Hakim pulled the truck to the side of the highway and parked in tears. Darius put his hand on his head and played with his hair, and Lionel was in tears looking out of the window. I heard everything that Hakim was saying. It sounded like a tortured existence he'd been living. Maybe Hakim thought I believed him a horrible person and should be locked away? I wasn't going to interrupt him while he felt like speaking about things. Talking about his parents seemed to upset him yesterday, and now I understand why.

But it was hard to listen with my own tears and thoughts blinding me. My heart ached with each breath I took. It was a growing burn that stabbed me when I gasped. There was so much I wanted to say, but Hakim needed to tell us as much as he could take. Darius seemed to not know much of this, and Lionel's smile was long gone. He was in tears the second that Hakim broke down. He does love his brother, and maybe this helped him realize.

Hakim stared straight ahead, thinking aloud, "Before, when I met a woman, I didn't have to do much to get it. After a few minutes of conversation, I'd twist her thinking, a kiss, maybe, then I'd have her legs open somewhere. But I can't do it anymore!

'MY sickness has nothing to do with getting my dick wet. That's only if a woman is crazy enough to play with 'ELYEUH.' If she puts on that collar or takes my money, she belongs to HIM. A smart girl will get her pussy eaten by the Master, and I'll send her on her merry way. But they want more…I don't want to fuck them…. 'ELYEUH' …wants to own them all. They keep coming back for more wanting to be with me, but I'm done.

'He collars them, and I have to tell them I don't love them, but they don't want to hear that shit after he's fucked them once! I hate myself so much for who I AM. I keep running, moving forward, so the past doesn't catch up with me. But the one time I wanted a woman to love…I found you…and I saw how lousy shit was for you, too, Mandisa…I know I'm wrong for being so selfish, but I knew we were made for one another when I saw that fucked up painting of that girl going to jump. I've been trying to end this shit…

'Maybe I was trying to kill myself with sex. I don't know what I think once I'm out of control. I've been tested so many times and nothing. So, sex won't work… Hanging myself didn't work either the 3 times I tried. I gave up trying to kill myself…Are you going to leave me?"

I was afraid of the thought of him being so promiscuous. What if he hadn't changed or gotten worse? How could I expect him to be faithful to me if he was always wanted more women? I had never heard of someone being with so many. I didn't know what to say to him as I glanced at the traffic lights zoom past, making the truck rock. It was so dark out there, and I had cried so much my eyes were burning.

"You can't…you can't leave…me, Queen," Hakim sighed, his voice low, raspy, and broken with sadness.

Hakim glared up out the window and opened the door, getting out! Lionel and I watched Hakim as he began to pace the side of the highway frantically. Darius opened his door, trying to get out, but Hakim slammed it shut, leaning against it. He refused to let him out.

I was terrified, and my face was on fire as my heart was pounding uncontrollably. Hakim stared at the traffic flying by with tears falling down his face. Darius started hitting the door, pushing, and kicking. He rolled the window down, yelling, "Hakim, Move! Let me out, Nigga! Stop playing!"

"Hakim, get in the car!" Lionel screamed as he opened the driver's door, trying to get out. Hakim slammed the door on his brother. "Let me out, Bro! What you doing, shit!"

I opened my door and took off my other shoe so I wouldn't fall. I carefully walked around the back of the truck and stood near the gas tank, looking over at Hakim. He was staring at each car and truck that flew by hypnotized. His back was rigid as he leaned against the car and looked like he was going to run in front of the largest car!

He noticed me from the corner of his eye as I took a step closer. He glanced over, sighing, "If you're going to leave me, just tell me now, Mandisa. I don't deserve you, and I know it. I've known it from the start. It was just hopeful wishing that someone like you could love a fucked up nigga like me. I ain't shit.

'All the money in the world can't change that. I was terrified if you got to know the real me, I'd scare you away. I've been trying to control so much in my life, and the more I master, the less control I have. You're so exceptional, and you deserve a King. I can't promise you I'll always be a nice person. I can't make you stay and love me...."

Darius climbed out of my door and tried to get past. I stopped him.

"Hakim, I love you. You are a sweet person. You are honest and respectful. Stop talking like you are crazy because you are not! You're hurting. You can't keep beating yourself up because of your mistakes. I won't leave you," I cried desperately, holding my chest.

"You don't have to patronize me, Queen. I can handle the truth," Hakim groaned, staring at the headlights of each car with wider eyes. "I've been running for so long, sometimes I really feel like Forrest Gump. I want to keep running until there's nowhere to go. Then I'll turn around and run in another direction until I just disappear. I fake my emotions so well now, but I haven't felt anything positive since I lost them.

'I want to fade away. Not many would miss me, but there might be at least 200 women at the funeral to make sure I'm really dead. ...I've only loved three women my entire life! Vivianne Clark-Dunn, Grandma Sophie, and you, Mandisa.

'I thought I could start over with a clean slate. It felt like we were made for one another. Now that I've felt this happiness, I can't go back! I don't care anymore! I just want you! I don't deserve your body, but if you give me your heart, I'll be so happy. Don't leave me? I won't go back…I can't live…in the darkness without your sunshine!"

"Hakim! Calm down, Bro. Don't talk like that. I love you, and Mandisa isn't lying. Lionel loves you, and you're scaring the shit out of all of us. He's in the car crying like a baby. Look at him! Look at us! We love you, man!" Darius yelled, grabbing Hakim and holding him.

Hakim looked at him, still crying, his eyes red, swollen, and miserable. Darius pulled his hair and hugged him. I stayed by the trunk, trying to pull myself together. I was hysterical now that Darius had him. I knew I was not strong enough to stop him if he ran. Hakim was intensely focused; his feet were digging down into the soft ground beneath his feet lower each time he looked back into oncoming traffic. Each time his locks swayed, Darius moved to get closer to grab him.

"Mandisa," Darius cried, holding out his hand to me. I took it, and he drew me over, and I grabbed Hakim's waist. Hakim trembled, in tears holding me. He kissed my forehead, and I rubbed his back.

"Don't leave me, please…don't go…I need you," Hakim pleaded, struggling to breathe through his sobs.

Darius grabbed us both as a gigantic truck flew past, nearly knocking me over. Hakim held me close, and his arms tensed as all those locks covered my face in the wind.

"I'm here, Hakim, okay?" I sighed, stroking his damp cheek as he sulked. "I'm not going to leave for anything. Anything…Do you believe me?"

"Yeah," Hakim cried, shaking his head looking at Darius. " I love you, Queen. Do you love me?"

"Oui, Yes, I love you, Hakim. Remember…? You're my fantasy boy," I reminded him looking up into his sad eyes. "I know you're not perfect. I am far from perfect. I do not care about what you did in the past, okay? All that matters is I have you now."

"I love you, Mandisa!" Hakim yelled in tears again. He frowned, holding me. "I want to make you happy! I want to be whatever you need.….I love you so much.…I'll do anything for you! I said I'd pay any price, and I meant that! I'm never going to be your everything.…but I can give you everything.…"

Hakim pushed me into Darius and tried to make me kiss him! Darius pulled away and looked at Hakim furiously!

"HAKIM!! That shit's NOT funny! Don't fucking play with me!" Darius shouted, moving away from the street toward the hood of his truck. He was so angry he was starting to cry again. Hakim pulled me over to Darius, and he pulled us together in a hug. It was so upsetting seeing Darius so afraid of me. It stung differently than Hakim. Was he upset with me? It wasn't my fault…I was so upset watching Darius run away. "You're FUCKIN trippin' if you think for one second that I'm- I've known you were gone, but this is too far, nigga!"

"It's okay…I know…I know," Hakim whispered to us. "It's not wrong. It's right. That's why it hurts so much to tell the truth. I love her, Cyrus…. You love her, too. ….We're the same, Cyrus. I know you…Just say it. Tell her how you feel!"

Darius glared and struggled to pull away from us, and I snatched his face and kissed his beautiful lips. He groaned for a second, then began crying and attempted to pull away. He fought me a second longer, and his hands slowly took my waist. Darius tenderly ran his lips across mine, and I discovered myself sucking his bottom lip. He violently wobbled his head, making his locks rattle, and let me go.

Hakim leered at Darius and asked, "Feels good, doesn't it?"

"But it's not right, Hakim," Darius groaned, shaking his head and pulling his hair.

"Hakim?" I cried, looking up at them. "That was mean. Darius and I are friends, and it was wrong to do that though I may feel he is special to me. How could you?"

"It's not mean, and I think that it's right. I love you, Queen," Hakim sighed, taking my hands. "Do you love me?"

"Yes," I answered honestly.

"I know I love you, Bro," Hakim told Darius. "I know you love me."

"Yeah," Darius replied, frowning with tight lips. "I love you, bro, but whatever you're thinking can't happen. I'm not gay! I love you, but not like that, Hakim."

"Nigga, ain't nobody trying to do no gay shit!" Hakim yelled, laughing. "I'm not gay! I'm making a point. I know you. You'll leave before you admit having feelings for the only woman I love. You don't want to hurt anyone. I can maintain when you're around me, and it's easier to keep me off Lionel.

'I've never been in love, and I need her, Cyrus. But I don't think that it would work with Mandisa for me unless you're around us. You run away because of this, and I'll be running wild after too long and fuck it all up. I don't want to lose her. So, I want to make a Civilized Contract of Relationship with you and Mandisa? If Mandisa wants us, she can have us both, and we'll marry her and take care of her. I'm tired of seeing you run from love too. Each time you fall and get heartbroken, you disappear.

'Not this time, Darius! Yeah, I said your government name. I'm not running from love anymore, and neither are you! You love her, you keep it real, and tell her the fuckin truth!"

Darius shook his head, frowning, saying, "If this is some sick-ass practical joke, I'm not laughing, Bro! Two niggas can't share one girl!"

"Who says they can't if she loves them both? If I need you here and she loves you, then it works so I can keep my fuckin wife happy! It would work for our situation, Cyrus," Hakim protested. I looked away, blushing suddenly. I couldn't believe what Hakim was suggesting! He was serious, and I was terrified of what Darius was going to say. I suddenly wanted a yes! I could love them both! I began to think that Hakim might be right about needing Darius. If I could….No, how could I dream of being so selfish?

Darius quickly moved in front of me and grabbed my hand. He made me look him in the eye, and I didn't want to see how upset he was. It made me want to hold him and kiss him until Darius was joking again. He touched my chin and made me look. He had tears running down his face and asked, "You love me?"

I couldn't lie to him like this. It was wrong to keep lying! That was what caused all of this!

"Yes, oui, Darius…I love you too," I whispered as I touched a tear falling from his cheek.

"What?!" Darius yelled, suddenly pulling away. His face wrinkled up in confusion, and he started marching behind the truck. "I don't understand what the fuck is happening right now! I must be crazy! I know….I fell the fuck to sleep…and this is a dream. You didn't say that to me. Take that shit back, Mandisa! You didn't mean it!"

"I can be honest about my feelings. Queen told you how she feels, but can you be honest with yourself and with us?" Hakim demanded, staring at Darius nodding. "I told you that it was going to take a remarkable woman to make me settle down. I feel like if you love her…You're going to stop hiding behind me and tell her for once, Cyrus!

'Or the alternative, you run, I run, and Mandisa will vanish. I need your help to save her. This isn't like Sami, Courtney, or Carla. Mandisa actually loves you, and I haven't touched her. You might need to imagine that a moment?"

Darius frowned over at Hakim, yelling, "No! I'm not running like you! I let shit calm down when ELYEUH thinks he can make a bitch out of me. You think you can control that shit with running, but it gets worse if you can't fuck. I was making sure you were safe, but you don't get to manipulate me with another game!"

"Cyrus, this is no game. I want a contract. I'm saying that if the woman I love is in love with a man, I need to be ordinary. I am willing to let him marry her. But the conditions are that he has to have a hand in helping me save her life and take care of her the same if not better than me. I think you're the only brother that I can trust to make this kind of arrangement. What King tells a Queen who to love knowing the brother has the best intentions for her too?

'It can work…If we all want it to work. As long as I have Mandisa, and I get it all in the end….I don't give a fuck what the world thinks," Hakim told Darius with a calm nod.

"You don't know what you're asking. We all have got serious issues, Hakim. It's not fair to do this to her. She's never had a boyfriend. You're going to make her choose between us in the end. What about you and me? We can't be cool if this shit goes bad!"

"She won't choose between us, Cyrus….Mandisa's already decided. Ain't that right, Queen? You want us both, don't you? You didn't want to hurt me by saying. That's why you kept dropping that trail of breadcrumbs?

'The texting, asking him about me, and it isn't wrong. You wanted me to tell you it's alright to love my friend, and I'm not letting you go? Right?" Hakim asked me. I looked at them together and nodded.

"Da fuck ya say?!" Darius said, looking down at me. His eyes were so large that he looked like he wore glasses. His eyes wandered my face a moment, and Darius looked me in the eye, saying, "You're a virgin! Why would you even think that way?"

"What does being a virgin have to do with how she feels about anyone? That's very animalistic of you, Cyrus. Obviously, she's agonized for both of us from the start. If you think the same about her, I don't see a problem submitting to her. I had never wanted to give control of my life to anyone before I met her….I'll do anything! I'll go against my dominant nature for her. I love making her happy. It makes me feel blessed making her smile.

'You're my brother, man. I know if you really love Mandisa, you won't hurt her. I don't want to hurt her either!

'That's why I'm swallowing all my pride to say…It's okay to love Mandisa, too. I need you. We all need each other to be happy, okay. It's not about sex! Now, tell her how you feel and stop being scared of me!"

Darius glanced from Hakim down at me, asking, "You're really in love with me?"

"Oui, Darius…I have loved you from the moment we met," I admitted, terrified of what was happening. There was no need to lie now that I had let my emotions run wild, and everyone was telling the truth. It would only harm us all further. I shook my head. "I was afraid to say so because it felt wrong, to be honest. That feels wrong to me now. If Hakim can tell me the truth about all the things that have shamed him, why would I lie when I know Hakim is right?

'It hurts to lie. I can see it hurts us all to lie about the way we feel. I could love you both if you loved me equally. I'm not going to run from either of you anymore. I'd rather run with you both."

"Come here, Mandisa?" Darius called me over to the side. As he pulled me near, Darius put his hands on my shoulders. "Hakim's not the only one with a past, okay? But I'm more than willing to leave it all behind if I can be with you, Queen. You say you love me. I love you, too. I have since the moment I laid eyes on you.

'None of this feels real to me, Mandisa. Seems like I'm about to wake up and be sad and alone. If there's the slightest possibility that I'm not dreaming, I just want you to know how I feel. I love you, Queen. I always will. If I wake up tomorrow and this didn't happen, I still love you in this memory. I'll never repeat it once I'm awake, okay? I'm too afraid to hurt anyone but myself. I hate doing it, but I'd rather break my own heart than anyone else's."

"You are not dreaming, Darius. I am standing here telling you that I do love you. Oui, I love Hakim too. I feel that I met Hakim, and he and I are both broken, and you make us both happy. It feels good to finally tell you both the truth. It does not feel wrong to love two men who love me, and I know they need each other to be sane in this crazy world. Fuck the world!" I giggled.

Darius stared at me in amazement and kissed my hands. He suddenly smiled and said, "A natural living breathing pure Goddess...I didn't think that shit was real that Kaliah talked about. Hakim...oh shit...I'm feeling light-headed!"

Hakim nodded, pushed Darius's shoulder, and hugged us both, saying, "Now, you understand why I knew she was made for me. She's going to give me the family that we need to be happy, and we're going to pipe her the fuck up! Antoine will elevate her spirits to heights beyond, and we're going to put some major waves in the industry once I start college. But first, we need to plot a way to get Dr. King out of Mami's mane. She's earned some time to enjoy her children without that tyrant killing her vibe!"

"I don't know how the hell you gonna get away with this shit, but I'm still in the pact, too. I'm with you...." Lionel added as he grabbed Hakim holding him from behind.

Hakim smiled to himself and said, "Just keep your ears open, mouth shut, and hands to yourself, and you'll live to see 16, Nigga!"

"Whatever, nigga!" Lionel said, laughing at Hakim. "You do realize that eventually somebody is gonna get fucked in this situation, and I'm hoping it's just Mandisa!"

"Nigga, I will kill you if you keep spitting that ignorance," Darius grumbled to Lionel. "There isn't a gay bone in my body, nor Hakim. I've been in the room when he's been with many women, and we never crossed swords. I think you should change your view of who the fuck you think we are, Lionel. We're men...and aware that we only want a woman sexually. I'm only interested in pleasing her and getting mine from her. That's all there is to it when it comes to multiple partner situationships involving sexual exploration.

'Do a bit more studying with Kaliah. I don't fuck with him because of Trisha, but we talk when I'm not pissed off at him for talking shit. He's my brother, but he rubs me the wrong way with his arrogant comments about my choices. He's not my fucking father.

'I think we need to get the fuck off the 20 before the law shows up asking questions wanting to search my shit! I got some Kaliah's finest in my dash. Let's Jet Jackson! Um, Queen, if you don't get my toes off that dirty ground! I paid for that pedicure, and I want to rub your feet until you fall asleep. Get your fine ass in the car!"

I laughed as Lionel picked me up and tossed me in the backseat, and climbed back upfront.

As Darius stood outside talking to Hakim, I felt much better. The both of them seemed to be much closer, and his concern for Hakim's well-being was genuine. Darius was hugging Hakim and trying to convince Hakim that he shouldn't drive. Hakim promised Darius that he was fine, and the moment had passed. Lionel tried to volunteer, and Cyrus died laughing and letting Hakim chauffeur home.

"How does this weird shit you trying to fail at work?" Lionel asked Hakim with a confused glance.

"Mandisa makes the rules. We're here to make her happy," Hakim replied, rolling his eyes.

"No one tells my Mami! I will wait until I feel it is a good time to tell her. No lying, we started this being honest with one another, and it won't work if we start lying or keeping secrets. No cheating...If you want someone else, you can leave. I'm not going to hold someone that wants someone else. I can handle the truth too. It may hurt to let go, but I would rather say goodbye than live a lie being made a fool of. I know what people will think of me. I have already been called enough names by my father or people on the internet. What's one more label? But Goddess sounds beautiful. I don't want to own anyone. If you are with me, then we do this for love and healing. It's not about lust. We can be bigger than than the modern marriage concept."

"That is exactly what I am saying, Queen," Hakim agreed, placing his lips on my forehead. "You are perfect. I had a feeling you would know where I was going. I want us to work so that I don't have to keep losing family. You're healing me, and we're going to free you together. You deserve to be happy, Queen."

As we drove back to Longview, I honestly felt much better. The boys were much happier and getting along well. Darius took off his expensive shirt and wiped off my feet, smiling.

"What?" He asked, gazing at my upset expression. "It's black, and it's just a shirt, Queen. I can't kiss these toes if they're dirty."

He burst into laughter and put my foot to his face, kissing it smiling again. Lionel stared at him and looked at me smiling, chuckling, "Freaky-ass, Niggas!"

"Jealous?" Hakim laughed, moving the truck back to the highway.

"Naw, my panties ain't getting wet," Lionel snorted at me.

"Shut up, Lionel!" I yelled, popping the top of his head.

"Oh!" Darius and Hakim laughed together.

"She's so violent! You might need to get a restraining order soon, Baby Brother. She's picking up our habits. Mandisa used to be so sweet before she met them Dunn Boys...Cyrus to the rescue!" Darius chuckled, spreading my toes and smelling them. "Oh, my Goddess....I am in Heaven!"

"You can't keep putting your hands on my brother, Queen," Hakim told me, shaking his head, driving, and frowning.

"Thank you, Hakim!!" Lionel agreed, touching his ponytail. "At least someone is looking out.

"That's my damn job!" Hakim laughed as he grabbed Lionel's hair, messing it up.

"Fuck you, Hakim!" Lionel yelled, fixing his hair. Lionel looked angry until he glanced my way, remembering before.

"Fuck me, too, Lionel?" I asked, frowning.

"Naw, you alright, Sis," Lionel replied, smiling as he held his head. I smiled back at him as he stared into my eyes. "What color panties you got on?"

"Ugh!" I groaned, laughing as I leaned down in my seat.

Darius smiled at me while softly stroking my feet. He suddenly leaned over and softly kissed my lips. He used both to cover mine playfully but made me have a giggle fit tickling my toes.

"I can't believe this is happening to me," He chuckled softly, staring down into my eyes. "You're all I've ever wanted, Mandisa. I've searched everywhere for you, and you pop up in Longview, Texas, of all places."

I rubbed his hand and pulled his head into my lap. I pulled his hair over my leg and played with his dreadlocks. He closed his eyes for a minute but opened them quickly and sat up nervously.

"What's wrong?" I worried as I playfully ran my nails across his palm.

"I can't fall asleep. I'll wake up, and none of this will be real," Darius sighed. "The only place I ever get the girl is in my dreams."

I grabbed his ponytail and pulled him back in place. I continued playing with his twists until Darius fell asleep.

"That's not fair, Queen," Hakim sighed, watching me with a smile.

"You will get your turn, Hakim," I told him, blushing. "Give him a break. He's been through enough today dancing to your music, Hakim. It must have been torture for you both."

I exhaled, peeking out the window. A snort told me that Darius was sleeping peacefully as I looked down at him on my thigh. He looked like a little boy. His face was so beautifully relaxed. My fingernails traced his lips and sulked as I felt a drop of warm drool in the corner. I wiped his mouth, and he kissed at my fingers but stayed asleep. I closed my eyes for what seemed like a minute, but the second I opened them, we were home.

Chapter Ten: The Art Of Peer Pressure

Cyrus

I felt gentle touches on my face, but I was far gone. It reminded me of the sweetest memories as a kid. I don't know about everyone else, but for me, my mother taught me the kind of woman I wanted to love. My father taught me the type of man I wanted to be with the woman I love. Daddy couldn't keep his hands off her and was always happy when she came through the door. He rubbed her feet after work, smothered her with attention, affection, and bought her anything he could afford. He never had enough after the bills, but Mama worked extra shifts so I could take dance classes. These memories are as bittersweet as my families' dark complexion, but they are all I have to push me forward. Her touch I sometimes miss more than the next blunt I smoke or sip I take. My mother's hands were tickling me awake for school.

"Osiris? Baby…get up!" She giggled while tickling my neck.

"No!" I yelled, laughing. "Stop, Mama, …I don't want to go to school!"

"If you don't go to school, you have to go with either Daddy or Mama to work. Then you have to make up all the assignments you miss. You'll be up all night doing work you could do at school today. I can't take you to the Square Garden to see the game tomorrow," She teased me, frowning. Her pretty brown skin was shining in the light with her brown eyes smiling, opposing her face. Mama was already in her chef's uniform, but her brown locks were still hanging free over her shoulders as she shook me again. "Come on, Osiris….let's get moving."

"What's for breakfast?" I asked, crawling out of bed and starting for the bathroom sluggishly. I hate getting up early, but I have to do it anyway, so I move super slow. Grabbing the toothbrush feels like lifting weights before I'm fully awake in the mornings. It's always been this way. Mama knew it and thought it was funny watching me stumble around and stare into nowhere before I woke up. "Help me!"

"Guess," Mama laughed, coming over to help me wash my face so I could stir.

"Um…Chocolate cake?" I laughed, asking as I opened my eyes completely. Mama shook her head as she started tying her locks beneath her scarf.

"No, strike one," She giggled, twisting mine back for me. She playfully scratched my scalp and ran her fingers to my shoulders. "They're getting long…Are you gonna grow them all the way out?"

"I don't know. The boys talk about my hair, saying it looks funny. Boys don't have long hair like this," I answered after drinking water.

"If you grow them out one day, they'll be really long, and all the boys will try to copy you, and the girls are going to love it," Mama told me, playing with my cheeks.

"Brownies?" I asked, watching her in the mirror. Mama was a big beautiful black woman, and my father loved her. She was the sweetest woman in the world, and he treated her like a queen though we never had much money. I loved eating everything she cooked, and it made me fat, but she didn't care. "Anything chocolate…"

"Strike two, Osiris. How were the dance lessons last night? I got in late from work and didn't want to wake you," Mama asked, putting my toothbrush away.

"It was fun! There are lots of pretty girls in the class, and they all want to dance with me because I'm good," I replied, smiling at her. I frowned suddenly. I hated it, and we had it all the time, but it was just my thing to get Mama talking every morning, so I could wake up. "Oatmeal?"

"Ding-Ding!" Mama giggled, helping me get dressed, and tucking my shirt. Her face lit up when she smiled, and it made me smile. Mama joked with me all the time and filled my life with happiness. Mama was never healthy, but she never let it stop her from doing anything she wanted, and that included having me when they told her it was too risky when she was weak. Daddy wouldn't tell me what was wrong with her. By the time I was old enough to realize how bad things were…it was too late. She was in pain when she woke up, and it started getting worse each day. "Let me take my pills, and I'll put some chocolate chips in your oatmeal? How's that, King?"

"You want me to get Daddy up to help you back in bed?" I worried, looking up at her face as it flushed suddenly and sweat formed on her face and neck.

"No! I'm walking you to school at least once this week. Between the treatments and work…I'm just getting tired. Besides, I need to talk to Mrs. Gibson about your reading problem. She needs to understand that you have Dyslexia. You're not stupid! I'm sick of her sarcastic voicemails talking about what you don't want to read. Where are your glasses, Darius?" Mama replied, frowning from the pain more than me as she held her side and began rubbing her hips.

I went to my room to get my glasses. I remember that I stuck them in my underwear drawer because I hated wearing them. They made me look like a nerd, but I needed them to see all the letters because my brain was underdeveloped. I didn't feel slower than other kids, but I'd make jokes or do anything to be overlooked when asked to read. It took me too long to get the words to come together. So anger was the result because it couldn't be rushed no matter how hard I tried.

My teacher told Mama about things, and she told Mama that she didn't have time to work with me and I should be put in Special Education classes. That pissed Mama off, and she advised Mrs. Gibson that the only thing wrong with me was that I needed to learn patience and support from others with the same issues. Mrs. Gibson told Mama that I needed a better school. We could not afford anything more than what was available, but Mama stayed with my teachers through the years. She did everything she could to make me feel normal when everyone treated me like a failure.

I'll never forget the fright I got when I heard the glass shattering in the bathroom followed by what sounded like a violent struggle. I ran back into the hall, and Mama had dropped her drink and looked up in my direction! She trembled to hold the door frame, and her eyes scared me. I panicked, and she held up her hand weakly, saying, "Don't step on the glass...go get Darius...Osi.."

Mama couldn't say anything else as her eyes rolled back into her head, and I ran screaming to catch her. I didn't care about the glass. She'd land in it if I didn't do something, so I slid in my socks, fell, and her head missed the glass landing on me.

Mama's previous treatment had utterly wiped her immune system, and everything made her sick. Mama couldn't sleep, wouldn't eat anymore. When she was exhausted from working, she'd pass out, then when Mama actually slept, she talked in her sleep, praying for me or talking to Daddy. She called him Darius, but I was Osiris, or she might have got us mixed up.

During the following treatments, Mama started losing her hair. It was a little here and there at first, but in 3 weeks, she shaved it all off. Mama was even more beautiful bald! It made her round face stand out. She even lost her eyelashes, brows, became so drained she had to be hospitalized.

Mama refused to eat, getting thinner and losing weight. She had tubes everywhere! Some to feed her, others keeping her hydrated, another filtering her blood after her kidneys stopped working, then a catheter because Mama was too weak to get out of bed.

It started as Fibroid tumors in her ovaries when she was young. She wanted a baby so she wouldn't have a hysterectomy like the doctors recommended. While pregnant with me, Mama was so sick they had to take me early because of my size. She had everything removed after me, but things got horrible. The cancer cells became very aggressive and spread. She fought the pain, fatigue and hid everything from me until she couldn't.

Three months, that's all it took—three months for her to wither away into nothing. I was almost ten when I watched my mother die. Literally, I was with her that last night.

#

When I got to the hospital with Dad that evening, he went to grab us dinner, and we'd sit with her until visiting hours were over. Somedays, Mama was sleeping the entire time, but that night Mama had her bed elevated and was watching TV sitting up when I walked into her room! It scared me to death to see her look over at me and smile like another day! I could tell how much weight she had lost by her thin shoulders and hanging skin from her arms as she reached out for me. I didn't care! That was my Mama, and I missed her! I grabbed her, and I know I cried. I hadn't had a hug from her in months or seen a smile. All I wanted was a smile, and she hadn't moved anything but her eyes.

"How has dance class been, Baby?" Mama asked, her eyes glowing with tears as she started rubbing my hair. "It's growing faster….Look so good, Osiris."

"You're up. Are you okay? You want something?" I cried. Mama shook her head and gave me her look, meaning spill it! "Dance class is okay. I go once a week so he can keep the insurance. He said that we had to make some cutbacks and sacrifices until you're well. I don't mind, Mama…you look better."

"I see," Mama said as she laid back. I moved her pillows. "Are you doing your schoolwork? Where are your glasses? Osiris, you're sweet, right?"

Mama seemed to be panicking, asking me so many questions at once. I smiled and replied, "Yeah, Mama, I'm good, no fighting, and my jokes made Mrs. Gibson laugh so hard she farted. The whole class was cracking up. I keep my glasses in my backpack. I only need them for reading, remember?"

"That's right, Baby. I'm sorry. Can you uncover my legs? It's warm in here," Mama recalled trying to hold in her laugh. "Mrs. Gibson, I hope she shited on herself laughing at you."

I laughed because Mama didn't curse! But she was roasting my teacher. When I moved the blankets and saw how thin her legs were, I remembered she was terminally ill but wasn't acting it. I could grip one with my hand, and It was like a bone covered in her skin. My Mama was always a size 20. I knew when I held her she was tired.

"Mama?" I called up to her, and she opened her eyes. "You think I should quit the dance lessons for a while?"

She opened her eyes a bit wider, and shook her head, saying, "No, you keep dancing, Darius. You were born to dance. I knew it when you started walking. No matter what you do in life…you keep dancing, okay? Will you go tell the nurse I need some ice for my water jug. I want a drink…but I want it cold."

"Yes, Mama," I said, taking the pitcher with me to the nurses' station.

"Hiya, Darius," Nurse Lindsay said as she glanced up from her charts, noticing me. "What you need, Cutie?"

I loved the nurses at Mama's hospital. They were the prettiest black women and Latinas I had ever seen. Nurse Lindsay was a lovely red-boned girl in excellent shape, and she was always glad to see me. She wore pink scrubs, but I loved watching her move around swinging her cute ponytail. She had a tight little body and an adorable face. Yeah, I was ten, but I was looking once I turned eight.

"Hey, Ms. Lindsay, Mama wants some water. Can I get some ice for her pitcher?" I asked politely as I smiled.

"I'll take care of it for you, Sweetie," Nurse Lindsay started taking the pitcher from me. She paused after taking a few steps and looked back at me. "Your Mama is NPO. She isn't supposed…Mrs. Jefferson is awake?"

"Yes, Mam, Mama was watching TV when I got here. She said she wanted some water but wants it cold," I replied.

Nurse Lindsay smiled down at me and raised her right eyebrow suspiciously, saying, "It's time for her to be repositioned anyway. We gonna see. It won't take long. You want to wait here for me? You gonna stay with her since she's alert?"

"Yes, Mam," I said, nodding. "Can I go get a blanket?"

"Go ahead, you know where they are. Nobody better say anything either. I'll come to get you once we check her and get her comfortable," She told me, smiling as she went into Mama's room, 1619, and pulled the curtain. I stood by the door, watching the other nurses reading charts, writing notes, and making their rounds. "We have a code BLUE! Code Blue floor 15, room 1619! Repeat! Code BLUE! Room 1619!"

I knew Nurse Lindsay's voice. The hospital staff ran into my mother's room, and I was pulled to the side. A team of doctors was in my mother's room. I only saw her face for a moment through the curtains before they tried to resuscitate her. Her lips were already blue, and her eyes looked glazed over in an instant. She was gone! I stood there watching as they tried to bring her back. Someone grabbed me, pulling me back into the hallway.

My dad held me crying as I lost it. I saw that white light that they talked about through my tears, looking at Mama. That's how I knew she was gone. My father picked me up in his arms and walked us home. Both of us were in tears all the way to Lafayette Street that March, a week before my birthday.

#

"Dar-i-us," I heard a sweet voice singing.

Then came the gentle tickling on my cheeks and chin. I shivered as my body responded, by my eyes stayed shut. It's always like this. It takes forever for me to wake up. A sudden quake from fingernails on the skin of my neck gave me chills, and I shot awake!

"I don't want to go to school today, Mama!" I laughed as I woke up, opening my eyes. It was dark as I looked up, but my eyes focused on Mandisa's face. She was so beautiful in the moonlight. Her gray eyes were brighter than the stars above as she smiled sweetly down at me.

"It is June, silly. There is no school until August," She giggled, teasing the whiskers on my chin. If I wasn't so dark, you could see me blush with excitement. Her accent gave my entire body chills. I offered her a smile as I sat up. "Are you awake?"

"My bad, Queen, I guess I fell asleep, huh? Sorry," I apologized, wiping my mouth with the back of my hand. I had drooled on her leg and left a wet spot on her beautiful new jeans. I sighed, shaking my head, embarrassed. I rolled down the window and lit the blunt. I have to wake and bake, so my brain catches up with everything else. I exhaled a long cloud of smoke out of the window and smiled as everything grew pleasant. "I got your leg wet…damn! When I get to sleeping too good, I relax, so I drool. I'll buy you another pair, I promise, Goddess."

"It is okay, Darius! It is only your drool. It will wash out," Mandisa giggled at me, watching me smoking. "You were so adorable I did not want to wake you. I fell asleep too. When you finish that, we will go inside, and you can meet Mami?"

"I'd love to meet your mother, Queen. I know she has to be amazing to have you for a daughter," I flirted, thumping my ashes, looking around, not seeing Lionel or Hakim. "Where's everyone else?"

"They went home to check for their grandparents and to take their things. They said they would be right back to say hello," She replied, eyeing me closely. I playfully offered her the cigar. She shook her head, giggling. "Why do you smoke so much? I understand why someone would smoke it. I want to know why you smoke it, Darius?"

I smiled at her approach. Most women caught an attitude the moment that I fired my shit up. Mandisa didn't judge, though it wasn't her thing. She wanted to know my reason for partaking. No one had ever asked me something so personal. It shocked me, honestly.

"It cures my depression, Mandisa. I smoke a lot, so my mood is elevated. I get down on myself and the past when I overthink, so I smoke to joke. Does that seem like a good enough reason?" I replied, thinking.

"If it makes you feel good, then I don't see why it's a problem. I think it is silly that parts of the world see THC and even Hallucigens as dangerous drugs. The 60s scared the shit out of Americans, huh?" Mandisa giggled, making a sweet face I'd never seen. I exhaled a puff of smoke through my nose and smiled, agreeing. Hakim was so very right about this woman. Mandisa was perfect. "I don't think I'm ready to experiment with that stuff with my heart condition and medications. But it doesn't upset me when I see someone use what they need to feel normal. Everyone is different, oui?"

"Oui, Cheri, you are so very correct. I love you, Mandisa," I replied, kissing her hand. "Jet-Amy?"

"Je t'aime, Darius," She blushed while watching. "Ze-TomA..."

"Je t'aime, Goddess," I repeated, making her smile. If her mother let her be a model, then I knew Mandisa was going to blow up! Looking at that face, sparkling eyes, long hair, skin, sweet heart-shaped lips, and now she was waxed and made-up like a woman. I'd never seen a woman so beautiful, and she loved me? I will say the more time that I spent with her, the more I wanted her. I was starting to feel like Hakim about the marriage thing. I wasn't sure if his idea was possible, but if there was the slightest chance that Mandisa was seriously going to ride it out with the both of us, I'd be a fool to not try. "I know I love you, Mandisa. You're everything a nigga could wish for. But what do you see in me? Hakim seems to be your type as far as physical appearances go, but you still look at me like I'm special or something."

"There is much physical attraction between you and me too, Darius. You are special to me. I think you are warm, funny, so handsome, and though you seem sad, you're still so much fun to be around. I don't know enough, so I won't assume. But you cling to Lionel and Hakim because they both are like you…or the other way around. Family members rub off on one another over time, oui? You act like them, and then they act like you, but you call it copying, and it's only your vibe connecting in harmony. So you reject it as something negative," Mandisa informed me, rubbing my knee.

"You keep talking to me like that, and you're going to wake up Jody, and I'm going to have to fight Hakim. Let's go inside before you meet baby boy!" I chucked, looking down at her manicure on my jeans.

"Jody? Baby Boy? You mean the movie, oui?" Mandisa asked, trying to put two and two together. Mandisa giggled, making a confused face. Suddenly Mandisa rolled her eyes and snapped her neck at me. "Nigga, who told you to light my candles? You're trippin!"

I died laughing at her imitation of Yvette. That shit was too cute the way Mandisa held her hand pointing at me. She playfully waved her nails at me and put her hands on those magnificent hips. Her eyes shot wide open, and she leaned closer to my face making me look her in the eye. I was gonna grab her and go crazy until I realized Mandisa was just playing with me! I was getting excited, and I liked that shit. I needed to get away, or I'd unleash the dragon, like Sisqo!

"I'm saying that I call my dick, Jody, and if you don't move your hand…You're going to meet him up close and personal, Woman!" I hooted, forcing her hand. "I'm not some punk, Queen. You can't put your hands on me and not get a reaction. Play with me too much, and I get serious. I'm trying to be good, so let's keep Jody in the crib, but I think your Yvette is spot on. Turned me on."

Mandisa died laughing as she looked at her hand. I grabbed her hand and let her feel Jody growing against my thigh, and her eyes shot up at my face. I smiled and raised my eyebrows playfully. Mandisa's face went limp, which is the opposite of what was going on with me. The moment her warmth touched me, I sprung to life. Yes, it was fully erect; she saw and brushed it through my jeans. When she felt it on her own, I knew she was curious. Once they were interested, it was only a matter of time before they wanted to see it. I only did that to show her she wasn't ready to deal with the fire I was packing.

Mandisa blushed and pulled away with a nervous giggle that drove me crazy. I laughed it off and let up the window getting out of the truck. We were parked on the street in front of her house. It was the same spot I parked last night. Mandisa gave me my car keys as she closed her door before I could reach it.

I stretched out my arms and legs, glancing at the flowers growing at night on the bushes. As I reached out my arms, my neck snapped over as Mandisa hugged my waist. Holy shit! This isn't a dream! Or, I was so high I forgot what I was doing for a second. I smiled, hypnotized, and followed where her heavenly body led me like a kid across the playground.

Her belly chains jingling, the clicking of her heels on the driveway, the swaying of her hips from the right with a wobble that made the left jiggle made me her hopeless puppy. Yes, woman, drag me…you can put me on a leash and make me your faithful pet. Just shake it for me and give me a kiss goodnight. I'll do anything you say to make you smile and give you these beautiful 14 inches until you can't take it anymore. I don't mind if you can't hang…just give Jody a kiss to make me happy. I really shouldn't have an erection about to meet her mother. Let me think about something else!

Something smelled really good when we got to the porch. My stomach growled so loud, recognizing the familiar scent of chocolate! Now I had an erection for a different reason. It was nearly 11 pm, and Mandisa's mother was baking something, and it was made of chocolate! I may need to make a contract with Mami!

The woman that opened the front door looked like Vanessa Williams from the goddamn Miss America contests! Her gorgeous face should have been in magazines! What the fuck! She opened the screen door, and I saw her round belly and nearly screamed! Mandisa did say that her mother was pregnant, but I forgot until I saw the miracle myself. My expression must have alarmed her because her starry eyes grew wide, and she covered her mouth.

"Are you okay, Cheri? You look like you have seen a ghost?" Queen Mother asked me with her soft accent. I nodded, unable to take my eyes off her lovely toes! She was wearing those adorable fuzzy slippers, and her toes were out. Her ankles were swollen, and I frowned, looking up at her face. "Queen, your new friend is silly."

"I'm sorry, Mami…I just hate to see a woman with sore feet. Your ankles look like they need a rest. You should put your feet up in your condition! What are you doing! You look like you're about to bless this world with another twin any second!" I laughed as I quickly grabbed her arm, helping her inside. I looked around at that living room as it hit me. There was this thrilling warmth filling that house, and I think it came from Mami. I didn't want to let her go once I grabbed her hand! "You may as well get used to it. You're my Mami, now! I smell chocolate, and I'm hungry!"

Mandisa laughed, following after me as I kidnapped her mother. Mami did not object, so I let her show me the way to the kitchen. Uh-uh, Cyrus loves older women, and Mami was smiling at me like she liked my black ass. That shit made me want to keep her.

"Darius, really? You're stealing my mother?" Mandisa asked me as I helped Mami sit and put up her feet.

"Hush, Queen! I like him. He's cute, and his skin is sexy! He's sweet too like chocolate pie!" Mami giggled, pushing my hand as I tried to pull off her slipper. I frowned at her playfully and ran my fingers over her toes. When I rubbed her ankles, Mami shut her eyes and nodded to me. "Shut up, Queen! He's mine!"

"Mami!" Mandisa giggled as red as a cherry from the doorway. "I've never heard you talk like that before!"

"I've never had a fine black man touch my feet before, Queen...It's a first for us both!" Mami giggled, looking at me, blushing.

"I ain't mad at cha, Mami. I'm Cyrus, Hakim's brother and Mandisa's new friend. I wasn't trying to be rude, but I hate to see a beautiful woman with sore feet. It makes me a pushover to serve and take care of any woman watching my mother work so hard. Ask Hakim? Grandma Sophie runs from me! She knows I will get her feet too!" I said, smiling. "But for real, Mandisa told me that you were expecting but seeing you is like...wow!"

"Oui, Oui, Darius...Cyrus...You are too sweet. You are a tall weed, aren't you?" Mami replied, blushing as I rubbed her feet.

I glanced over at Mandisa, pretending to be confused, asking, "What did she say about weed? Oh, naw, Mami, I smoked out in the car. But if you need some…I got you! I can get you some stuff to take all the pain away. Just let me know."

"Darius! Oh my God!" Mandisa screamed, pushing my arm.

Mami laughed, so I didn't understand why Mandisa was embarrassed by my offering to share pain meds with her. We all know that other shit isn't good for the baby. Kaliah's herb is excellent for anything that bothers you.

"You're funny, Darius, but no, thank you," Mami replied but made a very obvious gesture with her cute nose. Okay, I got you, Mama. You don't want Queen to know. I can dig it. She put her lovely fingers on her enormous round belly. Mandisa came and sat next to her. "I love your new look. You seem so grown up. I forget you're not a baby anymore sometimes."

"Speaking of baby, how long before the world's biggest girl gets here?" I asked, watching both their hands on her stomach.

Mandisa was crying as her mother covered her mouth, trying to breathe, "I'm due in September, Darius."

"You're telling me that you're going to purposely carry a full-grown person for another three months?" I questioned her, worried.

"Darius, No!" Mandisa snickered, turning red. "Please, Stop!"

"I'm just saying, Man-Di-Sa. Your Mama didn't have to hold your twin sister in so long! You needed a playmate growing up, not to graduate with now!" I teased, raising the vibe of those 3 women. The laughter made me so peaceful I didn't want to stop. I might have been Kaliah's weed, but I loved it! I had never received so much attention that felt so natural and inviting. "Alright, I'll stop before we end up in the hospital tonight. Then we'll have to take Amani to get her driver's license tomorrow."

Mami suddenly got up, laughing so hard that she was bright pink. She giggled, "I'm gonna pee on myself! I hate you, Darius! Driver's license…oh God…."

"Je t'aime, Mami!" I chuckled, offering to help her. But she waddled away quickly into the door down the hall. Mandisa was trying to stop laughing as I heard the backdoor open. "I'm gonna take her for real, Mami!"

Mandisa and I started laughing as we heard Mami have a giggle fit in the bathroom through the door. Hakim and Lionel arrived through the door as I stood up and washed my hands in the kitchen sink. Hakim was carrying all of Mandisa's things when he came through the door. I grabbed some of the bags as she showed us where to take things. Upstairs, I noticed all her pictures and paintings. When they talked about her work, they didn't say how fucking amazingly gifted she was with detail!

"Sit the bags on the floor near the closet. I will put things away in the morning," Mandisa told us as she turned on the light to her bedroom. I smiled, noticing her artsy and elegant space. Mandisa's family wasn't wealthy, but they were very well put together. Perhaps Daddy kept the money on lockdown to keep Mami under control? What kind of a man treats women such as this like slaves? She had a black panther on her bed that I was about to grab as I spotted her art space.

In the corner by the window, a painting wasn't entirely done being filled in. It was a girl in a yellow sundress rollerskating. The color, tint, and shade changes made it look like a disco with the mirrorball above. That girl was so happy and beautiful. But my jaw dropped as I noticed over in the golden light she had painted me as I skated with her just last night! I know it was me when I saw that detailed long hair and up close. It was insane! It was like a mental photograph of what I remember happening.

"That's us, last night? When did you paint this?!" I asked, amazed, staring at the eyebrows on the painting.

"I could not sleep when I got home last night. I have insomnia, and sometimes I cannot sleep for days, so I almost finished it this morning," She sighed, smiling at me. Hakim moved next to me and shook his head. He pointed to the wall behind us, making me look back. Mandisa had painted a damn picture of Hakim running! That shit was crazy! How could she get the faces to look so real? "I suppose I have more happy memories to capture the last few days. I don't feel inspired often, but Mami calls me Bob Ross when she sees me go for paint."

"This is the craziest shit, Queen," Hakim sighed, looking at the shirt I was wearing in the wind. I shook my head, glancing at Mandisa. "You did this in one night? You need an art gallery! People would pay big bucks to have something you paint off a whim."

"I don't want to sell anything. I like to keep the paintings as a way of gauging my life through the years. All the things I've seen and tried to understand about the world or myself: even the scary ones have somehow connected memories. I forgot exactly when I painted many," Mandisa told us honestly.

I couldn't take it. I had to see the rest of the infamous art that Hakim and Lionel told me about. As I stepped into the kitchen, Mami was taking her lovely meal from the oven. I quickly moved to help her with Lionel, who was eagerly standing by like a starving kitten hunched over the stove. I spotted that extensive landscape the moment my eyes saw the den. It really was impressive gazing at the lush greenery. There was even a distant cityscape below. But Mandisa was right there on the mountain summit, arms outstretched, shrouded in a horrid gown of distorted contrast, and prepared to leap to her doom.

I grabbed my phone and began to take photos of all her paintings, and I sent them to Kaliah. Something told me that he needed to analyze this shit. There was a painting that stood out more than that massive suicide warning! A little white boy had big silver eyes that seemed to glow so brightly they looked white. He was surrounded by darkness, standing in front of a door with a golden key around his neck. He was holding a lantern, but he looked blind, so why would he need the lamp? Behind that frighted little child holding the light were eyes everywhere watching from the abyss.

A little girl was next to that disturbing image, so beautiful with her blue eyes and brown skin, maybe just 3 or 4! She was dancing in a black room with a piano. There was very little light at all, but you could see the sweet angel, her halo, wings, tutu, as she twirled in a faint blue glow. That baby angel dancing looked like she was pregnant! Her tiny belly was poking out. Playing the piano was a barely visible man, but I could see his burned skin, torn flesh, and glowing red eyes! I kept trying to see his face, but it was so dark in the background I could only make out the outline of horns on his head and hooves for feet? Some of this shit was terrifying for spiritual eyes!

"You can see it too, Darius?" Mami asked, scaring the shit out of me while I was looking at the wrong shit! She saw my startled reaction and grabbed her belly. I laughed and gave her a hug. "I'm so sorry, Darius!"

"No, I was overthinking," I apologized, trying to shake off the feeling that overcame me.

"Your reaction tells me that you felt the same fear that I feel looking at them. You can see my baby's cries for help and understanding?" Mami asked me, her eyes dim almost green. "All of them tell a different story. Some are about her, others are about her emotions she cannot explain."

"I can see they are hiding a truth, but I'm not smart enough to understand what I'm seeing. I see things like my mother. Mama was afro-centric and admired anything created by black people. She used to take me to museums, theaters, and concerts when I was young. I can memorize things, but I hate reading because I'm slower than everyone else," I confessed to Mrs. King, getting a good picture of that last one for Kaliah. "I know someone that knows a lot more about this type of thing. He'll tell me what's up once he has a minute to get back with me."

"The fact that you said that tells me you see more than others. Many that have seen Mandisa's works in Paris looked at the pictures and saw beauty, Darius. I could tell you were different when I saw you start looking at different things than the others. You should give yourself more credit for your intelligence.

'The little things stand out much more than the larger subjects. Like those eerie eyes, the keys, roses, that baby, and the witch that haunts her nightmares with green eyes there!"

The painting that Mami was talking about was barely noticeable until she pointed it out. But when I saw all the black, Immediately I was angry! It was another dark painting, but it looked like you were looking through a doorway. There was a building outside, and Mandisa was standing on the edge! A woman in a long black dress looked like she was melting, that demon had big green eyes, and she had a knife trying to push Mandisa off the side! I panicked, taking a picture of it as Hakim stood over my shoulder.

"We need to talk once we're alone, Cyrus. I think you know what about," Hakim whispered to me, and I nodded, putting my phone away.

"Darius?" Mami called, getting my attention. "You said 'used to' and refer to her in the past tense. How long has it been since she ascended?"

"Ascended…I like that, Mrs. King. My mother ascended just before I turned ten years old. I don't have any other family," I replied, folding my arms thinking.

"What of your father?" Mami asked, trying to read my expression as I looked down.

"We don't get along anymore. Dad hates me, so I gave him his space and left. That was three years ago. When my grandmother ascended, I tried to contact him, but he wouldn't accept my calls. It's cool. He's dealing with everything his own way," I replied, raising my eyebrows trying not to overthink.

"I see…So you're young, wounded, and all alone like Hakim and Lionel. Their grandparents are very kind people but seem much too old," Mami groaned.

"No, I'm not alone. I have the Dunns and Kaliah. They're my family, Mrs. King. I love all of them like blood," I explained, attempting to smile. I didn't want to talk about it anymore.

Mrs. King nodded her curly ponytail and pulled me back into the kitchen. Hakim had Mandisa's cake on the table for Mami. She looked at it smiling, asking, "What have we here?"

"Hakim said Mandisa loves sweets, so he bought her a cheesecake to share with you and Big Baybah!" I laughed, teasing her. I glanced over at Mandisa as she came through the door. "I don't know what kind it is, but I'm sure it's delicious."

"Oh, Jah!" Mami giggled, looking at that pretty cherry-popped heart. "It is too lovely to eat! Look at that, Queen, isn't it beautiful?"

I took off my jacket and set it on the nearest chair. Suddenly I felt Mami grabbing on me!

"Darius! It's so long…Jah, look at it!" Mrs. King gasped, grabbing my…hair! I felt relieved for a second. I thought that maybe Jody had pulled a stunt. He's notorious for attacking goddesses at random when I'm high! I don't trust him as far as I can see that nigga!....LMFAO! "Are these extensions!?"

"Yeah, Mami, I get my weave touched up everi month cuz I don't like my new groff showing," I teased her, acting like my rachet self. I tossed it over my shoulder and put my hand on my hip. "No, it's all me. I've been growing it since I was five. Mama twisted it up, and it started getting long really fast. I've never cut it. My mom told me she started growing her hair when she became a Christian.

'I remember Mama saying something about the black men in the Bible, like Samson and Jesus were Nazarites and their strength was in their hair, so you never cut it unless it's to renew a covenant. My name means power in the face of evil. Michael Darius-Osiris Jefferson. But I never go by Michael. I haven't since my father and I stopped being cool.

'Osiris, but Cyrus became my nickname because Mama wanted me to have ties to Kemet. I love it, and it's dope. She was born into an Islamic family, but she met my father, became Christian, and never returned. Wrapping her hair when she went out was the only thing I ever saw her do that was Muslim."

"You miss her so much you can't bring yourself to part with it…She started it for you," Mami said, smiling up at me.

"I used to say I didn't want it long, but once she lost her hair from the chemo and shaved her head, I didn't want to cut my hair…ever. I guess you'd be right. I never thought of it being me holding on to her by keeping it. I've always felt like she was close, but I still miss her," I thought, watching Mami touch my crown. I reached inside my back pocket and pulled out my wallet. I gave Mami the picture of my mother and me.

"Look at you, Darius! You look so happy and proud. She's so beautiful, her eyes are so pretty like yours, and that smile!" Mrs. King exclaimed, handing it to Mandisa.

"Darius….she's so pretty and all that hair! It is as long as yours! Why is it so red? Did she color them?" Mandisa swooned, looking at Mama's hair.

"No, it changed colors in the sun and got lighter as it grew out," I replied smiling, looking at Mandisa's hair. "It was really brown and light like yours. She never had black hair. Mama wrapped it up every day in different colored scarves."

"You have her earthy eyes, strong nose, and round lips," Mandisa giggled, blushing.

"People used to say the only thing I got from my dad was my skin. But after I turned 13, I got his height," I chuckled nervously. "He's a giant chocolate man. When I was nine, his hands were so big that he could palm my head like a basketball. He used to pretend to dribble it all the time. My

Mama loved his black-ass so much she called him 'Sexual Chocolate.'"

Mandisa giggled again, staring at me, "Randy Watson? Your Daddy was Randy Watson!?"

Everyone died of laughter. I dropped my head, saying, "You gonna sit here and roast me in front of your Mama, Lisa McDowell?"

Hakim and Lionel both started clapping together….Lionel shook his head, saying, "That boy good!"

Both Mami and Mandisa had to stop Hakim from laughing so hard as I pretended to walk around the stage with a microphone saying, "Thank you, Thank you so much, everyone…Give around applause for my band, Sexual Chocolate! Give a round for yourselves….you're so beautiful."

"He's good and terrible," Hakim cried as Lionel kept clapping, making Mami scream. Hakim grabbed my hair. I called and ducked him. "Uh-uh, you gonna run now that I love you!"

"Oh, Baby!" I cried, grabbing Hakim. "I missed you so much! Why didn't you tell me you were back! I got your money, Daddy!"

Mandisa and Mami lost it.

"Eww, Y'all niggas are gay," Lionel laughed, impersonating Riley Freeman from the Boondocks. Mandisa died as she pointed to Lionel. "What?"

"Lionel, oh my god! You and Hakim! You remind me of those bad boys from that show! It is so funny that you sound like the little boy saying that!" Mandisa snorted.

Hakim frowned up and looked at Lionel and said, "So, I liked the Boondocks, and Huey Freeman is the most real. Maybe I imitated him as a kid because I thought that shit was dope."

"Maybe? Nigga, you watched that shit so much I liked it. But I can get how people would say we act that way. I love fucking with Hakim like Riley fucks with Huey because I know Hakim will fight me if I make him mad enough. It was fun when we were kids, but now Hakim is just ruthless like Easy-E!" Lionel groaned.

"This is why you should be happy you have girls, Mrs. King. I've had to be in the middle of this for years, and it's only going to get worse. You've been warned," I told Mami, eyeing Hakim and Lionel.

"Darius, you are not allowed in my home until after I have Amani! You are dangerous!" Mami laughed, trying to escape back to the bathroom.

Mandisa came over and nodded, blushing sweetly. Mami watched Mandisa look at Hakim and shook her head, giggling, "Hakim, I told you I'll kill you!"

"Mami, I didn't do anything! How could you?" Hakim chuckled as he showed Mami the paperwork for the modeling contract. "I looked over everything while the owner dolled her up, Mami. I checked his site at the house a moment ago, too. He's going to blow up, and Antoine's determined to put Mandisa in his clothes! She told me that she's always wanted to model, which would boost her self-esteem. Antoine seems to have a magical effect on her, don't you think?"

"She looks so happy, and her face is glowing! ..... Is this runway walking stuff? I don't think that Queen would like the pressure of those thin girls like in Paris," Mami replied.

I knew to stay quiet when the Master was at work. If Hakim was on it, then all we had to do was sit back and watch the man work.

"Antoine is not that typical fashion diva, Mami. He's interested in Mandisa for her figure. His shops cater to women with unique body styles. He thinks that Mandisa is the most beautiful woman he's ever seen, and he wouldn't care how her body changes. The man said he wanted to make future lines around her to put her on display as the Face of Zola…He calls her 'Paula,' the Lola of Zola. I think that 'Paula' is a bad bitch, Mami!" Hakim died laughing suddenly. "I think that as long as people know her as 'Paula' the bad bitch in pictures, then Mandisa will stay a sweet angel, but get some free clothes personally designed, her own money to save, a career of her own, and a major boost to her ego. I think that will help get her a step closer to defining her own lane without needing Daddy's approval. What do you think, Mrs. King? I know you have your thoughts."

"Of course, Hakim, come this way," Mrs. King replied, smiling as they went into the den with Mandisa.

"She's going to let Mandisa do it. I can tell…," Lionel whispered to me.

"Yeah, Mrs. King is the real deal. I like her, she reminds me of my mother a lot. Mami is sweet and loves her kids. Mandisa is blessed to have her. I'd take her any day," I sighed, folding my arms, thinking.

"Her food is killer! Last night she made me some…uh…crepes! Yeah, them shits were like Heaven on Earth!" Lionel added, nodding.

"Oh!" I yelled, remembering what I smelled before, and went searching. Mami had made some chicken wings and baked a tray of brownies. I grabbed one and quickly slammed it in my mouth. It was so fucking warm, fudgy, and there were chunks of chocolate melted in the center. Lionel suddenly pushed me. I grabbed the tray and held him back with my free hand. "Are you threatening me!? Uh-uh, my brother, you got to get your own!"

"Cyrus! Unass the chocolate!" Lionel yelled at me as I slammed number three in my mouth. "Really, Nigga, you just gonna put another in yo mouth like I ain't standing right in your face?!"

"I'm not scared of you, Lionel! We aren't at the Dunns! Hakim will kick your ass if you touch me in Mandisa's house. Sit down and have a wing, Bro! I'm in my fucking element!" I chuckled, having another bite. The sugary goodness in those little bites of chocolate heaven went precisely where I needed it to go. "Mami, I love you so much right now! Can I get in there with Amani? You can be my momma too?!"

"No! No, no, no more babies for Ninon! But you can be my son, too!" Mami laughed, coming back into the kitchen, taking the tray away from me, and giving Lionel a brownie. I slumped my shoulders, and she shook her head. "Darius, you are a pig! Look at your face!"

"What? Oh, this?" I asked, wiping my mouth. "I don't mind wearing my dessert...Who doesn't want a man that both looks and tastes as sweet as chocolate, Mami?"

"No!" Mandisa giggled. "You eat more than a black hole! Mami, I have never seen anyone eat like Darius! It is terrifying to witness up close!"

"Wait! Did you just call me black! I thought we were good, Queen? How could you?" I asked her, looking pitiful. "I resemble that remark and tape a fence."

Mandisa giggled, putting her hands on her fine hips, "Oui, yes, you do resemble it!"

Mami was blushing, covering her face telling me, "It is okay, Darius. When I was growing up, all the girls loved Prince and El DeBarge. I liked Rick James and Billy Ocean!"

"What!?" Mandisa screamed, blushing. "How did you fall in love with Dad if you love black men?"

"Hey, I liked rock music, and Thomas looked like Bret Michaels. He's got those sexy eyes and gorgeous lips. At first, I didn't like Tomny. He was a whore because he knew he looked good. But things got forced along, and he grew on me. The rest is history. Pretty eyes on a man always warm my heart," Mami told Mandisa shrugging.

Mandisa giggled nervously, "I never knew that about you. You always say 'Dad is Dad' or 'That's just the way it worked out.'"

Mrs. King frowned a moment to herself, then looked at Mandisa. I made a dumb face and acted confused.

Mami smiled and sighed, "Well, Thomas is a jerk! He's always been an asshole, but Tomny has soft spots. I know how to poke him to get my way most of the time."

"It was all that poking that got you Mandisa's twin," I mumbled, slamming a chicken wing in my mouth, being messy.

"Darius!" Mandisa hollered, hitting my shoulder.

Mami dropped her head laughing, "Darius, no!"

"Uh-uh! He was all in it! I know he was! Talk dirty to me, Baby…eww! Y'all are so nasty," I laughed, pretending to hump the table. "Did you hear the madness, Mandisa? Did they traumatize you? We're your friends. You can tell us."

"This is why I am happy I have no boys!" Mami laughed nervously, rubbing her belly, trying to escape. "I'm going to bed before I wind up in the hospital, Darius!"

"Don't have the baby in there yet! Her driver's test is in 3 more months," I reminded her as Mandisa helped her mother up the stairs.

"Nigga, you're crazy," Lionel laughed, hitting my arm.

"What? You saw her belly! They got it wrong. There are two babies in there," I laughed as Hakim wiped his eyes, putting on his glasses.

"You're in a hell of a mood, Cyrus," Hakim laughed, pushing my other shoulder. He sat at the table across from me, smiling. "What's going on with you? The only time you trip out is when you're really happy or nervous. What's up?"

"Mandisa's mom…she's so amazing! I see where Mandisa gets all that sweetness. Watch and see, Amani is gonna look just like her sister. Tiny little Queenie!" I chuckled, chewing the deliciously crispy Thai-flavored wing. Hakim stole a piece from my plate. "Uh-uh, nigga, no, you didn't! Don't ever touch another black man's leg!"

Hakim nearly choked chewing and said, "This is what I missed. It's like you're 12 again, Bro! You always raise everyone's spirits when you're around."

"It's been a while since we just vibed like this….it feels good. I don't know why I feel so good," I replied as I smiled at my brother.

"You happy as hell, and I bet I know the reason," Hakim said, taking another bite of his stolen wing raising his eyebrows.

"Man-di-sa!" Lionel sang, laughing viciously. "She's got both yall niggas zooming like the Commodores! (Pointing at me) Skyler Jett! (Then fingering Hakim) Lionel Richie!"

"Ha, ha, HA! Look who's named after the last motherfucker!" Hakim sarcastically taunted Lionel making him think. "Looking like a lanky Loyd Polite!"

Lionel rolled his eyes at Hakim, and I started laughing, "No, Baby Bro, you look just like him before he cut off all his hair on the cool."

Hakim was rolling as I gave him dap. He had tears in his eyes as he took another wing. Lionel groaned, "Ha, ha, Facial Hairless Trey Songz! You ain't got no chin chair or no tattoos, but those eyebrows got you sewed up!"

"Yeah, yah girl loves Trey Songz!" Hakim laughed, humping the table. "I make them sing…I don't do that shit."

"Fuck you, Hakim!" Lionel yelled as I took another bite smiling at them back and forth. "And fuck you, Calvin Payne!"

"Nigga! If you don't stop! There's gonna be a misunderstanding here! I don't look like Lance Gross, and you've been saying that shit since I was 15. It's getting old, Lionel," I warned him rolling my eyes.

Hakim dropped his bone on my plate, laughing, "You do look just like that nigga, Bro! You cut your hair, and you'd be twins….Identical twins!"

"Why do all dark-skinned brothers have to look similar to yall? I look better than Lance Gross, and I bet he can't touch the pussy like me. All this black-on-black hating has got to stop!" I said, staring at Lionel as he gave Hakim dap.

"Nigga, you're always bragging about your shit!" Lionel said, shaking his head.

"Because I have the biggest, Bro! I'm the King of the jungle, and the ladies be swinging from my head vines trying to jump all over Jody!" I chuckled, pounding my chest like Tarzan. "Cyrus's dick is addictive like crack, and I'll break a bitch's back!"

"You hear that shit, Hakim? You better get that pussy first, or it's a wrap for your ass! Everybody knows that niggas that love eating puss as much as you claim lacking not packing!" Lionel went in, making Hakim and me pause. Lionel was laughing so hard he fell on Mandisa's kitchen floor.

Hakim was laughing down at Lionel, "I'm not worried about Cyrus, alright. I don't need sex, Bro. That shit you're talking about is a myth. All brothers that love eating it aren't little men."

"I won't touch her like that, Man. I don't want to spoil it for you," I reassured Hakim.

"Can we stop this conversation, please?! We are in HER house. This is disrespectful as fuck!" Hakim whispered, frowning at us.

"Alright, I'm done. I don't need my chin checked like Lionel," I laughed.

"Fuch you, Cyrus! That shit still hurts," Lionel complained.

"You know you were lucky it was Hakim and not me that got your ass," I laughed, wiping my fingers with a napkin. Lionel started laughing, and Hakim looked away, scratching his head. "Oh, you both still on that I can't fight, shit, really?"

"No! No! Bro, but you're lucky Mandisa saved your ass, Lionel. I almost fucked you off," Hakim announced to him.

"Yeah…Your girl wants me…Yall, niggas are blind. Mandisa wants it so bad, but she is scared of me. I don't usually like Red-bones, but she can get it," Lionel sang, smiling. I pushed his melon head as I dried my hands.

"Whatever, Nigga, don't nobody want your bony-ass. Pussy hears you coming, and it locks up like a clam. That's why you've never tasted a pearl," I said, laughing.

"Nigga, I can call a number and have two on me right now. But I'm trying to take a fucking break before it gets too hot. I might get a few numbers and fuck, but I don't want no girlfriends. Bitches ain't gonna tie me down for the summer like yall dumb asses."

'I'm gonna have fun. Look at you spending your bread, sniffing after Mandisa, and you ain't even gonna get the pussy. What if her dad finds out? It's a wrap!" Lionel said, pissed off by his relaxed face.

"Bro, that shit ain't cool!" I warned Lionel about to seriously fuck him up myself.

"No, let him finish, so I can choke his bony brown ass out for the night!" Hakim said, staring at Lionel in disgust.

"Yeah, yeah, you both in love. But what the fuck you gonna do? You can't really think that shit is gonna fly? What you gonna do, Hakim, huh? She's a virgin. Girls like that, don't be trying to fool around like your sexed-out crazy ass. The minute you cross the line, she's gonna run away. One of you about to get hurt….and I think it's you, Hakim," Lionel added, looking at his brother.

"Is that right?" Hakim asked. Oh shit….that always was terrible. When he said those exact words, it was like he was accepting some imaginary challenge. It was his sarcastic way of saying, 'You don't know shit, nigga' I hated when those words came out of his mouth. "I said I don't need sex, and I meant that shit. I can wait as long as I have to. Tell you what…? You hang with us all summer, I keep an eye on you, and you keep an eye on me. If I fuck up, I'll buy you a car when you turn 16 in October?"

"You serious? I don't want to waste my time if you gonna pull a stunt on my ass," Lionel asked, getting excited.

"Dead serious, Bro! Any car you want! But there's a catch. You have to watch that mouth, and you can't fuck up either. You fight, get in trouble, or hurt Mandisa in any way; the bet's off. And I'll fuck you up myself," Hakim earnestly promised his brother.

Now I'm beginning to worry about who I'm dealing with. I can sense the exact same vibes that I get from 'ELYEUH' while Hakim is calm? He's playing too many games. Wait! Maybe Hakim was genuine. I needed to give him some credit.

"I'm in! You're getting me an Aston Martin!" Lionel laughed, shaking Hakim's hand. "All I have to do is chill and party with yall. This is gonna be the best birthday ever!"

"Easier said than done, Bro, don't forget. I've been celibate for almost a year and a half," Hakim reminded Lionel. A look of sudden realization washed across his face as I laughed. Hakim and Lionel looked at me.

"What? Don't look at me like that! I got a car, and I know how to act, so you can't con my ass into nothing. But she's a virgin, and I would never do her dirty. If she comes on to me first, that's a different story," I said, nodding. "I've been good a few months, but I'm due soon."

"You're sharing a girl," Lionel laughed, suddenly sounding more intelligent. "You can't sneak a taste without the other noticing! She's a virgin. She'll start acting differently once she gets some."

"It'll be fine," I said, smiling. "I love Mandisa, so it won't matter to me. Whenever it happens, it will happen. There's no rush. What did Mami say about things?"

"It looks like after Mami has a talk with Antoine tomorrow, she's going to make up her mind. Things look like everything is a yes me," Hakim said proudly.

"We need to talk to her mother about this shit with her father," I added, looking toward the stairs.

"I know, don't worry. Let's save it for another day. Let Mandisa and her mother have their moment about the modeling thing. I'll handle that part, alright? Besides, we can't tell Mami about us, not yet. She'll lose her mind and run us off," Hakim whispered quietly to me, looking over at Lionel. "Keep your mouth shut!"

"Nobody's gonna hear shit from me! You act like I can't keep a secret!" Lionel protested.

"You can't!" I laughed, but it was genuine.

"Whatever! Shit, when we gonna hit up a club or something? I don't want to be stuck all summer hanging with yall at Chuckie Cheese and shit!" Lionel grumbled. "We need to go to LA with Kaliah. At least he can be my wingman. His beige ass pulls the finest brown sistas! Beautiful grown women chase him, and he is turning down pussy left and right. 'Na Na mi got a wife!' Fuck that shit. Trisha is crazy as fuck and mean as hell. I would have left that ho alone a long time ago. She's pretty, but I can't have no bitch screaming at me 24/7 and fucking everybody that says hello. No, Sir!"

"I can co-sign that shit, Bro. I like a woman with a little attitude. Trisha is nothing but a big ball of pissed-off pussy. He knew that shit when he married her. I told him to run. I don't understand why he changed his mind the last time, but he took her back," I groaned, shaking my head.

"Kaliah told me he's done," Hakim added, making both Lionel and I stare at him.

"Since when?" I asked, chuckling sarcastically.

"Since he moved back with his mother and told Trisha he was done a few days ago," Hakim told me.

"That shit is too fresh. Kaliah's gonna turn around and step right back in it. Kaliah is a habitual shit stepper," I said, not trusting it. "He shows up, and I know Trisha is going to bring her loud-mouthed ass here. We can't handle her, Hakim! No!"

Hakim opened his eyes wider and sighed, "Bro, I love Kaliah. He's my brother, too, but he can't come here with us around Mandisa's fine ass!"

Hakim suddenly got up and went upstairs to check on Mandisa. Lionel glanced over at me, talking shit, "Look who's a hater now!? You worried too, Bro? Kaliah comes to the view shit might get deep, huh?"

"Shut the fuck up, Lionel!" I mumbled, frowning. Lionel was about to start some serious shit! Hakim did not want Kaliah here bringing Trisha. I was warming up to the idea of sharing Mandisa with Hakim because Hakim needed me far more than he admitted.

I was the only person besides Kaliah that could really stop him from falling off the celibacy boat and running wild. He got himself together, and I was glad. But he never said that he had things entirely under control. He was terrified that he would hurt that girl. I was there to keep his ass in check as always.

I knew a lot about Hakim, but I didn't know it all. What I heard earlier was sort of new, but no surprise. He'd really been a busy bee since we were young. I do not hate on him at all, but some shit he exposed me to affects me. But I couldn't stand by and watch him self-destruct. I kept some of his secrets locked away with all those old collars in my condo. No one knew where they were but me and ELYEUH.

It was best if that nigga stayed dead or asleep. There was no way Mandisa would ever trust Hakim if she knew the whole truth about how sick Hakim was deep down. It was much graver than they had seen when he lost his temper. That was just the warning that Hakim was gonna lose it. It's much worse once he's out. ELYEUH doesn't go away quickly once he's out, and he will try to fuck a girl before he goes back to sleep. So far, Hakim has only lost his temper a few times. It hasn't gotten nearly close to the danger zone. I honestly don't think that ELYEUH would hurt Lionel. He never wants to be near his brother when he's out.

#

When Hakim got his own car, we used to go to strip clubs everywhere or anywhere where women were gathering having fun. Typically, strip clubs were ELYEUH's personal shopping centers. I had been away for just a few weeks with Kaliah, but when I came back, Hakim was different.

When we walked into that club that night was the first time I met ELYEUH, and Hakim was 15 years old. Nearly everyone inside of that building knew who HE was. Hakim found out that a girl he liked named Nicole wasn't there anymore and got pissed off. We sat down at an empty table, watching another girl dance. I thought everything was excellent….NO!

I stared at the girl dancing on stage. She was cute. Tall, a bit lean for my tastes, light skin, green eyes, long blond hair. Her dancing was a bit stiff, but at least it was a show.

"Take it off, Bitch! Don't waste my time," Hakim yelled at her. His face was dead serious as he locked eyes with her waiting. She smiled and came standing onstage closer. Hakim looked up at her, folded his arms, and shook his head, frowning.

She climbed down on her knees in front of him, crawling around trying to get some paper. She smiled back at him and gave her barely covered ass a little wiggle. Her tiny red bikini made it seem like she was wearing less. But it was apparent she was new, nervous, and more worried about the money than the dancing.

"Do I look like a bitch now?" She asked, trying to touch Hakim, and he pulled away from her. He tapped my elbow.

"Cyrus, Maybe you can help this ignorant slut with simple science? What walks around on four legs, wiggles its tail in any male's face, and obviously is deaf?" Hakim asked me honestly.

"I don't know, Bro…It's your world," I replied, trying to see where this was going if he didn't want her to dance. I was looking for someone else to enjoy. "What?"

"This bitch, which ironically is in the position to get fucked like a dog, asking me if she looks like a fucking bitch! What the fuck makes you think I came here to watch a bitch dance? I said, take it off, Bitch!" Hakim demanded, taking off his glasses and putting them in his shirt pocket.

I clutched my glass as I noticed the sudden change in his tone. Hakim's voice dropped down with a lot more bass, and he had this dark gaze that looked like he was staring through you. Not just that but, you may not believe this shit, but when that nigga moves, it is so calculating you know that is not Hakim. Every move he made seemed to draw the eye, and other women were starting to listen, why I don't know.

"You can't fuck a stripper, Baby, besides you look too young to even be in here. What are you, twelve?" She laughed, becoming defensive tossing her wig around in Hakim's face.

Hakim raised his eyebrows, and the frown on his face made me worried about how close she was to him. He very calmly backed up in his seat and pretended to get her hair off his face. Hakim held up a Hundred dollar bill and clutched a wad in his other hand. His eyes were on the money, not the girl, as he said, "Is that right? Well, I'm 100 today, Bitch. Now, I bet you'll take it off or do whatever I say….?

'AND you don't give fuck about my age, now do you…BITCH?"

I frowned and stared over at Hakim. It was crazy! Suddenly he didn't even notice me sitting right there. The girl smiled at the bill he was holding and….Hakim slowly began to put his other money away.

"Whatever you want…You got my full attention," This pitiful girl said.

"Yeah, thought so…You've got mine for now, but the other red-bone over there has more ass than you…I love ass, so if you want to KEEP my attention, you need to either take it off and let me see it all, or you can show me something new. That won't be easy because I've seen it all, now, Bitch," Hakim chuckled. Hakim took that hundred and slipped the bill on the stage by her golden heels. "That's for getting me to talk. Usually, a bitch can't keep my attention long enough to get me to talk. I've been waiting 3 minutes now. So are you gonna dance, or should I cut my goddamn losses?"

"No! Don't go!" She screamed, moving closer and really shaking it for Hakim. She reached out, trying to get on him for a lapdance. Hakim pulled away from her, pissed off. The dancer was confused about what was going on. I believe we both were wondering what he was buying. Dudes pay to be touched inside a strip club. "What? You want something different?"

"I didn't say you could touch me, did I? I swear all you bitches are quick to jump for a dollar without asking what's in the fucking pool. I paid you for the 3 minutes. You haven't shown me shit, Bitch. So, unless you're going to give me what I want to pay for....you can find another simp with less than what I'm holding to help you with those financial issues that have you in here....Playing actress...I'm a director!

'I want some motherfuckin action, or I don't waste my time," Hakim told her. "I told you to take it off! Where the fuck is Nicole? At least her ass can follow simple instructions! She's got more body than your bony ass!

'I like my bitches thick, and I'm not paying you to piss me off! Get out of my face, Desperate Slut!"

Hakim hit the tabletop and stood up, finally acknowledging me. He motioned me to follow him.

"Nicole's not here! She's my sister! Don't leave….I'll do whatever you ask. Look, I'm taking it all off, okay, Look?" She hollered to us. Hakim glanced back over his shoulder, and you already know I was trying to see where this was going. She started taking off her bikini bottoms. Hakim went back and sat looking at her face, not her body, as she got completely naked! Mercy…Me…You usually have to be in a whole-in-the-wall club to get the girls to dance completely nude in the open.

"You're a stripper; please tell me you can actually dance, girl? You said Nicole is your sister, now you have my attention again. Okay, yeah, I can see it. Same skin and smile, but all that fake shit isn't working for me at all. If you're black, be black. I don't know any women like you with blond hair and green eyes! Strike one!" Hakim sighed charismatically, counting bills without looking away from her.

"You're HIM, aren't you? Nikki called HIM, ELYEUH. She said, you're mean, but you do nice things for girls. I got whatever you need. Cherry's here for you, okay?" She told him, nervously dancing near but not touching Hakim.

"I do nice things for girls that I like, and so far, I don't want you, Cherry! You ask the wrong questions and have yet to show me you can follow the most infantile instructions. I say dance, you dance until I say stop, Bitch! I tell you to take it off. You get buck naked, Ho! You let all these other punk-ass niggas treat you like shit, fuck you, and use you up for free. I'm different, Bitches! I don't need your love or respect! I want what the fuck I want, with no questions asked, and you can have something from me that half-stepping nigga will never give. I'll fuck the shit out of you, pay you for your time, and help you get the fuck out of the situation that brought you here….If I like you, Bitch!

'I'm Captain Save A HOE that doesn't want you. I'll save you, but your price comes with my hook. Since you can't follow directions, you must like it here? You are not ready to save yourself. So, you're lost, and I'll let you keep acting like you're about this life! I know a real ho when I see one, Bitch! You're scared and need to get the fuck out of here before I put you where you need to be."

You have to realize that the entire time that this nigga was talking shit to this one girl, everyone in the area heard what the fuck ELYEUH was saying. Many of the dudes there were confused about what the fuck was happening but watching Cherry. She was making more money than before, and Hakim seemed to do that on purpose.

I started to wrap my head around what was going on in his twisted head. In a way, he thought he was helping these girls that weren't really there to do what it took. He was picking the cute shy girls that looked afraid and pulling them away from the club...but he still was manipulating them. They wanted the cash, but once he fucked the shit out of them, they went crazy and came looking for ELYUEH and found a confused Hakim. He was tripping because he didn't remember these girls at all until they touched him. Then he was mad as fuck and trying to get the hell away from them. I went along with a lot of it because all the girls wanted it. All I did was keep the contracts for HIM and hold the collars of the girls he's brought. He won't look at them once he takes them back. Nicole's is the only one I have, and HE knows it.

Understand that a collar is not what you might be imagining. Most in a BDSM lifestyle will know that collaring someone for ownership does not literally mean wearing a collar. Hakim is not that sort of practitioner. When he goes for the kill, it means he decides that he's willing to pay more than a thousand dollars on a girl.

Instead of giving her the cash upfront, he buys her an expensive diamond necklace. If she returns the collar, then he gives her the money. But if she sells or keeps it...Then he fucks her until he gets bored of her. But he doesn't want any of them to come back once they make a choice. There is no in-between when it comes to the contract. Either you want to be fucked and collared, or you want freedom. If he fucks you after he collars a girl, she's going to come to find him. It's always like that.

Hakim Jahlil Dunn is my best friend, he's my brother, and I'd do anything to help him. Fuck that Nigga, ELYEUH! He really doesn't give a fuck. It's a game. He knows they want to fuck him, and in the end, Nicole is the only one he collared, but she gave it back, took the money, fucked him, and left him confused for once.

But I know if he gets out near Mandisa and fucks her, she'll do anything he says and never look at another dude the same. Hakim doesn't want to hurt her; he's in love. I believe it. But I'm so paranoid that I'm having a hard time telling who I'm dealing with. I've never seen him this bad. I think Mandisa may be having this effect on him. Love may not be a good thing for Hakim. What if ELYEUH and Hakim are starting to fight one another? That might be why I'm getting mixed signals. Fuck! He's getting better…I'm just gonna keep looking out. If things get too bad, fuck! I'm going to have to get Kaliah here. He'll be the only one that can get Hakim back if I can't.

Act Three

Chapter Eleven: Bitch, Don't Kill My Vibe

Hakim

The entire summer, we were together no matter what we did. We went to movies, skating, clubbing, shopping, concerts, or chilled here or there between our homes. Mandisa and my family were everywhere from Houston, Texas, to New Orleans, Louisiana. It was like being kids again without anyone having sex. We had weed, innocent fun, and life never felt so good. Lionel and I were getting along better than ever. Both Cyrus and I were head over heels in love with Mandisa. I didn't care that we looked like little boys chasing her around.

I know you don't believe me when I say this, but I don't have a jealous bone in my body when it comes to Cyrus. I honestly don't have a problem with him being all over Mandisa around me. People can't understand that Mandisa looks at me differently. She listens to me like I speak the gospel, plus she is so shy she's still afraid to touch me! It drives me insane that I have to chase her! I've never wanted to pursue a girl for attention. I would always find another if one didn't seem interested. It was rare one said no. The more Mandisa ignored me in public and was all over Cyrus, the more she thought she needed to be alone with me. I enjoyed letting her have her sexy dances and flirting with my brother. He didn't realize he was giving her so much attention that she thought she was neglecting Hakim.

I knew that if I let him in, he would keep her all over me. I have to pat myself on the back for that shit. It was so lovely to have my brother back, helping me get everything I wanted with a big ass smile on his face. Cyrus was getting what he always wanted, and I am glad I had a part in helping him leave the others alone. Now he could control his spending by focusing on Mandisa.

My girl, too.

That meant that he didn't have to spend as much as when he was playing the field. You see, I had gotten the entire family so wrapped up in showing Mandisa a good time that I could go along for the ride. Cyrus kept us laughing because he was happy, Lionel was calm because he was trying to get a car, and Mandisa rode the high waves. I was reaping in all her overflow of happiness. It motivated me to make this shit really last. If we had this much fun, not fucking…I'm going to have it all once she breaks that shy shell and lets us in. Which of us gets it first won't matter because she's so submissive and wants to make me happy. Cyrus, on the other hand, is jealous and always pulling shit. I laugh it off because it's funny. He isn't trying to start shit. I figured out he's just testing me to see if I'll lose it. That's another reason I need him around. He's keeping me on my toes.

Mandisa was so sweet, accepting, affectionate to us both. Sometimes it was like she could be two different women at once. We fell deeper in love with her every day. It was a beautiful thing, and Lionel was having fun because he was racking up his spending allowance. My brother was still loud, wild, and random but less violent and mean. I was starting to like being around Lionel. Shit, I may just blow the bet and get him the car anyway. But it would be my luck that he got the ride and went back to his old ways. That would make me fuck him off.

I'm not saying that being celibate was an easy decision because that shit is hard as fuck! As a man, this shit is torture. I'm just being honest with you. Sometimes when Mandisa and I were alone on a movie night, we'd start making out, and it would get heavy. I'd get terrified because once she touched me, it was as if I couldn't control myself. I made a promise, and I intend to keep it. But I hope you don't mind my manners when I say my dick was kicking my brain's ass. I had to excuse myself and run away from some situations. Mandisa caught on too.

Whenever I had to run, Mandisa knew why I was running. Cyrus had her calling me Forrest Gump now! That shit's not funny. They have no idea how bad I really am.

When I say I'm celibate, I mean no nothing! I can't even masturbate because it makes matters worse. I'd try to do the real thing once I was excited because I could! I would meditate or try to make myself sleep. Reading really helped a lot too. It got my mind off of things so I could focus on something positive. But somedays I had moments when I had to drink myself out of it.

With Mandisa dressing sexy like a gorgeous butterfly everywhere we went, niggas were always trying to get at her! I don't mean just our age either. All niggas that got anywhere around my wife tried to shoot a shot and had to be shut down by Cyrus, Lionel, or Me lastly if they didn't get the message the first two gates. I'll share her with Cyrus, but fuck them other niggas! They can't have my wife!

Mandisa was so naive it was as if she had no idea why she was being approached. Girl, you are the shit! Can't you see it? No....She can't see it. Mandisa still has no idea how beautiful she is. Even modeling with Antoine didn't open her eyes. When she saw herself in catalogs, posters, or even the internet, she would just laugh and say, 'That's not me! That's Paula!' I'd just shake my head.

Everyone that met that girl fell instantly in love with her. My grandparents thought she walked on water! Antoine, yes, Mr. Sugar Britches himself, looked at her sometimes like a straight guy. Everyone thought I was playing about that shit until they saw it for themselves. He got too close to that ass one too many times, and his fruity accent and feminine ways went out the door a few times. Just goes to show you, for some, it is a choice.

Mandisa's father called every Sunday evening, and we stayed near here or there because we were worried about Mami. When she talked to her father, it was a struggle. He'd say things that upset her. She never talked back; Mandisa accepted whatever the man said. When she'd mention anything fun she was doing, he'd say it was nice but tell her not to get attached to anything. He'd change the subject to her coming back to Paris. Mandisa would panic and get off the phone. The rest of the day, she would be so upset she wouldn't leave her room. It hurt me the first time it happened, and each time she talked to that man, it pissed me off.

Today, Mandisa accidentally dropped the ball in the middle of the game, the Sunday after my birthday. She mentioned my name and the birthday party to her father. Her father assumed all her friends were girls here. He knew "Hakim" was not a girl's name, nor was it white. Dr. King went off on Mandisa and broke her heart. He started screaming at her, saying that he was going to find them and drag her back. He had Mandisa so hysterical that it made me have a fucking panic attack. Mami had to grab the phone and play all her cards.

I was comforting Mandisa in the den while Mami talked to Dr. King in a heated argument, "Tomny! You cannot tell me how to raise my child! Your way is destroying her! No! No! I'm not going anywhere, and neither is Disa! School is about to start, and I am too close to my due date. I will not get on a plane. She will not stay Jah knows where, and you are never around! She needs friends, family, and fun to fix what you fucked up! You are driving all of us crazy! Amani deserves a chance to be happy, too! You have Mandisa losing her fucking mind! This is all your fault! Don't call her or me again! I want a divorce!"

Mandisa got up and went to the restroom down the hall. I waited a moment because Mami was so upset she held her tummy as if she was in pain and crying.

"This is the most fun she has had in her life, and I don't care what you think. I'm a doctor too! I can raise my girls alone, and if you think I've forgotten your little mess-ups, you're seriously mistaken! If you're going to be an asshole your entire life, then be one alone!" Mami told him, hanging up in his face.

I didn't think I was supposed to hear all of that. I went to check on Mandisa. She didn't respond when I knocked or tried to open the door.

"Queen!" I yelled through the door. Mandisa wouldn't answer. I knocked again. "Mandisa, talk to me, please?"

A moment later, she unlocked the door. Her face was red, her eyes were dark, and a frown on her face. She was so upset she couldn't say a word. Mandisa grabbed me and cried like a little girl. I picked the wrong week to send Cyrus and Lionel to LA to meet up with Kaliah. I had distraught women on my hands. I'd have to call them and let them know what was up. Moves had been made, but nothing was solid yet. It was too soon. I needed more time, shit! If Dr. King showed up now, we'd have to run, and Mami was in no condition for that shit. We'd be fucked. I needed to find a way to keep them safely here for now.

"Pull yourself together, Queen. We have to check on your mother!" I told her as calmly as I could. I held her and ran my fingers through her curls, attempting to calm her nerves. I pressed my lips to her forehead and made her look into my eyes. "Listen, Baby, you can't be in tears when your mother is hurting for all of you. You're the lioness that pulled me in to help you. I want to do that for you because I love and need you.

'You have to put the fear of that man aside so we can devise a plan that will stick. I want you free. You have to want it too. You won't get freedom if you're afraid to fight back with me. Mami needs you to grow up so you can help your sister. Are you ready? I don't want to rush you into anything you're not prepared to ride out. My first concern is your family's safety."

Mandisa made a choice, and I'm glad.

"I'm so sorry, Mami," I sighed, sitting with them in her room. "It's going to be alright. I'm here for you. Anything you need, I got you. I'll do whatever I can to help, but I need to understand everything. Help me?"

"You're a sweet boy, Hakim. It upsets me so much that HE will never know how much you love our daughter. He'd rather marry her off to some man than let her fall in love with someone like you," Mami cried, holding her side lying down. "I can't do this anymore. My girls deserve to be happy. I cannot go another 18 years of waiting, watching, and praying that HE doesn't hurt my baby. I can't do it, Hakim."

"He doesn't see how he's ruining your lives. I'm going to do whatever I can to keep Mandisa with me, Mami! Anything!" I told her, frowning. Mami petted my hand and nodded in tears while Mandisa tried to calm her down. Mami was about 2 weeks from her due date and constantly uncomfortable now. Amani was bearing down in her womb, and she was on bed rest. So we were staying close anyway. It had only been two months, but I had grown to love Mandisa's mother very much. She accepted all of my family without question, and we relied on her like our mothers. "You really want to get a divorce?"

"Hakim, if he insists on putting us through this madness, I have no choice. Mandisa's 18 now. If I hadn't have brought her here, bought her some time, he would have married her off much sooner. There is a method to this madness. You, I did not plan on, but it was a pleasant surprise. I'm glad she found someone that really loves her. You want to take care of her. I trust her with you, Hakim. Just promise me you'll make her happy and won't hurt my daughter?

'I don't know how much time I've bought, but he's coming here, Hakim. When he gets here, I don't know what he'll do. But she's not safe with me until I have a divorce filed.

'I've been a terrible mother, Hakim. I'm a failure because I've doomed her to my fate. Maybe it is not too late. You can take Mandisa and leave. When Tomny comes, you run. Once the divorce is final, I'll come to you with Amani. Just tell me where you would take her," Mami cried, rubbing my hand trembling.

"Mami, there's got to be another way. Don't cry, please? You say you trust me. If you're serious, give me a chance to build a plan?" I begged her.

"Hakim, my due date is coming. Once Amani is born, it will be too late. That's all the time Mandisa has. He's hellbent on getting her away from you now! Just tell me where you would go?" Mrs. King asked me, her eyes red with anger and fear. "Mandisa has run away before, she's tried to kill herself, and I can't fail her this time. I feel it will be a success if she attempts again. She's messed up because of HIM now. She has no idea who she is….it's all his fault!"

"Jamaica…I have a friend, Kaliah. He lives in Jamaica. He'll help us," I surrendered.

"Fine, I'll have her papers ready in case he tries anything. You keep them, so he doesn't get them and try to pull a fast one. But I have a feeling he doesn't need them. I'm going to find a lawyer," Mami insisted, nodding to me. Mandisa was quietly watching with the most confused look. There wasn't much that she could do but try to be tough for her mother. I got up and went downstairs to make the call I feared since I learned what her father was up to.

"Ha-KEEM!" Kaliah laughed in his high happy voice, answering the phone. That meant Lionel and Cyrus were near. Good….I needed to talk to Cyrus about things.

"Bro, we need to talk, seriously, right now!" I told Kaliah as I leaned against the kitchen sink and crossed my ankles.

"Wat di matter?" Kaliah asked, catching my tone.

"Where's Cyrus?" I asked, frowning and taking off my glasses.

"Right ere," Kaliah replied nervously.

"What's wrong? Where's Queen? She alight? Did Mami have Amani?" Cyrus started with the million questions messing with my head.

"Shut the fuck up a second!" I yelled, squeezing my eyes pulling myself together. "Sorry, we have a fly in the ointment! It's bad....Put me on speakerphone? I need to talk to all of you now. No outsiders! Seriously!"

"Yeah, Bro," Cyrus replied seriously. "It's just us at the compound smoking...talk."

"Dr. King is trippin! He's pissed off because he knows that Queen has a boyfriend now. My name got mentioned now he's trying to pop up and take her away," I sighed, closing my eyes stopping.

"Fuck no! Hell no!" Cyrus yelled. "She ain't going no got damn where, Hakim! We can't...hell no!"

"Chill, Cyrus, chill.... Kaliah, how's the house coming?" I asked, letting Cyrus hear what we'd been discussing.

"I got the best mi can, Bro. But it's coming along, aye? Already spent over budget, but mi make it perfect, Bro,"

Kaliah sighed worriedly. "Put some of mi money in helping, Bro."

"I appreciate it, Kaliah. We have to put an early time stamp on it. Mami is desperate. She wants us to run. But I'm going to find another way to help her.

'Cyrus can tell you anything you need to know, Bro. The house stands firm, but if my plan doesn't work, you'll have some neighbors," I told Kaliah, trying to think. "I want her comfortable, Kaliah. Spend all the money I've sent to you over the years. Blow the whole two million if you have to. I don't want her to be worried about anything. Make sure that there's room for her mother and a baby later. Her mom may have scared some sense in him, but I've got to make this work."

"Damn it!" Cyrus said, his voice shaky.

"Hakim, what you gonna do, Bro?" Lionel inquired with an angry tone.

"Don't worry, I'll fill you in when the time comes. I need to make some calls first in the morning. I'm relying on you all to stay calm and let me worry.

'Cyrus! Do not…I repeat…Do NOT call her and tell her anything. I'll talk to her. Just let me do me…you do you, alright?" I said seriously.

"Alright, Bro, we're just gonna play it cool," Cyrus agreed.

"Lionel, zip your fucking lips, Bro! You can't blow this! She'll be gone if word gets out! Don't fuck me on this!" I warned Lionel getting so emotional I was in tears.

"Hakim, I got you! No games," Lionel answered calmly.

"Kaliah?" I shed tears, frowning. "I'm trusting you, Bro. I know you can handle this. Take notes from Cyrus, and I know you'll make it happen. Please?!"

"Aye, aye, mi got yuh! Anything yuh need mi handle," Kaliah answered confidently.

I relaxed hearing he was on it. Cyrus would spend the money but miss the message. Kaliah understood what I was telling him. This house was going to be our great escape plan. But it was the last resort. No one could know where we would be, or it could still mean trouble. No, I had to keep Dr. King off of our asses for good if I would be happy with my wife. Mandisa would always be in fear of him showing up even afterward. He was a thorn in everyone's side that needed to be cut off. I love this rose garden!

"Alright, I need to calm down," I said, taking a breath starting to feel dizzy. "Fuck, I got a headache…This shit has been coming. Just thought I had more time."

"Bro, you alright? Calm down. Your voice sounds tired," Cyrus informed me, and I raised my eyebrow.

"I'll be fine...I'll call back in the morning after I make a few calls and handle some shit! I got this!" I laughed about to hang up.

"Bro! Maybe you ought to go home and take a nap? You're pissed and afraid. You might not be thinking straight," Cyrus suggested raising his voice.

"What the fuck did you say, Nigga? I got this shit! Just help Kaliah, and I'll handle Dr. King and his slave-master mentality. He's fucking with the real Master now!" I chuckled.

"Naw, Hakim...don't hang up the phone. Where's Queen? Is Mami alright?" Cyrus worried. I suddenly realized I was too excited and needed to calm down. But something told me that Cyrus was just trying to keep me away from Mandisa. I shook my head and let that shit go.

"Mrs. King is taking a nap, and Mandisa is probably upstairs with her mom," I told Cyrus, letting my thoughts wander. "Both of them are entirely rocked by this motherfucker, and I want to just make him vanish off the planet. But I know that will look so bad. Another brother losing his temper, going around the system, and killing a white man...?"

'Naw, the news will eat that shit up. I'm going to make sure that my wife is safe one way or the other. So I suggest you do what I say and stick with the plan. The house is the last legal way that I'm going to be happy! If Dr. King keeps fucking with my happiness, upsetting my wife, I'll kill his bitch ass and make it look like an accident."

"Ha-KeeM," Kaliah cried out with his deep serious voice getting my attention. I held the phone in my hand, hearing his words. "Go home, talk to har in di morning. It's late. You're emotional and exhausted! Listen to Kaliah….Aye?"

I remember blinking after I rubbed my eyes a second and frowned, saying, "Yeah…you're right…I'm tired. It's late, so I'm gonna head home."

"Alright, Ha-KeeM, yuh nah hang up tha phone until yuh at the house, Aye?" Kaliah asked me. Suddenly I was fucking offended, but I knew better than to piss Big Brother Kali off. He shows up bringing more pain than the Method Man!

"What? You don't trust me to go to my own damn house, Bro?" I asked sarcastically, cheerful.

"You can't be trusted right now, Bro. Just say night and head home," Cyrus added. I rolled my eyes. *This Bitch!?* No, I don't mean that…I'm really pissed off and worried…I hate when a motherfucker thinks they can tell me what the fuck

431

to do, and they can't whip my ass. I know he was taking my silence as a threat because he knew what set me off. "Hakim, Bro, you don't want to hurt Queen. Just go home."

"It's like that? You're lucky I'm drained, or I'll stay just to fuck with you. I know what you're thinking, and you're wrong! ELYEUH is not going to come out! I'm just stressed! That's all...You know I can't think straight....under extreme pressure....words come out," I warned Cyrus.

"Yeah, well, I can't see you now, can I?" Cyrus demanded. I smirked.

"Hakim?" Mandisa summoned me from the stairs. I glanced over, staring at her, still grinning.

"Queen?" I replied as I hung up the phone. "Are you alright?"

"Oui," She responded with an exhausted expression in her eyes. "Mami fell asleep. Hakim, who was that?"

"Kaliah, that's all, Queen. I was just making some arrangements. I need to protect you from the worst. Everyone is going to help in any way they can to keep you here. We don't want to lose you, alright?" I told her, caressing her silky, warm cheek.

"I've never seen Mami this upset before, Hakim. It cannot be good for Amani. She's so close to her due date.

Mami wants me to run away and leave her here alone. I can't do that. I will not abandon my mother," Mandisa clarified sadly.

I pulled her close and held her. I needed her and her softness. The world made me so hard that I hated everything sometimes. Mandisa was chipping away years of ice from my frozen heart, and I was not letting her go for anyone! I got Mandisa to talk, and she told me about her father and mother as much as she could.

Mami was a dance major in college, but part of the purchase was giving up dancing to help Thomas become a surgeon. His father was worried because Thomas wasn't motivated to finish school, and his first wife was useless. Ninon started dating him because he pretended to help her stay in school after her father died. Her mother needed the money, so Thomas had his father pay Mrs. Brown to marry her, promising he would take care of Ninon. Once the money was exchanged, her mother stopped talking to her, and Ninon was forced to follow through.

Mandisa told me about her father bringing his colleagues around her from the age of 8. He was grooming her to be the perfect wife for a doctor intending to sell into another legacy family of surgeons with a son old enough to marry. He was the only surviving son in his family, and he needed a boy to carry on the family name and traditions. So when Mami couldn't give him a son, he started mistreating her and cheating with other women. Mami started taking Mandisa and running, but he'd come to find them. When Mami tried to go home, Thomas would remind her mother how she took his father's money and threaten to sue her. So, she wouldn't get involved in their attempts to get away from him.

There were several doctors that Mandisa recalled, but one stuck in my head. This Indian doctor, Spencer Patesh. Dr. King obviously didn't want Mandisa married to a black man, but he was nearly convinced to marry Mandisa to this Indian Therapist in his mid-40s? He had his eyes on her since she was a sick baby. Mandisa said that Patesh was coming around when they lived in Africa. Then when she was 14, he visited and tried to make an offer. When she was at that age, her father started letting these doctors examine her. Something happened to her, and she can't remember, but it made her upset, and that's when Mandisa began getting worse. Her father suddenly wanted her to be near another doctor, much older in his 50s. Mami said no. He was some German Cardiologist that had a thing for pretty young girls. Mandisa remembers Spencer Patesh asking about these other doctors her father was exposing her to and seemed concerned. Her father told him to wait until she was 18.

The German doctor wanted her at that age and said no. Spencer Patesh kept coming around every year to check on her, then he suddenly vanished. The last time he came, Mandisa said he offered her father 5 million dollars!

But I know these men aren't trying to buy a wife to love! They all told Mandisa she would be the mother of their children, so she had to be perfect if they were paying. Dr. King was verbally abusing her to make her submissive to any man he chose to be her husband since she turned seven. She won't have a chance to go to college or have a career if that's the plan. Mandisa was going to be sold to be some old doctor's lovely sex doll. Once she's paid for, she'll do whatever he says, just like Mami. The bitter irony, I'm a black man in love with the half-white daughter of a slave master and a beautiful house worker. Now Master gonna sell my wife because she's not white!

I guarantee you that if she was white, he wouldn't pull this shit. But since her grandmother took that money, he feels like he can do whatever the fuck he wants to Mami and her kids! It sounds like he's running a modern-day slave auction. Oh, hell no. I'll outbid all you bastards and buy all their freedom! The idea was born right then and there! Now I just needed to make the calls to put it into action.

I felt the headache dying down, and a smile grew across my lips. I glanced down at Mandisa and rubbed her back.

"Mandisa, I love you so much. You know that, right?" I questioned her carefully as I took her hand. She stared at me and concurred.

"I love you, too, Hakim…I am so afraid. I don't want to lose you or live my life by someone else's rules either anymore," She wept as I nodded, stretching my fingers over the top of her hand.

"I'm going to fix this. I'm your king, Mandisa. I'm going to do whatever it takes to protect you and be there for you," I promised her as I hauled her into my lap, squeezing her. "You trust me, right? You know I don't want to hurt you, right?"

"Of course, Hakim. You have only been good to me since we met. I worry only that you will hurt someone else because of your feelings for me. Your temper is very frightening, but you have never given me a reason to doubt your word," She told me as I stared up at her. I rested my head on her shoulder, and my face touched her soft breast through her tee-shirt. I could hear her heart pounding, irregularly….here. There, there….there. Here….here...there…here…

I frowned as my hand rubbed her back, slipping under her pink tank top and massaging her soft, smooth skin tenderly. She looked down at me, and her cheeks blushed red. "Hakim…?"

"Don't say my name like that. You know what it does to me, Queen," I whispered against her skin, kissing her peach flesh smiling. I buried my face between her gorgeous breasts and inhaled. "I just want to touch you…that's all. Your body is so warm and soft. I could melt into you right now."

My fingers unfastened her bra and let my left hand make its way to the front to touch my prize. I was getting excited as I felt her nipple getting stiff. Mandisa got up and moved away. I sighed, watching her fix her bra. Her face was red, her eyes glowed peering down at me, but she didn't seem offended. All I wanted to do was pull her top down…and I would have….I thought I was going home a moment ago?

"I'm sorry, Queen. I got carried away," I apologized, squeezing my leg. My shit was starting to wake up, and I should have understood I'd lose it.

"It is okay," She said, beaming at me. "We've had a stressful evening. All of us….let's try to get some rest…okay?"

"Alright, Queen, I'll head home," I said, worried if I had fucked up. I went and grabbed my glasses off the kitchen counter and started for the back door.

"Where are you going, Hakim?" Mandisa catechized me.

"I'm going home, Queen, so you can go to bed," I reported looking over my shoulder, perplexed.

"Stay…you can sleep in my room with me. We can cuddle, oui? I'll leave the door open. Mami won't mind if we sleep on top of the covers. I don't want to be alone. I have nightmares after I talk to Daddy. You will make me feel safe, Hakim," Mandisa beseeched, taking my hand off the doorknob.

"Um…Okay?" I decided, allowing her to drag me back. It wasn't what I was expecting, but I'd take it!

I followed her to her room, and she lay on her bed. I got behind her and put my arms around her waist. We cuddled and talked for a few hours, and she fell asleep. She was so beautiful when she slept. Mandisa looked like an angel. What had she done to me? I wanted her so badly, but I couldn't hurt her. Every part of me wanted to love her. As I ran my fingertips across her relaxed face, she smiled, similar to a little girl.

I'm going to marry this woman if she has me. No doubt in my mind since I met her, and now I was determined. But first, I'm going to buy her freedom from the 'Good Doctor.' I don't care if it takes every penny I own! I can always make more money. I'll never find another woman that gives US a vibe like Mandisa. I laid my head on her behind and stroked her thighs through her pajama pants.

Her ass is like a memory foam pillow against my face! Ooh, my GODDESS! This ass is a perfect pillow just for Hakim. I drew myself closer and actually relaxed completely! I'm never sleeping without it again!

Chapter Twelve: Poetic Justice

Cyrus

Mami had Dr. King scared shitless! The idea that she would divorce him had the man acting right. But school, much to my dread, started, and we never let our guards down. We tried so hard to act normal, but it wasn't easy. Everyone was terrified that the baby would be born soon and Mandisa's father would show up out of the blue! Mami still had about a week left, and Mandisa was so nervous leaving Mami alone she didn't want to go to school, but Mami insisted she attend classes. We all agreed. If Dr. King showed up while we were at school, at least Mami could alert us and set 'Plan Exodus' into motion.

I lucked out and got three classes with Mandisa! Two of them included Hakim's crazy ass. He had five with her, so he used that to his advantage to keep ignorant niggas away from her. Lionel had one class with her. The only one that neither of us could talk our way into, Advanced Art and Design, was Lionel's watch.

English was our last class of the day. Hakim, Mandisa, and I had it together, and Mr. Lenord was a boring teacher! He was the typical white man, with only three black students, trying to get me to read? So sorry, that's not going to happen. Fuck, I hate private school!

It had been months now since I had seen a piece of pussy! I was losing my damn mind! But I had to play shit cool. Queen was still too afraid to take that step. The girls wear those cute uniforms. It doesn't help that Mandisa sits right next to me. Hey, Jefferson and King sit right next to each other in the alphabet! Hakim sat in front of us in the front row. It can be a good thing or a bad thing to share a class with Hakim Dunn. Depending on his mood, it could be a hell of a lecture or a fight if he got pissed off at someone in class. I was happy to be there to bear witness to the magic. He always had something to say when he didn't like the teacher.

This particular Thursday afternoon, I was nearly asleep because I ran suicides during basketball, a class I had with Lionel. Mr. Lenord was going on and on like Badu, but he was not making sense.

"Poetry! Raw human expression, this assignment will be about finding emotions and thoughts you've experienced in a poem and sharing them in class. I don't care about the author, but I want something real! Don't give me roses are red….blah!" Mr. Lenord said, pacing the front of the class.

I don't usually worry about the age of my instructors. I see them all as just people with a job. But for some reason, Mr. Lenord made me curious about his age. He looked like he might be in his late 40s, but his eyes were oddly older. It made him look like he was in his 60s when he looked around the room. I don't know how to describe these strange features he held in his gaze. It was like he was trying to hyperfocus his vision by staring longer than needed.

He had wrinkles all over his cheeks and jaws, his eyes looked too old to be whatever age he actually was, and it made him look like a predator when he stared. Hakim told me that when whites have eyes like that, it's probably because they are evil if you get that vibe looking in their eyes. You can pick up intention by staring into people's eyes. But I don't do that to people I don't like from a feeling. Fuck that! What if they can snatch your soul? I believe in shit like that!

My hand shot up, I waved it, waiting for him to stop glancing around the room like in Stand and Deliver. Yeah, that's who he reminded me of an old-looking, white version of Edward James Olmos or Danny Trejo? Why he seemed so damn interested in my face bothered the shit out of me. You know how I handle shit, right? You should know by now…Shame on you if you don't remember Cyrus!

"Yes, you have a question, Mr. Jefferson?" Mr. Lenord asked as he acknowledged me.

"Do-the-fuckin-ass-ign-ment!" Hakim coughed, falling forward on his desk, running his words together, making me chuckle.

"Mr. Lenord, do you consider song lyrics to be separate genres of poetry? Or is it too ethnic for me to sing or rap in this class?" I eloquently asked, articulating each word imitating his voice.

Mandisa's eyes shot over at me then back down at her notebook, quietly giggling to herself. I admired her blush and playfully pulled one of her loose curls from her matching navy headband. Mr. Lenord noticed my playing with her and frowned.

"No, I don't consider the music of any origins to be too ethnic, Mr. Jefferson. However, I prefer no curses or racial slurs in the works that you choose to share with the class?" Mr. Lenord informed me with a concerned gaze. He suddenly looked directly at Hakim and exhaled as Hakim sat up in his seat, frowning. Mr. Lenord's smile faded, and his green eyes grew as dark as his brown hair. As Hakim raised his hand. "Mr. Dunn, I don't want any trouble from you after last year. Can't we agree that you're more intelligent than most and hold the arrogant speeches and woke words for the hallway?"

"But most poetry, songs, or spoken word contains profanity. I think you're asking your students to give you a very watered-down human experience when you ask for raw emotion and then ask them to censor themselves. It's like telling a woman to take a piss while standing up but wanting the floor to be dry afterward. Some are talented enough to give you precisely what you want, but the ones that do make you wonder if it's a woman at all. You can't demand something fake and expect a tangible result.

'The real shit is going to throw you for a loop. I never take over your class, Mr. Lenord. I've been your student for 3 years. I make you teach better because you haven't considered your lessons enough to reach us yet. That Classical English Poetry is so dry and overrated, but they teach it as a standard, and whites co-sign it cause that's all you have…The past…

'Maybe if you thought outside of the breadbox, you'd become a much better instructor and stop putting people to sleep with the boring assignments. No offense, Mr. Lenord, but I know you always get offended when I say anything to you, so I'll shut the fuck up," Hakim chuckled, shaking his head and pretending to look at the list of approved authors. He quickly raised up his hand again. "Why is it that when a teacher tells us they're not racist, and I point out their racist behaviors and habits, do they get mad at me and not themselves?

'Can you explain that, Mr. Lenord? I just noticed you told Mr. Jefferson that you don't consider anything too ethnic. But none of the authors on your preapproved list are of color. Normally I'm fuckin offended that whites try to claim that they are the originators of any concept, but it pisses me off when one lies to my face. You still haven't added one black author after 3 years of hearing my mouth? I'm sick of you reading us Bob Dilan as a surprise. Folk, Rock, even Jazz music is just the Blues, and you stole that from us too when we flipped Gospel on you greedy bastards when you wouldn't let us in Country. You can't lie to me, Sir!"

"Mr. Dunn, should I prepare for you to call me a cracker, like the rest of the faculty here, or can I finish explaining the assignment? I don't want any trouble out of you and your new friend. Obviously, you know each other, and it's harming the other student's learning environment. I don't care what work you pick as long as you don't turn my classroom into Hakim Dunn's Def Poetry Read, like the year before. This is my English class! Out of respect for good Christian morals, we should all try to be nice," Mr. Lenord sighed, rubbing his forehead nervously. He was trying to hold his shit together because he was starting to sweat. Hakim was picking at him to see if he could get him to say something as racist as he was by using me.

"What respect do Christians have for Non-Christians? In fact, what relation does this country have for any alternative religious practitioners? You all expect us to respect your beliefs and shit, but you don't give a damn about us."

'I'm not a Christian, Mr. Lenord. You knew that shit when you said it! This entire country places so much pride in their religious affiliations that they don't fucking know which to believe. You all can't be right; someone has to be wrong. What's your denomination...? Do you realize that you're the active participant in your own mental enslavement in this capitalist system designed to keep you working this job and paying taxes so you can't pursue your dreams? Do you know why they don't tax churches because all the churches breed more taxpayers brainwashed to the system, and it's always been that way? Would you believe me if I told you that those higher up that claim to be good Christians have a warped sense of saving souls by sacrificing the weak to their ideal Jesus? They don't believe in the same shit as you. That's why you can't walk into a church where Donald Trump goes. But I bet you claim to be the same as him and share his vision?

'I think all of you are lost believing you can save anyone when you don't save your damn selves. You're a hypocrite playing righteous while hiding behind the guise of forgiveness and good works. But when it comes to money, suddenly, all that righteousness you preach turns to the suffering of others using greed and manipulation. No matter how much you try to convince yourself you're forgiven once you beg your imaginary white man for forgiveness, you're still a liar and a thief until you change.

"Confessing fixes nothing without a made-up mind and discipline that leads to changing habits. I'm offended every time someone says something ignorant around me, and I don't know why they keep insisting this is the most advanced English class this school has to offer. We read many old English classics and shit but can't seem to talk about anything written in English worth studying.

The only thing I've learned from you in 3 years is how to shut the fuck up and not speak my mind all of the time. So I'm mastering patience with you, SIR. You just so happened to catch me on a day when I didn't like anything you said."

"Why exactly are you here, Mr. Dunn? You're intelligent enough to have graduated years ago and left for college by now. You must not have everything figured out if you're wasting your time in my class," Mr. Lenord sarcastically asked, looking around. "There are many bright minds that actually benefit from the experience of being in my class when you're not disrupting it. I'm letting you have your moment because you chose to speak at the end of class, but my day is over."

"Well, you see, Mr. Lenord. I have a brother that is also a genius and skilled placed in high school at ten. He went to college at 13, and I'm following his advice. He told me that the experiences in school are just as valuable as the education you receive. I didn't want to look back and regret skipping ahead. Why rush something that is going to happen?"

"I understand that this class is the best offered at this INSTITUTION for a paying brother like me. Imagine that...I'm actually spending money that I earned to sit and listen to you tell me how you aren't racist, a dedicated instructor, a God-fearing Christian, and I'm supposed to also believe you aren't gay staring at all the men that come around, Mr. Lenord? I'm not pointing it out because I'm scared of you....I was just curious how your Christian values hold up against your preference of men?"

"Obviously, you seem very attracted to a few students, but I have never said a fuckin word. See, you did teach me something, Mr. Lenord. I'm learning every day from the white man what lies they tell themselves to get through the day. Once a liar, always a fucking liar!"

Hakim looked over me, grabbed his stuff as the bell rang, and I tapped Mandisa's arm. She was putting her things away nervously, watching Hakim and Mr. Lenord's staring contest. This was interesting. I honestly wanted to see what would happen if Hakim let loose on Mr. Lenord.

"You could have another instructor, Mr. Dunn. I don't understand why you insist on being in my class just to torture me in front of the other students?" Mr. Lenord sighed as Hakim shouldered his backpack.

"You don't get it. I know you now from observation…For three years, I've known you and insisted that you stay my "English" teacher. You're boring, don't know the lesson plan, you don't inspire us to read or write anything. You're gay, slightly racist, and confused about your values.

"You do realize I'm the only black man that you've taught since Mr. Jefferson showed up?"

"You taught me something about whites, and I assumed that my running off at the mouth when you kept being ignorant would teach you something about me. You learned how not to listen and how to continuously justify what's wrong with everything. People can tell you how you've got them fucked up, but some people need to be shown. But I don't want to get to that point with a teacher. You could earn my respect and maybe be a better person all around if you listened for once.

'You're not a teacher. You're a musician that gave it up and took a teaching job. Now music and being around kids are the only things that inspire you. Too bad you can't encourage them with this image you're projecting. Some people can be reached if they trusted you and your fucking word. Get a new job, or find a way to use what you love to connect with us?

'But don't hate me for telling you what your prayers won't answer. Thoughts & Prayer's is that superhero you religious people think will save everyone without taking any responsibility. I honestly don't hate you. I imagined that if you heard the black man in your ear for 3 years telling you how you were fucking up these kids playing like you want to help, you'd finally quit and go back to picking a guitar or bring one to class.

"That's all you really want to do. I know music is a great way to inspire some people, might keep Mr. Jefferson from drooling all over the desk. But class is over, Mr. Lenord. I'm done educating ignorant people. You'll have to tolerate me until graduation. I'll keep checking up on your progression, though."

I started laughing as I noticed a tiny twitch above Mr. Lenord's left eyebrow. Hakim wasn't smiling or frowning, staring at the man like he was worried. Mr. Lenord had nothing to say to Hakim. I like to believe that he considered the ass thrashing that Hakim had delivered to his standing ass. He suddenly turned on me.

"Mr. Jefferson, is there a problem? You're a new student here and obviously a close friend of Mr. Dunn. Ms. King is a bright new student, I see you together, and I don't want you influencing her behavior in class or distracting her from her studies with your jokes and outbursts. Some of the students are here to learn and participate. Since you refuse to read...Keep it quiet, or I'll ask you to leave," Mr. Lenord warned me.

"I asked a simple question that required the minimum of effort to respond. Why would you assume that the song I chose to share would be offensive to the class? Because I don't like to read aloud? I don't read, Mr. Lenord, but I'm far from dumb. I ask questions for clarity. My delivery may be off because I'm nervous, and the natural reaction is to seek a harmonious result if my question seems infantile, but that's how I express myself. But I did not disrupt your class. Hakim could save it if you listened to him for once. He may be rude when he makes a point, but it's an observation that should be noted. I've learned that from hanging around him for nearly 10 years, Sir," I explained, reaching for Mandisa's hand. "No one falls in love, breaks up, and just snaps their fingers and says, 'oh well, it was fun.'

"We get mad, sad, and confused at the same damn time. Whatever comes out when we express it...is what you get. How everyone handles it depends on perspective. The

Christian Bible is a very primitive guidebook to live your life by knowing most books are full of lies printed back in those days. But just like the men that printed those lies, you keep living yours. You contradict yourselves with every word that comes out of your mouths and expect the Bible to justify it? Alright...I'ma head out!"

He didn't seem to like the idea that I wouldn't look him in the eye. I couldn't do it. He was giving me the weirdest vibe the longer he looked at me. Now that Hakim mentioned he was looking too hard, I wanted to fuck him up. I think he caught my drift when he dropped his head and looked toward Mandisa. Whatever the fuck he was trying to find out, he wasn't going to get it from me. I knew there was something I didn't like about him.

Mr. Lenord called Mandisa to speak privately after class, and I didn't like what was up. I sat back at my desk as Hakim walked by but headed out into the hall. He didn't look at Mandisa, but he stared at Mr. Lenord for a second then looked over at me. I nodded quietly, waiting for Mandisa.

"Mr. Jefferson, the class was dismissed. The bell rang," Mr. Lenord reminded me and tried to motion me out of the room.

"I know, I'm just making sure no inappropriate student-teacher behaviors are going down," I chuckled, laying my chin on my hand staring at him. "Carry on, pretend I'm not here."

"Right…" Mr. Lenord sighed, shaking his head, nearly messing up his thin comb-over. "Miss King, you've written some of the most interesting papers I've ever read. You and Mr. Dunn are very gifted writers. I know you're friends in this class, but perhaps you'd be less distracted in another class of mine? My first-period English class is a much more focused group of students."

Mr. Lenord thought he would lore her into an all-white class away from Hakim and me! Why? She was an A student just like Hakim, so what difference did it make if Mandisa was with us? I'm sorry. I know Hakim said he was gay, but he touched Mandisa's shoulder, and I stood up loudly, almost knocking over the table. I glanced down at him, and Mandisa looked up at me. The look on my face must have told Mandisa it was time to go. I motioned her to come with me. She grabbed her things quickly and nodded to him.

"I believe I am doing fine in this class, Mr. Lenord. I will consider it if my marks slip," She told him, smiling sweetly. But I could tell by the look in her eye she didn't like being touched. She was always nervous around strangers, and he did not have permission to touch her. I suddenly did not like Mr. Lenord at all. I moved down to the door waiting for her, and took her hand as she waved goodbye. "Things are good here."

"She's fine where she is, Mr. Lenord, but thanks for looking out," I told him as I led her out into the hall. I needed to put as much space between him and us as possible. I wanted to turn around and fuck him up.

"Darius, what is wrong? You look so upset. Your face is pouting like Hakims! Do not do that!" Mandisa teased me as I pulled her along. I suddenly laughed as she made an evil face imitating Hakim's frown. I stopped and got my hug. "You two are so protective of me, and I love your concern, but you cannot fight everyone nice thinking the worse. He is our teacher, Darius. I have never been in a classroom, and I like this….Do not be a bad boy too. I cannot stop Hakim from running off at the mouth when he is in his feelings, but you have more control, do you not, Cocoa Puff?"

Oh God, when she talked to me like that…It made me feel 50 feet tall. That's right, Baby…put me in my place with your sweet loving charms. She was so very good with defusing the bomb that it began to turn me on. Hakim loved that shit too! When Mandisa put him in his place, he shut-the-fuck-up! She had us whipped, and I didn't care. Look at her in her uniform.! All tight on the hips, her vest was poking out, showing me why I love gold covering the breasts like a bird. I could mold a new hourglass from her figure and tapered waist.

She had to wear flats, but Mandisa wore custom-made tights, pantyhose, and socks Antoine designed to match her blue, gold, and white pleated skirts and solid jackets. They gripped her legs tightly in the perfect places that showed off the firmness of her calves, thighs, and behind.

Yes, you could see her behind poke out from that coat, and the skirt had to be hemmed lower because of her thick thighs....if she opened her legs...Mandisa loved black panties! I've seen all the pretty lace, golden designs, and I wasn't trying to see them! Let me keep going. She's wearing her clothes so well, thanks to Antoine.

She's so innocent and cute from Monday thru Friday, but on Saturday....

Mandisa puts away the school girl look and puts on the garb of the Baddest Bitch on the planet. Hakim is a wimp once she's dressed, and out of the mirror, and I'm her happy servant. No shame in my fucking game...She can have it any way she can take it, and I will deliver with no questions asked!

The idea of anyone else getting close to Mandisa pisses me the fuck off, and Hakim has it set up to where if a nigga tests me, he's coming. I'm the warning, and I have a gun.

Niggas still try knowing that shit. I'm no stranger to Longview! I've lived here for years, and most niggas recognize me. But that shit goes out the window once they take one look at Mandisa.

Suddenly, I'm the motherfucker with the paper trying to stop a REAL NIGGA from shooting his shot? That shit is hilarious! I love that terminology….REAL NIGGA….No, really…I hate that shit!

They won't teach you this shit in the streets. I had to learn the hard way as a kid. No black man should ever label himself as a REAL NIGGA. That's the equivalent of saying Proud Fool. I'm genuine because I'm proud of the shit that makes me feel real, but I don't know what REAL means so, I'm ignorant.

You only hear someone fake yelling about how real they are. But listen to brothers talking about doing wacky shit with broken hearts as a positive thing. That's why they want to be REAL. But the actual REAL NIGGAS are the ones that have their shit together and figured out they don't have to tell anyone how real they are. Their actions and lives inform you they're a true, REAL NIGGA.

What really messes me up is when the so-called REAL NIGGAS meet a brother with his shit together and has everything he wants. If he isn't trying to hear the ignorant shit the brother is kicking…suddenly he's a hater? I made my money, got the girl, but somehow that was a fucked up move on my part? Which somehow is stopping you from shining and getting what you want?

Ah, Nah!

That's so fucking stupid…Like watching a child cry for a toy that's a few steps away, and another child gets to it first. The other throws a tantrum and destroys everything in the room when he could have walked his ass over and got it if he wanted it bad enough. This is the fucked up mentality of men. I need what I want, and if you get it first and don't give it to me, then fuck everything, nigga. That's that crabs in the barrel shit I've heard old folks talk about round here. The old people in the south know some real shit to be so religious. Grandma Sophie told me about spelling words and how people are casting spells on people unknowingly.

Nigga, is the association of us to each other, right? They call us NIGGER, NIGGAR, but we say NIGGA talking to one another. I do that shit with other blacks, and I'm sad to say it's a habit I can't seem to break. We tried that flip it to Negus, but it doesn't stick. Anyway, a Nigga is a brother or a sista, and our verbal inflection of pronunciation determines if it's a good Nigga or a bad one.

Theory me this, Cyrus? If words are spells, and we control the delivery of the spell with our intention? Then doesn't that mean Nigga means whatever I want it to mean depending on the point I'm trying to make? When someone says something to you, you know they meant to offend you by how they say it? It never matters the word, right?

Huh?

It can sound like anything depending on how much energy we put into getting it out. So, with that now being known by most people, when we say REAL NIGGA…Overstand…

We are saying, "I'm very proud of being a black disappointment when I don't have my shit together."

We contradict the spell we intended to mystify the subject, and it backfires. The result is your ass having to prove how real you actually are. All kinds of fake shit about you start getting exposed. Fucking around with me is not the time to test your luck. If I get nervous and start laughing too much, I will pop a fake REAL NIGGA. Getting me mad is just going to get Lionel in your face, and once Lionel gets too loud, Hakim is going to fuck you up. If you can't see him coming, you'll be done before you realize. If you can survive the pounding he gives you, then hope he's not mad. He will beat you to death or shoot you.

I've saved a few REAL REAL NIGGAs from getting in their feelings over girls that ELYEUH fucked. He went to jail for putting two dudes through a gas station door. Then stumping a dent in a nigga's hood. I don't want to fight Hakim. Ever! I don't think niggas realize what they are asking for when they test him. You don't lie to the universe. It has a test for every damn spell you try to cast.

Want to know some really insane shit I learned?

Kaliah told me that subconscious thought, shit we don't even try to think about, has attraction principles. Even shit you didn't realize you were thinking about is coming to test your resolve. That fucking blew my mind when I saw how many times I thought about people, and then right when I came out of a thought, they called me or came by. I started finding those numbers 11;11, 456, and 369, shit like that everywhere.

That means we are constantly manifesting consciously with words and action, then subconsciously, with our known and unknown thoughts reversing or aligning with what we want. Kaliah explains shit like if we are all magnets, the north pole would be the brain and thought waves. The southern end is actually in the heart, and how we feel about our thoughts has its own pull. It interferes when the heart and mind are not on the same page, causing us to only attract what will teach us to change the polarity.

If we don't change our feelings and way of thinking, we'll just keep attracting new lessons. That's simple stuff a kid can get. But everyone wants to give it labels. Labeling shit is precisely what's so fucked up with the world. People need a title so they can feel someone is better than another. It's easy to compare something labeled differently, but without a label to project a feeling....people are just people.

That's kind of the way we're going with what we are doing. If Mandisa wants to have two husbands in the end, then it shouldn't matter what the fuck we call it. When she has a kid. It's gonna be mine or his. So the baby will have two daddies that love it and the mama.

Maybe if more people focused on the outcome of the union surrounding kids, then there would be fewer people jumping the broom to hang themselves with expectations. That's just my personal opinion, and we all know opinions are like assholes. We all have one, but only a few are gonna stick around to hear the shit that comes out! Then some are just too overly opinionated to stop giving a shit, like Hakim!

I learned when I was young from listening to my mother talking on the phone to her friends. Everyone has something they want to share but are afraid to say in a specific company. I admire Hakim for being ruthless, but he can be reckless, like Lionel. Lionel has no filter until he either hurts someone or they hurt him. But baby brother has been keeping it in a safe lane.

Mandisa has been joking with him a lot, and he is rubbing off on her. It's actually hilarious watching them have their fun. Lionel seems to enjoy having a sister to tease and talk to about women. He's getting softer, and Hakim rewards his behavior the only way he knows Lionel will respond. He's throwing money at his brother for being a good boy, and the results don't lie. I'm not saying Lionel is a gentleman. He's not changing that quickly.

#

"I don't like the way he looks at you, Queen. He's too touchy-feely," Hakim said, catching up with us in the parking lot near my truck. "I may have over-exaggerated the gay thing, but he was looking too hard at you, Bro. He's always staring when he thinks we're distracted. I've been watching for years. He may be bi-sexual. But he doesn't want Mandisa near you because he knows she likes you. He may not act on anything, but he's gonna know what I know now. He seems to be looking a bit too hard this year. That will make him think twice if the thought crosses his mind.

'The rest of the class now knows what I know, so hopefully, they will watch his ass when we're not around. That was the point of me running my mouth. They don't play that shit in any school, and I pay too much money to worry about Mr. Lenord's sexual preference. If he wants to keep his job, he will act like a teacher and stop daydreaming about touring. There are no groupies in his classes! Mediocre will only get so far when I spend my wealth."

"Hakim, he is trying to do his job. Be nice. Maybe you are right about everything. But what good does it do to tell him how much he hates his job? I think he knows he is unhappy. Your delivery needs work. Three years and he is teaching the same means you didn't reach him either," Mandisa corrected Hakim as he put his bag in his car. Okay, I didn't think of it that way either. I was enjoying Hakim telling him off. Mandisa clutched her ponytail up over her head and put her hands on her fine hips. "What good do your words do if they can't understand, you..? Don't go talking that shit, Hakim...Badu.."

Hakim smiled and blushed like a kid looking away. That shit was cute, and I was trying to keep my hands to myself. She giggled and shook her head, saying, "Everyone is going to teach us something, Hakim. The opportunity to reciprocate shouldn't be taken lightly. No one wants to hear someone that just blabs out facts with no compassion or overstanding of the affected outcome of the wrong timing.

'Don't waste your words unless you educate to inspire. What good does shaming anyone do? You, of all people,

462

should not want the karma of shaming people coming back to test you?"

"I'm going to buy you a ring so when people hear you talking like that, they know you're mine and the real thing! You probably want all those natural crystals and shit, huh?" Hakim chuckled nervously. "My Queen spits facts!"

"Uh-uh, Nigga! You want this pussy you gonna put a ring on it as big as Beyonce's! My beliefs are no excuse for you to think you get me for cheap," Mandisa wrinkled her forehead, glaring, and teased Hakim. My dick got hard as fuck as I hid in the truck laughing. "You didn't get me that outfit I wanted to wear for the 4th! I'ma tell my Uncle Sam on you, Nigga, You ain't no KING!"

Hakim dropped his head, laughing, "That shit is really adorable, Mandisa. Lionel is rubbing off on you. You looked mad like him when you said that."

"What about who?" Lionel asked, sliding down the front stairway railing on his uniform coat. He looked over, noticing a chocolate girl watching him. "What's up, Girl? You gonna hit me up later, right?"

She nodded, laughing as she ran off to join her friends watching from the bus stop. Lionel was smiling, watching her runoff for a second. She was a cute black girl I hadn't noticed. Probably because she looked too young. I forget that baby brother is only 15 sometimes when I hear him talk. Lionel acts like he's 25 and talks like he's 30. But he can throw a tantrum like a 5-year-old when his feelings get hurt. He looked over at Hakim as he put his things in the passenger seat.

"What Mandisa say about me?" Lionel asked, smiling viciously at his brother. "Did she ask you to put me in your contract yet?"

"Shut the fuck up!" I laughed as Hakim turned his eyes at Lionel.

Mandisa rolled her eyes and swayed over, getting in my truck giggling, "You are my brother, Lionel. Stop trying to get Hakim angry!"

Lionel chuckled, moving into the car as Hakim smiled, rocking his dreads saying, "We're gonna head home, change, and catch the GRANDS. Then we'll come to check on Mami. Call if you need us before we get there. It's casino weekend for them, so you know they want to talk about the slots!"

"I'll give Mandisa a ride home and make sure things are good before heading to change," I told Hakim starting my truck.

"Do you have a song or poem in mind for the English assignment, Darius?" Mandisa asked me with a dazzling smile as she played with my hair. I thought about it and shook my head, having no idea yet. She knew I hated reading aloud, so I was going to have to memorize whatever I chose. "You know lots of songs, oui? What feeling do you want to talk about? Think about it, Cocoa Puff. You got this!"

Hakim jumped up out of the driver's seat and ran over, trying to steal his kiss. I slammed on the gas and backed up, making him chase the truck before I stopped. He looked up at me and died laughing, "Cyrus, you knew I was going to do that! Stop being a hater, Bro!"

"I was just fucking with you! I stopped, didn't I?" I cackled as Mandisa tumbled in her lap, giggling. I loved fucking with my brother now that I knew I had him by the balls. It was too much fun! "I couldn't resist seeing you run Forrest, run Forrest, run!"

Hakim dropped his head, and Mandisa kissed him on the forehead, then the lips. Once Hakim got what he wanted, he was gone!

I will say that Hakim trusts me with Mandisa like no other. I worry about who we get from day to day, so you have to realize I can't trust him to do the right thing like Spike Lee. He doesn't trust himself either, which is why he is okay with her being around me all the time. I've never seen him happy, and it's a lot of fun meeting Hakim for the first time. His meditations and routine seem to help keep his mood swings under control. But things still piss him off and scare him. That's when we have to watch out.

At Mandisa's house, I sat with Mrs. King while I waited for Mandisa to change. I sat with her on the sofa in the den and rubbed her swollen ankles. She was so red in the face lying there. Lately, Amani was hurting her, and Mami didn't say much. Hakim and I had been giving her stuff to help, but weed can't stop labor pains when it's time. Mami was stalling, and I understood why she didn't want to go to a hospital. She was terrified of what would happen next. I could tell by the way she was holding her back that Mami would not make it.

"Darius, you are here every day. Are you lonely living alone?" Mrs. King asked, worried about me. She looked like she hadn't been out of bed all day, still wearing her pajamas. I shook my head, watching her struggling to sit next to me. "I am not complaining….You are a joy."

"I like being here with you….You're having contractions right now?" I started about to reach for my phone to call Hakim.

"All week, Sweet, oooh!" She groaned, leaning back into the sofa cushions suddenly.

"Mami, the pain is worse!" Mandisa cried, running down the steps and grabbing her mother's hand. Mami nodded as she tried to lean to a comfortable position. I stood up, realizing I was not ready to catch Amani. "Don't push, Mami! Breathe….take deep breaths…Darius!"

"Get the bag in the closet with the sheep on it and put it in the car," Mami told me, trying to shake the pain and sit up. Her eyes were getting wider by the second, and I panicked. "They won't send me home this time, Sweet One."

"Oh, shit!" I yelled as I saw her sweat pants and the sofa get soaked down to the floor! I jumped over the couch and ran to the closet near the front door, grabbing the pink bag. "I'll call Hakim and tell him to meet us at the North Hospital! The south is always crowded, and Mami will have Amani in the lobby if we go there!"

I carefully lifted Mami and got her in Mercedez. She wasn't as heavy as she looked. That or I was zooming on adrenaline. I was moving as fast as I could to get her lying in the backseat. Mandisa was grabbing things and trying to lock up the house. She sat with Mami keeping her calm in the backseat while I called Hakim.

"Bro, Mami's water broke! We're going to the hospital on the Nawf Side, Dat way! It's close to my place. We can't take Mami to the southside where niggas wait for a body bag!" I yelled, trying to control my growing excitement. Mami was groaning, and it was getting louder after her water broke. "Hakim?"

Hakim sighed calmly, "Take a deep breath and realize, YOU can't panic. Those women now depend on you to safely get them to the hospital—a good idea on the northside. We'll be there in a few minutes. You got this, Bro!"

"Okay, yeah…I got this…I can drive," I replied, starting the truck.

"Tell Mandisa to start timing her contractions…Just time how long it takes for another to start once one stops. That will give the doctors an idea of how close she is to pushing. Amani is going to move fast because she's so low in the womb," Hakim told me.

I put my phone over the speakers so she could hear what Hakim was saying while I focused on the road.

"Is she trying to push, Queen?" Hakim asked. Mandisa was watching her mother breathe and looked at me, nodding.

"Yeah, Bro! She's trying to push!" I yelled, frowning.

"Amani needs all the oxygen you can get to her now that the fluid is gone. You have to breathe so she's okay and doesn't panic, okay, Mami? Mandisa, it will help Mami with the pain if she focuses on inhaling deeply for your little sister and exhaling for herself to relieve the pain until the doctors can get to her," Hakim informed Mandisa. He was so calm while I was going crazy trying to stay in the lanes on the street! The more Hakim talked, the quieter we all got. I thought he would snap, but it was utterly unexpected to hear him in complete control with no emotion at all but concern. "You're doing good, Cyrus… Drive like we always cruise the roads. Amani is going to wait until it's cool for the fam. She's been nervous with all of us. Remember, she can hear and feel everything Mami does. As long as we keep Mami and Mandisa calm…Amani will wait."

"Right! We don't need her to pop out and try to take the wheel. I'm taking her to get her license tomorrow," I said, smiling.

Both Mami and Mandisa laughed as I kept driving until we got to the E.R. entrance. Mandisa ran inside to get help. They took Mami up, and I found a spot to park.

#

I was pacing the parking lot nervously, waiting for Hakim. A second passed, and Hakim flew into the back entrance and nearly jumped a curb parking nearby! He jumped out of the car and ran over so excited that I thought I was talking to someone else on the phone. Lionel was strolling as he came over.

"Why are you traveling in slow motion?" I asked him, glaring.

"Running fast ain't gonna make the baby come quicker. We might be here all damn night!" Lionel laughed, texting on his phone. "I just put that video on Facebook Live! Hakim's reckless ass driving already got us 400 views! I got my camera and a camcorder for this shit!"

"You dumb! You're not going to see Mami's twat or record anything for the world, Nigga!" Hakim yelled, slapping Lionel's hand.

"Eww, fuck naw! I just want to get Amani on film first. I've never seen a newborn baby before, and she's gonna look just like Mami! I ain't trying to see all that shit!" Lionel grumbled at Hakim, making a disgusted face wrinkling his eyebrows and nose up. "I ain't sick. That's my little sister! You think they got her in a room yet?"

"Give them some time….We can go to the gift shop and kill some time. I know they have some cute stuff for her room!" I suggested smiling, and Hakim nodded, agreeing.

Inside the gift shop, I found a wreath for her door, a grip of ballons, and a cute teddy bear thinking aloud, holding it, "I can't believe I didn't go shopping for Amani yet!"

"I got her all kinds of stuff the last time we went to Dallas. Mandisa and I picked out clothes, diapers, a crib, and anything I thought would help. Mami hasn't been able to move around to get anything. She's been sleeping so much the last few days," Hakim announced, watching me find more stuff.

"I've been so worried about getting her here. I guess I forgot everything she's going to need once she's here," I mumbled, glancing around. Hakim was gazing at the baby things with me; his face went completely blank. Everything was relaxed, like an amazed kid staring. I'd never seen him look like that before in the eight years I'd known him. "You feeling alright, Bro? You look kind of out of it."

Hakim looked at his phone as I recognized Mandisa texting. Hakim looked up at me, saying, "She's in room 624."

#

The nurses had put Mami in a private room. They gave her something to take the edge off her contractions. After four hours of constant pain and not much progress, Mami was exhausted, and Mandisa was worried. The doctor decided to take Amani by C-Section because the baby's heart rate was too irregular. Once they gave Mami an epidural, she was calm but not talking. She cried so much that I was crying. The hour was getting later, and it was after 10 when they came to take Amani. While they moved her, we grabbed things and went to the waiting room up front.

"You think everything is alright with Mami?" Lionel asked Hakim, concerned.

"If something were to go wrong, we're in the right place," Hakim replied, folding his arms thinking. He had the same lost expression as in the gift shop that made me stare.

I nodded, agreeing with Hakim. Mami and Mandisa were safe here. I tripped, feeling my phone vibrate in my pants pocket. I realized I was still wearing my school uniform and shook my head, checking my phone. My phone hadn't rung unless it was the fam. No one else was calling me, but I had four missed calls. I looked at my voicemail, trying to see if I had anything from someone I knew. I didn't recognize any numbers.

I called back the first few numbers...Dumb! The first two calls were from a girl I met at a gas station in North Carolina months ago on my way here! I hung up and deleted that number. The third call was from Ms. Mia at Club Gucci's. WTF?! We hadn't hooked up in 2 years. She left a friendly message asking how things were going. Wanting to know if I was going to visit the club IF I came back? Sad, she didn't realize I had been back for months.

The last call came from a number I hadn't seen before, but it was a Longview number. It had the 903 area code, so I called it back.

"Hi, Darius, how are you?" A happy female voice answered.

"Ase, Sister, I'm good, and how are you?" I replied, scratching my head, trying to place the voice.

"I am…. missing you. I've seen you around town a lot lately, but you never notice me. Someone has your attention. You never used to ignore me," She told me honestly, losing her happy tone.

"Who is this?" I questioned her, unable to make a connection.

"Samantha, I thought you would talk to me if I called from another number," She nervously giggled. I glared.

"No, I wouldn't have called it if I knew it was you. What do you want?" I demanded, annoyed.

"I just…miss you, Darius. We used to have fun together, remember?" She sadly asked.

"I have to go, Sami! I'm swamped, Ase!" I said, quickly hanging up the phone.

I couldn't believe I didn't recognize that trick! Sami always called when I came to town. I ignored it, but she was right. Mandisa had my full attention, and I had forgotten all the girls before her. I was so in love.

I could change my number, but that would fuck up all my business contacts. If my dad ever tried to call, this number was all he had. Even though he never called me back, I knew he knew this number. Now my vibe was ruined! Fuck! All those fucked up memories of that girl and her games....I folded my arms, thinking.

"Cyrus, Samantha Reed is still calling you?" Hakim questioned, glowering at me thoughtfully.

"I haven't changed my number in 6 years! I ignore her, but a new number. She caught me slipping! Every time I talk to her, she kills my vibe! Why would she call me this time of night?" I pondered, shaking my head.

I understood what she wanted. 'Darius, I miss you, wanna fuck? Can we go shopping? I love you, don't you love me? How's Hakim?' Ugh! Just let it go! I've got a great girl that wouldn't ditch me like Sami. Mandisa was my heart, and Sami was the devil after my soul.

It was after 11:15 pm, and Hakim was on pins and needles. We both had texted Mandisa and got no response! I broke down and called her when the nurses didn't help. It rang twice, and someone answered.

"Oui?" A male voice answered. I looked at the number and froze. "Bon Jour?"

I hung up and looked over at Hakim, saying, "Bro, a man that speaks French just answered Mandisa's phone!"

Hakim stared at me thoughtfully, his arms still crossed, and nodded.

"Aww, hell no!" Lionel yelled to me. "Dr. King's already here?!"

"Shhh," Hakim sighed, his face calm. "Give me your phone, Lionel, and stay quiet."

Lionel tossed Hakim the phone. Hakim dialed Mandisa's number and waited for someone to answer.

"Hello? Yes, may I speak with Mandisa King? Yes, well, I'm a neighbor. I noticed that she wasn't home when we came by to check on her mother. Is everything alright with the baby? She wasn't well earlier....Dr. King?!

'Very nice to hear from you, Sir. Yes, when did you make it to town? ... Wonderful, so did Ninon have the baby? Wow! Nine pounds and seven ounces, that's wonderful! Is she well?

'Great, my family was concerned. We check on her daily.... Of course, please put her on the phone? Thank you very much, Dr. King," Hakim very politely charmed the pants off of Mandisa's father, and that man was actually going to put her on the phone?

He glanced at me and slowly nodded. "Queen? It's me, Hakim, don't say anything but yes or no. Understand? Okay...Is HE alone? Okay, good....Can you get away for a moment... Damn it!

'Tell him you're going to the restroom and come down here. ...Shit! .... Alright, I'm sending Cyrus up there. Act normal. I can't come there yet.... No, I got you!..... I love you....Here he comes!"

Hakim hung up the phone, glanced at me, and raised his eyebrows. I was worried as hell as I took a deep breath and inquired, "What's the plan, Bro?"

"You two go, take the gifts to the room. Offer to drop Mandisa off at home and take her to school in the morning. Lionel, go get your pictures like you planned, but don't say my name! I'll wait here. She stays with us until I talk to Dear Doctor Daddy. I'll handle things. Mrs. King knows what to do...just be civilized, stay calm, and go along with everything that Mami says," Hakim informed us rationally, moving to sit down.

"I got this! Lionel, let's go!" I said, grabbing the bags. I went down the hall and stopped at the nurse's station. "We're family of the Kings. We came to drop off some things, and they're expecting us."

The nurse looked at all the gifts and pointed us to the room. When we got to the door, I froze up and whispered to Lionel, "Stay calm and let me work the room. I don't want him suspicious, Bro."

"Aight, not a word," Lionel replied, viewing me nervously as I hit on the door.

"Come in," I heard Mami answer. I opened the entry and walked in, smiling as I saw Mami sitting up holding Amani. My heart was tight when I saw her cuddling the bundle in her arms. Mandisa glanced up at me and smiled. I waved to her and everyone. Dr. King looked over at Lionel and me as we came inside. His expression was apprehensive as Mami stared up at us. I set all my attention on Mami and Amani so Dr. King would not make any assumptions.

"Mrs. King!" I sang as I shuffled closer.

I offered her a pair of slippers and a big bear for Amani.

"Darius! Lionel!" Mami called, waving me closer. I stared at Amani. She was so small, had curly brown hair like her sister and Mami. Her skin was toasty and gorgeous, but her eyes were shut tight. Her precious little jaws were suckling, but I don't think she was asleep. She was faking like I do when people talk, thinking I'm sleeping. "Come here and say hello, Darius! I know she will open her eyes for you. You are her boyfriend. She is a stubborn girl not letting us see her eyes."

"You bought all of this for Amani?" Mandisa giggled, peering at the bags.

"It's just some things for Mami and baby girl," I informed her as she examined her father.

"Tomny, this is Darius and Lionel. They are neighbors. They have been so helpful the last few months. They are sweet boys. I haven't had to lift a finger with them around," Mami flattered us, blushing.

Dr. King got up and strode over to me. His blue eyes appeared red and tired. His face was flushed as he looked me in the eye. Dr. King was shorter than me, but he looked me in the eye as he shook my hand, saying, "Dar-i-us, pleasure, thank you for helping with Ninon. She's been singing praises about you since I got here. I am glad you were there to get her here safely. I owe you one."

"I am honored, Dr. King, you have a beautiful family. Your wife is wonderful. She reminds me of my late mother,"

I informed him, grinning. "It's a pleasure to help her. May I hold Amani?"

Dr. King gazed up at me for a moment, then nodded. He didn't seem too bad, a bit stuck up, but not what I thought at all. He was maybe 6 feet 1 foot tall, lean, well dressed in a navy suit tie. His blond hair and blue eyes made him look young with no facial hair. I didn't see much to fear looking at him, but after hearing some of Mandisa's stories about his temper, I wasn't gonna risk anything.

I reached over, and Mami carefully handed me Amani. I held her close to me and caressed her head. Her adorable chubby face looked like an apple as I playfully tickled her tiny chin.

"Hey, Lil Mami, do you know who I am? Look at you!... You are a twin...So, I'm taking you to get your driver's license, then we can roll to the club, Girl," I teased her. Amani swung her tiny arm up and punched me in the bottom lip. She stretched, and her little head turned toward my face. "You saw that, right? Amani is about to catch an assault charge on day one! Really? I thought we had something real?"

Amani slowly moved her head and hands around, touching my lips. She opened her eyes, and I smiled at the beautiful sight. They were blue like ocean water as I stated,

"Look at you! Hey, Princess…She's gorgeous, and she has your eyes, Dr. King!"

He came closer, looking at Amani, and chuckled, "She's so beautiful, Ninon! She's perfect, Disa! Look at that…?"

"Darius, how did you do that?" Mandisa wept, beaming at her sister, taking her tiny hand. "She would not look at Mami or me."

"That's my future wife," I teased Mandisa. "We go back! She wants to drive my truck. I'm going to paint it pink for her and everything."

I carefully handed Amani to Dr. King, watching Mami motion me toward him. I gave Mami a hug. She smiled, rubbing my arms whispering, "You're doing fine. Ask to take her home?"

"Queen, you must be exhausted, and you have school tomorrow. Why don't you ride home with Darius? Tomny is here, so you go home and rest," Mami reported, concerned.

"Oh, yeah, Mandisa, we've been here for hours waiting. But we can bring you back after school tomorrow," I suggested.

"You do look tired, Queen. I do not want you to stress over your mother. We can catch up after school tomorrow, oui?" Dr. King agreed, but his face was grave as he settled.

Mandisa watched her father, and her eyes plunged as she concurred.

"You sure you don't mind, Darius?" Mami questioned as she stroked my hand, breaking my gaze from her husband. I didn't like the way he stared at Mandisa. It was freaky! Mami's eyes grew upset, seeing me.

"It's no problem at all, Mami. It's on my way. I only wanted to make sure you ladies were taken care of and safe. I've been dying to meet Lil Mami. I'll make sure Mandisa gets home, to school, and back here safe after school to see Mani-cakes," I reassured Mami with a smile.

"Good, then, Queen, we'll finish our conversation tomorrow after school. It will be Friday, and you can say goodbye to your friends. Then you can return to Paris," Dr. King stated, tapping Mandisa's arm.

Mandisa faked a smile and turned to her father. She grabbed her bag, gave him a hug, and said goodnight to Mami. As she said goodbye to Amani, she kissed her tiny foot and playfully nibbled her toes.

Damn! I wanted to do that too!

Chapter Thirteen: It's The Answer

Mandisa

"Queen, are you alright?" Hakim asked as we came into the Labor and Delivery waiting room door.

"I'm fine, now," I exhaled, walking to get away from my father. He would change his mind and come after me! I knew it by the way he talked to me. He was pretending because Mami had him scared, but he was still controlling everything. He did not know where we were staying, but it wouldn't be hard for him to find out now that he was here! "I was terrified when HE just showed up out of nowhere! He wouldn't let me out of his sight for a moment. Daddy took my phone, and he said that it was over. But Mami came to and took over the situation. He's going to try to get me on a plane…soon! We have to get out of here now!"

"Queen, it's going to be okay. Mami and I knew this was going to happen. I thought he would show up a little later. I had no idea he would get here tonight, but I knew he'd be here, Hakim said, catching up with me.

"What?" I asked him, seriously pissed off.

"We've got it covered, trust me?" Hakim said, helping me into his car. Lionel rode with Darius, following us. "We go get you things for school, you'll stay with us tonight in case he tries to come by the house for you, and tomorrow....I meet Dr. King. I'm going to fix this, okay?"

As I stared out the window, my heart was pounding wildly, and it hadn't stopped since Daddy walked into the room with Mami. I had no idea how he knew where we were or how he found out Mami had Amani. But Hakim was talking as if Mami had called and told Dad what was going on! I didn't know what to think anymore! I just wanted to get as far away from there as I could.

I got out of the car in the front yard and smiled at Darius pulled in behind us. He jumped out, grabbing me, asking, "Are you alright? You looked scared as hell, Queen."

I nodded, feeling better as Darius held me. Hakim was making me nervous with his cold and calculating demeanor. Darius made me feel safer now.

"Lionel!" Hakim yelled at his brother. "Come with me! Cyrus, help Queen. Take her home with you. We live too close. I'll be there soon. I need to grab a few things for tomorrow. No school. But we need to make sure it looks like you went, Queen, take everything you will need."

"Alright, Bro!" Darius agreed, watching them leave through the backyard.

We headed inside to grab my things. I was panicking about every move I made. I couldn't steady my nerves or relax. The thought that Daddy was here kept terrifying me. What were they thinking of calling him? Hakim had a plan that he hadn't informed any of us about, but Mami it seemed. He wanted me to trust him, but he didn't trust Darius or me. It made me feel like maybe this wasn't Hakim I was dealing with at all? He was too calm. He seemed to know exactly what to say and do from all sides. It was scaring the shit out of me because my father did that shit with my Mother! It felt like I was losing my fucking mind! Darius helped me get all of my clothes, shoes, and things. He helped me in the truck, but I didn't want to talk.

"Did you enjoy the bath, Queen?" Darius worried as I sat on his sofa, attempting to brush my damp hair.

"Oui, it was fine," I answered as he sat next to me, offering me a beer. He opened it for me, took a sip from his, and offered me a smile. I nodded and took a swig. What the hell, right? Who cares what I do now if tomorrow Daddy's going to drag me to hell kicking and screaming? I didn't like the taste of the beer, but I didn't care. I attempted to smile at Darius. "Merci, the water jets melted away the stress in my back. Do you have something here that will make me stop thinking about tomorrow?"

Darius smiled at me, lit one of his famous cigars, and took a puff saying, "You should relax, Queen. It's a celebration! Amani is here, and she's gorgeous! She looks just like you and your mother, but those eyes, wow! I didn't expect that. A black queen with blue eyes...the shit is crazy!"

"Amani is beautiful. When she is my age, she is going to be a heart breaker," I giggled as Darius blew his smoke in my face. He playfully wiggled his eyebrows and held out his blunt to me. Fuck it! I took it from him and put it to my lips. Darius's eyes grew colossal watching as I tried to smoke it. I coughed a few times, but the more I got inside…, the less I thought about things. I smiled and gave it back. "It is good...I feel...better."

"Now you overstand why those of us that get high from THC only want to get that shit off our heads so we can enjoy a moment! For me, it normalizes the parts of my brain that don't enjoy people. It's what Dr. Kaliah Morgan prescribes for Depression, the Indigo Shuffle is medicine for sensitive souls, and it works very well for Social Anxiety disorders," Darius chuckled as he took another puff with his beautiful brown lips and winked. I blushed and shook my head. "I didn't think you would actually smoke with me. I'm fucking happy as hell now!"

"It is only weed! I do not think I would ever mess with the hard stuff, but I don't think you would try to hurt me. I trust you, Darius," I giggled, making him gush shyly.

Darius held up his bottle, saying, "I think we should toast your mother and all mothers. I've never held a baby before, and watching your mother go through hell to get her here…Brothers like me respect women that go through that only to worry what's next. Mami has been through so much for you both."

"To the Goddesses, Darius. I look at my mother as my God. She put me here, raised me, and suffered for me like no one. All she asked was that I keep looking for something to love about being alive so I would not give up. How could I make up something more important than that?" I toasted thinking.

"You know, some brothers say that the black woman is God. But that's wrong, Queen. God is a masculine term of empowerment of the unknown forces that be. A man that encompasses the embodiment of what God represents can be called as thus. But you must give the woman more credit than just a portal for men to be birthed. She's higher than a god! She is creation itself! The source of all life needs males and females to coexist. The struggle lies in men giving women credit without ego. Money and power seem to inspire man's image of God.

'We have lost our reverence of the Source of Creation…the Balance…Natural Law and Order…Universoul Victims Unit….

'At least, that's what Kaliah tells me is wrong with society as a whole. Ego, materialism, division, fear tactics, hiding the truth with lies, and control, so men are too distracted fighting to change things and keep paying into the false illusion of security and protection for profit.

'That shit is facts…! You can see it if you look at everything with open eyes. It puts everything that's happened through history into perspective. That's why I know the revolution will only occur when people stop trusting the illusions projected by religion and government and start thinking for themselves. Keeping us divided has always been the American way, but they love to pretend to be United when they begin the shit that gets us the Evil Eye from other nations that know what's up over here.

'Hakim is always talking about how America's karma for all the lies is going to be its own self-destruction, and its enemies are going to fuck us up from the outside at the same time, so there's nothing left here. Those who believe we do no wrong and there is no healing that needs to be done will be the ignorant ones that push us to this destruction. Fuck that! I'll leave this country before I get bombed for the white man. He took this shit, and I will go back to Africa or anywhere else. I don't have to feed into the bullshit.

'Nothing here is really free, shit money doesn't make you unrestricted, and the best thing to do is change your attitude and move to a new latitude. Those that hate us can't keep blaming us if we leave. But no one wants us to go. We outnumber the enemy and are the biggest earners. We maintain their pockets. Hence they keep our minds empty to keep it that way to feel sorry for ourselves.

'Excuse me…I run off at the mouth when I get too relaxed, Mandisa," Darius explained, completely shocking me.

He was always joking and silly, but I knew he was intelligent. It was hard to get Darius to be serious most of the time about anything. I was used to hearing Hakim go on about things, but Darius was much more emotional and concerned when he talked. Darius wasn't focused, but it was a hell of a speech from just talking out of the blue! I was impressed as I gave him a hug shocking him. I glanced around his apartment, noticing all his stuff, and died laughing.

"How do you have all this stuff, and you're not old enough to buy it?" I asked, folding my legs.

"Money can buy almost anything if you know where to buy it," Darius told me, staring smiling sweetly. His brown eyes were much lower, and now that he relaxed, he was much more attractive. Darius smoked, thinking a moment. He made the most innocent faces when he was overthinking. With his hair tied back, he looked like a boy trying to understand something complicated. It was so cute I giggled to myself. "Mandisa, you're high….It's okay…You look adorable here trying to analyze me, but I'm doing the same thing to you, and it's so cute."

"Whatever, Nigga!" I giggled, pushing his arm away as he messed with my cheeks.

"Mandisa! How dare you! I am hurt and offended that you would address your man in such a way," Darius cried, frowning clutching his hand. "I love you, Girl! No one will ever love you like Cyrus!"

"Darius, stop it!" I groaned as he poked my hip, making my leg wobble. He stared at me and raised his eyes curiously a moment. "What?"

"You feel comfortable enough around me to dress like that? Those shorts are dangerously short, Queen," Darius told me, smiling at my thighs. "I mean…you like it….I love it. I'm just picking up some vibes from your choice of clothing."

"I can change! I have other things to sleep in. I wasn't thinking and put on the first thing. I forgot where I was or who was here until you spoke to me. I'm used to it always being just Mami and me," I explained embarrassedly. Darius laughed, pretending to be looking at the ceiling. "I will change. I don't want you uncomfortable with me in your home."

I went back into the guest room and found my sweat pants, and took off my shorts. As I folded them, putting them away, I turned around because I felt a draft, and Darius was standing in the door watching me! He didn't move but stood leaning against the frame with his eyes slowly scanning me. I blushed as I quickly put the sweatpants on, asking, "What are you doing, Darius?"

"I was just curious, that's all, Queen. We spend a lot of time together, but I've never seen you naked. I thought maybe I can see a little more so I can dream about it later tonight?" Darius replied, holding up his hands with a candid look on his face. He smiled a bit and stood up straight. "How about we play a game? Show me yours, and I'll show you mine…? I'll stand over here. I'll never touch you…?"

"Darius, that's not fair. Hakim has never seen me naked, either. Everything we have done, we never have to get naked. It's all innocent," I explained, blushing. I put my hand on my hip reserved. "Hakim has never asked me to take off my clothes, Darius. He tries to touch too much, but he always listens when I tell him to stop."

"I'm not Hakim, Mandisa….I'm asking," Darius retorted seriously. He bit his bottom lip and tilted his head slightly, grinning at me. "It's been a long time for me, Queen. I don't go this long without…Something. Hakim can meditate away his frustration, but I would rather think about your gorgeous body in full detail and …. do other things. If you get my drift? I promise…I only want to see?"

I stared at Darius for a moment. His eyes watched me intently; as he smiled, they seemed to glow at me with wonder. He let his eyebrows relax and made a cute face acting shy. I tilted my head back, sighing, "Darius, I'm not sure…It seems wrong for me to play this game with you and not Hakim. He will feel like we are keeping secrets?"

"I would not get upset with you for doing anything you thought would make him happy. If I show you whatever you show me, we'll be even. You stop, then I stop, so you can call it off if you get uncomfortable, Queen," Darius stated cheerfully. He reached up and took his hair down. "See, we're even. Your hair's already down. You go first, and I'll follow your lead."

Darius stood resting against the door, smiling beautifully with curious eyes. It made me feel shy, but it made him look so different when he took his hair down and pushed it back. Darius always wore his hair tied back or up in crazy braided styles. Staring at that beautiful dark man with his hair down reminded me of pictures and paintings of Zulu warriors.

I reached down, grabbing the bottom of my tank top, pulling it over my head. I sat it on the bed. Darius stared at my red bra, started chewing his bottom lip, and exhaled deeply through his nose. He nodded and snatched off his black teeshirt and held it in his hand. He had a black A-shirt underneath, but I could see a dark line just above the collar. I took a step closer and caught myself looking curiously.

"Is that a tattoo, Darius?" I asked, looking at the black lines. He sneered, waggled, and stuck out his tongue at me. "What is it?"

"Take off your bra if you want to see it? I'll take off my A-shirt, and then you'll see what's up. I'll even let you touch me," Darius chuckled, folding his arms making the muscles flex tensely in his chest, shoulders, and arms. Lionel had lots of silly tattoos all over his arms and chest, but he was so skinny. Darius and Hakim both had beautifully sculpted bodies covered in smooth-colored skin. Darius was the most beautiful chocolate man I had ever seen, and he knew it when we were alone. "You know...I have more than one? Only a few have seen them all. Hakim doesn't know about one I got recently. Wanna guess where?"

"This was a bad idea," I wheezed, catching myself about to reach for my bra.

Darius panicked and laughed, "Queen, that's how the game is played. You want to see something, and so do I. You have all the power if I can't touch you, but you can molest me."

"That sounds terrible, Darius! I don't want to molest you!" I laughed, covering my face.

"I'm not protesting being molested by you, Mandisa. Shit, it's not rape, if you yell, 'Surprise!' I'm hoping that you'll get inside of a huge chocolate cake and make my birthday one for the History books, but I'm only interested in what you're after in this situation, Queen," Darius joked making me giggle. But I knew that meant he was nervous as well.

"Fine," I said, reaching back and unhooking my bra. I slowly let go of the hooks, slid the straps off, set it on the bed, and covered my breasts, folding my arms. "There...happy?"

"Uh-uh...don't tease me, Queen. Move your arms, please?" He begged, tilting his head. "Your clothes hide your figure up top, but I can tell you have a spectacular body. Let me see?"

I trembled nervously as I slowly lowered my arms. Darius smirked, shut his eyes, and bobbed.

"Those are beautiful, nice, full, round, and perky. Mercy, they look delicious," Darius sighed as he took off his A-shirt. I blushed, gaping at the tightness of his magnificent torso! If Hersey's chocolate built a specific dark statue, it would be molded after Darius's six-pack and upper body! Every part of him was so smooth, and it looked silky. His stomach looked like small segments of a candy bar stacked beneath his smooth chest. There was a trail of dark hair beneath his navel that poked out a bit. His slender waist had sharp lines leading down into his waistband. He chuckled as my eyes exploded staring at that shit! "You can come closer if you want, Queen? I said I will not touch you. I would put my hands in my pockets, but that's not safe at the moment."

I moved closer slowly, and Darius stood up straight, towering over me, smiling sweetly as I looked at his magnificently chiseled chest. There was so much heat coming from his skin I could feel it just standing near. The tattoo on his chest was a heart drawn over his own, and it read, "Mama's Boy." I smiled, glancing at it. Darius spun around and pulled his hair over his shoulder, showing me his back.

"Ana" was beautifully drawn in the center of his shoulder blades. There were dark wings down his back and black feathers on his shoulders that ran down to the length of his hair. It was unbelievable looking at the lines that made those feathers seem to float away from his shoulders! They seemed so authentic on his skin, with all the black and brown fighting for light.

Darius spun back around, smiling down at me.

"It's beautiful," I whispered as I nervously pulled my hands back.

"I don't take off my shirts much unless I have a reason. I've got fat boy issues, Queen. Some shit is hard to fix when it comes to how we see progress. Sometimes, I still feel like I'm overweight and get self-conscious. I see that in you too," Darius explained, moving closer and letting me touch him. "You don't have to be afraid of me trying to handle you without permission.

'Well…your feet are always fair game around me, but I do not believe in forcing a woman into anything she doesn't want. You have perfect skin for a tattoo. It would stand out anywhere you put it. Turn around, Queen?"

I listened, turning my back to him, and I heard Darius sigh. I twisted my head, looking back, and he knelt down and looked up at my butt. He rubbed his forehead, smiled as he twirled his finger, and looked up at me. I turned back around and faced him. Darius stood up; his face remained calm, waiting.

I slowly reached for the waist of my sweats, and he nodded. I began to pull them down my legs to the floor. Darius poked out his lips and rocked his head, staring at my red lace boyshorts. He took a deep breath, exhaled, and licked his lips.

"Let me see it from the side, Queen?" He groaned, stroking his chin as he knelt back down. I turned to the side. "Yesh! That is perfect! Ooooh!"

I rolled my eyes, turning back forward as he lost his head, screaming, "I've never seen anything so perfect in all my life! Eww...you let Antoine see all that!? Ow! Shit! Fuck! I see why he Flippin and Flopping!"

"Darius!" I groaned, so embarrassed I was ready to stop. But I wanted to see since he got me out of my pants. Darius was always bragging about his gift. He was constantly rubbing it on me and getting me to touch on it. I knew it was gigantic, but of course...I wanted to see how Darius hid it! He lept up from his knees and pulled down his black shorts. Underneath, he wore blue boxer-briefs that were locked on his slender hips, gripping his thick legs, and though he was so slim ...that! WOW! "Oh, my god!"

Darius shook his head, demanding, "Why so shocked? I told you that it is the biggest! I let you touch it, so you didn't think I was lying. But I knew that once you have a visual, you'll put the picture together in your head about what you're getting. You really don't want to see me naked, Queen? Now that we're practically done. I figure, go for it...I still can't touch you."

"It's not that I don't want to see you, Darius. You are so sexy! I'm afraid things will go too far if I do not stop this game," I admitted as I took a step back. I could still feel all that heat coming from all that Hot Chocolate. Though Darius was cheerful and sweet, he scared me with that huge thing trying to get out of his underwear! Every breath he exhaled near me seemed to touch my skin and made it move! How could it be so long? It was rolled up inside his underwear like a fat snake waking up down his leg! Women want something this big? It was frightening. "Is it hot in here?"

Darius chuckled, pulling his Gucci waistband down his hip saying, "You're really not curious, Mandisa? I thought you wanted to see?"

"No..." I gasped, trying to breathe but unable to look away from his gorgeous skin. So why was he wearing blue underwear? God! "Darius, stop...I really don't want to see it...."

"Sure you do, Queen, look right here," Darius chuckled as he slipped his hand over, barely pulling his underwear down. Tiny lipstick prints were tracing down his hip and stopping at a baby panther sleeping on top of his thigh. I started giggling as Darius made the kitten look like it was purring, wiggling his hip. "See, I'm not scary. I just wanted you to meet, T'challa, Queen! ....Pet him!"

I died laughing as I heard a knock on the front door. I grabbed my bra and top, but Darius was standing there still staring at me, getting dressed. He slowly put on his A-Shirt, reached over in a drawer, grabbed some pajama bottoms, and left his shorts on the floor. He waited for me to pick them up, and I folded them and set them on the dresser. Darius smiled at me, nodded, and went to open the door.

Hakim came inside holding a bag and suitcase in both hands. He glanced at me on the sofa, brushing my hair, and smiled, saying, "Hey...."

"Hey," I replied sweetly, blushing as he came over, pressing his lips to mine. Darius's little game had my heart running wild, and my mind was wandering. I was trying not to touch Hakim too much and pulled away.

"Queen, are you alright? I know you're worried, but I told you I got you. Tell me that you trust me, please?" Hakim begged me sadly. His eyes looked me over, concerned.

"Of course, Hakim," I told him, but my eyes locked on his arms as he held his suitcase.

His uniform shirt was nicely fitted, and I could see his biceps, chest, and neck flex from the weight he held. Hakim was a brick wall under his shirt. I had seen his body watching him run. God…Damn! He was one tight brown boy with perfectly smooth skin everywhere. I shuttered and looked at my hairbrush.

Darius kept staring at me standing by the TV. He had a strange look in his eyes as Hakim knelt down nearby. I glanced at my hairbrush again, and Hakim took my hand.

"Queen, I love you. I'll do anything for you. I'm not going to lose my sunshine. Look at me," Hakim told me, rubbing my fingers with his hands. I could feel that warmth of his aura, just like with Darius. It was so intense I looked at Hakim and nodded. He stood up and frowned. "I'm going to go change. I'll be back."

"Alright, Bro," Darius replied as I glanced at him, then Hakim.

Hakim glared at us a moment and sighed back, and shut the door. I took my brush and stared at it a moment. I went back to brushing my hair a moment, but I looked down. My leg was trembling! I stood up and went to the door, and knocked.

No one answered, so I opened the door, and Hakim was on the phone. He turned around and smiled.

"Yeah, about eleven is fine. I'll be there, Man," Hakim said, then hung up the phone. He sat the phone on the dresser near Darius's shorts. "Is everything alright, Queen?"

"Oui, fine," I answered, smiling.

Hakim took out his contact lenses, washed his eyes, and dried his face putting on his glasses. He walked over to the bed and grabbed his clothes. Then, he stopped and looked over at me a moment.

"What's bothering you, Queen? You've been so quiet since we left the hospital. If you're afraid, you can talk to me," Hakim worried, taking my hand.

He set his things on the bed and stared at me, concerned. His lips pursed, and his eyes looked down at me through his lenses. Hakim's face was so soft and sweet when he was worried. He had a soft side he didn't let many see, and it was sexy. His eyebrows drew together as if he were in pain and asked, "Tell me what's on your mind, Mandisa. I wish I could read it, but I can't."

"I want to see your body, Hakim? Do you mind? I've been thinking you have been fighting so much to protect me from my own father. You have shown me so much of your heart. I want to see the real you," I whispered to him sweetly. Hakim raised his eyebrows and stared down at me.

"You've been playing with Cyrus....? He used to do that when we were younger to get girls to let him see something," Hakim told me, smiling. He reached for his things again, shaking his head.

"I really want to see anyway, Hakim," I insisted, locking my eyes on his face.

"Okay," Hakim replied as he reached down and started unbuckling his belt.

"No! Take your shirt off first, please? I want to paint the mental picture perfectly," I thought aloud, beginning to suddenly feel sad. This could be the last time I saw them. I wanted everything to go well, but I felt so helpless knowing my father was here. Maybe one day I'll look back on this and laugh, or someone will find a painting of me doing what I'm about to do…with the only two men I've ever wanted in my entire life. "If you do not want to do it…then…it is fine."

"It's not a problem at all, Queen," Hakim whispered as he froze. He slowly nodded, looking at me. I think that Hakim suddenly realized what I was trying to do. I was going to go ahead and get it over with if Daddy would take me away tomorrow. Hakim had his plan, but he did not include me in it. I couldn't give my complete devotion to him because of his secrecy, but I would give them both my body. Then I'd just have our time together for the remainder. But if I told Hakim that, he would lose it. He reached up for his collar button and paused. "You want to help me take things off since you want to see?"

I came over slowly and stared at him, blushing. I took a button between my fingers and unfastened it. Hakim stared down at me, smiling sweetly as I finished. I untucked the bottom, opened it, and slipped down his arms. He caught his sleeve and tossed it on the bed, and grabbed his undershirt, and pulled it off over his head, watching me.

Hakim's skin was so smooth. If Darius is a dark chocolate special edition, milk chocolate is Hakim's shade of brown. His skin loves the light, and it's always so ripped because Hakim rarely relaxes and doesn't have a pound of fat anywhere on his masterfully crafted body! He was all muscle with beautiful skin and the sweetest eyes and smile.

Okay, Darius was right; Hakim does have a face like Trey Songs. They have similar eyebrows and lips, but Hakim does not have a tattoo, scar, or pimple anywhere on his body. He takes excellent care of himself...He's a Gemini and remarkably conceded. Hakim has every reason to be stuck on himself. He is physically GODLY.

"Your body is perfect," I gasped, staring at his stomach and lean waist as he bent over.

"Thank you…I'm flattered you like it, really. Do you mind letting me see what's under your shirt?" Hakim asked, smiling putting his A-shirt on the bed. I quickly threw my tank top on the bed. Hakim's eyes shot over to me, and he laughed but stood up. "Ooooh….is that….RED? That is nice. My favorite color. That looks gorgeous."

Hakim took my hand, spun me around, and held me close a second. He chuckled playfully against my neck, I felt a flick, and my bra came undone! When Hakim spun me back around, his fingers traced my shoulders, and Hakim slid the straps from my arms, smiling. His eyes stayed on mine, his smile was very soft, and he put my bra to his lips and inhaled deeply. His eyes grew wide, and he moaned as he glanced downward.

"Oooh, look at you…!" Hakim whispered, taking a step back. "They look like two sweet grapefruit, but I bet they taste sweeter than an orange. Goddess, you are riper than a pineapple and juicier."

I was nervous watching as he rubbed his lips with his fingertips. Hakim took a step toward me, and I took a step back. I paused as Darius bumped into me. His chest touched my shoulders, and I felt his fingers trace my neck and play in my hair. Hakim stared into my eyes, getting my attention, and asked, "You want me to stop?"

Hakim came closer and grabbed both my hips. I gasped as my heart began to beat unpredictably while staring at Hakim as he flared his nostrils and bit his bottom lip. I held my breath as Darius ran his soft lips against my neck, and I shivered. Darius picked me up until my feet were not on the floor, and Hakim pulled my sweats down my thighs. Darius slowly lowered me as Hakim stared up at me.

"RED! FUCK!" Hakim moaned as he ran his fingertips over my knee and up my thigh.

"God!" I cried as Darius flicked his tongue inside my ear and pulled me into his body. My knees began to wobble, and Hakim followed where Darius led me. He seemed to be having fun watching me lose my mind! I was so overloaded with excitement I didn't know what to do! Darius was keeping me from escaping while Hakim followed, enjoying the chase. "Wait! Wait!"

"Not this time…I told you if you came on to me, then I was going to get it, Queen," Hakim whispered as he reached forward for my knee and pulled my leg up, admiring my panties. I screamed as Darius fell back and pushed me down on the bed. Darius smiled at me and looked at Hakim. "I know what you're thinking, and I don't think you realize who

I am, Mandisa. You don't know who you're fucking with, and Daddy will give me what I want. It's gonna be me that wins in the end! But since you want to fuck and I'm kind of stressed them, I'd love a taste…Thank you so very much for setting the table, Cyrus!"

"Hakim! This isn't one of your sick games! Stop playing! You're scaring the shit out of her! Did you forget, Mandisa is a virgin, NIGGA!" Darius told Hakim, laughing as slapped the shit out of him. Hakim glanced at me and died laughing. "You take shit too far, Bro!"

Hakim dropped his head as Darius held me, saying, "I'm sorry, Queen. Hakim is just playing with the wild boy shit. He was trying to figure out how to do this since you're so sure, but he's scared. I think that we should just flow. He said porn it up and see if you liked that fantasy? What do you want? We don't want to do this if you aren't going to enjoy it. Hakim is just an asshole because he knows we're all scared."

"I ain't scared, Cyrus! I'm hesitating because it's been a while, and I'm worried about what will happen afterward. I have a sexual addiction, Niggas! So once I fuck again, I'm gonna want some more. You ready?" Hakim said, moving back closer grabbing my hips.

For once, I wished they both would just shut up and finish what they started without fighting.

"Just flow like Darius said, we will worry about tomorrow when we wake up. I want to do this with you. But I am afraid I don't know what to do or what to expect. You're both so aggressive and want something different. Tell me what you like…what do I do?" I worried, wiping away a tear.

"I'm so sorry, Mandisa. I'm an asshole. I fucked this up for you, being me. I've never made love before. It's always been wild, so I have to relax too," Hakim chuckled nervously.

"Thank you very much for being honest with your Queen. You think I was going to let you do her dirty, Bro? She's my Goddess, too. I love her, and you're not going to fuck this up for either of us. This requires a certain level of control and finesse. Follow my lead, and I'll learns you something," Darius told Hakim, pulling me closer and smiling. "Can we start over and let me show you what this shit is all about?"

"For once, I'm going to follow his lead, but real talk….he doesn't last long!" Hakim teased Darius talking to me.

Darius raised his eyebrows, astonished, and said, "Long enough to get a big yes!"

Hakim put his hands on my knees and pushed them apart, grabbing my panties laughing. Darius winked down at me and said, "He's a hater. You sure you want both of us at once? I could-,"

I pulled Darius toward me and kissed his lips. My heart went crazy as I felt all the heat rush from my chest down below my thighs. My body shivered violently as Hakim's lips rolled up my thighs. He sucked my skin between his lips, and I held my breath as his hands grabbed the crotch of my panties. Finally, he paused, putting his hand over them, and flexed his neck, crawling closer on his belly.

Hakim looked up at me and frowned, snatching away the entire crotch from my panties, putting it inside his mouth, and kissing my thighs. I had never seen anything like that before, and it paralyzed me! He moved so fast and was so strong! I gasped as his tongue wiggled up my inner thigh. He was painting lines with the tip of his tongue until he reached his hand. Then, I was set on fire as his fingers began to massage my pussy and his tongue glided right inside of me!

"Oh Fuck!" I cried. Hakim pinned my legs open, so I couldn't move, and with Darius behind me, I had nowhere to run. Darius smiled, running his fingertips down my chest and beginning to stroke my nipples. I shivered as I felt Hakim suddenly slurp deeply, and my knees tried to attack his neck. It was so hot and getting stickier the more Hakim licked, making me groan and scream. Darius suddenly stopped using his hands and used his beautiful tongue to lick my nipple and suck it into his mouth, and I had never felt anything so remarkable in my life.

"That's right, Queen. Now you're starting to feel nice and warm. You have two kings turning up the heat. I'll let him have his fun for now. Maybe you can be nice to Jody and me since Hakim is so generous to you?" Darius whispered to me as he knelt nearby me. He took off his underwear, and Jody unraveled, hitting the bed! He took his erection in his hand and helped it over my face stroking it. "We can make a game out of this. You kiss, lick, and suck him for me. If you ever get me to tell you to stop…I'll buy you a car, Mandisa. You can pick out any vehicle you want. I'll pay any price if you make me bust like that. So far, no one has ever done it. You're not going to get it easily, but I just want you to try?"

Did he just tell me that no one has ever? I don't know why, but all of these games were starting to become fun. I opened my mouth and tasted it. It wasn't that bad. Just a little salty, sticky, and when I kissed it…Darius nearly lost his mind! His eyes stared down at me so big, as if he didn't think I would do it. I touched Jody and squeezed him in my palm, and he was thicker than my three middle fingers. But I tried to put it in my mouth anyway.

"Oh my God! Yes!" Darius cried out, watching. "She's a trooper! I think I'll keep her!"

I grabbed a handful of Hakim's locks as I felt his tongue begin to flick against my clitoris and my toes curled up.

My back slammed down into the bed covers, and my hips went crazy, and I gasped for air. Darius pulled away and kissed my lips.

"She's gonna blow!" Darius chuckled.

"Holy shiiiiit!" I yelled as Hakim lifted my legs higher so I couldn't run.

"Fuck!" Hakim moaned suddenly. "Why does it have to be so good? Cum for me, Queen, tell this mouth you love it!"

"Freaky-ass, Nigga!" Darius laughed, trying to put Jody back in my mouth. "I know...I'm sick too...just go with it! Two for one!"

"You can't wear a skirt around me, or my face is diving right here! I'm gonna eat this pussy six times a night!" Hakim groaned, sitting back, licking his face clean. He wiped his mouth and licked his hands frantically.

Darius laughed, biting his lips, "If I don't taste that, I'm probably going to go crazy like him."

Darius slid off the bed and crawled up between my thighs.

"Wait!" I yelled, trying to sit up. My head was swimming, and I had all kinds of insane sensations shooting through my body. Darius smiled up at me and rubbed his full lips against my lower lips. It was a totally different feeling than Hakim! Finally, my head flew down to the bed. "Oh, Shit!"

"Ha…" Darius laughed, sticking out his tongue. "Oh, my word? Yes, Sweet Pussy Pie!"

I felt lightning shot through me as Darius kissed my pussy with those lips. I could not sit still. I had tears in my eyes, and I could barely see now. Hakim came over, wiped my face, and smiled down at me. Then, he grabbed Darius's head and pushed his face into me, saying, "Boy, you better eat that pussy like it's your last meal, and you're Black Jesus!"

My back arched harder as Darius's mouth put more pressure sucking, and I sighed, trying to breathe, and it came out like a purr. Hakim closed his eyes and nodded, saying, "That's more like it. If you're not screaming, crying, or making sounds like that, it's not good enough. You get your face wet and eat that girl if you want her to need you! This isn't your first time. It's her's, Bro! You do that shit. You do it right every damn time!"

Hakim ran his fingers through his hair and walked away suddenly. Darius moaned and sucked my clit between his lips and rubbed them back and forth until my body exploded. It felt like everything locked up at once, and I couldn't breathe. Then, my hips began to jerk wildly against him, and he lost it.

"Fuck yes!" Darius screamed, tensing up. "Move those hips, Sexy woman! Now I know you can feel me!"

He rolled his tongue inside of me and pulled back as I came on his tongue. He moaned, kissing my thighs and gently stroking me with his fingers, and pushed inside and pulled out. He licked his fingers and stood up, saying, "Now that is sweet!"

I held my breath, trying to stop my knees from rattling, and my hips twitched every few seconds. I wiped my face trying to pull myself together. I trembled, feeling so delicious I thought I was melting from between my legs. I had goosebumps from head to toe, and everything that touched me made me moan or shiver.

"Queen, this is an intense experience, and if you want to stop, we can. We don't have to do anything else. I'm not a small brother. I want you to enjoy this, I can be mean unintentionally, but I can't do you like that," Darius told me as he sat next to me and rubbed my shoulder while I lay on my side.

I gasped as he pressed Jody into my back. He chuckled to himself and playfully slapped my butt with it.

"Wait, one goddamn minute, Bro....You expect me to follow you with that? I didn't know you were really packing like that! I'd be shy around niggas too," Hakim complained from the foot of the bed.

"It's not for niggas to see. I gave you a fair warning. Now he's yours, Queen," Darius told me, smiling.

"How do you hide it?" I asked him as I felt Jody's heartbeat against my behind.

"He's not this big when I'm not excited," Darius laughed, wiggling my behind against it.

"Uh, I'm not gay, but how big is that shit? That's inhuman, and I don't see how a woman could possibly handle anything that size, Bro," Hakim complained, shaking his head.

"I haven't met a woman that can handle it, Bro. It's 14 and a half inches in length—bout one and three-quarters thick. I became obsessed with measuring it once it got hard the first time. He stopped growing when I lost all the weight.

Good dick was hiding under all that belly," Darius chuckled to himself. That's why I am very picky about who I want to give my blessing to....She deserves a gift if she can hang with Jody for a few minutes.

'I've learned the difference between fucking and making love because if I fuck a woman wild, I know I'm going to do serious harm to her. I listen to a woman's body and never try to ram it home. She's going to start cumming the moment I get inside. The rest is her story. I'm going to love it all."

Hakim glanced at me and touched my knee, sitting down. He shook his head and said, "I've gotten what I wanted, and I can seriously wait before we go any further. I want to, but only if you're ready, Queen. It's addictive for me because it's so spiritual. The high of building the climax and holding it off....I'm not a small brother either. I'm not 14 and a half! But I can't get an accurate measurement."

Hakim pulled down his pants, and his penis hit his leg. He grabbed it and pulled it up; it touched his belly button and curved slightly to the left. I covered my mouth because I had never seen Hakim without pants and his legs and hips were gorgeous!

"I just need a taste, and I am good, Queen. I get excited about giving oral pleasure to women. I'm sick because I can have a sexual orgasm from tasting you. I can have one in many ways too. But it's more intense for me to give than to receive. Now that I've tasted you, Mandisa, it's going to be hard to keep me off of you. Oral sex is my form of crack, and I just relapsed, so I'm going to smoke your fine ass. If you want me to, I'll eat you all night, fall asleep, wake up, and do it again. I can't get enough," Hakim explained as he sat waiting for me to respond, wiping his left eye.

Darius nodded, adding, "Whatever you want, Queen. I'll love you no matter. No pressure, we can cuddle. I am happy as hell you went this far. Shocked, really…"

"Hakim," I sighed sweetly as I touched his elbow. He shut his eyes and smiled.

"Don't do that, Queen," He groaned as he shivered, looking away.

"I want you to make love to me—both of you. I'm tired of being afraid, and I love you. Unfortunately, if tomorrow comes and something happens…I might never see you again. But I can have this memory," I whispered, frowning as Hakim opened his eyes, looking down at me sadly.

"Queen?" Hakim sighed as his face turned red. "I told you…."

"If Daddy takes me away," I sighed softly.

"Mandisa...Don't think ..." Darius groaned, resting his chin on my shoulder. "You have to trust us. Hakim knows what he's doing. I trust him when it comes to important matters. The sexual stuff is a no-go, but when it comes to facts and money...He's yah boy to go to. You have to learn to trust that side of him."

"Just give me this, please?" I cried as I rubbed Hakim's sweet, round lips with my fingernails.

He closed his eyes and kissed my fingers. Darius pulled me back as Hakim grabbed my legs, climbing on top of me, pinning me down with his massive arms. He leaned back on his knees and lifted my calf to his lips, and kissed my skin. He glanced at me and sighed, "You're my wife! You're not going anywhere!"

Hakim leaned forward and kissed my lips. His tongue wiggled against mine, and he tossed my legs around his waist.

"Don't watch this part, Queen. It will be uncomfortable at first. But it is going to get better once you relax. Do you trust me?" Darius asked me as he laid my head on his lap and played in my hair.

"Oui, Darius...I love you...and I trust you," I answered nervously, closing my eyes. I felt Hakim pushing against me. The burning and pressure were so intense as he tore me open.

But it was quick! It was the sensation of him filling me up on the inside that made me gasp for air! I tensed up, and Hakim grabbed my hips and froze.

"Relax, relax, Queen, keep your eyes closed. Take a deep breath," Darius whispered tenderly against my cheek. "You're the most beautiful woman on the planet. I love your gorgeous energy, and I'm going to do everything I can to make you happy."

I inhaled, and I felt Hakim push his body into me more, and he moaned now deep inside. Finally, he gasped deeply, "Shit...I'm in...It's so tight...fuck!"

I felt so strange with him forcing deeper and filling my walls, stretching me wider.

"Worst part's over now, Queen, just relax," Darius whispered down to my neck, and I felt lips kiss my breasts. I moaned as Hakim slowly ground down lower, so deep that I felt a tingling sensation roll up my spine.

"Ooh," I moaned as I experienced a burning grow from deep inside of me.

"Ooooh, Queen!" Hakim groaned and started moving faster. "You're getting so wet...fuck...Haah! Don't do that! She's gripping my shit...Ooooh!"

I was on fire from head to toe as Hakim's hips went insanely fast, and I couldn't breathe when he dipped down and rotated his hips into me. His thrusts were powerful once he got excited, and his legs powered his every move.

Now I understood how it was possible! Hakim was a marathon man that probably could go as long as he could run! And he did not seem to get tired once he got going. If not for Darius being there, I think he would have driven me crazy. I don't know how many times Hakim made me cum. I lost count a long time ago when he was licking me.

Hakim tensed up and moved faster than he was already going and suddenly frowned, pulling his own hair! He screamed, bit his lip, and fell backward, hitting the floor, "Fuck! Shit! Good ass...pussy!"

"Damn! You killed him," Darius laughed, wiping my face. "If you make a brother cry like that, it means those walls tried to break him up. Let me see?"

Darius laid on his back and pulled my legs across his. I sat on his lap, and he lifted me and started pushing himself carefully against me. There was so much more pressure and tearing than Hakim, and Darius pulled me close and looked me in the eye. His face relaxed, and he began to breathe slowly against me. I found myself following his lead. He smiled at me and nodded, kissing my lips gently. His plump, soft lips caressed my cheek, and he kissed my neck. I gasped and shivered, Darius pushed up into me, and I froze.

"Breathe….Queen…I'm inside now…I'm not going to do what you think…I told you, Jody belongs to you. I'm going to lie here and let the two of you get acquainted…This is our dance, and you don't move unless you love the motion," Darius whispered, holding my hips and slowly pulling me closer, creeping deeper. I put my hands on his chest to balance myself from falling over, and he slowly moved his hips, drilling inside, and I leaked all over the bed. "Black Oil….Texas Tea…French Vanilla…Latte….I love that shit….You can take it…please do…."

"Ooh! Darius!" I screamed as he moved more, scaring me. He winked up at me and bit his bottom lip, and spun his hips in a circle. It moved around inside of me, and I think I wet the bed.

"I love you….Oh, Goddess! Fuck! You know you a freak for letting me do that to you, right?" Darius moaned, dropping his head on the bed.

He grabbed my hips and flipped over on top of me. I had to keep him back! He went crazy! I tried to slow him down, but Darius was lost! He was so deep that I knew he knew what he was doing. His body was like a well-oiled machine. Every movement was precise; he controlled the thrust, depth, and speed. It was strictly like when we danced the way he rode my waves of pleasure. He was so tender, excited, and attentive to my every movement. He tried to kiss every part of me he could reach with those gorgeous lips.

Each moan, scream, or cry was from pleasure, not pain. He met me at the peak of the mountain and led me back down to the valley. I closed my eyes as tears ran down my cheeks and filled my ears. Darius buried his face in my neck and whispered, "I'm going to give you everything I couldn't give the others that never loved me, Mandisa. I'm going to get you a car, house, ring, then I'm going to give you my baby! I'm going to spoil your fine ass! You're not going…anywhere! You belong to Hakim, but I belong to you! ….Fuck! I'm cumming!"

It felt like a bomb went off inside of me. My thighs quaked, my walls were vibrating and throbbing. I could feel Darius's pulse through my walls because he was inside so firmly. He was moving slowly but picking up speed, then quickly pulled out.

"Fuck!" I cried as the pressure let off, making me cum again. Spilling all beneath my back.

"I'm sorry," Darius whispered, kissing my lips. "Open your eyes, look at me, Queen. I'm sorry!"

He wiped the tears from my eyes, but I still couldn't see anything but the stars swimming around the darkness. Finally, I heard the water running, and I was lifted from the bed. He carried me close, and I was lowered into warm water. A warm towel wiped my face, and I opened my eyes. Hakim smiled down at me.

"Hey," He muttered with a beautiful smile on his face.

"Hakim?" I asked, looking around confused.

He kissed my lips, and his touch was so gentle and warm. There was so much passion in his fingertips I felt like I was catching fire from his contact! Hakim kissed my chin and held me closer. He smiled down at me, saying, "Woman, I'm so in love with you now. I'm never going to let you go. You may as well get used to being right here in my arms…This is your home now."

He pressed his forehead to mine and rocked me back and forth. I was so confused. I know I had my eyes closed, but if Hakim was my passionate lover…I saw Darius standing near the edge of the tub, smiling. He stepped down and came over. He looked worried as he asked, "Did I hurt you at all?"

"No," I replied as I touched his chin. He leaned closer, and I kissed his cheek and smiled. "I was so very emotional I could not control myself."

Darius sighed in relief, "I was terrified that I had lost it somehow. I told you the crying thing gets me. It got so good to me I couldn't control myself."

Hakim was nodding as I glanced back at him, "That was the best feeling I've ever experienced, honestly. You made me cum too fast. Normally, I can go! It's been well over a year, but an hour or two is easy before I feel good enough to release. You got me, and I'll take that loss with a smile....wow! ...Your eyes!"

"What?" I asked, looking at him confused. Darius came closer to me and smiled. Then, he looked away suddenly, like he was blushing.

"This light makes your eyes look like Amani. They look blue the color of ocean water, Queen," Darius confessed to me, smiling and looking away.

"Mami's eyes do that as well. When the light hits them at certain angles, they look different colors, but they are gray. Amani really had blue eyes like daddy. My babies might have blue eyes," I explained to Darius and Hakim, smiling.

"Oh, Shit! We didn't use anything!" Darius yelled, yanking his hair.

"It's okay," I giggled at his silly reaction. He looked like he was about to beat his brains out on the tub.

"Why? You want a baby right now?" Darius asked me nervously.

"No, silly-ass! I've been taking birth control hormones since I was 13 to regulate my cycle and clear my skin. Mami said it was safer than shots because I needed to keep my weight down for dancing. But I still got the hips and boobs because of them," I sighed, blushing.

"Thank you, Mami! So all that dancing and birth control pills, that's why your body is so womanly?" Darius laughed, relieved.

"Your mother deserves a standing ovation, Queen," Hakim chuckled, pulling his erection up from the water. I started laughing as he kissed my lips and forehead. "Damn it! How do I find something more to love about you every day?"

"Aren't the most special relationships the ones where you fall deeper every day? Rather than the ones where the reasons run out too soon? At first, it was a mere physical attraction, but the more I am with you…." I sighed.

"If you love me, you have to trust me, Queen, and you must believe in me!" Hakim chuckled sweetly. "It's more than your life that your father is trying to ruin. He's trying to destroy my existence and Cyrus's as well. I can't have him take you away from us.

'I'm willing to do whatever it takes to prove to your father that he's fucking up. Just have faith in your man. That's all I ask of you. I'm not going to fail you. We're going to be together. By any means necessary, Mandisa."

I noticed Darius nodding in agreement. I took a deep breath and agreed, "I believe you. I believe in both of you, okay?"

"That's all I ask of you, Queen!" Hakim sighed, relaxing.

#

I woke up from a dream early that morning….In tears!

Hakim, Darius, and I were together on a beautiful beach, and the sun was setting. Darius and Hakim found a beautiful kitten with the saddest eyes like mine. They changed colors in the light as it faded. The poor thing was wounded, but Darius and Hakim played with it. I held it in my arms and took care of him. He became my baby. It was so afraid of me, but it didn't run away. He followed me everywhere I went, and the more he chased me, the more I cared for my kitten. As the sun faded into the ocean, the sky grew dark, the moon came and bathed us all in dazzling light. My kitten turned into a strange man!

It terrified me the way he followed me. I didn't know who he was or what he wanted. But his beautiful eyes told me he was still my kitten! Hakim and Darius treated the man like he was still a kitten. They played with him and ran all over the beach.

He sat with his beautiful eyes on me, and I was overcome with happiness as he smiled at me. He held me close in his strong arms, and it was the most secure feeling I had ever experienced. It was like there on that beach with those three men; nothing could ever hurt me!

I awoke with tears in my eyes. I wanted my sad little kitten! It felt like I had lost a valuable piece of my heart once he was gone. I have often dreamed of cats lately. I don't know why, but cats seemed to be all around me. Darius had a panther tattoo, and Hakim bought me stuffed lions, tigers, and cheetahs. My room had so many cats now it was frighteningly sick. I don't know why lions speak to me. But something about my deep down desires and spirit tied me to these beautiful beasts.

Since I left Africa, I've met more lions than any other human beast. Strong people with deep roots, growing proud full manes of gorgeous hair. Each is deeply rooted in tragedy and tied to one another for survival.

Hakim, Darius, and Lionel were graceful, haunted, wounded. Yet, here I am, trying to nurse them back to life with love and friendship. But who was this kitten I was missing from the picture?

Who was he, and how could I help him?

I had no idea what was happening to me. But I was changing, and it was scaring me. Hakim saw it first, and he loved it. Mami mentioned it next. I didn't realize until the moment I lost my virginity. Now that Daddy was here, it seemed to trigger some metamorphosis. I needed to get over my fear before I did something stupid again. The first time it was pills. Then, all it took was a few of Mami's sleeping pills to nearly get me out of here.

"Mmmhmm, next time, you'll fly, Bitch…You'll fly…." I thought I heard a voice in the darkness as I glanced around, frightened.

"Queen, try to lie down and sleep. You don't want to see your father looking worn out," Hakim called up to me, grabbing my hips pulling me back down. He put his head on my behind and rubbed my back, trying to relax me. "Everything's going to be fine. I got this…I swear…."

"I trust you," I sighed, putting my head on the pillow. Darius put his chin on top of my head and played with my neck.

"I love you, Mandisa," Daris moaned, falling back asleep. I smiled and shut my eyes. "Fart on Hakim's head...I'll give you 100 dollars...."

Hakim lifted his head and said, "I'm not moving again. Let her fart. You love her feet so much that ought to be where you sleep, Freak!"

Darius's head shot up, and he chuckled, "Nigga, I would, but this bed is too damn little, and I don't want you kicking me in the shit. You are strong in the legs!"

"Go to bed!" I giggled, yelling.

"Okay, Queen, I'm sorry," Darius said, dropping his head back in place.

Hakim grabbed his pillow and laid down, glancing up and Darius frowning. I put my finger on Hakim's forehead and poked him in his third eye.

"I'm done...Night, Queen, I love you more!" Hakim said, hiding.

"Whatever, Nigga! We'll see!" Darius laughed, sitting up again.

"What?! What you got, Count Chocula!" Hakim groaned.

I popped Hakim and pointed at his place seriously. Hakim dropped down and pretended to go to sleep. Darius rolled his eyes and stared, waiting a moment for Hakim to come back, then laid down.

"Good night, Kings...." I giggled.

"You mean, Great rising, Suns? I'm as hungry as a hostage...I haven't eaten anything all day...." Darius suddenly started.

"Word up! We're not going to the hospital until later! So let's hit the IHOP! I'm starving, Bro! Come on, Queen!" Hakim shouted, jumping up turning on the light.

"Are you serious? It's 5 am!" I groaned.

"If we eat, we can fuck again before the nap, Queen," Hakim suggested.

"Where are my shoes?" I mumbled, sitting up.

"That is my motherfucking Goddess! Ooh! I got to get that ring!" Hakim screamed as he ran into the bathroom.

Darius smiled and shook his head, saying, "Mandisa, what are you going to tell Mami about the things you do with me? She knows about Hakim...How long do you think we can hide things...now that things are moving along?"

"We are taking everything one step at a time. This was a big step...Don't you think? Once things are safe, I will tell Mami about my choice to be with you both. She is going to get very mad. I know it. ...But it is my choice...Give me a little more time, Darius. All of this is happening so fast."

"You're right...I'm sorry for bringing it up...I was getting ahead of things...I really do love you, and I want to marry you too, Mandisa. This is real to me. I'm not playing," Darius replied, smiling sweetly.

"It's okay. I love you...I am not playing with your heart, Darius," I told him, playing with his hair.

"I believe you, Mandisa...Let's get going, so I can fill up my tank. Maybe when we get back, I can catch Cheaters!" Darius laughed, going to get dressed. "You'll love it, Queen. Ratchet TV is the best way to relieve stress when you've had a hectic day. Or we can watch the Jump-Out-Boys on COPs. It's always entertainment when it ain't your hood."

"You are silly. Can we get dressed so we can go and get back....? If you're serious...I do want a nap before going....but we can do it again....Can't we?" I asked worriedly.

"Oh, fuck yeah! Hell, yeah...Girl, let me shut the fuck up! You want dick?" Darius screamed, grabbing me and falling on the bed. He laughed playfully and relaxed. "I meant everything I said, Mandisa."

I nodded, smiling up at him knowing how Darius really felt for me. I was more in love with him now. But, I didn't tell him because he and Hakim were constantly having their little back and forth. I didn't want things to escalate between them.

They were having fun… and…It can work with both.…I didn't think it would…but I wanted to try. I have two kings! But I am not sure how Hakim plans on getting my father on his side. Daddy is so sincere that he does not want me with a black man. Daddy's so wrong about Hakim. Yes, he has a messed up past, a temper, and sexual urges to master.

Hakim was determined to fix everything that he thought was wrong once he realized his mistakes. He's a charming boyfriend that spoils me with everything from compliments, flattery, gifts, and he motivates me to take risks to be happy. If more people knew him, they would see how sad he is deep down and how much he needs the people he loves to keep him from spiraling out of control. I love him so very much, and I will never let Hakim Jahlil Dunn go. He's my fantasy boy. I belong to him.

But it is just as Darius said…He belongs to me. It feels like neither would be happy if I chose one over the other. But

they needed each other, so I suppose I held them together.
Hakim drew Darius to me now we are together, so I'm going
to trust in them and this path we have chosen.

But that does not mean that I am not afraid of what is to
come.

THE END.

www.ingramcontent.com/pod-product-compliance
Lightning Source LLC
Chambersburg PA
CBHW070336170726
48291CB00001B/72